Penguin Books

THE TRUE STORY OF SPIT MACPHEE

The gentle Australian town of St Helen had become accustomed to the eccentric lifestyle and periodic ravings of old Fyfe MacPhee, but when he takes in his young grandson, Spit, there are those who feel it is time to intervene.

For living in the wildly painted makeshift home by the river, Spit and his grandfather thrash out an existence in a raucous and haphazard fashion, but it is this very experience that brings out the best in Spit. A fierce individualist with a character as tough as the soles of his bare feet, the boy is beholden to no one and afraid of nothing.

However, this honest, freewheeling lifestyle cannot last and Spit finds himself the prize in an agonizing contest between Betty Arbuckle, who wants to save him for the Lord, and Grace Tree, who simply wishes to preserve that which she has come to respect and admire: his spirit. This evocative and moving story is a gripping read from start to finish.

James Aldridge was born in Victoria, Australia in 1918. He went to London in 1938 and worked as a newspaperman on the *Daily Sketch*. During the war he became a war correspondent in Finland, Egypt and then the Soviet Union. His first novel was written during the war. He later decided to leave regular journalism to have more time for his novels. He has lived in the United States, France, Switzerland and London, with two long visits home to Australia. His wife is Egyptian and they have two sons. He now lives in London. James Aldridge has written twenty-three novels as well as short stories, plays, non-fiction, and TV scripts. *The True Story of Spit MacPhee* won the 1986 New South Wales Premier's Award in Australia as well as the 1987 *Guardian* Award in Britain.

JAMES ALDRIDGE

THE TRUE STORY OF SPIT MACPHEE

PENGUIN BOOKS

PENGUIN BOOKS

Published by the Penguin Group
27 Wrights Lane, London W8 5TZ, England
Viking Penguin Inc., 40 West 23rd Street, New York, New York 10010, USA
Penguin Books Australia Ltd, Ringwood, Victoria, Australia
Penguin Books Canada Ltd, 2801 John Street, Markham, Ontario, Canada L3R 1B4
Penguin Books (NZ) Ltd, 182–190 Wairau Road, Auckland 10, New Zealand

Penguin Books Ltd, Registered Offices: Harmondsworth, Middlesex, England

First published in Australia by Viking Kestrel 1986
First published in Great Britain by Viking Kestrel 1986
Published in Penguin Books 1988
1 3 5 7 9 10 8 6 4 2

Made and printed in Great Britain by
Richard Clay Ltd, Bungay, Suffolk
Filmset in Baskerville

Without giving too much away I should admit
from the outset that I have stretched the
1928 Act which I mention here to its very
limit, though not beyond its real terms.
I have also borrowed a useful nickname from
an old friend, who would forgive me if he
were still alive. In any case it's not
about him or his family, it's all fiction,
but he would probably have enjoyed the use
I have made of the name we so affectionately
used on him.

1

BETTY ARBUCKLE, A PARTICULARLY GOOD WOMAN OF ST HELEN, a natural beauty and a devoted evangelist, was trying once again to do something about Spit MacPhee. Betty was worried that, with no real parental care, this wild, barefoot and growing boy (he was almost eleven), needed more help now than he could get from a grandfather who was already half mad and becoming increasingly so. When old Fyfe MacPhee had first come to St Helen, in the State of Victoria, most people had thought him a bit odd, but in the last few years he was generally considered to be as mad as a hatter.

Spit himself would sometimes have to fight boys or girls or even adults when he heard them give that little laugh and tap their heads when old Fyfe walked by. Though not always. It depended on how Spit himself felt about his grandfather, or how angry they were with each other, because sometimes (though rarely) Spit didn't care what they or anyone else said about him. Yet at other times, with the same boy or man who laughed, Spit's fists would suddenly flash out, or his bare feet would kick hard at a man's shins with surprising force if he thought that there was a case to answer.

What worried the lovely Betty Arbuckle was the obvious fact that the old man's madness was becoming permanent rather than spasmodic, so that Spit himself was more often left to his own devices, living as they did in a world of their own down by the river. To Betty Arbuckle Spit was like a stray dog that either had to be put down or taken off gently to some home that could care for him properly. She had always been worried about the boy from the day of his arrival in the town, but now that he was already ten, almost eleven, he needed a safer haven than his half-mad grandfather could give him.

That was why Betty felt very strongly about it, although she knew it was by no means the general opinion of the rest of the town. Whenever she had attempted to visit old Fyfe in his extraordinary little house, his quite crazy house by the river, she had been shouted at by both Spit and old Fyfe. She had been insulted in Scottish, even in Gaelic, and told to mind her own bloody business. She had been threatened with violence, and Spit himself had once emerged from the house and thrown a bucket of river water over her, drenching her from head to toe. A few hours later, still determined to do her best for the boy but refusing to be angry with him, she had returned with Sergeant Joe Collins, the policeman, insisting that he do something about the old man and his violent behaviour. 'If only for the sake of the boy,' she had said to Sergeant Collins.

Spit and his grandfather had seen Sergeant Collins coming. In fact Sergeant Collins had deliberately announced his noisy arrival in plenty of time for them to shut the front door on him. But he had called to them through the door that they ought to come out and apologise to Mrs Betty Arbuckle, or he would have to do something about it.

'Do what? Ye old fool,' Fyfe MacPhee shouted through the door. 'Get out of my garden, Collins, or ye'll get the same. And get ye away with that silly blasted woman. Get ye away with her . . .' It was a cry of bitter pain from old Fyfe.

Sergeant Collins wanted nothing to do with Betty Arbuckle, or with Fyfe or Spit, but he shouted through the door, 'Mind your language, Fyfe, or I'll put you in charge.'

'What charge?' Fyfe shouted back, his fists hammering on the other side. 'Get out of here, ye old fool.'

A few more heated Scottish insults began to escalate the situation, and Sergeant Collins urged Mrs Betty Arbuckle out through the gate, ignoring her protests. Kicking disgustedly at a lump of hard mud, Sergeant Collins told Betty, 'There's nothing I can do, Mrs Arbuckle. They haven't broken any law, and though old Fyfe is as mad as a hatter, I can't do anything about it.'

'But that boy is growing up like an African heathen.'

'That's not my business. If you want to do something about that you'll have to go to the Shire Council or the magistrate or someone. Not me. And anyway you had no right to come down here telling the old man you want to inspect the house and take the boy away.'

'I didn't say that.'

'No, but that's what you want. And that's none of my business.'

'It's not right . . .'

Betty Arbuckle's loveliness was always enhanced by her religious passion, but in her own kind of abnegation of it she did her best to disperse her loveliness by a blunt cut to her hair and by wearing dull and dowdy clothes and buckled shoes with flat heels. But even this could not spoil her beauty. In fact the more she tried to disfigure it the more she seemed to enhance it. Her house, her husband (he was the Water Board inspector for the town) and her two children were also encouraged to be barren, and the sight of Fyfe MacPhee's wildly painted little house on the river bank and his habit of walking around the town shouting at people in the middle of the night had long ago convinced her that Fyfe MacPhee, sane or insane, was something of a devil in the flesh.

It was true that old Fyfe could look the part, and what hinted at some sort of hell in his background was that nobody in the town knew anything about him, even though he had now lived in it for more than ten years. His secrecy, his shouting hostility to any kind of questioning, his sudden fits of madness, and finally the arrival five years ago of Spit as a five-year-old boy, were all facts looking for trouble. And as Betty Arbuckle walked up the slope, across the railway line and away from the little house, she was still arguing with Sergeant Collins that she must do something about the boy. She must somehow get him away from that dangerous old man and find him a place in her evangelical sect's Boys Home in Bendigo.

'For his own sake,' Betty said unhappily.

2

Fyfe MacPhee had arrived in St Helen not long after the First World War, and even then he had looked like an old man because he was small and grey and grizzled, with hard, wild eyes, a harsh voice that shouted everything in a bri-braw Scottish accent, and a battered old hat pulled tight on his head. Nobody had even seen him without that tight little hat which sat there as if it were part of his scalp.

He had arrived in O. Gilpin's Rolls Royce, which was not a limousine but a van that furnished supplies to the O. Gilpin stores throughout the mallee towns: a dusty but familiar visitor. After a few weeks, when the town's curiosity had been aroused by old Fyfe's behaviour, all that anybody could discover was that he had come from Manangantang. He had paid O. Gilpin's driver five shillings for the lift and had walked the last mile into town because the driver didn't want the manager of the local store to know that he had given anyone a lift. A few people saw him arrive – walking along the main road carrying a small suitcase and a wooden box which, in the light of what followed, contained his tools as a clock and watch repairer and an expert tool setter.

Fyfe lived at first in a small room behind Charlie Kruger's garage where he began his work as a watch and clock repairer and tool setter by going from house to house asking the women, who were usually the only ones at home, if they had clocks or watches needing repair, or if their husbands' razors needed resetting, or their chisels, planes or anything else with a double-edge needed re-shaping. But these were a reluctant necessity to his clock and watch repairing.

If one of the ladies said, 'Will you sharpen my scissors for me?' Fyfe would shake his head and shout, 'I am not a scissors sharpener. If they need to be set I'll do it and sharpen them for ye, but I'm no scissors sharpener.' He would not sharpen any plane or chisel or any other tool unless it was double-edged and needed to be re-set, and if someone persisted he would shout angrily at them and leave. But as he began to do a fair business at back doors he was soon to be recognised not only as the kind of tool setter that even carpenters would take their tools to, but the best watch and clock repairer in town and the cheapest as well.

He was considered no more than a bit odd because he never spoke without shouting, as if he had no other way of talking, even though he talked sense. But one day he had walked around the streets shouting nonsense for no reason. Afterwards he had locked himself in his room and emerged two days later in his normal, grizzled form. It was obvious then that there was something awfully wrong with him, but because it had not happened again for some time, some people forgot it and simply thought of him as being a little crazy. Thereafter, he was tolerated as a bit of a joke, and eventually he had made casual friends whom he could talk to: Tom Smythe the blacksmith, the two Benson brothers who looked after the telegraph poles, and Tom Yard who was a carter with a fine team of horses. But he shouted at them all as he did with everybody else. What he said to them was considered friendly enough, but with them too his shouting could seem quarrelsome and aggressive.

What became his craziest venture was his shift to the river bank. Fyfe had discovered on one of the shady banks of the little Murray river an old square boiler that had been there for years. After some enquiries he found out that it was owned by Tom Smythe the blacksmith, and that the river bank where it lay was under the jurisdiction of the State Rivers and Water Supply Commission. Fyfe bought the boiler from Tom Smythe, and paid two pounds a year for the use of a patch of river bank big enough for the boiler and a small garden. Then, after cutting a couple of holes in one side of it with Tom Smythe's help, he had turned the old boiler into a curious little house. The boys who swam in the river further upstream believed that it had once been the boiler of an old river boat, the *Mundoo*, which had sunk thirty or forty years ago in a bend of the river. But it was too big for that. It was really the remnant of an old plan to build a big pumping system for a canal to be drawn from the little river, a plan that had been abandoned even before the big pumps had arrived.

Fyfe MacPhee had worked hard on the interior of the boiler, and eventually he had built a little extension to the side of it which had become his workshop. And though the extension was a visible part of Fyfe's house, nobody had ever seen inside the boiler or the extension. Outside, he painted the boiler bright red and green, with a blue wavy line all around the sides. He completed the house with a picket fence and a sign on the front gate which said IN and OUT, which Fyfe adjusted every time he came and went. He planted a flower garden on the river side (the front), and a vegetable garden at the back; and under the big gum tree he kept chickens for eggs. The boiler itself was tucked into the shade of a big peppercorn tree and another tall, dry gum, and here old Fyfe settled down to live a strange and secret sort of life which meant keeping himself to himself.

He was, by now, nothing more than a town character who had unlucky moments of madness but was always harmless, although difficult to get on with because of his inability to talk in anything but an aggressive shout. Moreover he never seemed to listen, although somehow he did hear everything that was said to him. But there was one other aspect to his madness that encouraged the laughs at his expense. On occasions he would attack the outside of his boiler with a fourteen-pound hammer, hitting it all over its sides and top and bottom, knocking all its internal decoration to the floor, and shouting with each blow, 'Ye never had any steam in ye, no pipes, but I'll show ye . . . I'll show ye . . .' Smash would go the hammer, and after five minutes, when his fury was spent, Fyfe would become a broken old man, sitting on the step of the boiler holding his head, helpless now instead of the grizzly and bad-tempered and shouting old Scot the town was used to.

All this was before the appearance of Spit, who had arrived one day in early summer. The old man had disappeared for two weeks to return with a five-year-old boy whom the town discovered (by guesswork and a few captured hints) was his grandson, Angus MacPhee. Where the boy had come from, and what he was doing in St Helen with his grandfather, nobody knew. Most people thought the boy would stay a few days or weeks and then return to his mother, wherever she was. But he stayed on, and while he was there old Fyfe began to build another extension to his boiler. This time it was a proper little cabin, which he built solidly with timber and old windows and a serious door. He built it day and night, so that the people above the railway line would sometimes hear his hammer going at two o'clock in the morning. They knew better than to ask Fyfe why he was in such a hurry, but when he had finished it what the curious among the town's people saw was a tiny two-room house with a corrugated iron roof barely eight feet above the ground, but all neat and solid. As a final touch Fyfe painted it red and green, like the boiler, and painted the same wavy blue line all the way around it. To many of the town's people it was worth a Sunday stroll down by the river to see it, providing they didn't stop to stare, or provoke Fyfe into showing his temper.

While this was happening, the town made its first contact with the five-year-old boy. He was taken by his grandfather wherever he went, and the boy copied his grandfather in all things. He shouted aggressively because the old man did, and he spat (or tried to) because old Fyfe, who smoked a short cubby pipe, spat noisily and frequently. Inevitably the boy was soon known to the town as Spit MacPhee, and it was a nickname he didn't mind, which was lucky because when he eventually went to school he didn't have to get into fights over it. But in the formation of his character, which was already like his grandfather's, he would spit drily and emptily and forcefully to state his position. By the end of that summer he was a brown, bare-legged, barefoot copy of the old man who never seemed to restrain him, even though he shouted at the boy the way he shouted at everybody else. By the end of that summer Spit was left free to wander where he liked in the town, or along the river, or even across it on Pental Island. He learned to swim in a few days, and thereafter the river became his natural home. He was afraid of nothing and nobody, and was soon so well-equipped to look after himself that it persuaded some of the worried women of St Helen, notably

Betty Arbuckle, that in fact he was a little too good at looking after himself. Like eating people it was wrong for a six-year-old to be so recklessly free, and it was about this time that Betty Arbuckle first decided she would have to do something about the future of this boy who needed a proper home with proper care, which meant the Boys Home in Bendigo.

But then, one Monday morning, when Spit had been with old Fyfe for three months, the old man switched the sign on his gate to OUT, and taking Spit by the hand he caught the morning train to Bendigo – a large town one hundred miles away. Fyfe returned next day with Spit and a tall red-headed woman. It wasn't known at first sight who she was. All three were the last off the train because it was obvious that the lady did not want to be seen. But she was noticed anyway. Though it was the 1930s and the fashion then was short skirts, the lady wore a skirt to her ankles. Even more peculiar, she wore a brown veil that covered her face down to her neck so that only a few strands of her bright red hair were visible. She held Spit's hand in her own gloved hand, and Fyfe carried her suitcase as they walked straight to Tom Smythe's gig. It had been waiting for them, obviously pre-arranged by old Fyfe. The gig had a little oval step for mounting to the padded seat, but the veiled lady couldn't make it without Fyfe's help. Once up on the seat, still holding Spit's hand, Tom Smythe drove them to the little house by the river, and it was obvious then that she was Spit's mother and that Fyfe had built the little cabin expressly for her.

But once she was in it nobody thereafter caught more than a passing glimpse of her sitting in the back garden. She would sometimes sit there on a deck chair, holding a faded green parasol low over her head. Sometimes she was shelling peas or peeling potatoes or sewing, but more often than not she simply sat there as if that was all she could manage, never speaking to anyone, even when some of the ladies shouted a greeting to her. Sometimes Spit was seen spread across her knees, face down, kicking his legs, but nobody ever saw her face.

Eventually, a real explanation seeped through a report, in a Bendigo paper, that Mrs Mary MacPhee had been badly burned when her house in White Hills, near Bendigo, had caught fire. Mrs Joyce Andrews, coming from Bendigo to visit her sister in St Helen, had seen the case reported in the Bendigo *Advertiser.* The real tragedy was that Murdoch MacPhee, old Fyfe's son and Mary's husband, had managed to rescue the boy, but in returning for his wife and rescuing her from the back of the house, he had burned his lungs to shreds and was already dead on his way to hospital. Mary MacPhee had been badly burned on the face, legs and back, and she too had suffered some sort of lung injury from the heat and smoke. Only the boy had escaped untouched.

The town of St Helen was a normal town, and the sympathy for the MacPhees was natural and widespread. But unfortunately old Fyfe's shouted hostility to all questions or offers of help made any expression of sympathy difficult. It was particularly difficult for Betty Arbuckle, because now she had to think of the mother as well as the son. She too needed help and Betty was sure that personal salvation was the only way to rescue her. Never daunted by the devil in the flesh, or by setbacks, she had tried to call on Mary MacPhee only to meet old Fyfe, who happened to be digging in the garden. He threatened her with the spade and chased her off, shouting after her, 'Ye spying minnie. Y're after seeing her face, aren't ye, but if ye come down here again I'll throw you in the river.'

Spit was too young then to hurry her on her way with a bucket of river water, and Betty Arbuckle had not called on Sergeant Collins in those early days because she knew that Collins, like most people in the town, was on the side of the MacPhees. In fact, after some time, Betty had to admit that with his daughter-in-law there, old Fyfe began to control his temper a little, despite his threats to anyone who offered help. His sudden outbursts of wild shouting at anybody in the street and his mad attacks on the boiler stopped entirely. When it was time to start school, it was Fyfe himself who took Spit to be registered, and though Spit wore a clean, un-ironed smock, and clean pants, he still had no shoes. But at least he was off the streets, and because the river was rising he was not so much in it now but along its bank watching the currents. What did not change were the noisy exchanges, because Spit and his grandfather went on shouting at each other as if that was the only way they could talk to each other, and the people above the railway line would hear them exchanging early morning arguments at the tops of their voices every morning before school.

It remained like that – a rather neutral situation, until one cold, wet, winter's day in July, Mary MacPhee died. Initially only Dr Stevens and the Reverend Mackenzie of the Presbyterian church knew about it. Then, most people heard about it when they watched her funeral, attended only by Fyfe and Spit. It saddened many people in the town, and Betty Arbuckle wept for the woman whom nobody had actually seen in her terrible disfigurement, although it worried Betty that the boy might have seen his mother's badly burned face. That in itself was a frightful condemnation of what the boy had to suffer in those horrible conditions.

After the funeral old Fyfe and Spit had locked themselves up for two days and nobody had heard them shouting at each other. But it was only a matter of time before Spit was back at school and roaming freely again. Once more they shouted at each other, and once more Fyfe appeared from time to time on the streets, denouncing nobody in particular but simply walking around in a state of fierce invective. Spit was seven when his mother died. Now he was ten ('almost eleven' he would say when he was asked his age), and it was the accumulation of those three years of the boy's motherless condition that had persuaded Betty Arbuckle to try once more (the sixth time in three years) to do something about the boy, and it had brought her back that day to the little red and green boiler house on the river bank.

Something had to be done. The boy was now so fearless, so bold, so outspoken, and so equal to anyone, adult or child, so dirty (she was sure), so neglected by the old man and so lacking in any moral and spiritual guidance (he had never been seen in the Presbyterian church, or at Sunday school) that somehow he had to be saved from what was clearly and obviously an unChristian future. It wasn't fair to the boy to leave him like that. The beautiful Betty Arbuckle, with close haircut and buckled shoes, was more determined than ever not to be defeated by the swearing and insults of a mad old man. Soaking wet from Spit's bucket of water, she went home singing her favourite hymn:

Praise my soul the King of Heaven
To His feet thy tribute bring.
Ransomed, healed, restored, forgiven,
Who like thee His praise should sing.
Praise Him, praise Him,
Praise Him, praise Him,
Praise the Everlasting King.

Then her two favourite lines: 'Slow to chide and swift to bless. Praise Him, praise Him . . .' And finally her private addition to it: 'Give me strength, his soul to save.' Because salvation to Betty was God's pity, and she was sure that sooner or later she was going to save Spit from that Godless little house.

3

BUT THOUGH SPIT SEEMED TO BE A LEAF CAUGHT IN SOMETHING of a mortal storm, almost every boy in town liked him and admired him; and in return Spit himself was friendly to anybody who would accept him for what he was and could tolerate his habit of shouting rather than talking, and his routine gesture of dry spitting with his tongue. Spit's personal toleration of all and sundry was more like an equaliser between friends rather than the kind of mateship that Australians loved so much.

Girls were inclined to keep well clear of Spit, avoiding him as a barefoot ruffian. In response, Spit ignored the lot of them (though later there would be one exception to this). When he did get into a fight with boys his own age it was usually over a point of honour rather than a contest for some sort of superiority. If he was beaten by a bigger boy he never admitted defeat and would only accept his punishment on the understanding that there would be a return bout another day, which sometimes he forgot. In this regard he never bore a grudge, although he had his likes and dislikes. Among his very few dislikes were the son and daughter of Betty Arbuckle and her husband, Frank, who read the water meters and checked the town's water supply. He was also responsible for keeping the water mains in good condition.

Like Betty, Frank Arbuckle had been saved in his youth because (like Betty) his parents had also been saved. But whereas Betty was sustained in her salvation, Frank was overwhelmed and beaten by it, exhausted and helpless in it. Betty got life and vigour from her faith, whereas Frank followed silently behind – easily frightened, worn out, and only able to do the best he could. Like his ten-year-old son

Ben, Frank was an easy victim for Spit's retaliations whenever Betty Arbuckle attempted to get into old Fyfe's house. Spit's usual response was to choose a moment in the night, find some remote corner of the town, and lift one of the small water mains' inspection covers. Then he would jam a piece of wood into the ball-cock that was used as a valve when sometimes the mains had to be tapped. The flood that followed was not easy to stem but needed quick attention, and Frank Arbuckle always knew who had done it. To all Frank's complaints Sergeant Collins always gave the same reply: 'You catch him at it, Frank, and I'll see he gets punished.'

'The little devil is too cunning for that,' Frank Arbuckle said. 'But I'll get him someday, Joe.'

But Sergeant Collins knew that Frank Arbuckle was as much afraid of Spit as he was of his wife, and of old Fyfe, and of his own twelve-year-old daughter, Joannie. So he would do almost anything to avoid Spit under any circumstances.

Spit, for his part, didn't spare the Arbuckle children: Ben his own age, and Joannie who was older. He terrorised Ben simply by waiting from time to time until Ben happened to be fifty yards in front of him in the street. Then Spit would shout, 'Look out, Ben, I'm after you.' And setting out on his fast bare feet after the fleeing Ben he would roar his threats, never trying to catch him and never intending to harm him, but out simply to remove him from consideration.

But one day, instead of fleeing at full speed, Ben ran a little way in his heavy, black boots and then suddenly stopped and turned around to face Spit, who was amazed. Spit got ready for a fight, but instead of offering resistance, Ben was in tears.

'Why don't you leave me alone, Spit,' he said. 'It's not me, it's my mother. So leave me alone . . .'

This so startled Spit who, recognising a *cri de coeur* despite himself, didn't know what to do except to shout in reply, 'Well I'm after her, Ben, so you'd better tell her to look out.'

'I know, Spit, but I can't help it.'

Ben's tear-stained face was already too much for Spit, and the best he could manage in retreat was, 'What does she think she's doing?'

Thereafter he left Ben Arbuckle alone. Joannie, though, was another problem. Spit could not threaten her with violence, and Joannie would stand up to him and accuse him of being dirty, smelly and mad like his grandfather. Spit's reply was usually a shouted insult about her mother being a crank, which didn't frighten Joannie so that Spit had to resort to one or two 'bloodies' or something worse. Joannie could stand almost anything except bad language, and as a rule she covered her ears and ran away. Joannie was even prettier than her mother, but she didn't have her mother's resolute innocence. She always wore a pinny, her hair was tied in two curious little horns above her ears, and like her mother she wore buckle shoes and thick stockings. But like her mother she couldn't dim her own prettiness, and like her mother she firmly believed that the Lord Jesus needed everyone to turn a shamed and obedient face to the world and acknowledge their sins in order to be saved.

'You were born wicked, Spit MacPhee,' she would cry out as she fled.

But apart from the Arbuckles and a few other people who tried to interfere, Spit made a point of never threatening anyone without cause. If the men, women, boys and girls of St Helen left him alone, he would leave them alone, and in those sort of live-and-let-live conditions he was given a fair amount of good-natured respect, even from adults. What helped him was his dour self-confidence, because he was always rather serious for a boy. When he stood at the back door to face Mrs Evans (or Mrs Jackson or Mrs Ellison) to say to her, 'Do you want to buy a fish, Mrs Evans?' he was making an offer that had to be accepted or rejected without any nonsense. If Mrs Evans asked him how much he wanted for the Murray cod he would give his price. But if she made a mistake and asked him, 'Is it fresh, Spit?' he would shout, 'What do you think it is, Mrs Evans? I just caught it.' If he chose to take offence he would take his fish and walk away.

In this particular case Mrs Evans mentioned it to her husband and said, 'He really is a bit mad, Bert. Just like the old man.'

'I don't know, Dot,' Bert said. 'If you start doubting Spit's word you know what to expect – a blast from the furnace.'

'Well, I wish he wouldn't shout the way he does.'

'That's the old man in him,' Bert said. 'The kid's never

known anything else. You can hear them shouting at each other any day of the week when you walk along the railway line. Day or night.'

Bert and Dot Evans were among the people in town who liked both Fyfe and Spit, despite the fact that Spit teased their dog, Patchy, which put Spit and Patchy into a curious relationship. Patchy would always bark fiercely and instantly whenever Spit came or went up the slope to and from the boiler house. It was enough for Patchy to hear Spit's raised voice, even in the distance, and a fit of barking would follow. But if Spit went through the Evans' front gate to offer a fish for sale Patchy was all over him with eager paws and licking tongue. Dot and Bert even took a quiet delight (being childless) in knowing when Spit came and went because of Patchy's bark, and they were among those in town who thought that Betty Arbuckle had no right to march down to the boiler house to make trouble for them.

'Betty's been after young Spit ever since his mother died,' Dot said.

'So what the devil does she think she's going to do with him, if she gets him?' Bert asked her.

'Send him off to that Boys Home in Bendigo she's always talking about,' Dot replied. 'The trouble is that old Fyfe is getting madder and madder every day, and some day he's going to go right off his head. The other day he tore up all the flowers in his garden and threw them into the river, and he and Spit were at each other for hours afterwards.'

'It's the kid who is looking after the old man these days,' Bert said. 'But I wonder, Dot, if they even know what they're doing. They don't seem to know what else they can do but live that half-mad life down there.'

That was where Bert and Dot left the problem, as most of the townspeople did whenever they gave a passing thought to the old man and the barefoot boy living in their red and green house on the river bank. That is, all except Betty Arbuckle.

4

The town knew almost everything visible about Spit and old Fyfe except what went on behind the front door of the little red and green boiler house. Spit now slept by himself in the boiler, and Fyfe had moved into the little cabin extension he had built for his daughter-in-law. To some people in town it was considered shameful that such a bright and active boy had to live in such a place, but others said it was nothing more than a sort of gypsy caravan made of riveted steel plates. Every boy in town envied Spit, but he had to defend his boiler against his grandfather's need to attack it from time to time with a fourteen-pound hammer. He would wrestle with old Fyfe, get a grip on his arm and simply hang on, wrapping his bare legs around his grandfather's spindly knees, shouting, 'No you don't, grandfather. Leave off . . . Take it away.' It worked if Spit was there, but sometimes he would come home from school and find that his grandfather had been at work with his hammer, and everything inside the boiler was in shambles.

Spit's life was divided into various separate parts. Living on the river became for him the source of life itself. He fished in it and swam in it. He set crayfish nets in it, long lines and shrimp tins. And he spent a lot of his time studying and trying to puzzle out the course of every curve and current in the little Murray, the depth of every hole, and where there could be perch or bream; or most important the tasty Murray cod. Whenever he caught a cod, even at night, he would try to take it alive and kicking to houses along the railway line. As late as nine o'clock there could be a knock at any one of the back doors along the line and Spit would be offering his catch hanging on a tether. He knew all the Catholic families along the line so he would try to offer them a fish on Thursday night or Friday morning early.

What he had become a specialist in was the big crayfish that lived in the little Murray. He knew better than anybody else in town where to lay the crayfish drums made of old bicycle wheels and chicken wire. He used a sheep's head from the butcher's for bait, and when he had caught two or three he would take them to one of the two hotels in town and demand five shillings each for them and get it. That became his own money, and he saved it in a tin which he hid in a curious little locker in the underside of the boiler where his grandfather couldn't find it in one of his fits of unpredictable destruction.

Inside the house or the boiler he had his duties, some given him by his grandfather, others taken on unplanned simply because they were necessary. Old Fyfe was calmest and quietest when he was bent over his bench, magnifying glass pushed into his fire-rimmed eye, and the fine tools of his craft gripped delicately in his short, square, quivering fingers. Almost from the first day that he had brought Spit with him from Bendigo he had allowed the boy to peer through the eye-piece at watches and clocks, whole or in pieces, and eventually he had given Spit an old clock and a set of clockmaker's screwdrivers and a pair of fine pliers and let him do what he liked. Spit had little difficulty taking the old Westlox Big Ben apart, but in the more complicated business of putting it together again he and his grandfather had shouted at each other, and only by trial and error had Spit put it all back, aged eight, with deft fingers. He could now assemble simple escapements in pocket-watches, and often did so for his grandfather; but he was not allowed to touch wrist-watches or old time-pieces.

When someone from the town brought a watch to old Fyfe for repair Spit would often receive it and write out the little tag in his heavy large left-handed writing. He would take money, and sometimes give an approximate date for completion, and would often have to shout at his grandfather to get it done in time. On occasions the old man would abandon his bench for days on end, and that was usually when he wandered into the town, talking to himself, shouting at anybody who took his fancy, gesticulating and making incomprehensible demands on unlucky neighbours in such braw

Scots that they couldn't understand him and sent him packing with a laugh or a joke. Though violent in speech, old Fyfe was never physically violent except when Jack Taylor and Peter Mayfair, both in their early teens, had tried to snatch off his hat. At first Fyfe had brushed them off like bothersome flies, but when he realised what they were after he had ripped a paling from Mrs Burns' picket fence and lashed out at both boys and chased them down the street shouting, 'Ye think I'm mad, ye naughty dogs, ye carnal little beasties. But I'll show ye.'

Next day Spit had confronted Jack Taylor, who was twice his size, and warned him to leave his grandfather alone. 'And don't touch his hat. You leave that alone, Jack.'

'Okay, Spit,' Jack said. 'We didn't mean your old man any harm.'

'Well you'd better watch out,' Spit warned. 'He'll make mincemeat of you if you go after his hat.'

'Okay, okay . . .' Jack said, taking it too as a warning from Spit himself.

In fact only Spit knew the agony and pain his grandfather suffered after one of these bouts of madness. The worst of them was not those he suffered in the street, but inside the house when he would suddenly crouch on the floor with his head between his knees, groaning and hitting the top of his head with his fists, while Spit looked on, helpless, aware that he must not say or do anything until the agony had passed. If it happened at the wrong time Spit would have to prepare the lunch or the dinner, or water the garden with buckets from the river, or light the oil lamps which he kept filled with kerosene, or put people off if they came for their watches or their re-set tools.

After one of these bouts Fyfe MacPhee would usually say in a drenched voice to Spit, 'How long did me noise last this time?'

'A couple of hours, grandfather,' Spit would reply. 'You got up twice, and then you were on the floor again. You couldn't get up.'

'You didn't leave me did ye?' the old man would shout anxiously.

'Not me,' Spit would reply at the top of his voice.

'Are you sure?'

'I tell you I was cleaning the wicks, and filling the lamps.'
'I saw ye . . .' the old man would roar.
'Well, that's what I was doing, wasn't I?'
'I know what you were doing.'
Thus they would return to their usual behaviour, to their endless giving and taking in response to each other.
What they had to share they shared without decision. Every Saturday morning at dawn Spit would light a fire under the copper near the big peppercorn tree and fill it with water from the river. Then Fyfe would throw in all the clothes that needed washing, the sheets and shirts and shorts and anything else handy. After twenty minutes boiling he would lift the washing out piece by piece with a wooden stick, wring it out, and hang it all on the line between the trees. Spit also had to light the kitchen fire every morning and prepare the porridge at night in a black iron pot. Fyfe had once kept half a dozen hens and a few pullets for the eggs, but he had cut off their heads in one of his fits and thrown the headless bodies, still wriggling, into the river. It was one of the few times when Spit was in tears. He had come home to find the devastation, and because he had known every hen and pullet by name, and was used to them eating out of his hand, he had considered them his pets. But he said nothing to his grandfather and the old man was surprised the next day when he went out to get the eggs and realised what had happened to the hens.
Sometimes old Fyfe would bake bread – hard, dry, bannocky bread, but Spit preferred white bread, and he would insist on bringing it home after school from the baker's, or he would catch one of the delivery vans on the other side of the railway line in the early morning.
But buying and selling were part of the second category of his life. This was Spit in town. He did most of the shopping for butter and jam and meat, and he would collect the four-gallon tins of kerosene for the lamps in a little cart he had made from a fruit box and a pair of old pram wheels. He would also use the cart to bring home horse manure from Mr Walker's stables for his grandfather's garden. But most of his carrying was done in an old leather hunting bag he had found under the boiler, and he carried it over one shoulder, so that it reached almost to his ankles. He wouldn't carry fish in it but

he used it for anything else he sold in season: potatoes or tomatoes or beans from Fyfe's garden, and because they were usually perfect vegetables there were always women at their back doors who would buy them because Spit always chose households near the centre of the town which didn't have their own vegetable gardens.

He sometimes had problems with the vegetables when Mrs Andrews, for instance, always asked, 'What have you got today Spit?' and when he said, 'Peas,' she would say, 'Let me see them.' Normally this could have produced a vigorous response from Spit: what did she want to see them for? But Mrs Andrews had always said to him, 'And how is your grandfather, Spit?' which was enough to remove her from one of his sharp rejections.

Spit had his other friends in town. He would sometimes turn the blower on the forge for Tom Smythe the blacksmith, and he would hitch a ride with Bob Taylor the baker in his horse-drawn cart, or a dink home on Jack Burrow's bike as he delivered the meat. But though he kept his stocky, barefoot distance with most people, he had no real enemies. Even Mrs Betty Arbuckle was not so much an enemy as a crank, and when his mate, Crispie Cornforth, told him that Betty Arbuckle was after him again, and was determined to get him to the Boys Home in Bendigo, Spit shrugged it off and said, 'She doesn't know what she's doing. My grandfather'll make mincemeat of her. And anyway how does she think she's going to get me off to an orphanage in Bendigo when I am not an orphan?'

'That's what she's after though,' Crispie said.

But to Spit Mrs Betty Arbuckle wasn't really a menace, she was simply a permanent troublemaker who made his grandfather angrier than usual. Once out of the way she was out of mind, except when he decided on the spur of the moment to pick on Joannie or Ben.

There were two more categories to Spit's life in St Helen which, when his real troubles began, were an established part of his special environment. One was his life at school, and the other was his friendship with Sadie Tree.

School to Spit was a winter period when the river was swollen and he couldn't fish effectively or lay his crayfish drums or swim across to Pental Island. He didn't mind school, he could even like it, and he could always sit still long enough to tolerate lessons because he had always been used to sitting still with his grandfather on the step by the river, or in the house, or on the seat in the vegetable garden or even at the workbench. The only real trouble he gave Miss Masters, his teacher, was the boom of his voice and the size of his writing. Spit always writ everything large – big bold letters which too soon filled a line and a page. No discipline that Miss Masters put on him could reduce the size of his letters, and being left-handed he held his exercise book sideways to write towards him. Though Miss Masters never tried to make him write with his right hand, she had tried consistently to correct his letters by insisting that he keep the book straight.

'That way,' she told him, 'you can see what you're doing.'

'Yes Miss,' Spit said, 'but then I can't do what I'm seeing.'

'You're too stubborn,' Miss Masters would say in despair.

'Yes Miss . . .' Spit would boom.

Miss Masters had long ago given up trying to soften his voice although sometimes it was unbearable, but she did her best with Spit. She always knew when old Fyfe was going through a quiet period because Spit's primitive homework was then reasonably disciplined. But during the bad patches Spit would ignore all homework and take his punishment without resentment or concern. Next year Spit would pass into the first grade of the secondary school, and Miss Masters, a grey-haired professional who always kept two pencils stuck into her thick grey hair like antennae, was concerned for him because he was the only boy in her class who still did not wear shoes or socks; and that would not do at the higher school. But she knew there was little that she could do about it because she couldn't talk to old Fyfe. Nobody could. She could only hope that they would solve the problem between them in their own way.

'You're always a problem, Spit,' she would sigh, but not without affection.

'Yes Miss,' Spit would boom back.

Out of the classroom and out of school Spit was a come-and-go friend to most of the other boys, but when he played cricket or football with them he gave the game everything he had. This was often effective, though not always so, particularly at cricket when he wanted to hit every ball for six. If he connected it worked. If he missed the ball everybody nearby ducked in case the bat left his hand in its wild swing. If he was bowled out he always spat dispassionately at the wicket and handed the bat over to the next man.

His closest friend, Crispie Cornforth, was a country boy who rode to school on a bike from a poor and salty farm five miles up the little Murray. Spit would get a dink home on Crispie's bike but they would always part at the railway line, and if he met Crispie out of school on a Saturday it was usually on Pental Island, not at the farm. Their friendship depended on no surroundings, and they knew it.

But Crispie was the only person in town who had ever questioned, indeed dared question Spit about his grandfather.

'What does he do it for, Spit?' Crispie asked him one summer's day when they were lying on the hard cracked mud of the big river, out of sight and sound of town and people, fishing and making the best of a hot day on the big river. 'I mean why does he go around shouting at everybody?'

'He's got something wrong with his head,' Spit replied.

'Everybody in town thinks he's crazy.'

'That's what they think,' Spit said. 'They don't know anything about it.'

'My old man says he ought to be locked up.'

'Well ...' And, with his usual habit of defending his grandfather, Spit turned his head and spat at a passing bee. 'If they lock him up I'll go and burn the place down. They don't know anything about it, Crisp, that's all I'm saying.'

'Well, I always say, "Hello Mr MacPhee," and you know what he says back to me?'

'No,' Spit said. 'But I'll bet he lets you have it.'

'He always says, "You've got big ears, Willy Wastle."'

'He likes you,' Spit said.

'Why does he call me Willy Wastle?'

'That'll be his name for you, Crisp. He does that all the time. Sometimes he calls me Tam Glen or Davie Bluster,' Spit said, and they both laughed at the old man's wild sport with their proper names.

They were good friends – planned to be for life, but one day Crispie didn't come to school. He didn't come the next day, and on the fourth day Miss Masters told the class that Crispie had been bitten by a tiger snake in one of the canals near his house, and he had never recovered. He was being buried that day, and Spit decided on the spot that he would never forget Crispie and would never have another friend as long as he lived.

It was early summer. Spit was still 'not quite eleven', and now that his real trouble was about to begin he had no Crispie to support him. In the end it would be Sadie Tree who would become the other part of him – like Crisp, only being a girl Sadie was different.

5

Sadie Tree lived in a house downstream, where the little Murray and the big Murray joined. Her father, Jack, owned a Dodge tourer and he was the Pastoral and Livestock Inspector for the district: a strict, soldierly man who, as an Anzac at Gallipoli, had discovered something good in the best moments of soldiering. In the attack on Suvla Bay he had taken charge of a machine-gun position when all the officers and sergeants had been killed, and he had done it well enough and bravely enough for a General to raise him from Private to Officer in the field. Since then he had kept his faith in soldiering and in old soldiers as the best thing in his life. He was the Secretary of the St Helen's branch of the Returned Soldiers League, and his first loyalty in the town (apart from his family) was to any man who had been a soldier. Old Anzacs always knew that he would help them if he could, they could count on him, but this belief in the comradeship and pride of arms made something of a disciplinarian of him at home, although for his luck he had married a silent and obedient and gentle wife, Grace, and now had a silent and obedient and gentle daughter, Sadie, both of whom accepted his discipline, and respected and loved him nonetheless. In the end, Spit's predicament would make a change in this mix of modesty and discipline, but that was to be the end, not the beginning.

Sadie was a quiet girl and a clever girl who watched everything, saw everything, and said so little that she was hardly noticed even by girls her own age. Nobody resented her and nobody bothered her, and those who did notice her said that she got her silence from her father, the strong silent Jack. But if Sadie had inherited his silence (it was really her mother's) she did not have his strength, because Jack was used to having his own way so that Sadie and her mother always gave into him, as if it was the normal and the right thing to do. There was never any conflict in the Tree family.

Spit liked Mrs Tree because she was always silently there. She was often alone with Sadie when her husband was away on one of his inspections, and she would sometimes walk by herself, or with Sadie, along the river bank and stop to admire old Fyfe's garden. But neither she nor Sadie would ever say anything at all to old Fyfe. They left him alone if they passed by when he was in the garden. When Spit, in turn, offered Mrs Tree a fresh cod at her back door on a Friday (they were Catholics) and wriggled it fiercely under her nose, she would smile, almost laugh, and wait without saying anything for Spit to name his price. She would always accept it, pay it, and take the fish without saying a word except to say, 'Thanks Spit'. If Sadie was around when this was happening Spit hardly noticed her, although he was often faintly aware that she was always inspecting him as she did everybody else. But she would say, 'Goodbye Spit,' as he left, and that always startled him because he would shift a little on his bare feet and shout back, 'G'day, Sade,' and then forget her a few moments later.

It was the river that eventually made them friends. Spit's passion for watching the currents and sending small, flat, pointed 'boats' along the river carrying messages to unknown destinations, took him often along the bank downstream to pass by the Trees' house, which was not right on the river but a little way back from it nearer the railway line. Spit would write his left-handed messages on old newspaper saying, 'Help. I'm shipwrecked. 20 *longtude,* 62 *latude.* Come quick.' His grandfather had once given him a hard and shortened version of *Kidnapped.* Tying the message around the mast of his little flat boat he would swim out to the middle of the river, launch it, and then walk along the bank to follow it through the swirls and eddies until it either lost its message, got stuck on the opposite bank where it was too far away to swim to, or finally disappear for ever into the faster mainstream of the big river.

He loved to guess or calculate the complex twists and turns in the currents and eddies, or puzzle over the reasons for their endless variety, and he was absorbed one day in one of his little boats when a voice behind him said, 'They always end up under that big tree, near the bridge.'

Spit, surprised by the sudden and very quiet arrival of someone behind him, swung around and found Sadie Tree standing with her hands behind her back watching him.

'How do you know?' Spit said.

'Sometimes I follow them when they're in the big river.'

'Tell us another one,' he said disbelievingly. He knew that once they were in the big river they either got swamped by the fast current or were lost to view. 'You can't see them in the middle.'

'Yes, you can,' Sadie said. 'They always come in on the other side near our place. Then they go around and around where the posts are, then they cross to the other side again and come back near the bridge.'

'You can't see them across the other side,' Spit insisted.

'Yes you can, with my father's field glasses.'

'What do you mean?'

'You can see for miles through them.'

'Tell us another one,' Spit said.

'Honest, Spit. Wait here and I'll show you.'

When she came back with the field glasses – a worn but good pair of military 8 x 30s – she showed Spit how to focus them, and then handed them over.

'You're right,' Spit said generously. 'You can see everything.'

Sadie blushed and put out her hand for the field glasses. But Spit wasn't going to part with them so quickly. They were hanging around his neck and he meant them to stay there for a while.

'If we run for it we'll find the one I just put in,' he said and set off along the river bank without waiting to see if Sadie was following.

She followed, and in thus proving the accuracy of her observations, she and Spit established their mutual fascination for the weird behaviour of the river. But it was a private discovery and it became at first a secret friendship. Sadie knew that her father would object because he thought Spit wild, and in need of discipline. So rather than create a situation which would end in a downright denunciation of it,

Sadie kept it to herself. That is, she told only her mother.

Mrs Tree thought about it for a moment and then said, 'Don't tell your father. He'll only tell you to keep away from Spit.'

Implied in this response was Mrs Tree's permission for Sadie to talk to Spit if she wanted to, because Mrs Tree liked him and trusted him. And, in allowing it, there was also a silent contract between them which left Jack out of it, even though he liked to rule the house even in his absence. But it was not a serious conspiracy. Grace Tree respected and admired her husband, and Sadie loved her father, but because neither one had any particular friend they depended on each other to keep for themselves some of the fragments of their own lives – the unimportant fragments which mother and daughter considered harmless and inoffensive to Jack. After all, Spit was only a small boy, and Grace Tree had always felt, like Betty Arbuckle, that some day Spit was going to need help, although she wasn't quite sure what sort of help it would be. Certainly not Betty Arbuckle's Boys Home, she knew that much.

It seemed natural thereafter for Spit to devise a system of sending messages downstream to Sadie, rather than addressing them to unknown and unlikely persons. At first it was a trial run of one little flat pine boat which they both followed, and the message on this one was written by Sadie and read, '*I am sick. Send me a doctor,*' which Spit had instantly rejected.

'If he's sick, all he has to do is walk up to the railway line and ask somebody in one of the houses to get Doctor Stevens. So what's the use of that?'

'What's the use of saying you're shipwrecked?' Sadie said. 'It's the same thing.'

'No it isn't. Nobody's around when you're shipwrecked, so you can't ask somebody up the railway line to help you.'

'You can't get shipwrecked in a river,' Sadie insisted.

'What do you mean? What about the old *Mundoo* where the boiler came from?'

'That was years ago. There aren't any river boats on the little Murray anymore, so nobody would believe you.'

Spit conceded the point because his private world had finally been penetrated, and his imagination now had a companion.

They operated their message system successfully all summer, so that in the end Spit was writing genuine messages to Sadie. 'I am going swimming tonight.' Or 'I am up at the old Point. Home at six.' When Spit went swimming off the steps near the boiler (he never swam with the other boys higher up) Sadie would sit on the hard mud steps and watch him. She couldn't swim herself, and when he tried to persuade her she said, 'Not me, Spit. I'm afraid of the water.'

'But it's dangerous living by the river and not being able to swim. What if there's a flood?' he told her.

'My father doesn't want me to go in when he's away,' Sadie said. 'That's why I'm afraid, I think.'

'He won't know.'

'He'd find out.'

'What does your mother say?'

'I don't know, Spit. If you ask her she might let me.'

'Me? Why should I ask her?'

'She trusts you. Only don't tell anyone else.'

Spit as a plenipotentiary was blunt rather than diplomatic. 'It's no good if she can't swim, Mrs Tree,' he said, and this was his one-and-only argument.

In fact Mrs Tree agreed with him. 'But I'll have to be there, Spit. At first anyway, and she's never to go in unless you're near her.'

'Okay, Mrs Tree,' Spit agreed.

With Mrs Tree sitting on the mud steps, and Sadie in a new bathing suit, he taught her to swim. His methods were not persuasive but impatient, as if it astounded him that she couldn't just walk straight in and do what he did.

'Just paddle your arms and legs,' he shouted at her.

Mrs Tree listened and watched and took the girl's punishment for her, but she said nothing. Sadie was twice in tears, shouting (for her) at Spit, 'I can't. I can't . . .' which Spit treated with anguish and contempt. 'Yes you can,' he said. 'You're not even trying, Sadie. Look.'

To demonstrate the ease of it, Spit was under and over the water and halfway across the river and back in a violent, skilful, splashing demonstration of how easy it was.

'I'll never get it,' Sadie said.

'Go on. You just have to do it.'

In the end she did it, so that in those first miraculous strokes of a dog-paddle Sadie accepted thereafter a lifelong debt to Spit. Her mother too was so pleased that she insisted on Spit (dripping wet) sitting in the kitchen and drinking a glass of raspberry vinegar. It was the first time that Spit had been invited to sit in anybody's kitchen, and though he was always bold in the grip of a new experience, he was about to leave quick. But then Mrs Tree offered him a second glass. Anything more than the essentials was manna to Spit. He would sometimes buy an icecream or an aniseed ball because he had a sweet tooth, or a snowball for a penny, but this was a different kind of indulgence so he said, 'Yes thanks,' and Mrs Tree gave him the second glass of the thick red cordial. Sadie had been watching him and smiling, still happy with her first few strokes in the water.

'Can we do it again tomorrow?' she asked him.

'All right,' Spit said. 'But you have to learn to put your head under. It's no use learning to swim unless you can put your head under.'

'All right, all right,' Sadie said. 'I'll give it a go.'

Mrs Tree watched them both, and in a moment's pause between Spit's long draughts of the red vinegar she said, 'How old are you, Spit?'

'Eleven,' he said, and then as if in this silent kitchen he had suddenly heard the violence of his own voice for the first time, he said it again a little quieter, and he retreated too. 'I'm eleven now, Mrs Tree,' he said, 'but I'll be twelve next birthday.'

'I thought so,' Mrs Tree said. 'You're the same age as Sadie. She'll be eleven in January. When is your birthday?'

'Last week – the fourteenth,' he said.

It was, in its way, another tie, and instead of wanting to get out quick Spit looked around him at the kitchen and, seeing an old, marbled, mantle clock above the fireplace, he said, 'We can fix that if it stops.'

'I know,' Mrs Tree said. 'But it's still going strong. It belonged to my father.'

'It probably needs cleaning,' Spit said.

'No. I think it's all right,' Mrs Tree said.

'Well . . . if it stops,' Spit said threateningly at the clock.

'Don't worry,' Mrs Tree said. 'We'll have it around to your grandfather in a jiffy.'

Though Spit and his grandfather seemed only able to shout at each other, Spit was also used to long silences with old Fyfe, so it was easy for him to sit in this kitchen of silence with two people who said little or nothing at all. He had finished his raspberry vinegar and he was aware that Mrs Tree was looking at him the way nobody else in the town looked at him, although he didn't know what exactly it meant. Sadie seemed simply to be waiting for him to do something or to tell them something. When he finally decided it was necessary he said to her at the top of his voice, 'I'm going fishing tonight by the willows. Do you want to come?'

'In the dark?' she said.

'Of course. That's the best time, up by the willows.'

'What will your grandfather say?' Sadie asked him.

Spit looked surprised. 'Nothing,' he said. 'I'm always up there. Sometimes he comes with me.'

'Is he going with you tonight?' Sadie asked.

'No. He's . . .' Whatever Spit was about to say he changed his mind about it. 'Do you want to come?' he said to Sadie.

Sadie was readily frightened and yet she was also determined. 'Can I go?' she said to her mother. 'Just for a little while.'

'But it's so dark,' her mother said. 'You won't be able to see your way near the river.'

'That's nothing,' Spit said. 'I know the way blindfold.'

Mrs Tree looked worried, but she too had her own way of making a difficult decision. 'You'll have to hold her hand, Spit. I shan't let her go otherwise.'

'You mean just on the way up there?' Spit said.

'Yes. And when you're at the willows, Sadie has to sit right away from the river. No paddling or swimming. I want you to promise me that.'

'That's all right,' Spit said. 'It would frighten the fish anyway.'

Mrs Tree was still worried but she said to Sadie, 'Do you really want to go?'

Sadie pulled in her lips nervously and nodded.

Spit said he would come at seven o'clock, and he would give a special whistle, which he demonstrated piercingly. Then, saying in a business-like way, 'I have to go home now,' he was up and out in a few seconds, leaving Sadie and Mrs Tree feeling rather sorry in their quiet kitchen that they had suddenly lost a noise and a force and a small attack on their isolation, which left them feeling rather empty.

'It's such a pity,' Mrs Tree said to Sadie.

Sadie didn't ask what was the pity, but her silence and her slight frown asked the question anyway.

'He's a very nice boy, considering all the problems he and old Mr MacPhee have had to live with.'

'He doesn't seem to mind,' Sadie said.

'I don't think he really understands,' Grace Tree said but did not go any further. She shook her head a little and left it there.

At first nobody was aware of Spit and Sadie's friendship. It wasn't difficult to keep it modest enough to be unobtrusive, and it gave them a chance to enjoy themselves. Sadie was a good pupil, and it wasn't too long before she was swimming more than a few strokes and learning to dive and keep her head under water. Spit also taught her how to fish, how to bait with worm or mussels, and how to cast the line out. She knew where all his crayfish drums were, a secret that Spit normally kept to himself, because someone in town was sure to take a look at them and maybe steal the crayfish if they knew where they were. He couldn't get her across to Pental Island because that was going too far for Mrs Tree's comfort. But Mrs Tree no longer walked along the river bank at night waiting anxiously when Sadie went with Spit to the willows, or to inspect his crayfish drums. She had given Sadie an electric torch, but after trying it out one night when it was particularly dark, Sadie said to her mother, 'It's not much use, Mum, because when your eyes get used to the dark you can see a lot more than you can see with a torch. And Spit can see everything.'

What became a habit, too, was Spit's visits to the Trees' kitchen, although he would never accept their invitation to eat his six o'clock tea there. 'I have to eat with my grandfather,' he would say, and they didn't press him. But he knew, without being told, to keep away when Jack Tree was at home, although he was now curious about Mr Tree. Previously he had taken no more notice of Jack than he had of most of the adults in town who either greeted him, ignored him, or treated him and his grandfather as freaks. Occasionally Jack Tree – deciding to notice him – would say 'Goodday, Spit,' in his crisp, upright, disciplined way, and Spit would return the greeting equally at the top of his voice.

So, like everyone else in town, Spit kept his distance from the Tree household when he had to. But the day that he saw Mr Tree by the river looking carefully at the water's edge, Spit considered himself to be on equal ground. The river was his domain. He watched Mr Tree without greeting him, and when he was finally noticed Mr Tree said, 'Hello, Spit. It's still pretty low, isn't it? It isn't rising at all.'

'It hasn't started yet,' Spit said.

'It's been a long summer,' Jack Tree said.

To Spit the longer the summer lasted and the longer it took for the river to begin its autumn rise, the better. But for Jack Tree, and his district stock and pasture problems, it was a question of water in the Riverrain where the dairy herds were. Jack would always look back on these long dry summers as harbingers of drought, and if the weather didn't change soon there could be trouble.

'You haven't noticed any rise at all in the last week or so?' he said to Spit.

Spit always kept a willow sprig on the very edge of the river at right-angles to see if it was rising or falling, and he could report to Mr Tree that the river had fallen another two inches in the last week. 'It's still going down,' he said.

'They're keeping the weir wide open too,' Mr Tree said thoughtfully. 'So we're going to be in trouble. How are the fish?' he asked Spit.

'All right,' Spit said. 'Do you want to buy a cod?'

'You shouldn't catch so many,' the soldier replied. 'You're depleting them.' And he was on his way up the slope to his house when Sadie came running along the river path from upstream calling, 'Spit, it's your grandfather. You'll have to come quick.' Then she saw her father and stopped where she stood.

Spit said, 'Goddamn,' and was off, running like a muscular,

fleet-footed hare along the path, with Sadie and Mr Tree following him. They found old Fyfe lying twisted-up on the very edge of the river, his hands clamped tight over his ears, his face distorted as he groaned and swung his head from side to side, and his legs stiff and straight. He was shouting something that was too broken to understand.

'He's having a fit,' Mr Tree said, kneeling over him.

'No he isn't,' Spit shouted. 'It's not a fit. Don't touch him.'

'We'll have to get him inside.' Mr Tree said.

'That's no good,' Spit said. 'Just leave him alone. Don't touch him.' And Spit tried to push Jack Tree out of the way.

'He'll fall in the river if you don't move him,' Jack insisted as Spit kept pushing him off.

'No, he won't. Just leave him alone, and go away. Go away.'

Sadie and Mr Tree stood for a moment, undecided, watching the old man's suffering. But then Sadie said, 'Come on, Dad,' and she pulled at his arm. 'Spit will do everything.'

'He needs some help.'

'No, he doesn't,' Sadie said, pulling at her father. 'You've got to leave them.'

Reluctantly, Mr Tree allowed himself to be led away by Sadie as Spit took one of the buckets of water, always waiting at the river bank for kitchen use, and threw it over his grandfather. Fyfe groaned a little and ground his teeth but then he subsided, and as Mr Tree followed the fleeing Sadie up the slope they heard Fyfe shouting, and Spit replying angrily, 'You're too near the river, Grandpa. You've got to get up.'

'Poor Mr MacPhee,' Sadie said miserably as they hurried around the big trees to their fenced-in house to get to the back door instead of the front.

'He's a tough old bird,' Mr Tree said. 'Although I've never seen him like that before.'

'Why is he like that?' Sadie asked her father. 'Is he really mad?'

'Not all the time,' her father said. 'But he's getting worse, and some day he's going to go clean off his head. No doubt about it.'

'What'll happen to Spit then?' Sadie asked. 'What'll he do?'

'Betty Arbuckle will probably get him,' Mr Tree said.

'But she'd send him away to the Boys Home in Bendigo, wouldn't she?'

'Probably.'

'That's not fair.'

Mr Tree was surprised to hear so much sudden conviction from his daughter. 'It doesn't have to be fair or unfair,' he told her severely. 'It's just the way it is. Spit needs some discipline, and that's the sort of place where he'd get it.'

Sadie didn't accept it, even though she knew she must accept it.

'You keep away from that old man,' Mr Tree told her. 'In case he gets dangerous.'

'Yes, Dad,' she said, and when they had joined Mrs Tree in the kitchen Sadie said nothing at all about old Fyfe because if anything was to be said about it her father would do the saying.

That night, when Sadie had gone to bed, Jack Tree told his wife what had happened. 'The old man was lying there like a grizzly bear in agony,' he told her. 'His hat was off, but he had on a sort of felt skull cap which looked as if it was glued to his head.'

'Last week,' Grace Tree said, 'Mrs Evans told me he was seen walking around the town in the middle of the night, shouting at all the dogs and opening all the front gates, with Spit walking behind him closing the gates again.'

'You keep the back door locked,' Mr Tree told her.

'But he's harmless, Jack,' Mrs Tree said quietly. 'He could never hurt anybody.'

They were sitting in Mrs Tree's spotless, linoleum kitchen. While Mrs Tree labelled the glass jars of her preserved apricots, Mr Tree was saving electricity by working on his reports at the other end of the kitchen table – not only a soldierly man but a neat man with a neat moustache, organised papers, and a dry pipe in his mouth which he sucked but didn't smoke.

'You're not to take a chance,' he ordered his wife. 'The old boy could easily turn violent.'

Mrs Tree didn't argue, but she inspected her husband carefully for a moment before saying, 'We really ought to do something about that boy, Jack.'

'What do you mean – do something? Do what?'

'I don't know,' Mrs Tree said. 'But he and old Fyfe can't go on much longer the way they are. Spit is a nice boy, and someone should help him.'

'How?'

'I don't know how,' Mrs Tree said unhappily. 'But there must be some way.'

'Leave him to Betty Arbuckle. She'll do something. The best thing for him is probably that home in Bendigo.'

'That's not right Jack.'

'Well, right or wrong, there's nothing you can do about it, Grace, so leave him alone. He's a grubby little devil, and he's like the old man. He can look after himself.'

'He can't be grubby if he spends so much time in the river.'

'Keep him away, that's all I'm saying. Don't let him hang around.'

'He doesn't hang around.'

'Then what are we arguing about?'

Grace felt guilty now. She wanted to tell her husband more about Spit, but Jack had made his position too firm and clear to do it now. Nonetheless, when he went off again on one of his inspection tours she allowed Sadie to go on swimming and fishing with Spit. The trouble was that other people had seen the children together, the Evanses, Mrs Andrews up the slope, the station master's wife, and Mr Moon the butcher. Sooner or later it would all leak out.

It was Sadie who told her more than anyone else could possibly know about Spit and his grandfather, because Sadie had been watching and listening and thinking about them, and she had reported everything she had seen and done to her mother. Sadie had not only seen inside the boiler, but she could now sit quietly in Mr MacPhee's workroom with Spit and watch them together. It had been quite simple. She had said to Spit after they had been swimming one day, 'Can I see inside your boiler house?'

Spit's first reluctant reply was, 'I dunno . . .' But Sadie simply waited as if she knew he would change his mind, and he did so. 'All right,' he said. 'But no telling anybody.'

'No. I won't tell anybody.'

Spit took her through the front door of the house, through

the workroom where old Fyfe was working on a clock, and into the extension which finally opened into the boiler itself. What she saw amazed her, because there was nothing else like it in the town of St Helen. The inside walls of the boiler were painted yellow, and though rust from the rivets had streaked the sides, the whole interior had its own painted designs – not the wavy line of the outside walls but a black fish, a lily-like flower with a green stem, something that looked like a firework bursting, and a red tomato. She had never seen anything like it. Spit's narrow, wooden bunk with an old quilt on it was at one end under a cut-out window, and at the other end she could see a table painted bright red, and on it a bundle of old books, mussel shells, lines, and the bits and pieces of clocks and watches. She could not take it all in at a glance, but afterwards she remembered a flower pot with a fern in it, an old acetylene bike lamp, and a painted kerosene tin which had been cut into curls and twists around the top. It was full of old wire and pieces of wood and horseshoes and dried crayfish claws.

'It's fantastic,' Sadie said. 'It's great, Spit. It's absolutely great.'

'Don't say anything about it,' he said. 'That's all.'

'No, I won't. I swear.'

It seemed quite simple thereafter for Sadie to sit in the extension, which was where Spit had his own bench and where she could watch him shape the little pine messenger boats, make sinkers for his fishing lines out of lead slugs, and (another of his secrets) fit spokes into a rusty bicycle wheel which he would eventually add to the rest of a half-built old bike which still needed a front wheel, handlebars, two pedals and a seat.

'But where did you get it from?' she asked him.

'I got this and that from the back of Sykes' bike shop, and some at the blacksmith's, and here and there and everywhere.'

Spit almost forgot her sometimes as she sat on a small three-legged stool; and when his grandfather shouted at him, 'Ye maun put the potatoes on, or ye won't be eating supper,' she moved with him into the small kitchen at the end of old Fyfe's workroom where she helped him peel the potatoes. Spit was a quick impatient peeler of potatoes, and he filled a cooking pot from a bucket of river water on the floor. He put it on the wood stove, which he poked fiercely, and then shouted at his grandfather, 'You didn't put any wood on the fire.'

'Well put it on now.'

'That's what I am doing.'

Sadie listened to them and whispered to Spit, 'Why are you always so angry with each other?'

Spit didn't lower his voice but said indignantly, 'We're not angry with each other.'

'But that's how it sounds, Spit. Everybody thinks . . .'

'They don't know anything about it,' Spit said, and he was putting two mutton chops in a wire folder to grill them when he said, 'Do you want a chop?'

'No, thanks. I'll have to go home in a minute for tea.'

She left reluctantly, but thereafter she would come and go to the little house without any difficulty. Old Fyfe had looked quizzically at her once and said with a sort of grim laugh, 'How are ye dressed, Jean Armour, aye sae clean and neat.'

Sadie, in her own advice to herself, had always been frightened of old Fyfé, but in the little house with Spit she lost all her fear of him, and though she didn't understand what he said to her most of the time, she always smiled at him and one day said to him, 'Can I watch you mend the clocks?'

The old man's face, grey as it was and grizzled as it was, and so often pained, ground itself into a smile. He stared at her for a moment. 'Stand there,' he said.

'Give her the glass,' Spit said to his grandfather.

'You be quiet, ye cairn . . .'

'I was only trying to help,' Spit shouted back.

Sadie listened and watched, unafraid, and the old man pointed to the clock he was working on and said, 'Ye don't need the glass. It's the clock of Mrs Andrews, and if ye look at the coggies there ye'll see all her powder, pink and dirty, and look at her grey hairs that she brushes into the clock. All in a bedroom, the clock stays, and it maun tick with its face down.' He showed Sadie the scratched glass of the clock. 'And all that grease on her face. She's winding it up wi' her fingers thick with that awfu' gruel.' Mrs Andrews' face-creamed finger marks were stained into the clock where she held it to wind it.

'I never thought . . .' Sadie began in amazement.

But old Fyfe had lost interest in his demonstration, and Sadie stood still to watch his quivering hands working with the diminutive screwdrivers, holding them miraculously still long enough to undo the minute screws. The old man crouched over his bench, a tiny figure. It was neat and clean, and she could smell the fine oil he used on the clocks he was repairing. Sometimes it seemed to be a quiet, rumbling fury, and other times it was more like a Scottish bee buzzing. Noise, in fact, seemed to be his only relief, as if it were a desperate diversion from whatever was going on in his head.

Like that, Sadie learned to sit and watch not only old Fyfe's clock and watch repairing, but the way he re-set planes and razors on his oilstone and with the tiny grinder, using a strop to finish them with.

While she watched old Fyfe, Spit would sometimes behave like a housewife, sweeping the floor or cleaning the stove; or he would leave her when he watered the garden or chopped the wood for the stove, and she began to love the place. But she was surprised one day when, helping Spit with the spokes of the old bicycle wheel, she heard her mother calling her.

'Oh, my gosh,' she said, handing Spit the pliers with which she was holding the spokes in place for him. 'What time is it?'

'I dunno,' Spit said, 'but – maybe your father's come home.'

'Goodbye, Spit,' Sadie said as she rushed out. 'Goodbye, Mr MacPhee,' she shouted. And, calling over her shoulder, she said, 'Be back tomorrow.'

But in fact she would not be back on the morrow, because that night old Fyfe burned down the house, and Spit's days of security and safety were finally over.

6

Spit had awakened to hear his grandfather banging and opening and then banging and opening again and again the front door. At first Spit lay still and did nothing because it was not unusual for his grandfather to wander around in the middle of the night making a noise and shouting nonsense. Sooner or later it would stop and the old man would drop exhausted on his bed to sleep it off, groaning and twisting and covering his head but eventually subsiding. But this time it seemed different because Spit could see a reflection of a light through the boiler's window. Instead of simply shouting, his grandfather was also singing, which he sometimes did when he was working at his bench, but never in the middle of the night.

Spit got out of bed, and still wearing the old shirt he slept in and pulling on his trousers, he went through the house and found his grandfather holding the front door open and wrenching violently at it as if he wanted to tear it off its hinges.

'Grandpa,' Spit shouted at him. 'You've got to stop. You're making too much noise.'

But he knew his grandfather couldn't hear him. What puzzled Spit was the hurricane lamp which his grandfather had managed to light. It was on the path leading to the gate. Deciding quickly that it was the best thing to do, Spit picked it up but didn't blow it out. Old Fyfe was still singing, but sometimes he laughed the grim and curious and agonised laugh which was often a sort of punctuation to his shouting. When Spit tried to pull his arm he held the door tight and shouted, 'I'm awfu' cold . . . awfu' cold.'

'You can't be cold,' Spit told him.

'It's an auld auld killick,' Fyfe said in his agony. Then he left the door and walked down the path to the gate, which he also tried to pull off its hinges. It was too well made, and Fyfe suddenly crumpled to his knees and held his hands to his ears and began to moan.

'It maun kill me, cairgie . . . It's awfu' bad . . .'

'Come on, Grandpa. Come back inside,' Spit said anxiously, aware that though it looked like the old man's usual behaviour in such moments, this time there was something else that was different and disturbing. Spit held up the lamp and caught a glimpse of tears running down his grandfather's face. Then, in a quiet, almost normal but pained voice, his grandfather looked up at him and said, 'Go away, cairgie . . . run away, d'ye hear me. Run away from me. Go on . . . Go on, I tell ye.'

Spit had never before heard that sort of calm if desperate sense in his grandfather's voice, and he didn't know what to make of it. 'Go on w'ye,' Fyfe shouted as if he was trying desperately now to contain some terrible danger that could not be held off much longer. 'Run off, cairgie, and don't come back. Don't ye come back, do y'hear . . .'

Spit understood the words but he couldn't grasp the meaning or the reason. He shifted from one bare foot to the other, holding up the hurricane lamp so that he could see his grandfather's upturned face. What he saw was a subterranean terror in the old man's eyes, and it was the first time in his life that Spit felt frightened by his grandfather's behaviour.

'What's the matter, Grandpa?' he said. 'What's wrong?'

'Will ye go . . .' the old man groaned.

Spit knew that he had to stay; above all he had to stay. 'I'm not going anywhere,' he said. 'You've got to get inside. It's no use shouting out here. You've got to go in.'

The old man's face made some final tortured gesture towards sanity, clawing at it, trying to convince the boy. Then it broke into madness as if everything he had been holding back had finally defeated him and had now overcome him. He no longer saw. He no longer recognised. He seemed no longer to have any link with anything except the awful torture in his own mind. And, seizing the lighted lamp from Spit, he walked slowly up the path and threw it through the open door of the house.

It was too unexpected for Spit to stop him doing it, and as the lamp glass smashed and the kerosene spilled and caught alight Spit ran straight into the flames. Without thinking about it he tried to damp them out with his bare feet. When he felt the burning pain of it he looked around for one of the buckets of water that were usually kept near the stove. One bucket was empty and the other one only half full, awaiting a fresh refill in the morning. He threw the half bucket of water over the flames which made no impression on them, so he rushed out and down to the river to fill one of the buckets on the banks. By the time he had struggled back to the house with it, the whole floor was alight and also the curtain that divided off his grandfather's bed. He threw the water over the floor but again it made no impression, and though his grandfather was standing in the doorway looking at the flames and shouting, Spit ignored him and ran back to the river once more for water. But this time he knew as he threw it on the flames that it was hopeless for him to go on alone.

'Grandpa, get out. Don't stand there,' he cried.

The old man didn't see or hear, and Spit pulled him out of the doorway. Then he set off down the river and up the slope to the house he knew best, Sadie Tree's. The back door was a wire screen door so there was no use hammering on it. Instead he shouted, 'Mr Tree. Mr Tree. Our house is on fire. Mr Tree . . .'

It took a few minutes, but Jack Tree heard him and called out, 'Who is it?'

'It's Spit MacPhee. Our house is on fire. Will you come and help me?'

'Did you call the fire brigade?'

'No, I can't.'

'All right. I'll do it.' Mr Tree shouted from somewhere within. 'Go up to the Andrews on the other side, and Tim Evans. Get their help. I'll be down.'

Spit was off up the well-worn path to the railway line, and he repeated his cries at the back doors of the Andrews' house and the Evans'. Then he raced back to the house and found

Jack Tree already there and the fire so fierce now that it was sending sparks high in the air and crackling fiercely. Mr Tree was running back and forth to the river carrying buckets of water which he threw over the flames, but now it was obviously out of control.

'Where is my grandfather?' Spit shouted.

'Down by the steps. Get some more buckets.'

'It's no use,' Spit cried. 'It's no use any more.'

'Do as you're told,' Mr Tree ordered. 'Get the buckets.'

They were joined by Mr Andrews and his son Jolly and then Mr and Mrs Evans and Joan Gillespie their neighbour. There were only enough buckets and kerosene tins with wire handles for six people, and though they all poured water onto the fire it was obvious that it couldn't be put out. By the time the volunteer fire brigade had reached the railway line, and were on the river bank with a hand pump, there was not enough left of the house to bother about. As the fire began to subside in the ashes, the only thing left standing was the charred boiler. By now, too, there was a little crowd of people from the houses along the railway line. They had all done their best, but it was Mrs Tree and Sadie who went looking for Spit and found him, dripping wet, fifty yards along the river bank holding his grandfather half in and half out of the water.

'Did he go under?' Mrs Tree said. 'Is he drowned?'

'No. He fell in,' Spit said. 'But I got him out.'

With Sadie's help from above, and Spit pushing from the water, Mrs Tree pulled old Fyfe up on the bank.

'He's sick,' Spit said. 'He fell in. He didn't know what he was doing.'

Old Fyfe was now lying so twisted and helpless that Mrs Tree said to Sadie, 'Go and get your father. Quick.'

As Sadie ran off, Spit said, 'He didn't know what he was doing. He just threw it in . . .'

'Threw what in?' Mrs Tree said.

'The hurricane lamp. He just threw it in.'

'He needs a doctor now, Spit. He's unconscious. Are you sure he didn't go under?'

'No, he didn't. He'll be all right,' Spit insisted.

'But he looks bad, Spit. He needs help,' Grace told him.

'I tell you he'll be all right,' Spit insisted.

When Mr Tree arrived, black and wet, Mrs Tree simply pointed to old Fyfe and Mr Tree looked closely and nodded.

'We'll get him up to the house and I'll get Doctor Stevens,' he said. 'You stay here with him, Grace, and I'll get the others to help.' He dropped a hand on Spit then and said, 'Your house is gone, Spit. There's nothing left of it.'

'Oh no . . .' Mrs Tree said.

'It's all right,' Spit said, fighting back. 'My grandfather will build another one.'

'Maybe. Maybe,' Jack Tree said. 'But you wait here until I get back.'

Spit had to push away Jim Evans' dog, Patchy, who had escaped and was pawing and licking him as he stood guard over his grandfather. 'Get away, Patch,' he was saying as Jack Tree and Jim Evans and two others returned and lifted old Fyfe off the ground and set off up the slope with him.

But Spit was already ahead of them, trying to stop them. 'Where are you taking him?' he said, blocking their path.

'He needs a doctor,' Jack Tree told him. 'We'll take him up to our back verandah and get Doctor Stevens.'

'He can stay in the old boiler. It didn't burn down.'

'It's burned out, Spit. It was all that paint on it. And anyway it's half-full of water,' Mr Tree said. 'In fact you'd better come with us too. You can't stay down here.'

'Come on, Spit,' Mrs Tree said. 'We'll look after your grandfather.'

Spit, confused now, followed them up the slope, holding on to his grandfather's wet shirt. And Sadie, walking beside him, whispered, 'Maybe he was drowning and you saved him?'

'No, he wasn't. He just didn't know what he was doing.'

'How long was he in the water?'

'Only a little while. His head didn't even go under.'

'Did he jump in?' she asked softly. 'Is that what he did?'

Spit didn't deny it. 'But he didn't know what he was doing.'

Spit would never remember afterwards all the details of that night, but in its sequence he would remember the long wait in Mrs Tree's kitchen for Dr Stevens to come, and Mrs Tree and Sadie sitting silently beside him.

When Dr Stevens finally came and looked at old Fyfe, he told Spit that they would have to take his grandfather away to the hospital. This time Spit didn't protest because he knew that it was out of his hands now. What had changed his mind was the sight of his grandfather when they had laid him out on the floor of the Trees' verandah, and he had seen his grandfather under the electric light. Spit was still holding his grandfather's shirt in a tight grip, but he suddenly let it go when he saw his grandfather's face. It wasn't the grey, grizzled, fierce and combative Scot's face he had lived with for so much of his life; instead it was a white, shattered old man, helpless, almost lifeless, with the fire gone out of him so that his twitching mouth and staring eyes and his clawlike hands had invented a substitute who looked nothing like his grandfather. Spit knew that they had to take this one away, and when they had carried him out to Dr Stevens' car Spit didn't go with them, he waited at the door until he heard them drive away.

'You'll have to stay here the rest of the night,' Grace Tree told him. 'You can sleep on the old cane bed on the verandah.'

'I have to get back,' Spit said, opening the wire door to go.

She held him back. 'What for?' she said. 'There's nothing left, Spit. So wait until tomorrow.'

'I want to see if my bike's all right,' he said.

'Spit, you haven't got a bike.'

'He was building it himself,' Sadie said, 'from bits and pieces.'

'Well you can't do anything about it tonight,' Grace told him. 'There's nothing more you can do. So wait here and I'll get some covers for you. And Sadie – you go off to bed now.'

Sadie glanced quickly at Spit but didn't say anything to him because he wasn't looking at her or listening, and as he sat down at the kitchen table Grace went out to get the covers for him.

When she came back Spit had his head in his arms on the table. She thought he was crying, but when she touched him on the shoulder she realised he was asleep. 'You'll have to sleep in this,' she said to him when he lifted his head. She gave him one of her husband's old shirts. 'Your clothes are still wet.'

'I'm all right,' Spit said, and when he lay down on the cane bed on the verandah, which she had padded with blankets for him, Grace didn't argue with him but let him be, and in a few moments he was asleep – so heavily asleep that Grace sat on the couch near him for a while looking at his face which, in sleep, had lost its self-sufficiency and its rather serious and confident air, and was now the face of an eleven-year-old boy who was finally vulnerable and exhausted.

'You're going to need all the care and attention you can get this time,' Grace said to the sleeping figure and, sighing as she left him, she added, 'But it shouldn't be from Betty Arbuckle.'

When Jack returned he found Grace asleep in a chair near the kitchen stove, and when he told her the kettle was boiling dry she said, 'It's the second time. What happened? What about old Fyfe? Is he all right?'

Jack washed his hands and sat at the table and watched her making tea. 'When we got him to the hospital the old man sat up and began to fight and shout. He's completely round the bend this time. They had to hold him down.'

'What does Doctor Stevens say?'

'He doesn't think he's got much chance of coming through this one.'

Grace thought carefully for a moment before saying what she had to say. 'What about the boy?' she said. 'What will happen to him now?'

'I'll see Sergeant Joe Collins in the morning. The police will have to do something about him, or the council, or one of the churches.'

'Or Betty Arbuckle,' Grace said unhappily.

'I suppose so. He's a Protestant, so they'll have to look after him.'

Again Grace hesitated and then she said, 'Couldn't he stay here for a while, Jack, until they sort it out?'

'What are you talking about?' Jack Tree said. 'It's not our problem.'

'It wouldn't hurt for a day or two.'

'Not here,' Jack Tree said. 'How's the tea?'

'It's drawing,' she said and poured it. 'But he can't go back to that boiler any more, and Betty Arbuckle lives on the other side of town, miles from the river.'

'What's that got to do with it?'

'He's used to it down here. It's where he lives.'

'Yes, but not in this house. Have some sense, Grace.'

'I meant just for a few days, until they know what to do with him.'

'Joe Collins will find something.'

'But it's a shame, Jack, to just turn the boy like that over to the authorities or to Betty Arbuckle. Betty'll send him away to that Boys Home.'

'It'll have to be done sooner or later if the old man's locked up. So there's no use getting soft about it. He can't stay here, and that's all there is about it.'

Grace didn't argue because she couldn't argue. But she knew that her husband was right. If old Fyfe was finally and completely mad, then sooner or later Spit would have to be cared for by some sort of authority. A few days on the back verandah wouldn't be of much to him.

'He really is a nice boy,' she said. 'That's the pity of it.'

'He's a tough little bushie,' Jack said, 'and he'll survive anything. So don't worry.'

'I'm not sure about that,' Grace said sadly. 'He's not as wild as you all seem to think he is.'

She washed the tea cups and listened to her husband cleaning himself in the bathroom. She took another look at the sleeping Spit, and it seemed to her that with the smell of smoke and fire and damp on him, Spit too had been burned to the ground. How, she wondered, would he emerge from the ashes this time?

7

When Spit woke up at dawn he knew instantly where he was, and without having to think about it he was out the back door and down to the river to see what was left of the house and the boiler. What he expected when he reached it was exactly what he saw – an ugly pile of charred wreckage, a chimney still standing, some smouldering timbers, sheets of twisted corrugated iron on the ground, and nothing left of the house or the extension except the boiler. Nonetheless, it was a shock to see it in broad daylight because when he stood and looked at it he knew that his home had gone.

He walked cautiously into the mess. The buckets which Jack Tree and the others had used to fight the fire with were lined up near the front gate, which still stood, although the fence and flower garden had been trampled down. The gate sign said OUT and Spit pushed it to IN as he passed through it, feeling the damp sharp ashes under his bare feet. He was afraid to continue because of the broken glass and the nails. Remnants of clothes and curtains, and his grandfather's stuffed chair, were still smouldering.

It was the boiler he wanted to get to, and by raking his way through the mess with a piece of wood he reached its gaping side. The extension had been burned to the ground, and now there was only an open hole leading into the boiler. When he put his head inside it he realised for the first time that the fire had ruined the inside of this too. His bed was burned, so were his table and the boxes. The walls were black and charred. The wooden floor had gone. Instead, there was a pool of black water in the iron bottom. The little windows at both ends had been smashed, and he had to avoid the broken glass underfoot. What he saw now was the boiler almost back to its natural state.

His original intention had been to cook himself some breakfast and afterwards to clean out the boiler. But there was nothing to cook. Although the stove was still there and the chimney still stood, the Coolgardie food safe was a twisted, empty wreck. Eggs and butter and jam and porridge and tea had all gone to the flames, and the kettle had lost its handle. He found a pair of old shoes his grandfather usually kept for working in the vegetable garden and, flopping about in them, he set about rescuing what he could of his grandfather's equipment, and whatever clocks or watches were left. He raked out his grandfather's tools from the mess of damp ash – the vice and clamps and the lathe and grinding wheel, and he put them into a box which he had found intact in the garden. But none of the clocks and watches in the process of repair were worth bothering about, although he found Mr Temple's razor. He then set about emptying the water from the boiler with a bucket, and he was still at it when Sadie walked down the slope.

'What on earth are you doing?' she said.

'Cleaning it out,' he told her. 'I can fix it up a bit if I can get rid of all this water.'

'Your breakfast is ready at our place,' she told him.

'I'm not hungry,' he said.

'But you can't fix the boiler now,' she insisted, 'so come on. My mother's waiting for you.'

'Is your father still there?'

'Yes, but he won't do anything to you.'

'Well . . . I want to see my grandfather, and he'll probably try to stop me,' Spit said.

Sadie sighed. 'No, he won't, Spit. Anyway you have to have breakfast.'

It was sound logic, so Spit pulled his feet out of the old shoes and went up the path with Sadie. When he entered the kitchen, Jack Tree was at the table eating bacon and eggs. He looked up at Spit and said, 'You'll have to wash before you sit down at this table, Spit. You look like a blackfeller.'

'Sadie,' Grace said quietly. 'Give Spit the towel I left on the couch, and then both of you come and get your breakfast.'

Spit had never before washed under a running tap in a basin, and when he saw the colour of the water as it left his hands and face he tried to clean the basin too until Sadie said, 'Never mind that. Just wash your face and hands.'

Even so, the towel received a fair residue of the black and the grey from his face and hands. When he was seated at the kitchen table he looked boldly at Mr Tree and said, 'What did you do with my grandfather?'

'He's still in the hospital. Where did you think he was?' Jack said.

'I don't know. Are they going to let him out today?'

Mr Tree shook his head. 'Not today,' he said.

'What are they keeping him for?'

'He's too sick,' Jack Tree said.

'He'll get over it all right,' Spit insisted. 'He always gets over it.'

'This time it's not so good.'

'Am I allowed to go and see him?' Spit asked.

'You'd better talk to Dr Stevens about that,' Jack said. 'But your grandfather won't be able to do much for you now, Spit, so you might as well get used to the idea.'

'I don't want him to do anything for me,' Spit argued. 'I'm going to fix up the boiler myself, and we can live in that.'

Jack Tree – dressed for work in his collar and tie, and with his hair brushed and his face spruced – was in no mood for Spit's nonsense. 'You can't do a damn thing to that boiler,' he said to Spit, 'so don't even think of trying it.'

Spit's instinct to attack as the best means of defence sustained him. 'Anyway I'm going to fix it,' he repeated grimly. 'I don't care what anybody says.'

'You can't live down there any more,' Jack Tree told him, 'so you'll only be wasting your time. Joe Collins will fix up some place for you to live for the time being.'

Grace Tree knew she had to stop them, and she put a plate of bacon and eggs and a cup of tea in front of Spit and said, 'We'll see about that when you've had your breakfast.'

'We are not going to see about anything,' Jack told her. 'I'll take Spit around to Sergeant Collins, and Collins will fix him up with a place to sleep.'

'But Jack . . .'

'No, Grace. Have you got any other clothes?' he asked Spit.

'No. But I'm not going to Sergeant Collins.'

'Somebody'll have to look after you.'

'I can look after myself,' Spit shouted angrily.

Jack Tree stood up. 'I'm not going to argue with you,' he told Spit. 'I'm taking you to Sergeant Collins.'

'Not me,' Spit said and he was off the chair and out the back door before Jack Tree could catch him.

'Oh Jack,' Mrs Tree said. 'Look what you've done.'

Jack Tree was so surprised to hear protest in his wife's voice that he lost his temper. 'Of all the crazy ideas you get sometimes. I'm only trying to do what's best for the kid and now, by God, I'm going up to get Joe Collins.'

Mrs Tree said nothing and Sadie finished her breakfast in silence. But when her father had driven off in the Dodge she slipped out quietly and went down to the river to see if she could find Spit. She thought he would be hiding somewhere, but he was emptying the boiler again, and when she warned him that her father had gone to get Sergeant Collins, Spit said, 'Don't worry. He's not going to catch me.'

'But what are you going to do, Spit? Even if you can fix the boiler how are you going to cook your food? And where will you get your money from?'

'I've got some money. I'll be all right, as long as your father doesn't try to catch me.'

'But I think he's really trying to help you, Spit.'

'Well if he comes down here with Sergeant Collins, I'm off.'

'I suppose you're right,' Sadie said. 'Give me a pail and I'll help you.'

'I've cleaned up the glass, but if you come in here you'll only get dirty.'

'I don't care,' Sadie said, and taking off her sandals and tying her plaits across the top of her head she followed Spit's method of scooping up the water with an old enamel jug and throwing it through the smashed window. She was hurling a half-full jug of water out of the boiler, almost the last of it, when she saw her father and Sergeant Collins coming down the path under the big trees.

'It's them,' she called to Spit. 'They've come.'

Spit was at the other end of the boiler, his shirt was off and he was now barefoot like Sadie. He dropped the jug he was using and, saying 'I'm off, Sade,' he ran out through the ashes and down to the river where he dived in. By the time Jack Tree and Sergeant Collins reached the bank he was halfway across the river, and because there was a current he was carried downstream.

'Come back, you little dingo,' Sergeant Collins shouted.

But Spit was well on his way to Pental Island, and when he scrambled up the bank on the other side he stood there for a moment to get his breath.

'What do you think you're doing?' Sergeant Collins called out to him.

'You're not going to get me,' Spit shouted back.

'Listen, Spit. If you want to see your grandfather you'd better swim back here. You're not going to see him if you don't come back right now.'

'That's not fair,' Spit said.

'That's the way it is, so get back here.'

'Are you going to lock me up afterwards?'

'What would I do that for? I'm not going to hurt you, so come back here and I'll take you up to the hospital to see your grandfather.'

'Don't do it, Spit. They're tricking you,' Sadie called out.

'Sadie!' Mr Tree said, and for the first time in his life he smacked his only daughter across the legs. 'Put your shoes on and get back home,' he told her. 'What are you doing down here anyway?'

'I was helping Spit,' Sadie said defiantly and ran off to collect her sandals and retreat up the slope.

'Come on, Spit,' Sergeant Collins called again. 'Your grandfather wants to see you.'

Spit hesitated, then he began to walk upstream. 'All right,' he said boldly. 'But that's all I'm going to do. I'm going up to see my grandfather. That's all I'm doing.'

'Then come on, I haven't got all day.'

Spit chose his spot and plunged into the river, and when he reached the near bank he was exactly at the steps.

'Have you got another pair of pants?' Sergeant Collins said.

'No. Everything was burnt.'

'He's got a shirt somewhere,' Mr Tree said, 'so put it on and let's go.'

Spit picked up his shirt from the gate and walked up the

slope between Mr Tree and Sergeant Collins, who kept a vigilant eye on him because he expected Spit to run off again at any moment.

'We'll have to do something about you, Spit,' Sergeant Collins said to him. 'You're becoming a bit of a stray.'

'Leave it till later, Joe,' Mr Tree said quickly.

'But I've got that damned Betty Arbuckle on my back already,' Sergeant Collins said under his breath to Jack Tree.

Spit was put in the back seat of Jack Tree's Dodge tourer (though only after Jack had covered it with a piece of canvas from under the front seat) and he watched the town pass by, crouched forward and gripping the side support of the hood. He knew that he was more or less a captive now, and that what happened next would depend on his grandfather. He knew, too, that there was no point asking either one of these men how his grandfather was, because nobody would ever know that except Spit himself. They were always wrong about his grandfather.

When they reached the low, cottage hospital and were walking up the path under the shady trellis of sultana grapevines, Sergeant Collins said, 'Now behave in there, Spit, and for heaven's sake talk quietly. Don't do any of your shouting. It's a hospital.'

'I know,' Spit said. 'I know what to do.'

In the dark, aseptic place Spit rubbed one foot on the other while he waited for Sergeant Collins and Mr Tree to come back. They had been taken away by Sister Campbell with whispers and quick, sharp looks at Spit. In fact Spit had the impression that Sister Campbell was annoyed with Jack Tree. She said to him, 'Not the boy, surely.' And Jack had said something in reply that Spit didn't hear. In a few moments she came back and told him to 'come along'.

'You're all wet,' she said to him, looking at his trousers.

'I was in the river,' he said.

'Haven't you got another pair?'

'They were all burnt,' Spit said.

'It just isn't right,' Sister Campbell muttered, not at Spit but at the world that surrounded him. 'I'm sure we've got some trousers here that will fit you.'

'I'll be all right,' Spit said, and when Sister Campbell

opened the door of a rather cool, dark room with wooden Venetian blinds, he couldn't see anything for a moment. Then he saw dimly his grandfather, lying on a bed.

'Open the blinds,' Jack Tree said to the sister.

'It's not right, Mr Tree,' Sister Campbell said.

'Yes it is. He's got to see his grandfather sooner or later.'

Sister Campbell pulled a cord and the slats of the green Venetian blinds opened. In the light of day Spit saw what was left of his grandfather. He had almost forgotten his last view of him on the Trees' verandah. Now, in a confirmation he didn't want of his grandfather's disintegration, Spit saw that he was strapped by the wrists to the iron bedstead. And though the wild look in his eyes had returned, the rest of his face no longer had anything alive in it. It was worn out, wasted, gone. Even when his grandfather had suffered one of his attacks before, when he couldn't see or hear anything and would finally collapse in agony, Spit had always seen a man alive under the agonised and troubled shell. But looking at his grandfather now, he knew that in this dislocated and distorted face, and in the violent, uncontrollable jerks and twists of his body and the tortured mouth, there was nothing that he could depend on to rescue him.

'You said he wanted to see me,' Spit shouted accusingly to Sergeant Collins. 'He can't talk when he's like this.'

'He kept talking about his cairgie. That's you isn't it?'

'He didn't want to see me at all,' Spit said. 'He never does like this. What did you do with his cap?'

Spit had never seen his grandfather without his skull cap, and now that his head was bare he saw why that cap had always been in place. Instead of hair, Fyfe MacPhee had a dark raw stain on his crown and two deep scars in a simple cross – from the top of his scalp almost to the neck, and the other way almost from ear to ear. It was another destructive dimension to his grandfather that left Spit with very little hope for either his grandfather or himself.

'You just tricked me,' he shouted at Sergeant Collins.

'Listen, Spit. It was the only way.'

'We wanted you to see him, for your own sake,' Jack Tree told him. 'And here's Dr Stevens. He'll tell you what's up with him.'

Dr Stevens dropped a hand on Spit's shoulder and said to Jack Tree, 'I'm not sure if it's right to tell him, Jack.'

'We won't be able to do anything with him, or for him, if you don't tell him the truth,' Jack Tree replied.

'All right,' Dr Stevens said reluctantly, and told Spit to come with him.

Spit had to run to keep up with Dr Stevens who was six feet four inches, and when they reached the little surgery of the hospital Dr Stevens closed the door and told Spit to sit down.

'No thanks. I'll stand up,' Spit said.

'I know how you feel, son, but everybody's trying to do their best for you.'

'I don't want them to do anything,' Spit said.

'I'm sure you don't. But you're going to need help now.'

'No, I'm not. I can look after myself.'

'All right. All right. But I've got to tell you about your grandfather. Do you know what he's got under those scars?'

'No. He always keeps his cap on.'

'He didn't tell you how he got them?'

'No. He never told me anything about it. Not about things like that.'

'Well, we don't know either. But under those scars he's got a silver plate in his head. Sometime or other he was badly hurt, and they put in the silver plate to protect his . . . his . . . his brain box, if that makes it simpler for you. Do you understand me?'

'Yes . . .'

'But as he got older, and his skin and muscles and nerve structure shrank a little, or lost their tension, that silver plate has been pressing harder and harder on the soft stuff in his head, where all his sense and his feeling comes from. It must have been hell for him, and he must have known he could do nothing about it. In fact it was so painful that I wonder he managed to survive this long.'

'Can't you fix it?' Spit asked.

Dr Stevens hesitated, wondering what to say, how much to tell the boy. He was a kind man who was always hurt by this aspect of his profession. 'I'm afraid not,' he said slowly. 'It's done real damage this time, and all we can do is see that he doesn't suffer any more excrutiating pain. Although even that is doubtful. He's in terrible pain now.'

Spit's voice rose. 'Why did you tie his hands to the bed. What did you do a thing like that for?'

'Because he can't control himself and he could hurt himself.'

'Can't he come home? Can't I look after him?'

Again Dr Stevens hesitated. 'Not this time,' he said, reluctant, and saying what he had to say word by word. 'I'm afraid, Spit, that he'll never come home again. That's what I've got to tell you, old son. He's not mad, you and I know that. But his brain now is being destroyed, and he will never be normal again, not even for five minutes. They wanted me to tell you this so that they can fix you up with a place to live, and someone to look after you.'

'You mean they all want me to leave the boiler?'

'That's right. There's nothing left of it anyway, is there?'

'You're not going to let me see my grandfather any more?' Spit said.

'You can see him any time you like. But we'll have to do something about him, Spit. We can't keep him here.'

'But he's all right,' Spit insisted again. 'And he won't hurt you.'

'He's too sick,' Dr Stevens said with a shake of his head.

Spit was sure now that they were aiming him away from his grandfather. 'You want to take him away,' he said. 'Don't you?'

'We'll have to, Spit. He needs a different kind of hospital now. They can look after him better in Melbourne than we can here.'

'Melbourne . . .'

'That seems to be the only way,' Dr Stevens said with a sigh. 'In the meantime you'll have to move in with someone.'

'They can't make me, can they?' Spit said, and this time he was appealing to Dr Stevens to join his resistance movement and confirm his right to be left alone.

'I'm afraid they can,' Dr Stevens said. 'That's the trouble, old son.'

Dr Stevens was known in St Helen not only for his long-legged lankiness but for his belief in raw foods and for his refusal to eat fish or meat or even eggs. Which explained his slow and careful way of speaking and his well-known patience with dogs and children and sick women and with his Nash motor car. 'I'm sorry for you, Spit,' he went on, 'but we can't let you run around loose.'

'Who's going to run around loose? I can fix up the boiler.'

Dr Stevens smiled. He was a mildly sad man, so that what he said was mostly in sorrow rather than a threat. 'They just won't let you do that, so come on and we'll see what Sergeant Collins and Jack Tree plan to do with you.'

When they went outside Sergeant Collins and Jack Tree were waiting under the vines in the shade, and Spit knew that these two men had already decided what to do with him.

'We're taking you over to Mrs Arbuckle,' Sergeant Collins told Spit. 'She'll be able to look after you for the time being.'

'I'm not going to Mrs Arbuckle's,' Spit said.

'Oh, yes you are,' Sergeant Collins told him. 'If you don't do as you're told, young feller, I'll lock you up.'

'You can lock me up any day,' Spit said.

'Mrs Arbuckle's all right, Spit,' Mr Tree said. 'She's a bit of a crank, but she'll be as good as a mother to you.'

'Not me,' Spit said firmly. 'I'm not going to stay there.'

'Listen, son, you don't want to end up tomorrow in that home in Bendigo do you?' Mr Tree said to him. 'Because that's what'll happen if you don't do as you're told. You don't want to be taken away, do you?'

Spit was biting his top lip, knowing that he had no way out.

'Why don't you make the best of it,' Mr Tree told him. 'It's the only way.'

'I'll only do it,' Spit said, loud and desperate, 'if you don't take my grandfather away.'

They all looked at Dr Stevens. He hesitated, as he almost always did. 'All right, Spit. We won't take him away. We'll do what we can for him – for a little while anyway.'

'What if you trick me again?' Spit said.

'Nobody's going to trick you again, Spit,' Dr Stevens said. 'I can promise you that.'

There was nothing more to say because the adults were now embarrassed, and Spit was trying to hold himself together. They were halfway to the gate, Spit and Jack Tree and

Sergeant Collins, when Sister Campbell ran out of the hospital and called after Spit and told him to come back.

'What for?' he said.

'I found a pair of trousers for you,' she told him.

'Mine are all right now,' he said, staying where he was.

Sister Campbell joined them and she felt his pants. They were still damp but dry in places. 'You don't want them?' she said, holding up a pair of very short pants.

Spit shook his head but Sister Campbell rolled them up and gave them to him anyway. 'You might need them when school starts,' she said.

Spit was not in a thanking mood, but he put the trousers under his arm and climbed into the back seat of the Dodge.

He was still holding himself together when they left him at Mrs Betty Arbuckle's clean, bare and untainted house, with a final word from Sergeant Collins to behave himself. 'And remember,' the Sergeant said, 'if you try to run away, or refuse to do as Betty tells you, we'll pack you off to Bendigo on the next train. It's for your own good, Spit, so for God's sake do as she tells you, otherwise I can't help you any more.'

Betty Arbuckle greeted him at the back door as if she had been expecting him, as if the anticipation of years had finally been justified and rewarded.

'What's your real name, Spit dear?' she said to him.

'Angus,' Spit said. 'Why?'

'Because you have to have a proper name now.'

Instinctively, Spit saw this sudden need for a proper name as a threat to what he had always had been in St Helen – no more nor less than Spit MacPhee. He knew he was staring a Boys Home in the face.

'You call me Spit,' he said threateningly at Betty Arbuckle. 'That's my name.'

Betty, surprised at the vehemence, said, 'All right, dear, if you want me to.'

Somehow, still intact, he followed Betty Arbuckle through the wire door and along a corridor to the back verandah. Spit had left the short pants Sister Campbell had given him in the Dodge, and what broke him now was the pair of Ben Arbuckle's old short pants that Betty had ready for him on the bed in the wide verandah where, she said, he would be sleeping. There was also a pair of boots on the floor and a pair of darned grey socks on the bed, and when Betty told him to put on the nice pair of clean, dry pants, and the socks and boots, Spit tried grimly but could not prevent the tears that slipped out of his squinted-up eyes and ran down his cheeks. They surprised him and angered him, because he could not remember having cried before. He knew it was a stupid and traitorous mistake for his eyes to do that to him, and in defying them he knew he was never going to put on a pair of Ben Arbuckle's old pants or boots. He wasn't going to do it.

Seeing his tears, Betty said, 'Oh dear,' but didn't press him. She was about to suggest a moment's prayer but she changed her mind about that and said, 'You don't have to worry, Spit. You can stay here as long as your grandfather is in hospital. And if he joins the Lord Jesus we'll make sure you get a proper home. You don't ever have to worry about that again.'

Knowing that he couldn't make a run for it, Spit stood silently and defiantly still; but he couldn't contain himself for long and he said, 'I'm not putting on any of those pants or boots of Ben's.'

'We can think about that tomorrow,' Betty said firmly.

Spit didn't argue, but began instead to edge his way out.

'Now Spit,' she said to him. 'Where do you think you're off to?'

'I'm going down to the boiler to get my grandfather's tools. Somebody'll take them if I leave them there in my cart.'

'You're not to go back to that boiler,' she said to him. 'And I don't want you to go anywhere near that river. You won't need those things of your grandfather's, so you can leave them there. I want you to promise me not to go near the river ever again.'

Since Spit's entire recollected life had been spent on what was to him the lifeline and sanctuary of the river, Betty was threatening his heart, his soul, his life and his liberty. Her house was a mile inland from the river, surrounded by other dry houses and other dry streets, and whenever he had been in this part of town his only desire had been to get back to the banks of the Murray as soon as possible.

'What's the matter with the river?' he said to her.

'It's best that you begin to forget all about that place where you lived down there. It only made you wild and Godless, like an African heathen. You've got to start afresh now, Spit, because soon you'll be coming to Jesus, and you won't need to go down to the river again. You can't live like that any more, and I know you *will* come to Jesus if you don't ever go anywhere near that place again.'

'Jesus has got nothing to do with it,' Spit said indignantly.

Betty Arbuckle had a temper, but because her voice was always soft, the best she could manage in anger was a hurt forbearance. 'That's a terrible thing to say,' she said. 'Everybody needs Jesus.'

Spit had no argument to that, and she went on, 'Now go and find Ben. He's gone to the Co-op to bring home a fourteen-pound bag of potatoes, so you can help him carry them. But don't you dare go near the river.'

Spit, still mesmerised by Betty Arbuckle's force and persuasion, walked out of the house on his bare feet and pointed himself aimlessly at the Co-op because he didn't know what else he could do. He knew he was now living under a threat, because Betty's plans for his future were so strong that she, more than anyone else, had convinced him that maybe his grandfather would never recover, even though she had not mentioned his grandfather. Moreover, he was very frightened of her forgiveness, because she bore him no grudge for the bucket of water he had thrown over her. And, without knowing why, she made him feel that he had now done something even worse, and ought to be punished for it.

'She's a cootie, a damn black cootie,' he was muttering when he saw Ben Arbuckle coming down the street.

Ben in his boots was hopelessly entangled with the fourteen-pound bag of potatoes. Seeing Spit he dropped them and was ready to make a run for it. But he recovered and stood his ground and tried to look defiant.

'What are you going to do?' he said nervously to Spit.

'Nothing, Ben. Your mother told me to help you carry the potatoes.'

Ben, still suspicious and ready to run, said, 'She did?'

'Yes. I'm going to stay at your place. Just until my grandfather gets better.'

'I know.'

Spit, without plotting it, knew that he needed an ally in Ben because he was about to defy Betty Arbuckle and go down to the river. 'Why don't you make yourself a cart to carry things like that?' he said to Ben, kicking the thick brown paper bag of potatoes.

Ben, hot and sweating, sat on his haunches. 'You've got to have wheels for a cart and I haven't got any,' he said.

'Why don't you go around the town and ask people if they've got any old prams they don't want,' Spit said.

'Ask who?'

'Anybody. All you do is knock at any old back door and say have you got some old pram wheels.'

'What's the use, Spit? I haven't got any tools anyway, and my father won't let me touch his.'

'I've got some of my grandfather's tools down at the old boiler, and if I go and get them I'll show you how to make a cart.'

Ben, still wary of Spit, while at the same time begging in his boots and smock for toleration and friendship, couldn't quite believe what he was being offered.

'Do you mean you'll help me?' Ben said.

'What do you think I mean? I'll go and get the tools now if you like. D'you want to come?'

Ben now kicked the potatoes. 'I've got to get these home,' he said, 'and anyway I'm not allowed to go down to the river, particularly down to your place.'

'She won't know. You can give her the potatoes and then duck out quick.'

'Somebody'll see us and tell her,' Ben said.

'Well, we can say we just happened to be down that way. And I'll bring up my cart and you can use it any time you like.'

Friendship, co-operation and co-existence – Ben now had the choice of all that, even if it meant dire consequences at home. It was the biggest offer – the best ever made to him in his Sabbatarian life, and he took a quick and desperate hold of it before he could change his mind. 'All right,' he said. 'Only you'd better keep out of the way so she doesn't see us together.'

'I'll carry the potatoes, if you like,' Spit said, and with his stocky, muscular arms and his practised body he lifted the awkward, bulky bag to his shoulder and said to Ben, 'Is there anywhere I can hide my grandfather's things?'

'You mean at home?'

'Yes. In your back yard somewhere.'

'Under the house,' Ben said. 'Nobody goes there except me, although I'm not supposed to crawl under there because my father's afraid of fire.'

'Nobody'll hear us,' Spit assured him.

'All right,' Ben said with far more courage than he thought he had.

It worked well enough. Spit hovered a few houses away while Ben took over the potatoes, hurried up the path through Betty Arbuckle's neatly clipped runway of burning bush and, calling out to his mother, 'Here are the potatoes,' he dropped them on the two little steps at the back door and joined Spit, who was already on the run when he saw Ben clumping out of the gate in his heavy black boots.

Spit would have kept it up all the way to the river, but Ben was neither a fast nor a willing runner, so they had to walk by the post office, Ben nervously watching everybody in sight and trying to keep a little behind Spit, whispering to him, 'Watch out, Spit, there's Mr Thompson.' Or, 'There's Mr Andrews. He's seen us.'

'Come on,' Spit said impatiently, and when they had crossed the railway line and could see the boiler he was surprised to see fragments of burned wood being flung through the broken window.

'Somebody's there,' Ben said.

Spit was already ahead and when he reached the boiler he was not surprised to see Sadie Tree inside it.

'What do you think you're doing?' he said to her.

'Don't you want to clean it up?' she said.

'Yes, but Sergeant Collins says I'm not allowed to now.'

'That's what my father says,' Sadie told him. 'But I knew you'd be back.'

'They're going to lock me up in Ben's place,' Spit said, aware that he was exaggerating, though not by much.

'What's *he* doing?' Sadie said in surprise, pointing to Ben with a fragment of burned-out bed. 'Won't he tell his mother?'

'No, he's not supposed to be here either. I just came down to get my grandfather's things. They won't let me see him if I don't do what they want. If I don't stay at the Arbuckles they'll take him away. So it's no use cleaning out the boiler, Sadie.'

'Are they going to send you away to Bendigo?' Sadie asked.

'That's what they keep saying,' Spit said. 'But I'm not going down there. I'm not leaving my grandfather.'

'I found a lot of other things in the ashes,' Sadie said, 'and I put them in the buckets.'

'Can I see inside your boiler?' Ben asked, waiting outside.

'You might as well,' Spit said with a shrug. 'There's nothing left anyway.'

Ben, like the others, had always envied Spit his life in the boiler, and now that he was suddenly standing inside it, even in its burned-out condition, he knew that he was enjoying a privilege that Spit would not share with everyone. In fact he was surprised to see Sadie Tree here – and so friendly with Spit. But he didn't say anything about it. He simply stood and wondered at the difference, at the life that Spit must have lived here and, as a gesture to it, he longed to take his boots off but did not dare do it.

'We'd better hurry, Spit,' he said, 'or we'll be late for dinner.'

'Won't you be coming down here any more?' Sadie said.

'I don't know. Mrs Arbuckle says I'm not allowed to, but I don't know, Sadie. Does your mother know you're here?'

'Yes, but my father's gone to Nooah.'

'If I can't get down here will you look after everything for me?' Spit asked her.

'I'll come down every day,' Sadie said.

Together they packed Spit's cart with the box of Fyfe's tools and what Sadie had found and saved – a silver picture frame, pots, knives and forks, enamel mugs and basins, and a little silver parrot that old Fyfe had kept on his workbench.

'And this too,' Sadie said. 'Look.' Sadie took from her pinafore pocket a little enamelled and lined box with scissors, a nail file, needle and a thimble in it.

Spit looked at it for a while, never having seen it before. He gave it back to Sadie and said, 'It must have been my mother's.'

'What'll I do with it?'

'You'd better keep it for me,' Spit said.

'I might lose it.'

'No you won't,' Spit said, and he told Ben to go ahead with the cart. When Ben was on the way up the hill Spit told Sadie about the hiding place under the boiler where he kept his own money.

'All you have to do is push the side of this piece of metal under the boiler and it drops down,' he said, demonstrating it for her. It was obviously part of a system that had once had some use in the boiler's original purpose, but now it was a rare hiding place which the fire had spared. Spit took a little cocoa tin out of the hole and showed Sadie his money, all in coins. 'Two pounds four and six,' he said. 'I was going to buy tyres and a seat with some of it for the bike, but I'll leave it here now because I don't know where I can hide it in Ben's place. But don't tell anyone . . . I mean your father.'

'Don't worry,' she said as Ben called out to him: 'Come on, Spit, or we'll get into trouble.'

'See you later, Sadie,' Spit said as he slammed the little door shut and raced up the slope to help Ben with the cart.

They were more than an hour late for dinner which surprised them both. Frank Arbuckle was at the gate; he had been working in the garden, watching the street. He took out his pocket-watch and said, 'Where have you been, Ben, and what's all that?' He ignored Spit as if he still didn't know how to deal with him. 'You're not bringing that stuff in here,' he said to Ben.

'It's my grandfather's things,' Spit said boldly. 'Somebody would have pinched them if I'd left them down there.'

'All right. But get inside, both of you,' Frank Arbuckle said. 'You're in trouble. You were told not to go down to the river and you took Ben.'

'He had to help me,' Spit said.

'We didn't do anything wrong,' Ben said to his father.

'Your mother will decide that,' Frank said sadly. 'But you're both in trouble.'

They went inside to the back verandah where the Arbuckles ate their meals, and Ben stood wide-eyed and expectant before his mother while Spit, an alien here, didn't know what to anticipate.

'So you went down to the river,' Mrs Arbuckle said, upset for their wrongdoing rather than their lateness for dinner.

'I had to get my grandfather's things,' Spit said again.

'And you of all people went with him,' she said unhappily to Ben.

Ben said nothing, and Spit knew that Ben was almost in tears, though not quite.

'You're wicked, both of you. You've been tempted. Disobedience is like telling a lie, which is a sin in the eyes of the Lord and you know that, Ben, even if Spit doesn't.'

Ben said nothing, his wickedness inescapable, his joy in a rare and surprising friendship gone to ruin.

'And you're dirty, Ben. Look at you.'

Ben was smeared with black ash, his smock stained, his boots blotted; whereas Spit, used to handling dirt, was clean.

'You have to be punished, the pair of you, so you can either do without your dinner now, or Frank will give you both a good hiding. Take your pick please.'

Spit had to think about it for a moment. Apart from an occasional strap at school he had never been beaten or slapped by an adult. His grandfather had never touched him because that was not the way they had lived. Though they had always shouted at each other, there had never been any question of obedience or disobedience needing punishment, so there was something here that Spit didn't like and didn't want and resented. On the other hand he was very hungry and he said, 'If he wants to give me a hiding, he can do it any time he likes.' He looked across at Ben, hoping for some support.

Ben had been so rarely disobedient that this was a new experience for him too. He had lived his life unable and unwanting to escape obedience, or the moral guidance of his forceful mother. Moreover he was afraid of all violence, so that in character he should have missed his meal rather than taken a hiding. But Spit's offhand acceptance of a hiding, together with a new hope in a friendship restored, gave Ben enough courage to say, 'I'd sooner the hiding than miss my lunch.'

Betty Arbuckle, in her Australian way, was not without a sense of humour, and she also knew her son. 'Are you sure you want to be brave?' she said to him.

Ben kept his eyes down, knowing that if he looked up at his mother he would collapse.

'You're a very bad influence, Spit,' Betty said calmly, 'and you won't like it,' she said to her son. She called Frank and told him to get the strap.

'I thought they were going to do without their dinner,' Frank said to her.

'They decided to take a hiding, so we'll have to make it clear to Ben that he must not be led astray. And we have to show Spit that he can't lead others into temptation. You've got to learn not to be wicked,' she said to Spit.

'What's wicked about it?' Spit protested. 'I was just . . .'

'Please don't answer back,' Betty Arbuckle told him in her troubled voice. 'And don't shout at me like a navvy. You'll have to change your awful ways, Spit, and I'm only thankful that Joannie's not here to see what you've done to Ben.'

Frank Arbuckle had his razor strop in hand, a long double layer of leather with a metal hook at one end and a thickened handle of leather at the other. It was gashed with the cuts of a mishandled razor, and oily with lubricants like old Fyfe's own strop. Spit looked at it, judged its effectiveness, looked closely too at Frank Arbuckle who seemed unhappy and nervous, and decided that it was bolder to bend over willingly and submit rather than struggle and make it difficult.

'Bend over the chair, Spit,' Frank said.

Spit did so without hesitation, but Frank's first blow surprised him with the force because he had forgotten that Frank Arbuckle had a lot to remember him by. Spit had made too much trouble for him with the water mains to be easily forgiven, and Frank was not going to let this opportunity pass. In Frank Arbuckle's delayed punishment Spit felt the strop scour his flesh: *one, two, three, four . . .*

'How many, Bet?' Frank Arbuckle said. 'Is that enough?'

'I don't know, Frank. Give him at least half a dozen, so that he learns his lesson.' Betty was firm, but she wouldn't watch.

Spit flinched each time but he bore the half dozen successfully, though he knew that one or two more could have wrecked his determination not to cry out. As he straightened up he caught sight of Ben's face, and though he said loudly, 'You didn't hurt me,' Ben was unconvinced, and after two blows from his father he was in tears.

'I told you, Ben,' Betty Arbuckle said, almost in tears herself. 'I *told* you. And it's for your own good because you must not be tempted.'

Spit watched the blows, and though they were serious enough they were not as forceful as the ones he had taken on his own backside. But since it was simply a matter of an eye for an eye now, Spit didn't mind Ben's milder punishment because he knew that at the first opportunity he would block a water valve again.

What puzzled Spit was Betty Arbuckle's concern over dinner that he should get enough to eat. She offered him more potatoes and peas, and encouraged him to eat. She was a good cook, better than Spit's grandfather, and better than Spit himself who knew how to roast a leg of lamb. She was lavish with the bread and butter pudding, which normally Spit would not have looked at. He did not like milk. But he had to admit that Betty Arbuckle had made a delicious pudding of it. A cup of hot, sweet tea and Spit was satisfied, waiting now for Ben who was a slow and careful eater.

When Ben had finished, Betty Arbuckle gave them both a small square of torn white cloth, part of an old sheet, and she told Spit to wipe his hands and his mouth clean before she thanked the Lord for what they had received.

Spit followed Ben's example, and though he knew that grace was usually said before a meal rather than after it he listened as Betty Arbuckle thanked the Lord Jesus for His benefice, for His grace abounding and for His harvest of good for their bodies' health. He didn't bend his head or close his eyes, like Ben, but he watched Betty Arbuckle, fingers tightly laced together, her head held high in some secret esteem, her eyes closed, and Spit saw a beautiful woman in a moment of ecstasy. He could remember his mother, but only in confusion – his mother with an unblemished face and then his mother with the disfigured face which she had tried to hide from him, although he had seen it enough to remember it. After her death his only contact with women had been his business affairs at back doors, or an exchange of greetings, or lately his friendship with Sadie and her mother. But it was this woman whom he had insulted and punished, and who had punished him in return and threatened him, and who now had a veto on everything he did – it was this one who puzzled him with her conventions for sin and her begging appeals to the Lord to save her from wickedness. She fascinated him and frightened him, and he wished his grandfather would get better, even if he couldn't re-build the boiler. He wished above all that he could run away, because he knew for sure now that Betty Arbuckle's determination to do what was best for him would sooner or later end in the Boys Home in Bendigo, and he didn't know how he was going to escape that.

8

HE DECIDED IN SELF-DEFENCE AND AS A TEMPORARY MEASURE TO do as he was told. He managed to get through the rest of the day helping Ben in the garden, mowing the lawn and trimming the already trimmed hedges. The interior walls of Betty Arbuckle's small house were bare of anything from floor to ceiling, because to Betty a picture on a wall was a wicked indulgence. Yet her garden plot was a gem, as if in suppressing her own temporal beauty she had to protect its equal in nature with roses, violets, pansies, zinnias, lilies, dahlias, little vines, passionfruit, and a neat lawn. It was one of the loveliest gardens in St Helen, and Spit liked it.

At night, sitting next to Ben's sister, Joannie, who moved a few inches away from him because she whispered to him, 'You smell,' he had to repeat the words of the grace after the meal, and before Betty Arbuckle put him down in the hard but comfortable little bed made of an old door with a mattress on fruit boxes, she insisted that he say, as a fledgling in prayer, that now he lay himself down to sleep he must pray the Lord his soul to keep, and if he should die before he was awake, he pray the Lord his soul to take.

He could accept that, but what was still difficult for him were clothes and the socks and the boots he would have to put on in the morning if he was going to be allowed to see his grandfather.

'We have to begin right, Spit,' Betty Arbuckle said in a kindly way. 'So, starting today, you won't be running around like an African heathen any more.'

Spit had never worn boots and grey woollen socks in his life and he felt like a stranger to himself as he set out for the hospital next morning, his borrowed boots hitting the dirt pavement like horses' hoofs. He didn't mind the pants and the smock now, but the boots did something to him because he felt that as long as he wore them he was being tricked and betrayed.

'They're after you, Spit,' he muttered to himself as he clumped noisily into the hospital, almost into the arms of Sister Campbell.

'Good heavens, Spit. What have you got on your feet?' she said.

'Ben Arbuckle's old boots,' he said.

'Well take them off. It's too hot to walk around in boots. Did Betty Arbuckle tell you to wear them?'

Spit nodded.

'Oh heavens,' she said. 'Then leave them on, but she ought to have known better. Come on. We've put your grandfather in the little room outside in the garden which we usually have for fever patients.'

She led Spit through the hospital, out through the shaded verandah which was covered in bougainvillea and where there were three patients who said, 'Hello, Spit.' He went on through the back garden of fruit trees and vines to where there was a neat, green, wooden shed with a corrugated iron roof sheltered by two big gums.

At the door Sister Campbell, who was efficient and crisp because nurses were supposed to be efficient and crisp, stopped Spit before going in.

'Don't look too long at your grandfather,' she told him. 'It's better not to remember him this way. He won't know you, so it's no use trying to get a reply from him. Just don't expect . . . don't expect too much, will you?'

'No,' Spit said boldly, 'I'm not going to ask him anything.'

'Still . . .'

Sister Campbell opened the door, and inside it was dark, but she didn't open the blinds. By the light from the door Spit could see the bed, and his grandfather's face on a pillow.

'We've given him something,' Sister Campbell said, 'so he isn't strapped down any more.'

As his eyes became accustomed to the dim, almost dusty light Spit saw that his grandfather seemed to be in a very deep sleep. His tension was gone, and though his face now was grey and unshaven, it seemed finally freed from the pain of his life.

'Is he better?' Spit said in a whisper.

Sister Campbell shook her head. 'No. But at least he's not suffering any more.'

'When will he wake up?'

'Not today, maybe not tomorrow.'

'How is he going to eat?' Spit whispered again.

'Don't worry about that,' Sister Campbell said.

Spit watched his grandfather breathing. It was thin, light, fragile and transparent breathing, simply in-and-out, in-and-out, and he knew that it was the most his grandfather could manage. There was nothing else left of him.

'I suppose he's going to die, isn't he?' Spit said simply, although he looked up at Sister Campbell wanting a denial.

'Let's go outside,' Sister Campbell said, and she took him out into the sunlight. 'You know more than anybody how much your grandfather has suffered, Spit.'

'I know all that,' he said aggressively.

'You know that he really couldn't stand it much longer.'

'Dr Stevens told me all that.'

'Yes, but now we've given him something to stop the pain, Spit. It'll help, but he may never wake up again. He has suffered too much, more than a human being can stand, so now it's better that he doesn't have to suffer all that pain any more. He's an old man and it's time he was spared any more pain.'

'He's not so old,' Spit protested.

'Then he's lived a long, hard life, if you like. But it's over now, Spit, and there's nothing we can do about it. We just want him to quietly go to sleep.'

'You mean he'll never wake up at all?'

'No. He'll never wake up again.'

'Why? Can't you do something?'

Sister Campbell shook her head and Spit shooed away a fly that was bothering him.

'I didn't want you to know any of this, Spit, but since they did it to you anyway it's best you know now that he's going to slip away from us very peacefully.'

'Can I come back this afternoon?' Spit asked.

'Of course. But for heaven's sake take those boots off and

I'll tell Betty Arbuckle to let you go around barefoot.'

'It's all right,' Spit said and this time he walked right around the hospital garden to get out. Once on the street he clip-clopped in his boots through the town and down the slope to the river, where he sat on the mud steps near the boiler, dangling his feet in the water which he sometimes did for relief. This time he remembered too late that he still had Ben's boots and woollen socks on. He was like that when Sadie Tree found him.

'What on earth are you doing?' Sadie said to him.

'Nothing,' Spit replied.

'You've got those awful boots all wet,' she pointed out.

'I know that,' he said. 'I forgot.'

'Did you get into trouble yesterday?'

'Yes, we both got a hiding.'

'She'll give you another one when she sees those boots,' Sadie said.

'No she won't. They'll be dry by then,' he said.

'Have you seen your grandfather?' Sadie asked, squatting down near him.

Spit dabbled his feet and nodded.

'Is he all right? Is he better?'

Spit didn't say anything but lay back with the sun on his face.

'Is he getting better?' she said again.

'They gave him something,' Spit said, and for a while they were silent. 'He's asleep.'

'What are you going to do now?' Sadie asked then.

'I don't know,' Spit said. 'I suppose I'll have to go back to Ben's place.'

'I wish you could stay with us,' Sadie said.

Spit got up and stamped his squelching boots. 'Listen to them,' he said, and Sadie laughed as the water squirted through the lace holes. 'I'm going to look at my crayfish drums,' he told her. 'Do you want to come?'

Sadie followed him, and when Spit pulled out the first drum and found a large crayfish in it he didn't know what to do with it. 'You can have it if you like,' Spit told her.

'I can't carry it, it'll nip me.'

They were standing under a willow tree that drooped over

the river, and Spit pulled off a long, thin, supple branch of the weeping limbs and tied it gingerly around the crayfish's big claws. Then, wrapping it tight in a bundle of more willow and leaves, he went on to the next drum and the next, until it was time for Sadie to go home for lunch.

'Aren't you going up to Ben's place for your dinner?' Sadie said.

Spit was hungry but he knew that he couldn't face Betty Arbuckle or Ben or Joannie or Frank Arbuckle, even to satisfy his hunger. They were too much of a confirmation in the flesh that he would soon be on his own, and he didn't want that confirmed now. In fact he wanted it denied, and the only denial he had was here, where his life had been and where he wanted it to go on.

'I'm not going back there till tonight,' Spit said.

'What about your dinner?'

'I'll get some of the tomatoes left in the garden.'

'I'll bring you back some bread and butter,' Sadie said as she took the wrapped-up crayfish from Spit and walked up the slope. But when she came back after lunch with two jam sandwiches Spit had gone. She guessed that he was somewhere up river, so she walked around the Point, along the edge of the Italian pea farm and found Spit sitting under Mr Walker's mulberry tree on the river bank, eating mulberries and cutting out one of his little sailing boats.

'I've got six ready,' he said, 'so we can put them in here and see where they are by tonight.'

'The river's beginning to rise fast,' Sadie told him.

'Yes, I know.'

'It won't be long now before summer is really over,' Sadie said.

Spit didn't seem to be listening any more, and when he suddenly got up to go the last thing he said to Sadie before he set off into town to see his grandfather was, 'You chuck the boats in. Sade.' He pushed the pile of little boats into her hands and cut across the Walker's lucerne paddock to take the short cut into the town and to the hospital.

He had been so quick about it that Sadie was left alone with her jam sandwiches, which she decided to keep for him in case he needed them later. After putting the little boats in the water and watching them for a while, she soon gave up because it was not much fun without Spit there to follow them with her.

9

It was Dr Stevens, not Sister Campbell, who took Spit to the fever house and told him that he had to be a brave boy.

'Why?' Spit asked, trying to keep up with Dr Stevens' long legs.

'Well, Spit, you can take a look and that's all.'

Spit didn't understand, but when Dr Stevens opened the green door and stepped in ahead he said, 'Now take a look, but don't be upset. He's gone and there's no more pain now.'

Spit understood the words less than the sight of his grandfather, who was hardly recognisable: a tiny, shriven, hundred-year-old ghost, who nonetheless was so peaceful and relaxed that Spit was frightened and wanted only to get out. He knew it was the end of his grandfather, and that this was finally what it all meant as he ran away from the fever house.

By the time Dr Stevens had caught up with him Spit had already removed from his thoughts the image of that figure on the bed. Instead, he had fixed permanently in his mind the memory of a grandfather bent over his work bench, muttering or shouting, his skull cap tight over his head as he filled in their lives with noise and abrasion, and then got them through each day as if each day had to be fought for.

'Are you all right, son?' Dr Stevens said to him.

'Yes, I'm all right,' Spit said.

'Don't worry, you'll be looked after,' Dr Stevens told him. 'They'll find you a home.'

Spit's only clear intention was to get as far away from the place as quickly as possible, and as he started off around the hospital rather than through it, Dr Stevens said, 'Come through this way. I want to talk to you.'

'I'm going around here,' Spit told him, and wriggling out of

Dr Stevens' friendly grip on his shoulder he was too quick for the doctor to stop him as he ran around the garden and out the main gate.

Spit would never know why he decided to go back to Betty Arbuckle's. There seemed nowhere else for him to go, except back to the boiler, and he knew now that his life in the boiler was over forever. He thought of going to Sadie Tree's place, but maybe Mr Tree would be there and anyway there was nothing they could do for him anymore. Moreover he didn't even know what he wanted of anybody. The powerful certitudes of Betty Arbuckle seemed to be the only certainties there were now, and as he stood on the back step of the house, reluctant to go in, he shouted: 'Are you there, Ben?'

Ben wasn't there but Mrs Arbuckle was, and she opened the wire screen door and said, 'So there you are, dear. We were worried about you.'

'I got Ben's boots all dirty,' he announced aggressively.

Betty Arbuckle pushed him gently inside. 'You've been to the hospital, haven't you?'

'Yes.'

'I know what's happened, Spit,' she told him. 'Dr Stevens telephoned me. You'll have to be a brave boy now and put all your trust in Jesus. He's always there, and you'll know how good the Lord can be. Sit down and I'll give you a cup of tea.'

'No thanks,' Spit said, and he was surprised to see tears in Betty Arbuckle's glittering and almost happy eyes.

'Your grandfather has gone to join his one and only friend,' she said to him. 'Poor Spit. But it's a happier, happier place he'll find with Jesus, and I'm so glad for him, Spit, so you musn't cry.'

'I'm not crying,' Spit said, fascinated by the way she was trying to get a grip on him with her joy and her sorrow, which trapped him for a moment in the way she wanted it to.

'Now you'll have a proper place to live,' she told him cheerfully. 'I have written to the Boys Home in Bendigo and I know there is a place for you there, so try and be a good boy until they let me know when they can take you. It shouldn't be more than a week at the most, so I'll look after you until then, and I'll try to help you come to Jesus because you'll never be alone as long as you come to Him. Do you understand me?'

'Yes,' Spit said. 'You're going to send me to the Boys Home in Bendigo.'

'That's right, and there'll be lots of other boys there like you, so you'll be very happy there.'

Betty Arbuckle had such a tight grip on his arm that he wondered if she was going to lock him up until she could send him off to Bendigo in the train.

'Go and clean off your boots,' she told him in a hopeful, encouraging way. 'The brushes are in the box under Ben's bed.'

Spit knew then what he had to do. He went through the kitchen to the verandah and sat on the floor. He took off Ben's boots, the socks, and the smock, and he put them neatly on the bed he had been sleeping in. Then, waiting until he heard Betty Arbuckle busy and singing in the kitchen, he walked quietly through the back door, closing it carefully after him. He crawled under the house to take from his grandfather's things a frying pan, a billy, a plate, and a knife and fork. He bundled them into a sugar bag and, still being very cautious, he walked his quiet way out into the street. Once there he used his liberated bare feet to run all the way to the boiler.

He took some money out of the box under the boiler, flung his bag over his shoulder and went back up the slope to the shops. He bought two loaves of bread, potatoes, eggs, jam, tea, matches and sugar. He was so intent over his purchases that when Tim Evans in the grocer shop asked him where he was going with this stuff, he said, 'It's not for me, Tim,' and got out quick. At the boiler he packed his fishing lines into the bag with the food, rolled the lot up into two half-burned and badly holed blankets, which were covered in ash but dry now, and tying them up he hid them under one of the gum trees and went along the river and up the slope again to Sadie Tree's house.

'Sadie . . .' he called softly at the back door.

But softly to Spit was loud enough to be a shout. He could hear Sadie practising the piano, and he waited a moment and called again.

Mrs Tree came out the back and said, 'Hello Spit. What's up?'

'I just wanted to talk to Sadie,' he said. 'I want to tell her something.'

'She's practising.'

'All right,' he said, turning to go.

'How's your grandfather?' Mrs Tree asked him.

'He's dead,' Spit said.

'Oh Spit. That's awful . . . Come in and sit down.'

Spit stayed where he was. 'I just want to tell Sadie something,' he said. 'Can't I see her?'

He had no other way of talking but boldly, and Sadie, hearing his voice, had abandoned the piano. She joined her mother at the back door.

'Spit's grandfather just died,' her mother told her.

Sadie looked at Spit and didn't say anything and she watched him shifting nervously from one bare foot to the other.

'Can I tell you something?' he said to her.

'All right.' Sadie didn't ask her mother but simply followed him through the garden and down to the boiler.

'I'm going across the little river to Pental Island,' he told her. 'I'm not going back to Betty Arbuckle's because she wants to send me away to that Boys Home in Bendigo. So I'm getting out. They're not going to get me.'

'But how will you live over there? There's nothing there, Spit.'

'I'll be all right. But if I need something will you get it for me with the money left in my box?'

'Yes, but how will I know?'

'I don't know, but if I need something I'll try to sneak across first thing in the morning. Or I'll put a message on one of the boats so you can look out for it when it ends up near your place.'

'But they're sure to be looking for you, Spit.'

'I know. That's why I'm going across the river to the bush. They won't get me over there. Only don't tell your father.'

'I won't. But they'll be looking everywhere for you and sooner or later they'll guess you're over there on the island somewhere.'

'Even if they get me I'll run away again,' Spit said. 'I'm not going to that Boys Home in Bendigo, that's all I'm saying.'

'I'm sorry about your grandfather, Spit.'

'Well . . . he didn't know he was going to die so it's not his fault.'

'I know it isn't, and I'm going to ask my father if you can live with us.'

'He'll only be after me, like the others. Don't tell him anything. Don't tell anybody.'

'I wish I could swim well enough,' Sadie said, 'then I could bring things across the river to you.'

'Don't even try, the way you swim. It's too dangerous, and the river is really rising now. Anyway I'd better get going before they come down here looking for me.'

'How will you get all these things across?' Sadie asked as Spit picked up one of the two blanket rolls.

'I'll go across on my back holding one of them up. Then I'll come back for the other one. It's easy.'

But as Sadie watched Spit walk up river and then jump in with the roll he held over his head she knew it wasn't easy at all, and as he kicked himself across on his back she saw the roll dip in the water when he couldn't hold it high enough. She watched him struggle on the other side as he threw the roll on to the bank. He came back and landed twenty yards down-stream. But he walked up river again and jumped in with the second bundle, and halfway across he shouted, 'I'm all right now, Sadie.'

'But it'll be dark over there in the bush,' she called to him.

'That won't hurt,' he called back, and when he had landed the second bundle she watched him climb up on the bank, pick up the two rolls, and start walking to the big clump of trees across the island and along the big river.

10

It took the town a little while to realise that Spit MacPhee had disappeared. By the time everybody in St Helen knew about it there were rumours that he had drowned himself or hidden in one of the trains going to Melbourne. He had been seen from one end of town to the other, but nobody could offer any real facts to Sergeant Collins whose duty it was to find him. The river was a logical place to look for Spit, but where exactly?

The first news of his absence had come from Betty Arbuckle who had waited for him at six o'clock tea time, and after questioning Ben and ringing the hospital she realised by eight o'clock, when it was fully dark, that Spit was being wicked again. But it was ten o'clock before she told her husband Frank to go down to the boiler to see if he was there.

'He won't be there, Bet,' Frank said. 'He'd know that I'd come and get him by the scruff of the neck if he was there.'

'He may be hiding there, just crying,' Betty said.

'He won't cry,' Ben told his mother.

'You get back to bed,' Betty told Ben, who had heard the fuss and was in the kitchen to see what it was about.

'I'll go down to the boiler,' Ben volunteered.

'No you won't. You get back to bed,' his father said sharply.

'Well . . . I'll bet he's not there anyway,' Ben said boldly.

'You don't bet in this house,' Betty told him, and took him firmly on his way to the verandah.

'I won't sleep,' Ben told his mother defiantly as he got into bed. 'Not until Spit comes back.'

Betty Arbuckle was not in a mood to deal with her son's new rebelliousness, so she tucked him up and returned to the kitchen to tell her husband to go on. 'You'll have to look somewhere,' she said.

Frank Arbuckle put his boots on and walked through the dark streets to the railway line, then along the line to the path leading down to the river and the trees and the boiler. It was a dark night and he stumbled once or twice, but he found the boiler among its ashes, looked inside it, called, 'Spit where are you?' once or twice, and then went back home to tell Betty, 'He's not there. He's up and gone, Bet.'

'But he must be somewhere,' Betty said unhappily. 'He can't just sleep in the street.'

'Spit can sleep anywhere.' It was Ben again.

This time he got a quick and surprising slap across the backside which brought tears to his eyes and quick obedience, but he was mumbling in protest as he went back to bed, 'I told you so. I told you, didn't I?'

It was almost eleven o'clock and by now Betty Arbuckle was sure that Spit was not coming back at all. 'I'll ring Sergeant Collins,' she said. 'He'll have to do something.'

'What can he do?' Frank said. 'If Spit has disappeared it'll take more than Sergeant Collins to find him at this time of the night.'

'He might have fallen in the river,' Betty said.

'In that case he's well on his way to Adelaide by now, swimming like a fish.'

'That's enough, Frank,' Betty said. 'You ought not to be heartless about it. I'm going to ring Sergeant Collins.'

That was the first step in the town's discovery that Spit had run away. And, as the first man to hear about it, Sergeant Collins' attitude was predictable.

'That damned little dingo,' he said. 'Why can't he stay put somewhere. I don't even know where to look for him at this hour of the night, Mrs Arbuckle. But you can bet that he's safe and secure somewhere. He knows how to look after himself, so don't worry. He'll turn up all right.'

'But I have to worry, and you ought to do something.'

'Well you tell me where I can find him and I'll go and get him. Leave it until morning and I'll be after him first thing.'

'You ought to be able to do better than that,' Betty Arbuckle said angrily.

'Tomorrow morning,' Sergeant Collins told her and hung up.

'He's right,' Frank Arbuckle said, and in an unusual act of defiance took off his boots and told Betty, 'I'm going to bed.'

Betty Arbuckle, determined in her conscience to do something, walked to the front gate, looked under the house hopefully, turned her eyes to the clear and starlit sky above and asked the Lord Jesus to protect the wandering boy. Then she went to bed.

It was another two days before all the town became involved in Spit's disappearance, but not everybody in St Helen recognised Spit's problem. Those who were curious but not particularly concerned assumed that with his grandfather's death he would end up in an orphanage anyway, which meant Bendigo or even Melbourne itself. That should be the end of it. But there were plenty of others who realised that Spit had disappeared because he didn't want to be taken off to an orphanage, and though his disappearance seemed like a hopeless gesture of defiance, there was plenty of sympathy and support for him. Also enough confidence in Spit's character to believe that he could look after himself.

But where was he?

Sergeant Collins spent a wasted day looking into all the turns and twists of the river bank upstream and downstream, and into the two deserted houses and the old lean-to that Spit had used sometimes to store his crayfish drum in during the winter. He asked the Italians who ran the pea farm if they had seen Spit; then the Walkers, and at the other dairy farms that bordered the little river. The one person he didn't ask was Sadie Tree who was the only person in town who knew where Spit was. But when he asked the boys and girls who normally used the Point for a swimming hole if they had seen Spit (he never swam there anyway) they all told the Sergeant, 'He's over on Pental Island, somewhere on the big river.' In fact they didn't know for sure where Spit was, but they knew that the island and the big river were Spit's territory, so where else would he be?

It was something that Sergeant Collins also knew but was reluctant to accept because it meant rowing a boat across to the island and searching the strip of bush – the tall old eucalypts – that bordered the big river. Even then, unless Spit could be surprised in his sleep, the chances were that he would hear or see anybody looking for him, and could easily hide somewhere if he was determined enough. He knew every inch of the bush along the big river.

'That little wombat is so bloody determined, God knows where he is,' Sergeant Collins told his wife as he sat down to tea after his wasted day.

The next morning, when Sergeant Collins crossed the river in the boat he had borrowed from the power station, Spit was fishing from a fallen tree on the big river where he could see all that was happening. He saw Sergeant Collins rowing across the river, and rolling up his lines he buried them with his bed rolls under a pile of leaves and ran along the edge of the bank as fast as he could go.

Spit felt safe enough as he picked his way along the river bank, but he was always alert for any one of the three threats to his bare feet which, though hardened and almost always suffering a missing toe nail or a bloody big toe, could be attacked on the ground. He was afraid of the poisonous black or brown or tiger snakes that lived in the grass or under the trees or on the river bank, and were often difficult to see until you almost stepped on them. He could not forget what had happened to his friend Crispie. He was also afraid of the big goannas which were like prehistoric monsters and were often aggressive and could run as fast as he could it they wanted to. But the nuisance which always made him yelp or swear were the hard little seeds – three-pointed spikes called bindi-eyes which lay on the ground almost anywhere in the open, and jabbed deep into his flesh if he stood on them. He had to hop several times to extract a bindi-eye as he ran, but he knew he was safe because he could move faster than Sergeant Collins, and could hide in dozens of places among the trees or on the river bank.

When he had plenty of distance between him and Sergeant Collins, he heard the Sergeant calling out to him, swearing sometimes and adding the threat: 'You'd better come out now, Spit, because we'll catch up with you sooner or later, and then I'll lock you up, you little devil, for wasting my bloody time.'

And finally, but more effectively: 'Your grandfather's

going to be buried tomorrow, so you ought to be there, Spit. You can't miss the old man's funeral.'

Spit could still see Sergeant Collins who was dabbing his face with his wet handkerchief. It was a hot day, the Sergeant's jacket was undone and his cap was on the back of his head. He looked around from river to bush as if he knew that Spit was not far away.

'Come on Spit, be a sport. Nobody's going to hurt you,' he was shouting.

Emboldened by the Sergeant's obvious disarray, Spit shouted back, 'It's just another trick, and I'm not coming back.'

He turned then and ran as fast as he could through the tall gums to the river bank where he could still watch almost everything that Sergeant Collins did. As the Sergeant retreated to the little river Spit followed him all the way until the Sergeant was back in the boat and rowing across the little river to St Helen.

Spit returned then to his fishing because he had discovered that he was going to be short of food sooner than he had expected. He was forever hungry, he had finished the bread and all but two eggs, and because it was late in the season the fish were not always biting, so he had only caught one Murray cod and a couple of small perch. But now he made his fire on the river bank where it was safe and couldn't be seen from any distance. He had made, in his life, many fires, and cooked many a fish and boiled many a billy. It was easy and routine now. But he had to be careful. He climbed to the top of the bank from time to time to see if Sergeant Collins or anyone else was on the way back. Finally, when he had eaten the last of the cod and the last hard end of his white bread, he sat on top of the bank sipping hot sweet tea and thinking of his grandfather, wishing without any admission of his final and ghostly loss that his grandfather would be waiting for him in the boiler house again, and that their life there would go on forever.

But he knew he had to fight for himself now, and he cursed (in his best all-round selection) Sergeant Collins not for being the local policeman or a particular enemy but because he was the agent of everybody else who was out to get him. Finishing his tea he stood up, took the last dregs of sugar out of the enamel mug with his finger and said aloud, 'They're never going to get me.'

He washed out the mug and the billy and the plate in the river, covered the ashes of his fire, and began to dig with his feet in the soft sand and mud, looking for the big river mussels which were the best bait for Murray cod.

Now that he was discovered, and having carelessly revealed himself to Sergeant Collins, he decided to move further up the big river. Packing his two blanket rolls he slung them over his shoulder and made his camp in another clump of gums where he could still see anybody crossing the little river, although it was much farther away now. Since there was nothing to do but fish, he fished, and sometimes he sang one of the Scottish songs his grandfather had taught him, although he didn't understand the words because they were too Scottish to make any sense of. When it became dark, which always settled quickly now that summer was almost over, he made his way back to the little river, smacking the path in front of him with a stick so that he didn't step on a coiled up and sleeping snake. He swam the little river, climbed out cautiously, found a fragment of wood among the ashes of the boiler, cut a little boat from it, found also a fragment of brown paper, wrote '*2 bread and some eggs*' on it with a blackened splinter of burnt wood, made it into a sail, and set the boat on its way down to Pental island by the time Mr Evans' dog, Patchy, put his visit on record, although nobody paid that much attention to connections like that except Sadie.

He knew that he had to be particularly careful with his camp at night, in case Sergeant Collins or someone else decided to sneak up on him in darkness. He made his fire under an overhang on the bank and he doused it when he had cooked his last perch and boiled his billy. He slept in his blankets, hidden under a fallen gum near the overhang, although he knew that snakes often lay along that particular tree when they sunned themselves.

He slept nervously alert, and spent the next day avoiding not only Sergeant Collins but Jack Tree and Frank Arbuckle and Tim Evans who had organised themselves into a posse to search out the bush along the banks of the big river. Seeing all three hunting him like a bushranger it became a challenge to Spit, and though he found little difficulty in avoiding them (sometimes he got around behind them and simply followed them) he was worried at the end of the day when he heard Sergeant Collins say to Mr Tree, 'We're in for some rain, Jack, and the poor little beggar will probably come in, once it starts to pour.'

'I'm not so sure,' Jack Tree said. 'He's a barefoot barnacle and he's not likely to be afraid of a little rain.'

'It's going to get awfully muddy, and if we get a bit of wind it's also going to be pretty miserable. In any case we'll bring Doug Stewart and half a dozen others tomorrow and we ought to get him somewhere sooner or later.'

'Maybe . . . maybe . . .' Jack Tree said doubtfully. 'In any case doing it this way is a dead loss. He's probably watching us right now, and laughing up his bare sleeve.'

'Maybe he'll get hungry,' Frank Arbuckle said, 'and that'll bring him in. Don't you think?' he appealed, knowing he would have to face Betty on his return without Spit.

'I don't know about that either, Frank,' Jack Tree said. 'He's better at catching fish in this river than anyone else in town. Anyway, let's go. We're just wasting our time doing it this way.'

Spit had heard enough and he did a wide circle around his pursuers to pick up his blanket rolls and then head for one of the thickest clumps of gums where he could shelter best from the rain when it came. He had not noticed the sky to the north-west because the timber and his concentration on his pursuers had obscured it. Now that he took a good look at the sky, he saw in the shadow of the setting sun a silhouette of thick black clouds etching a flat line along the distant horizon, and he knew it was going to be a bad night.

Rain, when it came to St Helen, was always a visible aggressor behind a waning in the sky, and its first splashing gum-drops were usually sudden and heavy once the thick clouds were overhead, particularly in late summer. He knew that this time it would probably arrive in the middle of the night, and he wished that he had brought his little tomahawk that he normally used to cut kindling with. It was still there in the garden shed. Now, when he reached the triangle of thick gums where there was some overhead protection, he tried to construct a lean-to with dead limbs and thick grass against one of the trees. But he knew it was hopeless so he returned to the river bank, found a sandy edge with an overhang under some exposed roots, and decided to sleep out any storm here if he had to.

But first he must cross the little river again to get the bread and eggs he had asked Sadie for. It took time to cover the longer distance to the little river, but he swam as quietly as he could, aware now of the faster currents of the rising river. He waited at the mud steps in the darkness for a moment before running quickly to the shelf under the boiler.

'Good old Sadie,' he said softly as he felt the bread and eggs and something else – a tin of sardines. They were all together in a sugar bag and there was a note tied with string around the sardine tin which he couldn't read in the darkness. He heard Tim Evans' dog bark, and somewhere above the railway line he heard a motor bike. It was enough to hurry him on his way, and he set out higher than usual to allow for the faster current and swam on his back, holding the sugar bag as high as he could. But again it got wet and he swore at Sergeant Collins for trying to trap him. At this moment he wasn't thinking of Betty Arbuckle and the Boys Home, he was far more concerned with the men at his heels.

He beat his way back under the threatening sky to his shelter beneath the roots of the big gum tree, and it began to rain as he tucked himself into his blankets. He heard the storm slowly rumbling overhead and he looked up at the big tree which, he knew, could topple over at any time once the winds began.

'But not tonight,' he begged the tree. 'Any old time, but not tonight.'

11

What Spit didn't know, after a night of thunder and lightning and heavy, windy rain, was that in the dull muddy morning there was a large following of his unseen and unknown friends behind the cortege of his grandfather's funeral. They had to bury him without Spit, even as ten men of St Helen went across the river in a phalanx to track him down. They were going to catch him this time, even if they had to hunt for him all day and all night. But thirty people of the town followed the funeral, and though some said it was really a gesture to the defiant Spit, hiding in the bush, for those who were there it was more a gesture to the strange and tortured old man who had done his best for his grandson, even as he tried painfully and often hopelessly to keep some remnants of his sanity intact.

Betty Arbuckle was on foot, and though she was here to bury the old man, she was more concerned about Spit's future than she was about Fyfe MacPhee's shadowy death. Nonetheless she was overcome; she was in tears, her lovely face always beautiful in its passion as she declared in her heart that she was deputising for Spit in the eyes of the Lord who would forgive his absence.

On the other hand Grace Tree, holding Sadie by the hand, walked self-consciously but determinedly at the very end of the little procession feeling out of place. She too was trying to formulate her own concern for this serious and wild little boy who had disturbed her own family. At the cemetery gate she sent Sadie home. Thereafter she stood at the back of the gathering to listen to the Reverend Mackenzie, the Presbyterian Minister, make his fiery appeals to the Lord to take up the departing soul of Fyfe MacPhee and make the best use He could with it.

Being a Catholic she was not at ease with the Reverend Mackenzie's Calvinist appeals to the Lord, although she considered him a fine man with nothing but good in his heart. But she was glad that she was here for Spit's sake, and looking across the open sandy grave at the tear-stained face of Betty Arbuckle, she too knew that it was Spit's life that was now the problem. Like Betty she was thinking more about Spit than the old man who was being returned to earth.

Grace left the ceremony before the others. Walking back to town, avoiding the fresh puddles along the muddy road, she was thinking about Spit. She had always known where he was hiding without having to think about it. The reason for his sudden flight seemed so obvious that she was surprised that the whole town didn't somehow organise itself to save Spit from being sent away to a Boys Home that was miles away in Bendigo. Now she was worried about him fending for himself on Pental Island, particularly at night. Like everybody else in town she knew about the snakes, but she had enough confidence in him to decide that he was safe enough for a few days at least, barring accidents.

She had also guessed that Sadie was helping him, and she didn't question her daughter or try to interfere. But when her husband had returned yesterday with Sergeant Collins from the first fruitless search of the bush along the river, she had said to him when he began to complain about the little devil wasting everybody's time: 'He shouldn't go to an orphanage, Jack. That's what is causing the trouble.'

'Well what else is there for him?' Jack Tree had said.

'I don't know,' she replied. 'But surely something can be done for him.'

'Maybe Betty Arbuckle will take him over,' Jack Tree said as they listened to a mosquito searching them out in the darkness as they lay in bed.

'But it's Betty Arbuckle he's running away from.'

'I don't know why,' Jack Tree said. 'If she decided to take him over it would be a pretty good thing for him. She's a kind woman underneath all that evangelical soap.'

'I know she's kind, but kindness is not enough. He deserves more than that, Jack. Even when he was with her for a few days Betty Arbuckle was trying to turn him into a copy of her own Ben, and that just won't work with Spit. Anyway if you do catch him and take him back to her he'll only run away again.'

'That's why he's better off in a proper place in Bendigo where it is a damned sight more difficult to run away. No bush down there.'

'It's wrong,' Grace insisted. 'It's terribly wrong.'

'I don't know why you're so worked up about this boy,' her husband said. 'For heaven's sake stop thinking about him. It'll turn out all right, so stop it.'

'I can't,' Grace Tree said in her firm, quiet way and her surprised husband wondered again at her stubborness, although he decided not to pursue it in case her defiance persisted.

That had been yesterday. Today, as she walked away from the funeral, she hoped that even ten men wouldn't be able to catch Spit, even though she had listened to the storm last night and pictured Spit huddled somewhere on the island, wet and afraid, and feeling friendless and miserably alone. She was sure that in his heart her husband had been as worried in the night as she was, but his solution was not hers. She was determined not to accept the easy and obvious way out of the problem for Spit. 'It's wrong,' she told herself once more as she saw Sadie running up the slope to meet her.

'They caught Spit,' Sadie said breathlessly, 'but he got away and tried to swim across the big river to New South Wales. Dad and Mr Arbuckle are taking the boat down to the big river so they can get across to New South Wales and catch him if he does get across.'

'Poor Spit,' Mrs Tree said bitterly. 'I wonder what on earth he thinks of us all, chasing him like an animal.'

Spit, at the time, was not thinking of the population of St Helen at all but of the big river that was in full steam ahead of him – too full and too fast and too wide.

He had come through the wet storm last night rather well. His little caved-in bank under the gum tree roots had been fairly dry, and the thunder and lightning had not bothered him too much. There was a strong local theory that in a bad storm snakes, seeking protection, would crawl into the blankets of anyone exposed enough like Spit to the elements, so he periodically had to shake his blankets out to make sure that no snake tried to get in with him. When the wind had broken off a small dead limb from the gum tree and dropped it on his blanket he had leapt up in a moment of terror, swinging the blankets across his feet in a panic until he had seen the broken limb. He could swear effectively and fluently for the fear in his heart, and after telling weather, sky and tree what he thought of them, he flung the broken limb into the river, rolled himself up in his blanket and again went to sleep.

He was in a fairly good position in the morning to make his fire, and though everything was damp and dripping, the sky was blue again and he found enough dry sticks and leaves to get the fire going. He boiled his billy and toasted the bread. He missed butter, but when he opened the sardines he said, 'Good old Sade,' and read her note. It said: '*Tomorrow I leave you eggs and butter. Do you want some chump chops?*' He took a blackened stick and wrote '*Yes*' on the same paper and put it in his trouser pocket to be delivered that night.

He stored his goods and chattels neatly under the roots and took his lines with him down river to a deep hole which he had not yet fished. He spent most of the morning failing to catch any fish, while keeping his eye on the little river crossing. But when he had run out of mussels he walked a hundred yards down river to a little sandy patch where there was also an edge of some noisy rapids, and he was digging in the mud with his toes, concentrating on his search for the big river mussels, when he saw Ted Jackson, the butcher and fireman, and Andy Frith who delivered the milk, standing on the shore. He realised that he had been careless. The stony crackle and bubble of the shallow rapids had drowned their noisy approach so that he had lost his first line of defence – his ears.

'Come on out, Spit,' Andy shouted at him. 'It's time to go home.'

Spit didn't say anything. He looked for a way out. The rest of the big river was too wide and fast to get right across, but he knew that if he dived in he could catch the downstream flow and make some sort of an escape. He ran along the sand bank, over the rapids, and dived in. As he swam with the fast current downstream he could hear Ted Jackson calling out to someone that he was in the river, going hell-for-leather downstream.

Spit kept his eye on the banks as he was carried downstream, but he was surprised when he was swept around a bend to see Ron Jackson, one of the best swimmers in the town and one of the fastest runners as well, waiting on the bank and taking off his shoes and trousers and shirt ready to dive in.

Spit knew that he could not outswim Ron Jackson, but he headed across the river anyway, trying to escape him. He was barely halfway across in the current, already carried fast downstream, when he felt Ron Jackson's arm around his neck.

'Come on, kiddo,' Ron said to him as he tightened his grip around Spit's neck. 'The game's up.' Ron was a film addict and his language had to fit the situation. But he was young and friendly to Spit and he was one of the adults whom Spit would call by his first name instead of Mister.

'Let me go, Ron,' Spit said to him as they struggled together in the water. 'You're choking me.'

But water and swimming and struggling were not good for an argument, and it was only when Ron had pulled him up on the bank two hundred yards downstream that he said to Spit as they both caught their breath, 'You can't run away in this town, Spit, so it's no use trying.'

He kept a firm hold on Spit, and by now six of the other hunters had arrived, including Sergeant Collins, Jack Tree and Frank Arbuckle. Spit expected at least one of them to cuff him, but Sergeant Collins said, 'You're as slippery as Ned Kelly, Spit. But you got careless, like all bushrangers.'

'I'm not a bushranger,' Spit said. 'I haven't stolen a damned thing.'

The others laughed and Jack Tree said to him, 'We don't want to hunt you down, young feller, but we can't have an eleven-year-old running around alone in the bush. It's for your own good.'

Spit knew they were trying to do something for him and he knew all these men: Sam Allenby the greengrocer, Billy Andrews from the power house, Peter Macrae who was the shunter, and all the others. But he also knew at a glance that the only real swimmer among them was Ron Jackson, and Ron had gone back to get his trousers and shirt and shoes, two hundred yards upstream where he had left them.

Sitting on the bank getting his breath back Spit watched Ron Jackson through the trees, and at the moment when Ron was putting on his trousers Spit stood up slowly and before the others realised what he was doing he had jumped into the river again, and this time he was determined to get across to New South Wales where there was thicker timber and he could outrun Ron if he got enough start.

But unluckily this was one of the places where the river was widest and fastest, and it was another mile to the junction of the little river. So Spit knew that he was going to be carried downstream more than across. His real problem was to use the stream in his favour before the rivers joined; but above all to get as far ahead of Ron Jackson as he could.

He heard Sergeant Collins shout, 'Ron, he's back in the river. Get down here quick or we'll lose him.'

It was then that Sergeant Collins told Jack Tree and Frank Arbuckle to hurry back to the little river, get the boat, and row across the big river to cut off Spit's escape into New South Wales.

12

When Sadie saw her father and Frank Arbuckle launch the boat on the other side of the little river, she had been sitting on the steps waiting for someone to appear with news of Spit. When she called out to her father, he told her what had happened and as he began to pull the boat downstream to the junction of the big river, he called out to her, 'You go off back home, Sadie. You're not to hang around waiting for me to come back. Go on . . .' he called out as he disappeared around the bend.

But Sadie was not hanging around waiting for her father to come back. She was telling herself unhappily that she was waiting to see if they caught Spit, and she was going to defy her father and sit on the mud steps to see what was going to happen now. She was running up the slope to the house to get her father's field glasses when she saw her mother crossing the railway line on her way back from the funeral. Sadie continued on up the slope to tell her what had happened.

'He could drown in the big river, couldn't he?' she said to her mother as they both hurried back to the boiler steps.

'He could,' Grace said, 'but he's a strong swimmer and if he doesn't exhaust himself he'll be all right.'

'I hope they never catch him,' Sadie said as they reached the steps to wait again for someone to reappear with news of Spit.

'The only trouble is,' her mother said, 'he can't stay out there forever, Sadie. Although I wish they could have done it some other way.'

'What'll happen to him when they bring him back?' Sadie asked.

'I don't know, I really don't know. But if they try to send

him back to Betty Arbuckle he'll only run away again. So I don't know what is to become of him.'

'Maybe Sergeant Collins will have to lock him up?' Sadie said.

'I wouldn't put it past any of them,' Mrs Tree said unhappily. 'Even though they all think they're doing their best for the boy.'

'It's unfair,' Sadie said.

'Yes, it is,' her mother replied, and she sat down near her daughter to wait.

Half an hour later they saw the rowing boat coming heavily upstream, and in it were Jack Tree, Frank Arbuckle, Ron Jackson and Spit.

'Oh, they got him,' Sadie said bitterly, standing up.

As Sadie and her mother watched the boat approaching, the rest of the hunters and seekers emerged from the clump of gums on the island to wait to be picked up.

'Where did you catch him?' Sergeant Collins called out to the boat.

'Ron caught up with him,' Frank Arbuckle replied. 'And just in time. He was almost done for.'

When the row boat reached the steps Ron Jackson jumped into the water and stayed there because he was in his underpants. Jack Tree manoeuvred the boat so that Frank Arbuckle could get Spit up the steps, and seeing his wife and Sadie he said angrily, 'I told you to go home, Sadie. Now get. And quick. We had to take Spit's pants off him so he wouldn't run off again, so turn your back and run straight up to the house.'

Sadie had seen Spit huddled in embarrassment in the back of the boat without realising why. Bursting into tears she ran up the slope to the house. When Frank Arbuckle tried to get Spit out of the boat he resisted violently, and now Mrs Tree saw that he too was in tears, not, she knew, for his defeat but for his naked humiliation.

'It's all right Spit, I won't look,' she said to him, turning her back. Then she added angrily to her husband, 'Jack. Give him back his trousers.'

'Not on your life,' Jack Tree said. 'He'll be off like a shot.'

'No he won't. Do as I say, Jack. I'm telling you,' she said so firmly and angrily that Jack Tree hesitated only a moment before telling Frank Arbuckle, 'Give him back his pants, Frank, but keep a good grip on him.'

Mrs Tree waited until they had landed Spit then she turned around to face her husband and Frank Arbuckle.

'Spit, come here,' she said to him.

Spit, weakened by his humiliation, did as he was told. Mrs Tree didn't touch or comfort him or look at him in his humiliation, even with his pants on. She was looking straight at her husband.

'Where do you think you are taking him now?' she asked him.

Startled by her temper, her posture and her sudden defiance, Jack Tree said, 'I don't know, Grace. We'll let Joe Collins decide that.'

'No, you won't,' Grace said. 'He's not moving from here. I'm going to take him up to the house, and he's going to stay there until we've sorted this all out.'

'Don't be such a fool,' Jack Tree said to her. 'He'll run off again the first chance he gets.'

Grace Tree looked at Spit now and said, 'Will you run off again Spit if I promise not to let them take you back to Mrs Arbuckle's or send you away?'

Spit was also surprised by Mrs Tree's anger and temper; and because he was beginning to recover himself he knew he had an ally, for the time being at least.

'All right,' he said. 'I won't run off. But just so long as it isn't a trick.'

'It isn't a trick,' Grace said.

But Frank Arbuckle resisted. 'He's fooling you, Grace. He'll duck off again the moment your back is turned. You don't know him.' Frank was hurt by Grace's remarks about his wife, and he also had to face Betty empty-handed.

'You might not trust him, Frank,' she said, 'but I'm willing to, and you're not going to take him away simply because you don't believe him. He's staying with me, and I'll take full responsibility for him until something sensible is decided about him. Come on, Spit,' she said firmly and, walking ahead, she didn't bother to turn around to make sure that Spit was following her.

But he followed, and as they went up the slope Spit heard Ron Jackson calling out to Sergeant Collins, 'Did you bring my pants and shoes, Joe?' And Joe Collins reply, 'No, we clean forgot.'

Ron swore and said, 'What a pack of bloody fools . . .'

Spit thought that pretty good, and though he liked Ron Jackson, he was glad in view of that first grip around his neck that Ron had to go back for his trousers, although he was also grateful to him for having reached him in midstream, because Spit knew that he was almost done for when he felt that sudden, tight forearm around his neck for the second time.

13

WHATEVER SPIT LEARNED LATER ABOUT THE NEXT FEW DAYS and weeks in his life, he knew little about them at the time. He was aware that something was being fought out over him, so that eventually the whole town seemed to be taking sides. He was aware too that he had caused serious trouble between Mr and Mrs Tree, so much so that Sadie was unhappy about the continuing though often hidden dispute going on between her mother and father.

'I wish they wouldn't quarrel,' Sadie had confided in him after a week of it and when Spit was doing what Jack Tree had told him to do – cut kindling wood for the fire.

'What are they arguing about anyway?' Spit asked her.

'I don't know. They've never argued like this before.'

But Sadie knew, and Spit guessed that he was the cause of it. He didn't know what he could do about it himself except to run away again, but he had promised Mrs Tree so he could not do that. And there was no need to do it yet anyway. What made both Sadie and Spit particularly aware of the trouble was Grace Tree's stubborn resistance to her husband's usual habit of making decisions and then assuming that they would be automatically obeyed.

It had now become a simple issue of what to do with Spit. Grace Tree had first of all consulted Sergeant Collins and asked him what he intended to do about the boy, now that he had no home.

'He'll have to go off to that Boys Home in Bendigo, Grace,' Sergeant Collins told her. 'I don't see any other way. But in fact it isn't my decision. You'll have to go up to the Shire Office and ask them what they are going to do with him. It's more their responsibility than mine. And you'll also have to cope with Betty Arbuckle, if you're thinking of anything else. She already wants me to go and get the boy and bring him back to her place.'

'Don't you dare,' Grace Tree said in her quiet way. 'He's not leaving my house.'

'All right. All right,' Sergeant Collins said. 'I'm fed up with the whole business; always have been. You settle it with the Shire Office and I'll do whatever they tell me.'

Grace Tree went to the Shire Office and spoke to the only man she knew there, Pat Stillman – the dark and affable Pat Stillman who told her that there was no way locally that Spit could be looked after. There was no place and no organisation that could take care of him. So the logical place, no matter which way you looked at it, was the Boys Home in Bendigo.

'That's awful, Pat. There ought to be something else.'

'Unless you want to take him over yourself,' Pat said and laughed. 'In that case you'll have to look into the legal side of it before we could agree to anything. But that I'd love to see,' Pat said and he laughed again, because he was a determined laugher at everything, including himself. 'I'm a round peg in a square hole,' he loved to say to anyone admiring his untidy and crowded office, walled-in with square pigeon holes stuffed with files and documents.

It was when she was walking home from the Shire Office that Grace Tree made up her mind. She could not, physically, have any more children of her own, but even if she were able to have them it would not have altered her resolve. It was a startling decision, almost frightening, but she knew what she must do. She would adopt Spit. That was the simplest and cleanest solution and she knew it was right. That is, if they (whoever 'they' were) would let her adopt him.

14

GRACE'S FIRST OBSTACLE WAS HER HUSBAND, AND WHEN SPIT AND Sadie had gone to bed that night she said to Jack, 'I'm going to try and adopt him, Jack. He's a good boy and Sadie likes him, and I trust him because he has always been very honest. So I'm going up to the Shire Office tomorrow to see how to go about it.'

'You'll do no such thing,' Jack Tree said incredulously. 'You must be out of your mind to think of it. I forbid it.'

'I'm not out of my mind at all, and I'm going to do it.'

Jack Tree was seated at his roll-top desk making out his complicated reports on herd testing, a task that his wife would not normally have dared interrupt. But Grace stood at the side of his desk looking so close-mouthed and determined that Jack Tree was nonplussed.

'I'll tell you this,' he said, taking off his spectacles with a snap. 'Even if you want to adopt him, you haven't a ghost of a chance because Spit is a Protestant and you're a Catholic. They'll never let you do it.'

Grace had already considered this most obvious of problems in a country as divided and as passionate as Australia was by sect and prejudice, but she had not come to that problem yet so she had pushed it out of her mind.

'I'll face that when I come to it,' she said, 'but I wish you would think about it,' she told him, appealing to him now as if she would be quite willing to return to her docility if he would only agree. 'He's still so young, and whatever you think is wrong with him now, you can do something with him. I like him, Jack, and I don't want him to end up in an orphanage. It would be so wrong, and you know it yourself. Think of Sadie, if something happened to us.'

'If you start thinking that way you'll end up with all the lame ducks in the town at your doorstep. I'm not going to turn this place into a charity.'

'I'm not asking you to. I'm simply asking you to let me adopt him and bring him up properly.'

'It wouldn't work.'

'I'll make it work.'

'You would spoil him. He's already twisting you around his little finger, though how on earth he does it I don't know. Or even why.'

'That's not true, and you know it. I'm thinking of the boy.'

'All right, then. I have a suggestion.' Jack pointed his spectacles at her which was usually intended to intimidate her. 'Will you do what I tell you?'

Grace hesitated and said for the first time in their married life, 'I'm not sure, Jack. But what are you saying?'

'Will you go and talk to Betty Arbuckle and see if you can persuade her to adopt Spit instead of sending him off to that home in Bendigo?'

'I'll do no such thing,' Grace said angrily. 'Betty Arbuckle is a very kind woman. She means well. But Spit is not for her. He would simply turn against her and become a criminal or run away or do something terrible.'

'And what makes you think you could do any better with him?'

'Because if I were a child I would sooner be our Sadie than Ben or Joannie Arbuckle.'

'Well I can tell you this, Grace. Betty Arbuckle is not going to stand aside and let you adopt a Protestant boy like Spit MacPhee. She'll fight you tooth and nail.'

'Then I'll fight her tooth and nail. I've made up my mind, Jack, and I only wish you would too.'

'I have. And I say No.'

'I think you are wrong, and if I can adopt him I know that you'll change your mind.'

'Have you considered for a moment what his influence would be on Sadie?'

'Sadie is a very quiet girl. She doesn't make friends easily because she is too quiet. But she likes Spit and I know he would always look after her, so I'm not worried about that. I didn't tell you before but he taught her to swim, which I thought was a good thing, living so near the river.'

'He what?'

'He taught her to swim.'

'Why, for God's sake, didn't you tell me?' Jack said angrily and yet helplessly.

'Because you would have stopped her.'

'I give up,' Jack Tree said in exasperation. 'Do what you like, but don't expect any help from me.'

Grace Tree stood quietly for a moment, troubled that she should be so determined about something which affected her husband as profoundly as it was affecting her, perhaps more so. If he wanted a son, which he couldn't have from her, he obviously didn't want Spit as a substitute. Yet she was sure he would change his mind if she succeeded in adopting Spit. And, falling back on her old habit of silence, she left him to his work, although this time her silence was not an admission but rather a denial of his authority, which surprised and troubled her as much as it did her husband.

15

GRACE WAS NOT SURE HOW TO GO ABOUT IT, BUT SHE PUT ON A print frock and a straw hat and went back to Pat Stillman at the Shire Office. She had no way of going about it except the simplest and the most direct.

'Pat,' she said. 'I want to adopt Spit MacPhee, so how do I go about it?'

Pat tried not to interfere in anybody's life, even his wife's, but because of his round-peg-in-a-square-hole joke about himself he had the reputation of being a soft and helpless man. In fact he knew and liked his job and did it well.

'Hang on a bit, Grace,' he said. 'I wasn't serious yesterday when I said you might take him on yourself.'

'That's all right,' Grace Tree said. 'But I'm serious now so how is it done?'

Pat became thoughtful; and here in his small dark office behind the Shire Hall he was less inclined to laugh at everything because he was safe here.

'Well, I'm not too sure, but I'll look it up for you and find out all I can. But are you really sure about it?'

'Yes.'

'What does Jack say?'

'He said I could do what I liked, although he wouldn't help me.' She knew that was not quite the whole truth but she was not going to open up any little doors to her private life for Pat Stillman or anyone else.

'Hmmmm . . . Hmmm . . . But did you stop to think that you are a Catholic and Spit's a Protestant, and you know what it's like in this town. The Protestants won't like it.' Pat was a Catholic himself so he was talking within the family.

'They may not like it but all they want to do is send him off o a home in Bendigo and that's wrong. Anyway I don't think hey all want to get rid of Spit like that. I know Dorothy Evans vouldn't think like that, and plenty of other Protestants. But 'll face that when I have to. What happens first?'

Pat laughed. 'Good on you, Grace,' he said. 'I'll do what I an. But I'll bet that first of all there'll be a lot of forms. You an bet your life on that. But I'll look into it and let you know.'

'Thanks, Pat,' Grace said and stood up because she knew here was nothing else she could do here.

'One thing,' Pat said as she waited for a moment. 'If I were ou I wouldn't tell anyone what you are doing. Not until you ave to, because the further along you are before they start etting worried, the better.'

'I have no intention of telling anyone at all,' Grace said.

'Not even Spit himself,' Pat told her.

'I wasn't going to do that either. I'm not going to build up is hopes.'

'You're full of surprises,' Pat said slyly as she left. 'But vatch out for the dingoes, Grace,' he called after her. They're always looking for lost strays like young Spit AacPhee.'

She wasn't sure what he meant by that, but she guessed that e was warning her to trust nobody but her fellow Roman Catholics. But what she first had to contend with, as she vaited out the weeks for her intentions to reach some sort of hape, was Spit himself. She discovered that Spit was not a irl, and though it was an obvious realisation, nonetheless it vas the one she had to deal with first. She and Sadie had lways been very close, and without having to think about it he could pull things on and off Sadie, walk in and out of her oom at any time, put her in a bath, push her into bed, plait er hair, touch her and tell her or discuss with her what she ught to do, or ought not to do.

But she discovered that she was shy with Spit, which urprised her. Why should an eleven-year-old boy make her elf-conscious? She did her best not to let it show. But trying to it a ready-made Spit into a ready-made household that was uite unprepared for him was more difficult than she had hought, particularly when there was nothing sure about his uture. If it had been certain that she was going to be allowed to adopt him she could have started from scratch. But because there was still a shadow on him, still a likelihood that it wouldn't be possible and that he might be taken away from her, she felt unsure and limited in what she ought to start, or even what she could do for him at all.

All this too in the face of Jack's resistance and some from the town. When her idea of adopting Spit became known in the town she felt rather than heard the opposition of those who thought it wrong for a Protestant boy to be adopted by a Catholic family when there was a perfectly good Protestant home waiting for him elsewhere, even if it was an orphanage. And, to add conviction to this sort of opposition, she knew, as every Australian knew, that there had always been certain rules to the sometimes savage game which both sides played with their religion.

But she refused to think of Spit's adoption as a religious battle. A Catholic orphanage to Grace was no better than a Protestant one; it could even be worse. This was true also of her opposition to Betty Arbuckle. It was not because Betty was a Protestant, but rather her ideas on restraint and abnegation, and her passionate method of conciliating her God by de-naturing herself and all those around her. To Grace it was simply wrong, particularly for Spit.

So whichever way she looked at it, Catholic or Protestant, Grace knew that none of it would benefit Spit if it became an issue of religion. What surprised her, as her intention became known in the town, was not the obvious degree of hostility to it but the support she got from women whom she hardly knew, including Protestants among them. When she met women in the street like Mrs Finch, the Stock and Station Agent's wife, who was a good Methodist but who had never spoken to Grace before and Mrs Finch said, 'I hope you can save young Spit MacPhee from that awful Bendigo home. It would be terrible if he had to end up there,' Grace felt that her isolation was not as serious as she thought it was. When other women, and even men like Mr Williams the draper said the same thing to her, she had a quiet woman's satisfaction in listening to them. But she had to be worried and unhappy about Jack because he refused to understand, and she knew he was even less likely to understand when he saw the long form that Pat Stillman had unearthed for her to fill in – the form that outlined the statutory and legal requirements which were going to make Spit's adoption far more complicated than she had imagined.

What finally disturbed her was a visit from Betty Arbuckle as she was cleaning a cod which Spit had caught that day. Grace had never curtailed Spit's life on the river, nor his fishing, nor even Sadie's companionship. But Jack had forbidden Sadie to go too near the water now that it was high, and he had ordered Spit in a soldier's voice not to take her any further up river than the boiler, so that when Betty Arbuckle came, unannounced, dressed in a long, dark, heavy frock and buckled shoes, Grace felt as if she was something of a libertine for allowing Spit and Sadie to be together on the river bank enjoying themselves. And she had to pay the price for Betty's radiance – for Betty's light and passionate eyes and for her almost ephemeral beauty. Being a plain woman, Grace Tree couldn't help but admire and envy the face that God had given Betty Arbuckle, even though she disagreed with the spirit that went with it.

16

'WHY DIDN'T YOU COME AND TELL ME YOU WERE GOING TO TAKE the boy away from me?' Betty Arbuckle said in a hurt voice. 'You know you had no right to do that, Grace.'

Grace Tree felt defensive, but she told herself that she would have to do her best. She must somehow match this curious woman's childlike conviction which had always seemed impenetrable and inviolable. Grace remembered her as a girl at school, and she had been the same then as she was now, almost unchanged except in fulsomeness. 'I didn't take him away from you, Betty,' she said. 'Spit ran away on his own account.'

'But Frank told me that when they rescued him from the river, you told him he was not to come back to me. You forbade him.'

'I did no such thing,' Grace Tree said, dropping the fish and the knife she was using, and standing up. She had been bent over the little table near the outside tap where she often peeled potatoes or cleaned fish. 'I did say he was not going back to your place and that he was not leaving here; but that's what I told those men who were dragging him naked by the scruff of the neck. All I told Spit was that he could do what he liked. And he chose to stay here. So please don't come here accusing me, Betty. You are wrong.'

'I'm not accusing you,' Betty said. 'But you know that I have always been worried about the boy, and for years I have been trying to help him. It was only his grandfather who made it difficult. Now we have a home for him in Bendigo, and I think you are wrong to interfere. You musn't try to keep him. It is best for him if he is properly looked after in a proper place, instead of running around like a poor, unfortunate, barefoot,

African heathen.'

'That is what I think too,' Grace Tree said. 'But I don't want him to go to a Boys Home in Bendigo. I don't think that's the best thing for him and I won't let you send him there.'

'But everybody knows that your husband doesn't want him,' Betty insisted. 'So he won't be happy here. He would only turn bad. He needs all the things that will help with his own salvation.'

'Don't worry about that,' Grace Tree said. 'Jack will change his mind.'

'But Spit's one of us, Grace. He's not one of yours.'

'I don't think Spit is one of anybody's at the moment.'

'But you'll try to convert him, you always do.'

Grace was still determined not to get Spit mixed up in a religious quarrel and she said, 'Does it matter what religion he is, Betty, as long as he has a good home?'

'But that's what a good home is. There's a terrible difference between us. The Lord Jesus is not . . .'

'Stop,' Grace said. 'Stop it, Betty.'

Betty Arbuckle and Grace Tree had been standing face to face in the sun, and for Grace it was a disturbing experience. Like most people in the town she had always, since childhood, considered Betty a bit of a crank, if only because Betty herself made such a point of elaborating her evangelism into a punishing oddity. But standing close to Betty, watching her face as it advertised her feelings, and looking into her crystal clear eyes, Grace knew that Betty was a naturally innocent woman who longed for the rest of the world to be innocent with her. Or, failing that, to be made innocent through salvation. And, in her passion for Spit's future, Betty was also sure that what she wanted for Spit was his real welfare and his real salvation, so that without knowing why, Grace said to herself in a puzzled, incredulous way: 'What a terrible pity. She would have made such a marvellous nun.' But, dealing here with the subject of a barefoot boy, Grace knew that Betty's innocence and passion and conviction were very down-to-earth, and she would probably be unbeatable if she went ahead with her plans for Spit to end up in a Boys Home in Bendigo.

'I can't let you do it, Grace,' Betty was saying to her, and Betty was now at her most obdurate. 'I can't let you interfere.' And after a brief search into each other's souls over a Murray cod, Grace knew now for sure that she was facing a real opponent who would fight her to the end.

Picking up the half-gutted fish she said, 'You think I am wrong, Betty, and I think that you are wrong. But I have to do what I think is right. I know that Spit is better off with me, and I am not going to let him go to any home in Bendigo. That would be cruel.'

'Then I'll have to make you give him up,' Betty said in her soft voice. 'You're a good woman, Grace, but your faith is in your priests and your Pope. Our faith is in salvation, and I'm surprised that you don't understand the difference. A boy saved for us becomes a vessel of the Lord, and Spit can only be saved if he is taken to the right place and taught the right lessons and given a chance to save himself.'

Betty Arbuckle turned to leave, but Grace followed her to the gate, feeling rather like a disciple in the steps of the Master. 'I don't think it is salvation that Spit needs,' she said to Betty, 'but a decent home, which is what I thought of giving him.'

'I'm sorry,' Betty said, upset now by Grace Tree's unusual stubborness, 'but you have no right to do this to the boy. I shall pray for you to give him up, because I am sure that right is on my side. And I am sure that the law is on my side too.'

As she watched Betty walk away like a heavenly body up the slope, Grace was not so much afraid of her influence with the Lord as she was of Betty's secular determination to use even the law if necessary. She knew that Betty would go to almost any lengths to do what she thought was right for Spit, and that meant the Boys Home in Bendigo rather than a Catholic family in St Helen.

'We'll just have to see,' Grace said to herself and went back to cleaning the fish which was one of Spit's silent offerings to the house he now lived in.

17

FILLING OUT THE FORM THAT PAT STILLMAN HAD GIVEN HER Grace did her best with the obvious questions about her and Jack's age, family, financial condition, social background, and religion (both their own and Spit's). They were the sort of questions she hated answering, and she knew that Jack would hate them too. Yet she was sure that when the time came she would get Jack's signature on the form. In fact she had to get it because the adoption application had to come from Jack as head of the family, rather than from Grace as the wife.

What made difficulties for her were the questions that needed permission of the natural parents, because the form assumed that adoption was mostly concerned with unwanted babies, rather than eleven-year-old orphans. Or, if the parents were both dead, she needed a signed release from the nearest relatives. Without that the form was invalid, which meant that her only recourse to the information she needed in order to write 'no surviving relatives' would have to be Spit himself. She could remember the fuss about Spit being left alone with his grandfather when his mother had come and gone so quickly and tragically, but it was only a hazy memory of casual rumours. She remembered Dorothy Evans telling her that there were no other relatives left. So Spit himself would have to be asked.

The trouble was that she didn't know how she could do it. Spit was still a problem, and she didn't want to open up his silent wounds. He had kept his word not to run away again, but she knew that he was being cautious with her, although she understood why. Even in her house he was in a sort of limbo. Sleeping on the verandah he was not quite in the house and at the same time not quite out of it. In studying him so that she could know how best to deal with him she had slowly unravelled some of his private rules for himself, which made Grace almost as cautious with him as he was with her.

Her first duty had been to clothe him, because he had come to her with nothing more than a pair of torn trousers and a shirt. She had discovered that he usually slept in an old shirt, so she had cut down one of Jack's rejects for him. She had been a little nervous about giving it to him as a first offering, but Spit had taken if off-handedly without any fuss. She had then bought some cotton lengths and run him up two new shirts on her Singer, which he had also accepted with his own sort of pride, but without demur. Her trial attempts at making up trousers with an old sheet had defeated her, so she had bought him one pair of khaki shorts and also a grey woollen pair because school was about to start. She had taken him to Williams the draper, and bought him socks, sandals and a school cap which, on his thick, fair hair was a lost cause.

Grace's only way of coping with his impersonal acceptance of her practical gesture was to repeat to herself a simple sentence that covered everything that Spit did: 'He's a strange boy.' But she also knew that his years of self-sufficiency and his loud and childish equality with his tortured grandfather had made him more than just a tough little boy who should be treated as one. Whenever he did any service about the house it was not in gratitude to her, nor even a favour, but was an unthinking contribution to what had to be done. He chopped the wood for her, which saved Jack a daily chore. She had watched him swinging an axe which seemed to miss his bare feet by inches, but though she had winced and turned away at the prospect of a miss, nonetheless she knew that he wouldn't miss and that she must let him do it. When he helped Sadie with the dishes, his tendency to clatter and treat the cups and saucers roughly bothered her, but she said nothing. He watered the garden for her, but unlike Jack, who was economical with water, Spit lavished it on everything in sight. He would walk – never run – up the slope to the shops if she wanted thread or an extra pint of milk or bread, and in this too he was neither willing nor unwilling. He simply did it and when Sadie went with him it gave her a deep sense of satisfaction to see them go up the slope together without any thought now of being anything but a natural brother and sister. That was when she felt most deeply Jack's reluctance. Why couldn't Jack see it as she saw it?

Finally, she had discovered that, apart from the thick grime-ingrained soles of his bare feet (his sandals would be only for school), he was a very clean boy, although she had to persuade him to use the inside bathroom rather than the outside tap.

'Where did you wash when you were living in the boiler?' she had asked him.

'Outside,' he had told her.

Summer or winter (she discovered) Spit and his grandfather had used a basin of river water on a table outside, and Spit's idea of washing himself was to stand naked to the waist over a basin and, having soaped his face and neck, simply douse himself with a mug full of water. He wouldn't tell her how he did it below the waist, but she suspected something similar, and because there had been no chip-fed hot water heater in the boiler house, it had always been a cold douche. She let him go on doing it in his own way outside; but she persuaded him to finish his lower parts in the bathroom, although he insisted on locking the door.

What surprised her, although she knew she shouldn't have been surprised, was her discovery that he had no naughtiness in him. It was not because he was good. In his certainties he seemed incapable of being silly or childish, even in his childish behaviour, which was another aspect of his self-sufficiency. But he had his faults, and the one that she knew she would have endless trouble with at home was his loud voice and his often aggressive answers of one harsh word in reply to a simple question. She knew that it was the way he and his grandfather had always spoken to each other, but she was a quiet person herself and it bothered her. She tried to correct it by speaking to him in a softer voice than her normal soft voice. She hoped that this would persuade him to speak quietly. It didn't.

But these were annoyances rather than serious faults. What she had to deal with was a brand of wickedness which genuinely surprised her. One morning when he was chopping the wood and a hard lump of mallee root had split off and hit his shins, his instinctive response had been a long line of such bad language that it shocked her. It was not the casual and childish kind of schoolboy curse, but an adult and shameful list of the worst. She didn't say anything to him, but she asked Sadie as she sat on her bed that night, 'Have you ever heard Spit swearing?'

'Never,' Sadie said, shocked that her mother asked her such a question. 'He never swears.'

But Jack had also heard him swearing at the Evans' dog, and he had told Grace that he would have to teach Spit a severe lesson – which meant giving him a good hiding.

But Grace said, 'You're not going to touch him, Jack. It won't teach him anything. On the contrary, it would only make it worse.'

'That's a lot of tommy rot,' Jack Tree said. 'If you don't stop him now pretty soon he'll be using the same language in this house and I won't have that. I won't have it, Grace, so don't start protecting him.'

Grace had not told her husband that she too had heard Spit in full flow, and she knew that she would have to do something about it. 'I'll talk to him,' she said.

They were waiting for Sadie and Spit to come in for lunch. Sadie had been to her piano lesson, and Spit had been trying to sell what was probably the last catch of the season to the houses along the railway line.

'You can't treat Spit the way you treat Sadie,' her husband said. 'He's a tough little beggar and he's not going to listen to kind words and a soft voice.'

'I'll talk to him anyway. And afterwards, if you do hear him swearing, you can beat him as much as you like. But you're not to touch him until I've told him not to do it.'

'How will you know whether he's swearing or not? You weren't there when he was telling off Tim Evans' kelpie in language a bullockie wouldn't use.'

'I'll take his word for it,' Grace said. 'And you'll have to sooner or later. You can't always mistrust him.'

'By God,' Jack Tree said angrily. 'I wish I'd been given some of this treatment when I was a kid.'

Grace smiled at her husband. 'Never mind,' she said. 'Because now you have a chance to give it to somebody else.'

'Well I'm damned if I'm going to let you joke about it,' Jack said. 'You're dead wrong, Grace, and that's all there is about it.'

Grace knew very well that she could be wrong, and what weakened her resolve was Jack's blank wall facing Spit's blank wall. As they ate their lunch of chops and potatoes and peas, she watched them both to see if she could detect even a glimmer of communication between them. Jack ignored Spit, and for his part Spit kept quiet throughout lunch, answering her questions or Sadie's unusual chatter with loud monosyllables. Grace knew he wasn't going to give anything back to Jack, neither a friendly word nor a whole sentence that Jack might use against him. Listening to his stiff, childish, serious voice in its bold disguise (the only way Spit knew how to talk), Grace knew how difficult it was going to be to break him down – with Jack or without Jack.

'He's still expecting to be tricked in some way,' Grace decided, and after lunch when she organised Sadie to hunt for all the empty jam jars so that they could make some mixed pickles, she took Spit into the garden to help her pick the last of the green tomatoes on the dried up plants, and she asked him why he didn't like Jack.

'He's all right,' Spit said in his untouchable way. 'I like him all right.'

'Why don't you talk to him?' she asked.

'He doesn't talk to me much,' Spit said, busy with the tomatoes, deeply involved in what he was doing as he always seemed to be in anything he did.

'Well, try and talk to him, Spit, because we're going to need his help soon.'

Spit didn't ask her why they would need Jack's help, and again she was aware of his suspicion and his childish caution. But she still had to settle the problem of his swearing. 'Why do you swear, Spit?' she said to him.

Spit looked up in surprise. 'What makes you think I swear?' he said.

'I heard you swearing like a trooper the other day when you were chopping wood.'

Spit didn't like that. 'I only swear to myself,' he said. 'I don't go around swearing.'

'Do you know what the words mean?' she asked him.

'They don't mean anything.'

'Oh, but they do mean something. And it's better that you don't know what they mean. So please, Spit, don't swear any more. Even when you think nobody is listening. Jack heard you, and the more you do it the more careless you'll be with it, and I don't want Sadie to hear that kind of language.'

'I don't swear in front of Sadie. She didn't say so, did she?'

'No, she said you didn't. But don't swear at all. That's what I want you to promise. And you'll have to keep your promise because we're going to have a lot of trouble if you don't.'

'All right,' Spit said, concentrating on the tomatoes. 'I'll stop swearing.'

'That means you don't swear at all, even when you're alone. No swearing. Not the way you swear.'

Spit could be obliging and he said, 'Don't worry. I'm not going to hurt anybody.'

Grace was not quite sure what that meant but she accepted it as a promise. Encouraged now by this strange companionship she always felt for him, she asked him if he had any relatives left.

'Anyone anywhere?' she added. 'Did your grandfather ever mention any?'

'I had an uncle once,' he said, 'but he didn't last long. He got killed a long time ago.'

'Was that the only relation you had?'

'Except for my mother and my grandfather.'

'Do you remember your mother?' Grace asked him, on her knees in the tomato patch but more interested in Spit than in the green tomatoes.

Spit was watching her now. 'My mother got burnt in a fire,' he told her.

'Yes, I know. That was so sad.' Grace hesitated, still not sure what to say to him. But then she made up her mind.

'You know, Spit, that I'm trying to adopt you?'

'Yes. I know,' he said.

'You know? How did you know?'

'Mrs Evans told me, and a lot of other people asked me. A lot of people. Jack Ellison asked me yesterday.'

'Then why on earth didn't you come and ask me if it was true or not?'

'I don't know,' Spit said. 'I thought it might be another trick.'

'I wouldn't trick you. Don't you know that?'

'I didn't mean you. I meant them.'

'Who?'

'I don't know. I don't know . . . It's no good asking me . . . It's Mrs Arbuckle and all the others. They'll trick me again if they get a chance.'

'I don't think they want to trick you,' Grace said to him. 'They want to do what they think is best for you, and that's why I'm trying to adopt you. I wasn't going to tell you because I didn't want you to think I had worked it all out. I haven't. I have to get Jack's signature on the paper, then I have to take it to the Shire Office. But I can't do anything at all without Jack, which is why I wanted you to get on with him a bit better.'

Spit was silent. She did not expect any gratitude from him because she knew where his attitude came from; she knew that years ago he had he had been forced to acquire a childish skin of stoicism so that he could cope with his grandfather, and at the same time help him to survive as a boy. But she suspected that he was secretly frightened now, aware that he was a wisp of nothing, and that his only defence against everybody else's plans for him was to keep himself to himself. There was nothing else he could do.

'Jack doesn't like me much,' he said dispassionately.

'It's not that,' she said unhappily. 'Jack's a kind man, Spit, but he's a bit rigid, and he doesn't like things to disturb his life. Sadie and I learned that a long time ago. But when he sees something is right he'll stick by it. And sooner or later he'll see that we are right, don't worry.'

'All right,' Spit said, and once again Grace knew that he had gone as far as he could.

But that night when Grace sat down at the kitchen table, just before sunset, and carefully opened up the adoption form to write into it that Spit had no living relatives, she knew she was about to change the light and shadow of her own life, and she half-wished that when she handed in the form tomorrow that nothing would come of it. She was frightened of what she was undertaking. Until now she had never felt lonely or separated from Jack. On the contrary, she had always been satisfied with his set of rules for Sadie and herself. She had thought of them as no more than the ministry of a rather stiff man who was trying to order life decently, knowing that he was married to a very quiet woman who had no rules of her own except a desire to live from day to day without harshness or conflict. She had always been satisfied with the kind of protection and care that Jack gave her with his certainty that he knew best.

But now, for Spit's sake, she was undoing the pattern of it.

'I hope to God I'm doing the right thing,' she said because she now had to get Jack's signature on the adoption form, and how was she going to manage that?

Grace had no guile, she was incapable of scheming, particularly against her husband, so that when she decided to use Sadie she was not thinking up a quiet little plot of her own. She was trying to influence Jack, she told herself, the only way she knew how. As she waited for Sadie and Spit to come back from the railway station with the two boxes of laboratory test phials that Jack had sent them for, she looked around at her home and knew how valuable it was, and how safe and secure it had always been. Even the mustardy smell of it at the moment made the point.

18

GRACE HAD SPENT THE AFTERNOON PREPARING AND BOILING THE marrow, cauliflower, cucumber, tomatoes and onions for the mixed pickles she made every year for Jack. Sadie had helped to wash and cut and salt the vegetables, and Spit had fed the fire and scattered the peel and skins to the hens, and then stirred the mixture of mustard and vinegar as she poured the vegetables into the big copper kettle. Now the sideboard was packed with twelve jars of mustardy pickles, and the kitchen was still heavy with the air of pickling which Jack always liked. When he came in after six o'clock and said, 'I could smell those pickles halfway to Nooah,' she was pleased, because they needed that reminder of the their old peace and security, even in the smell of cauliflower and tomatoes and onions and mustard and sugar and spiced vinegar.

But the evening meal was not familiar, nor was it relaxed, and she was glad when it was over, when Sadie and Spit were helping her with the dishes and Jack was at his roll-top desk. It was quiet and dark outside, and it was only a matter of waiting now for the right moment to send Sadie in to her father. Grace was on the point of doing it when the Evans' dog began to bark, and because she knew how that dog annoyed Jack she decided to wait. It was a persistent and worried dog, and the barking went on long enough for Spit to say, 'What does he think he's barking at?'

'It's not you this time,' Sadie said.

'Maybe he knows I'm in your kitchen,' Spit said.

'He's not that good,' Sadie told him, and they heard someone at the back door calling out in a loud whisper, 'Spit, are you there? Spit, can you hear me?'

'Who on earth is that?' Grace said.

'I don't know,' Spit said and went around the table to the back door, with Sadie and Grace at his elbow. When they looked into the darkness all they could see was a small figure with a cart.

'It's me, Ben Arbuckle.'

Ben's defiant whisper suggested a father and mother ready and waiting in the shadows to catch him. 'I brought your things back, Spit. I've got them in the cart.'

Spit had been missing his cart and the small store of family possessions he had left under the Arbuckle's house. He had thought once or twice of going back in the middle of the night to get them, but he had decided against it because Mrs Arbuckle might be waiting to catch him, using the cart and his grandfather's things as bait.

'Come in, Ben,' Grace said to him. 'Don't stand out there in the dark.'

'Well . . . I don't know, Mrs Tree,' Ben said.

But Grace insisted. 'Come on in,' she said, and went down the steps to take Ben by the arm and bring him into the kitchen.

The usually neat Ben was in a mess. He had no boots on, his smock and trousers were dirty, and his legs and arms and face were smeared with the mallee dust the town was built on. Spit knew why he was dirty. Ben had obviously crawled under the house in the dark to get the bits and pieces of his grandfather's things.

'You haven't got your boots on,' Sadie told him, pointing to his bare feet.

'No,' Ben said. 'I threw them in the river.'

Spit laughed, but it was Grace who noticed that Ben's dirty face was smeared and streaked as if he had been crying, and she asked him if his mother knew that he was here.

'No, and I'm not going to tell her,' Ben said.

'Do you want a piece of cake?' Grace asked him.

'I'm not allowed,' Ben said, but then changed his mind. 'All right,' he said, and he turned to Spit and told him that he had borrowed his cart a couple of times. 'But I've got some wheels of my own.'

'Where did you get them from?' Spit asked him.

'From Billy Cotsman. I've hidden them under the house.'

'What about an axle?' Spit said as Ben bit into the cake Grace had given him. 'They're not going to be any good without an axle.'

'Billy didn't have one, but I'll get one somewhere.'

'All you have to do is get the fruit box and the axle,' Spit said. 'But if you want me to help you build it you'll have to get the stuff down to the old boiler yourself. I'm not going up to your place.'

'All right,' Ben said, and with his mouth full of cake he backed out as if his defiance was rapidly running out. Grace saw what was happening to him and hurried after him, catching him by the arm before he could run off. 'Are you sure your mother doesn't know you came down here?' she said to him. 'Is that why you've been crying?'

'She doesn't know anything,' Ben said. 'I got into trouble for throwing my boots in the river.'

'What did you do that for?' Grace said.

'Well . . .' But Ben's defiance was now exhausted. And shouting, 'S'long Spit,' he was off on his bare feet, not to the gate but to the nearest part of the fence which he scrambled over as a last gesture of resistance to good order.

'Poor old Ben,' Spit said.

'What do you think he's up to?' Sadie asked. 'Why would he throw his boots away?'

'I don't know,' Spit said. 'But it's not his fault. He can't help it.'

'That's why Tim Evans' dog barked,' Sadie said as they went inside.

'What do you mean?'

'He thought it was you with the cart.'

Spit was delighted. 'Well I fooled him that time, didn't I?' he said.

Grace listened, and when they were in the kitchen she sent Spit to check the front gate in case Ben had left it open when he brought the cart in. 'Otherwise the dogs will get in,' she said.

Alone in the kitchen with Sadie she gave her the adoption form and said, 'This is what I had to fill in so that we can adopt Spit, so take it in to your father and ask him to sign it.'

Sadie knew about the adoption. She knew about the tension

it had caused between her mother and father, but mother and daughter were so close that they both knew what had to be done, so she took the form in to her father.

When Spit came back Grace, who was tense now and nervous, sat him down at the kitchen table and asked him if he had a birth certificate somewhere. 'Because,' she said, 'I think I'll need that too.'

Spit shook his head. 'I never saw one,' he told her.

'Do you know where you were born?'

'In White Hills near Bendigo,' Spit said.

'Then I suppose I'll have to get your certificate from Bendigo,' Grace said, not quite sure that what she was saying really mattered. She was simply talking in order to talk while she waited for Sadie to return.

Sadie, standing behind her father at his desk, had hesitated to interrupt him. He disliked being interrupted when he was filling in the long yellow form of stock lists, or the weigh bills of the summer's wool clip shipped out of the town. But Jack looked up at his quiet daughter and felt for a moment the affection that always touched him when he was aware, as now, of Sadie's natural and delicate shyness. He took off his spectacles.

'All right,' he said. 'It must be something you want badly, so what's up?'

Sadie was about to say that her mother wanted him to sign the form, but she changed her mind and said, 'I just wanted you to sign this form about Spit. That's all.'

'What form?'

'So that we can adopt him.'

'Did your mother put you up to this?'

Sadie shook her head. 'No, it's me. I want us to adopt Spit so he can stay with us. It's my own idea as much as Mum's.'

'It's an idea I don't think much of, Sadie, and your mother knows it.'

'But it won't hurt you,' Sadie said.

'Do you know what it means if we adopt Spit?' he asked her.

'Yes. He'll have to live here with us all the time. I know that,' she said.

'That's not even the half of it,' Jack said. 'We'll have to

bring him up like a son. We'll have to be responsible for him, no matter what he does . . .'

'He won't do anything wrong, Dad. Not if he can help it.'

'Even if he doesn't, your mother will have to look after him all the time. Did you think of that?'

Sadie could keep very still and she was very still now. 'She won't mind. She likes him.'

'And you'll have to live with him every day. If you up and decide one day you don't like him any more you won't be able to send him packing off to Bendigo. Once I sign that paper Spit becomes as important to me as you are. Do you want that, Sadie?'

Sadie, like her mother, knew that she had to stand her ground. 'Yes,' she said. 'If you don't mind, I don't.'

'You want me to treat him like a son?'

Sadie compressed her lips, but this time all she could manage was a vigorous nod.

'Well I'm damned if I know any more,' Jack said in despair. 'I don't know what you see in him.'

Sadie, finding her courage again, said, 'Spit has never hurt anybody, and he never will.'

Jack was trying not to be impatient with Sadie but he laughed his dry, impatient, military laugh. 'I'll bet he's had more fights in your school than any other boy his age,' he said.

'Spit only fights when they say something about his grandfather. Everybody likes him. And he knows how to do everything.'

Jack's response was a surprise even to himself. He did not snatch the form from her hand and tear it up, which is what he wanted to do. Angry with Sadie's resistance and angry with Grace, he wanted to make a punishing remark to his daughter, one that he knew would get a submissive reply. 'So what do you think you're going to do young lady,' he said, 'if I refuse to sign that form? What will you do then?'

Sadie, facing defeat, was silent for a moment. 'Nothing,' she said. 'I couldn't do anything, could I?'

Jack knew that he had won his private little contest but, looking at his daughter's calm face which was trying to give nothing away, he knew that her eyes (uncontrollably wet), and her lips grimly (for her) compressed were an argument and a conviction that he could not face up to any more. It was too much.

'All right. All right,' he said. 'Give me the form.'

Taking it from her he turned it over, found the place where he had to sign, dipped the pen, scrawled his signature and gave it back to her.

'Give it to your mother,' he said.

Sadie was so surprised that she simply took the form. Uneducated in gestures and untaught in affection she said, 'Thanks, Dad,' and feeling very sorry for her father she took the signed form in to her mother in the kitchen.

19

GRACE WAS NOT SURE WHAT SHOULD HAPPEN NEXT BUT SHE WAS surprised when she gave the form to Pat Stillman at the Shire Office only to have him hand it back to her.

'You'll have to take it to the county court office,' he told her.

'What on earth for?' she asked him.

'Because it's the court that will decide if you are a fit and proper person to adopt and care for that poor little orphan, Master Spit MacPhee.'

Grace wished Pat wouldn't joke about it because suddenly it was irritating. 'Why didn't you tell me that before?' she said to him.

'Because I didn't know. We've never had a legal adoption in this town before, and it was only when I wondered myself what happened next that I found out. I got that form from Henry Fennel at the county court, he's the clerk of the court, and even he didn't know. But then he found out, and so I found out, and now you've found out, and pretty soon everybody else will find out.'

'You mean it will have to be some sort of court case?'

Pat shrugged. 'All I know is that you've got to go before a county court judge, and he will take everything into consideration,' he said in a sepulchral voice. 'That's what Henry says.'

In love with his stuffed office, lovingly in command of his square pigeon holes that told him how much water was used in the town, how much the roads and footpaths cost to repair and what were the regulations about drains and fires, Pat was smiling at Grace because he couldn't help it, even though he was sorry for what he was about to report to her. 'There's now another little fly in your ointment, Grace. Betty Arbuckle is doing exactly what you're doing.'

'What do you mean?'

'She wants to adopt Spit herself. She was here yesterday asking for one of these forms, and she wanted to know if you had already made an application.'

Grace had always known that Betty Arbuckle would do something drastic, but she had not expected Betty to put in a rival claim for adoption. It shocked her. It was all right for Betty to think of Spit as an orphan in need of the care and protection of her evangelical Boys Home, but Grace thought it cruelly personal and wrong for Betty to want to adopt Spit herself.

'Why would she want such a thing?' Grace said. 'She knows that Spit ran away from her, and I'm sure she doesn't really want him.'

'She wants to save his soul,' Pat said with a laugh.

'Don't laugh, Pat. It's serious. Spit would hate living with Betty in that house. He would only run away again if she tried to make him stay with her. He'd never stay.'

'Are you sure that your little switch-ditcher would stick it out with you, Grace? He's a wild kid.'

'He's not wild, Pat. He's had to look after himself, and it's made him a strange little boy, but he's certainly not wild. I know that much about him.'

'Well, he certainly seems to have dug himself under your thin skin, and now that he's getting himself between Betty Arbuckle's teeth God help the both of you.'

'Spit's all right,' Grace insisted firmly, 'and I don't know now what I'd do if they took him away from me, Pat. That's how I feel about it.' Grace was surprised that she could say such a thing to Pat Stillman who was no more than an old acquaintance from school. But she needed to talk to someone about it.

'What do you think I should do now?' she said, appealing for help even though she knew that he couldn't give it.

'Take that form to Henry Fennel down at the court house and he'll tell you what to do with it.'

'Henry's a Protestant, isn't he?'

'Yes, but he's pretty dinkum, old Henry.'

'But that means Betty will have the advantage, won't she?'

'I don't know, Grace. Anyway it won't be Henry Fennel who decides it. It'll be Judge Laker.' Pat still had the form in his hand, and he turned it over and glanced at Jack's signature. 'You didn't forge it did you?' he said teasingly.

'Of course not.'

Pat laughed. 'Then you must have hit him on the head with a sledge hammer,' he said. 'Knowing Jack . . .' he added.

'I didn't think it was going to be so complicated,' Grace said, taking the form.

'That's because you think life's a bowl of cherries,' Pat said, 'whereas it's really a whacking big basket of unbreakable monkey nuts.'

'Thanks anyway,' Grace said and left him in his square pigeon holes, escaping the smell of his carbon paper and cigarettes and the mallee dust and the onions that Pat seemed to eat raw, even for breakfast.

She knew Henry Fennel by sight and she couldn't imagine him giving her much help. He was a short, tight, springy man with eyes that told you not to treat him in any way but seriously. Gingery, with a small moustache and rimmed pince-nez spectacles, he seemed to Grace to be a friendless sort of man. She remembered him as a boy, several classes ahead of her at school, who didn't seem to want friends and didn't have a nickname, so that when she knocked at the door of his little office and he shouted, 'Come in,' she was already sure that he would dismiss her in some way if he could.

'Hello Henry,' she said nervously.

Henry Fennel's serious eyes behind his spectacles flashed their serious warning. 'Hello, Grace,' he said.

Grace looked around her and knew that Henry, as the clerk of the court, was a very square peg in a very square hole. Everything here was in order: rows of curious files tied with blue tape, a neat desk with neat papers on it, a bookshelf with large green books that seemed fitted to size. She decided that she must not waste this man's time; or rather she must not give him the impression that she was wasting his time. She came straight to the point.

'I've come to give you this form,' she said. 'Pat Stillman told me this was the place.'

He took it without comment, spread it carefully on his desk after moving aside the papers he had been working on and, with a sharp pencil in his hand, he checked one by one the questions and answers. When he came to Jack's signature he looked up.

'You should have printed your husband's names under his signature,' he said.

'Oh, I'm sorry.'

'Does Jack have a middle name?'

'Yes. Edward.'

'All right,' Henry said. 'I'll print it in for you.' And with a clipped almost bouncy action he took pen to paper and printed Jack's full name under his signature. 'You want it dated today?' he asked.

'I suppose so,' Grace said.

He added the date and looked up. Grace waited, but he said nothing more.

'Is that all I have to do?' she asked.

'You'll have to be present when the application is considered by the county court. But we'll call on you when we know the date and time.'

Grace hesitated. 'I know that Betty Arbuckle has made an application . . .' she began.

'I can't say anything about that,' Henry interrupted in his clipped voice.

'I don't want you to,' Grace went on quickly. 'All I want to know is if they'll stop me adopting Spit because of my religion.'

Henry looked at her without saying anything, and Grace knew then that in the cold blood of his honesty he would give her a fair chance.

'I know you're a Protestant . . .' Grace began.

'That's got nothing to do with it,' Henry said sharply.

'I know that, Henry. But you know that I'm a Catholic and Spit is a Protestant, so can't you tell me if that's going to make it impossible?'

Again Henry hesitated. 'I don't know. But religion does count. It always counts. And in a case like this it could be decisive. So if I were you, Grace, I'd get some legal help.'

'How?' Grace asked. 'What sort of legal help?'

'You'll need someone to argue your case if you hope to have even half a chance,' Henry said slowly. 'So I would advise you to get a barrister – a lawyer – to appear for you.'

'A lawyer? But that would cost money, wouldn't it?'

'Certainly.'

'How much money?'

'That depends on the man, and the sort of arguments he'll have to prepare.'

'I see . . .' Grace said. 'But who on earth can I go to?'

Henry's cold eyes had never left her face, and Grace had stared back at him as if in their different shades of honesty they had found a direct route between them.

'That's not for me to say. It's not my business to advise you. But . . . if I were you I would go and ask Edward Quayle if he would help you.'

'Mr Quayle? But he's a Protestant.'

'Nonetheless, if you want your case argued, and argued in your favour, he's the man I would go to in a situation like this.'

'But surely he hates Catholics. You know all about him and Lockie MacGibbon.'

'Never mind that. He's the one who might give you a chance. And I would get to him quick before someone else does.'

Grace looked back at those threatening eyes as if, in all these years, she had missed the value of the boy and the man behind them.

'All right, Henry,' she said. 'I'll do as you say.'

He returned the form. 'He'll need this,' he said, and as she left he called after her, 'Whatever you do don't tell him I sent you.'

Wondering now if she should wait and consult Jack before she took another step, another plunge into what was becoming a multifarious mess, she walked slowly down the main street until she reached the little sign that said, *Edward Quayle. Barrister and Solicitor.*

She stopped for a moment but walked on past it, quarrelling with herself about the expense, about Jack, about the deepening complications she was getting into. It was the possible expense of it that she must decide on first. She was determined not to ask Jack for money, which meant that the fifty pounds which had been left her by her Aunt Cissie, which she kept in the Commonwealth Savings Bank, would have to pay for the lawyer. She wondered if that would be enough. And, as well, would she have to pay something to the court or the State for adopting Spit? Turning back, she went into Mr Quayle's office, having decided that if she began to question anything now she would probably give up the whole idea of adopting Spit.

In the first little office it was Tom Quayle, Edward Quayle's younger son, she saw. He was sitting at a tiny desk writing vigorously. Even in his penmanship Tom looked like an athletic boy who should be anywhere at all except in an office when the sun was shining outside.

'Hello Tom,' she said. 'I've come to see your father. Is he in?'

'Yes, he's in, Mrs Tree,' Tom said. 'But I think he's working on something. What's it about?'

'Well . . .'

'It's all right. I work with my father,' Tom said.

Grace liked Tom, but he looked so young and out of place that she was reluctant to explain anything to him.

'All right,' he said, 'I'll see if my father is busy. You wait here.'

Grace waited while Tom went into another little room, and though she could hear voices she couldn't understand what they were saying until Tom put his head around the door and said, 'Come on in, Mrs Tree. Come in.'

What Grace found was another modest room, neatly but hopelessly over-stacked with files and books and papers so that there was little room left, even on the floor. She knew then that Edward Quayle – represented here by his office – was a man who cared little for anything extra to the law and order of his profession, so that he would not expect anything more than the bare information needed to get his work done.

'Good morning, Mrs Tree,' Edward Quayle said in his English voice, flinging his spectacles on his desk. 'Please sit down.' He pointed to a hard chair near his desk, and he swivelled his around to face her. 'Tom,' he said, 'if Mr Jackson comes in, tell him I shan't be a minute. Now,' he went on.

'What's on your mind, Mrs Tree?'

She handed him the adoption form. 'I want to adopt young Spit MacPhee,' she said, 'and here's the form I had to fill in. I've been told that it had to come up before a county court, and I think I'll need some help with it.'

'Why? Isn't it straightforward?'

'I don't know, Mr Quayle,' Grace said.

She waited while Mr Quayle looked at the application. He turned it over. 'It seems all right,' he said. 'Why would you need my help?'

'You see,' she said, realising now why Henry Fennel had sent her here: Edward Quayle was the same kind of man as Henry himself, except that he wasn't gingery. But he was red-faced. 'Somebody else is making an application to adopt him.'

'Ahhh . . .'

'It's Mrs Betty Arbuckle.'

'I see.' Mr Quayle seemed to be making a quick summation of the problem. 'That does make it a little more complicated,' he said.

'Yes, and there's one other thing,' she went on.

'Yes?'

'I'm a Catholic and the boy is a Protestant. And Mrs Arbuckle is a Protestant too. That will make it difficult for me, won't it?'

Edward Quayle sighed, and later he would say to Grace that according to the Greeks a man usually sighed when he didn't want to feel the inevitability of pain. But obviously he understood. 'It will certainly make some difference,' he said, and before she could say anything further he held up his hand. 'In fact this may not be able to come to judgement at all. There may be some stipulation about it in the legislation on adoption – religion being what it is in this country. Particularly with a child. It's most likely, therefore, that a mutual religion will be a requirement for court consent, whatever else is concerned.'

'Even though it would be wrong for the boy to go to someone who happens to be a Protestant?'

'Right or wrong may not have anything to do with it, Mrs Tree. It's possibly a negative requirement you will have to face. That is, the boy simply may not go to you because you're

Roman Catholic. But this doesn't mean that he will go automatically to someone else.'

'In other words he could even end up in the Boys Home in Bendigo.'

'Wait . . . wait . . .' Edward Quayle said. 'I don't know yet what the law says about adoption, I am only warning you before you go any further that you could be disqualified from the outset.'

'That wouldn't be fair,' Grace said.

'It may not even be the case,' Edward Quayle told her, 'but you asked me about the possibility of religion being important, and I am simply warning you in answer that it may be decisive. I cannot say what it is in law until I've looked into it. And if you want me to look into it I'll do what I can. Although I am rather busy at the moment.'

'I'm worried that Betty Arbuckle will get her application in before mine, and that she will . . .'

'Don't worry. If it can be argued before the court I'll see that your application is there. But I'll have to look into it, and if I need any more information from you I'll send Tom down to get it.'

Grace stood up. She half closed her eyes and said what she had to say. 'Will it cost a lot of money, Mr Quayle?'

'Money? Well, it depends on what I have to do.'

'I've got fifty pounds of my own money.'

'It won't be that, Mrs Tree. It will never be that. Just let me look into it, and I'll tell you what your chances are, and what you have to do. But don't worry. It won't cost you a fortune.'

Relieved, Grace thanked him and went out through Tom's office, sorry now that she had not opened up more to Tom, who could at least have listened.

'It's about Spit MacPhee,' she said now to Tom as she stood by his desk for a moment. 'I want to adopt him.'

'I guessed it was that,' Tom said. 'And what does old Spit have to say about it, Mrs Tree?'

'Nothing much,' Grace said. 'I think he's as confused as I am.'

As she left Tom and walked out into the street she realised that she had forgotten that Edward Quayle was a Protestant, which seemed to prove Henry Fennel right. In any case she felt relieved that it was now in the hands of an expert, even though he was considered to be a bigoted sort of man, not always liked by many people in the town.

20

WHEN THE SCHOOL YEAR FINALLY STARTED, SPIT FELT LIKE A stranger to himself as he put on Grace's home-made shirt, new grey trousers, grey socks and sandals.

'I'm sorry about the sandals, Spit,' Grace said to him that first morning, 'but you'll have to wear shoes and socks sooner or later, and you're too old now to go to school barefoot. I think they'd send you home if you turned up with no shoes on.'

'It's all right,' Spit said, looking down at his feet. 'I don't care about the sandals.'

What he *had* cared about was Grace Tree's efforts to get the soles of his feet clean. She had made him sit on a chair near the outside tap, and she had scrubbed the soles of his feet with a hard brush. Spit had submitted to it in silence. But he wasn't used to anyone washing him or fussing over him, and though Mrs Tree didn't fuss he had almost enjoyed the experience of sitting there with his feet in her aproned lap, and that bothered him.

But it was only when he was on his way to school that he knew his old carefree life was coming to an end. It was the clothes and the shoes and the new school bag and the house he now lived in, and Sadie chattering at his side. Pressed, housed, fed and looked after – the Spit MacPhee who accepted Mrs Tree's care and attention was not the Spit MacPhee who was expecting to disappear again at any moment. And something else frightened him. On Sunday, at nine o'clock, Mrs Betty Arbuckle, with Ben at her side, knocked at the kitchen door and said to Grace, 'I've come to take Spit to church.'

Spit, who normally spent most Sunday mornings scouring the town for anything he could find to help him rebuild his workshop in the boiler (which he had been working on now for weeks), was not at that moment wandering around the town. He was making a kite out of old newspapers on the kitchen table, so that when he heard Betty Arbuckle he dropped the scissors he was using and said to Sadie, who was mixing a flour paste, 'I'm off . . .'

'No, Spit,' Sadie said. 'Wait.'

'What for?' Spit said. 'She's after me again.'

'Don't worry,' Sadie whispered. 'My mother won't let her get near you.'

'She won't be able to stop her,' Spit said.

In fact Grace was trying to cope with her own surprise, opening the door and suddenly seeing Betty there. It always confused Grace, because Betty's beauty was forever a shock when it arrived on you like that, and Grace was speechless for a moment.

'Why on earth should you come here to take him to church?' Grace said when she had recovered.

'Because I want to be sure that you don't take him to Catholic mass.'

'What a thing to say,' Grace told her.

'Then he must come with me, Grace,'

'Why?'

'Because you haven't been sending him to church or to Sunday school, have you? And you know that is wrong.'

Grace as always felt at a disadvantage with Betty Arbuckle, and the best she could manage was an excuse. 'But Spit doesn't go to any church at all. He's never been to any church.'

'Then how can you expect him to grow up a good Christian if he doesn't go to church. It's wicked.'

Grace knew that Betty Arbuckle was right, and it was a dilemma she had been trying not to face. Sadie went to mass, not every Sunday, but often enough to justify her upbringing as a good Catholic. Grace herself and Jack were not very regular churchgoers, in fact Jack almost never went to church at all. They were, to that extent, pale Catholics but they were loyal ones nonetheless. In fact she had found it difficult even to encourage Spit to go to a Protestant church. It went against her Catholic grain, but here was Betty Arbuckle making a necessity of it. Grace needed a quick ally so she called Spit.

'What for?' Spit said to her.

'Just come here a moment,' Grace said. 'I want to ask you something.'

Spit, beside her, looked over the threshold of his safety at Betty Arbuckle who said to him, 'Spit, dear, I've come to take you to church.'

Spit was ready to take off but Grace stopped him.

'Did your grandfather ever send you to church, Spit?' she asked him before Betty could say anything more to him.

'No. Not me.'

'You have never been to any church, have you?'

Spit looked from Grace Tree to Betty Arbuckle and wondered what made them both so determined to get him. 'I went to the Presbyterian church a couple of times,' he said slowly, 'when the Minister came down to get me, and when my grandfather didn't know what he was doing. But my grandfather didn't send me to church, and that's all I'm saying.'

'What your grandfather did wasn't your fault,' Betty Arbuckle told him. 'But now you are on your own and you'll grow up a heathen ignorant of the Lord if you don't go to church.'

'I'm not a heathen,' Spit said. 'I'm a Presbyterian.'

'Yes,' Grace said quickly, 'He's a Presbyterian. He doesn't belong to your church.'

'Then I'll take him to the Presbyterian Church,' Betty Arbuckle said. 'But he must go to church.'

'Not with you, Betty,' Grace said firmly.

Betty looked at Spit's Sunday bare feet. She neatened her small, black, straw hat which would have been an ugly mistake on anybody else, but surrounding Betty's face it became a perfect frame for her immaculate beauty. 'Spit,' she said firmly, 'you now have sandals to wear, I've seen you with them, so please go and put them on and I'll take you to church.'

They had all been so concentrated on each other that none of them had noticed Jack's presence. Joining them on the step he said to Betty, 'What do you think you're doing, Betty?'

'I've come to take Spit to church,' Betty said,

'You've come all the way down here knocking at our back

door for that?' Jack said.

'Yes.'

'Listen, Bet,' Jack said grimly. 'You may think you can come down here and tell us what to do but you're way off the mark.'

'I'm not telling you what to do, Jack. I'm telling the boy. It's a sin . . .'

'The boy lives here, and if anybody is going to tell him what to do we'll do it ourselves. It's nothing to do with you.'

'But you'll never tell him to go to his own church. You know you won't.'

'Whether we send him to church or not it's got nothing to do with you.'

'I've brought Ben with me,' Betty said. 'He can go with Spit.'

Ben, booted and smocked, was now in the same arena as Spit. Why were they all so keen to get hold of Spit MacPhee? It was more than Spit's bare feet. He glanced at Sadie. She smiled at him. Spit smiled at nobody. He was out of it. He would do what he wanted to do, and Ben showed his admiration by saying boldly, 'What were you and Sadie making?'

Spit still had the scissors in his hand, Sadie's pinafore was dusted with flour, and nothing could have given Ben such a feeling of hopeless envy and longing as much as scissors and flour on a Sunday morning.

'We were making a kite,' Spit said, 'but we haven't finished yet.'

'You shouldn't do that on the Lord's day,' Grace said to him.

Jack gave Spit and Sadie a little push and said to Grace, 'Go inside, all of you. I'll deal with this.' When they were inside they heard him say, 'Now don't waste your time, Betty. Go and preach the gospel somewhere else. But don't come here telling us how to be good Christians. You don't even know what Christianity is.'

Betty's 'Oh' was audible in the kitchen, and they heard her retreating down the steps and disappearing up the path.

Jack joined them in the kitchen and he stood still for a moment and looked at Grace as if she was little better than the children with her. 'I told you she would be after you,' he said, 'and you didn't listen.'

'I think she was just trying it on, Jack.'

'Well she's going to try a lot more on,' Jack told her. 'In fact she's asked J.C. Strapp to present her own application for adoption to the county court.'

'Who told you that?' Grace said, hardly believing it.

'Never mind,' he said. 'You've got Edward Quayle, and she's got J.C. Strapp. So you can guess who's going to win that battle.'

Edward Quayle was known in the town as the poor man's lawyer, and J.C. Strapp was considered a rich man's advocate.

'But how can she afford it?' Grace said miserably.

'How can you afford it?' Jack said.

'I told you, I'll pay for it out of Aunt Cissie's money.' When, yesterday, she had told Jack that she was asking Edward Quayle to help her, he had groaned in exasperation and complained of the expense, but she had told him then that she would pay for it out of her own money.

'All right, all right,' Jack said, returning to his work. 'It's your problem so you'll have to deal with it in your own way.'

'Yes, I know,' Grace said slowly, and catching sight of Sadie and Spit who had their eyes on her, trapped as she was in this undesired confrontation, she said to them, 'Get on with your kite, you two, and please clean up your mess when you've finished.'

21

Now that she knew about J.C. Strapp, Grace was worried about Mr Quayle. In the weeks of waiting and now, only five days before the court hearing which she had been ordered to attend, he seemed to have done nothing except send his son Tom to talk to Spit and then take him down to the ashes of the boiler house. She had asked Spit afterwards what they had been doing there, and Spit had said, 'He was looking for any kind of papers my grandfather left, a tin box or something like that, only we couldn't find anything. He found one of my grandfather's badges, that's all.'

'What sort of badge?'

'Tom said it was a soldier's badge, but I don't know. I never saw it before. It was all green.'

'Is that all he did?'

'He asked me a lot of questions.'

'What sort of questions?'

'He wanted to know where my grandfather came from, and if he had any bank books, and all sorts of things like that.'

'Is that all?' Grace said.

Spit seemed reluctant. 'Well, he kept asking me questions, and then he said he was going up to the hospital to see Doctor Stevens.'

Grace knew that Spit disliked being questioned about himself or his grandfather, and she had not persisted. But she was disappointed that Tom Quayle had not returned to question her, although she wasn't sure what sort of help she could have given him anyway.

But finally, on the day before the court hearing, Edward Quayle did telephone her and asked her to come to his office. 'As soon as you can,' he said.

Grace put on her print frock and hurried up the slope into town. When she walked into Mr Quayle's office Tom was not in the little ante-room, but Mr Quayle called out, 'Is that you, Mrs Tree?'

'Yes,' she said.

'Then come in,' Mr Quayle said, and without looking up from the papers he was reading he half stood up in a polite gesture and pointed to the hard chair near his desk. 'Sit down please,' he said, and then he looked at her and said, 'I suppose you have received notification of the hearing tomorrow.'

'Yes, I got it last week.'

For a moment Edward Quayle seemed to hold his breath, and then he went on, 'Mr Strapp, who will represent Mrs Arbuckle, has approached the court and suggested that the hearing be held not in a court room but in the chamber where sometimes the court sits for hearings in camera. The point is that it does away with any atmosphere of a court or of a legal dispute. Do you object to that?'

'I don't know, Mr Quayle. What do you think?'

'I think it's a good idea, so if you have no objection I will agree.'

'All right,' Grace said.

'Unfortunately there's one thing I must make clear,' Mr Quayle said, holding up a blue covered document. 'This is the 1928 Adoption of Children Act of the State of Victoria. It's a new Act. Only a few years old. It is the first this State has ever had governing the conditions of adoption, and I'm sorry to say that under this Act, and what seems already to be the interpretation of it, you don't have very much hope of adopting the boy.'

Grace told herself that she had always expected this. She had always known that everything would be against her if it had to be judged by a court of by law or by someone else.

'But why?' she said angrily. 'What makes you so sure, Mr Quayle?'

'I'm never one hundred per cent sure of anything in law,' Mr Quayle told her. 'But as far as the interpretation of this Act is concerned, and its application so far, the problem of what they call *matching* makes your application almost dead before it is alive. I half warned you about that. Remember?'

'What do you mean – matching?' Grace asked.

'In all previous cases, without exception, and in the wider interpretation of this law, the religion of the child has had to match the religion of the adoptive parents, regardless of any circumstances that might favour adoption. In other words, it doesn't matter how good your case is, religion is a decisive factor. I told you I thought this might be the case and now I am sure of it in law.'

'I don't care what the law says,' Grace told him. 'It's not right.'

'Nonetheless, I did warn you that the law is the law,' Mr Quayle said.

'Yes, I know you did. But I thought you were going to do something about it.'

'I have been looking into it, Mrs Tree, and all I can say is that all precedents and judgements are against you. The point is that if I know the position in law so will Judge Laker who will decide this case. And I doubt very much if he will want to set a contrary precedent in your case, knowing that it would cause a lot of religious controversy and would probably be overturned by a higher court anyway.'

'You are not just saying all this, Mr Quayle, because you don't want to take it up.'

Grace saw Edward Quayle's brick red face turn a deeper rouge, and he slapped his hand so fiercely on the table that she jumped. 'Mrs Tree . . .' he said. 'Mrs Tree, I shall forgive you that uncalled-for remark,' and she felt the anger and contempt in what he was saying, 'because you are obviously under some strain about this boy. On the other hand if you don't want me to go on with your application we can end it now.'

'No. No. I'm sorry, Mr Quayle, I just meant that you're a Protestant, and perhaps you don't want to represent a Catholic if that's what is causing all the trouble.'

'Religion is the issue of your application, Mrs Tree,' Edward Quayle said coldly. 'It is not an issue in my professional support for your application. If I am to represent you, then I represent you regardless. Is that understood?'

'Of course.'

'Then you wish me to go on?'

'Yes, Mr Quayle. I'm so confused.'
'I appreciate that.'
'But what can you do if the law says I can't adopt him anyway?'
'We can always argue, Mrs Tree. Or we can give it up. It's a simple enough choice.'
'But there's not much hope is there?'
'No. I have to tell you that. Even your own case is far from perfect. For instance you don't have the support of your husband in this, do you?'
'How do you know that?'
'I spoke to him, Mrs Tree. He is the formal applicant, not you, so I had to know his feelings about it.'
'What did he say to you, Mr Quayle?'
'That it was all your idea and yours alone, and that he only agreed to sign the form because your daughter asked him to.'
Grace was now able to discipline herself, and she said grimly, 'I suppose that will count against me too, won't it?'
'Naturally, if the other side makes a point of it.'
'So it seems to be quite hopeless. Everything . . .'
Edward Quayle sat back in his chair and rubbed his greying chin with his short square fingers. 'The only strength you have for your case, Mrs Tree, is your conviction and faith in the boy. You, and I gather your daughter, really want to keep him, don't you?'
'I don't know what I would do if they took him away now,' Grace said, 'and my daughter Sadie would be heartbroken.'
'You want to have the boy under any circumstances? Is that right?'
'Of course. Just so long as they don't take him away.'
'Do you trust me in this, Mrs Tree? Have you recovered yourself?'
'Of course I trust you, Mr Quayle.'
'I must be absolutely sure that I have your full confidence so that you will understand that what I am doing is best, even when you may not like it or understand it.'
Grace was already ashamed of her doubts about this man, and she didn't hesitate now to say, 'Yes I'm sure you'll do your best, Mr Quayle. It's all right.'
'Even more than that, Mrs Tree, I want you to understand

that what I can do is probably all that can be done. Will you accept that and leave it to me?'

'Yes, if you say so.'

'Very well. Make sure that the boy is properly dressed when you come to court. And with his shoes on.'

'Don't worry.'

'Are you willing to let your daughter Sadie speak up for the boy?'

'If that will help.'

'Then that's all, Mrs Tree. Be at the court chamber at ten o'clock on Wednesday. On time please because this judge doesn't like anyone to be late. And make sure a note has gone to the school explaining the boy's absence in case the judge asks about that.'

'Of course.'

'Then good day, Mrs Tree.' Edward Quayle stood up and sat down again.

'Goodbye, Mr Quayle,' Grace said, and emerging into the street she realised that Edward Quayle's persuasiveness seemed to be so strange that she wondered what he really meant when he said, 'Leave it to me.'

22

AT FIVE TO TEN TOM QUAYLE WAS WAITING AT THE DOOR OF THE court chamber and Grace found herself in a little room that was almost bare, with three tables shaped into a U at one end and a long solid bench at the other. At one of the tables Betty Arbuckle, her husband Frank, Mr J.C. Strapp and another man (Strapp's assistant, Jock Stone) were already seated.

'You'll have to sit here, you two,' Tom said to Spit and Sadie. And leaving them on the bench where Ben Arbuckle was already in place, he took Grace to the table on the other side of the U facing Betty Arbuckle.

'I thought it would be just a lot of questions,' Grace whispered to him. 'I mean – not in front of Betty Arbuckle.'

'The whole thing is a bit odd, Mrs Tree. But don't worry.'

'Where is your father?' she asked him.

'He'll be along. Don't worry,' Tom said.

But when Judge Laker came into the chamber from a back door, with Henry Fennel at his elbow, and they sat down at the head of the U near Mrs Price the stenographer, Grace was worried, particularly when Judge Laker said, 'Where is Mr Quayle?'

'He'll be along in a minute, your honour,' Tom said.

'But he's late,' Grace whispered, remembering how Edward Quayle had told her that this judge didn't like anyone to be late.

'If my father's late,' Tom whispered back, 'then he's deliberately late. Anyway, here he is.'

As Edward Quayle walked on his short legs into the chamber to join them at the table he was saying, 'I'm sorry for my tardiness, your honour, but there were some difficulties.'

'All right, Mr Quayle,' the judge said, 'at least you are here, for which we must be thankful.' He picked up what looked to Grace like her application. 'You are representing Mr John Edward Tree, are you not?'

'That is correct, your honour.'

'I don't see him, so where is he?'

'That was one of my problems, your honour. Mr Tree is our local pastoral and livestock inspector, and very urgent work keeps him away for the moment. But I hope to have him present later on. In the meantime Mrs Tree is here beside me and she will be able to answer any questions the court wants to put to her.'

'You haven't made a very good start, have you, Mr Quayle?'

'No, sir. I haven't, I'm afraid.'

'Very well, let us begin. You, Mr Strapp, are representing . . .' he picked up the other application form, 'Mr and Mrs Frank Arbuckle.'

'Yes your honour, they are both here.'

'Then there is nothing more to delay us. But before we begin I must make some serious observations for all those present here.' He looked around him like a schoolmaster addressing a wayward class. 'This is not a trial,' he said, 'it is a court hearing. But because of a unique situation in which we have two applicants applying to adopt the same boy, I have decided that they will both be present to hear the other's case. I have never heard of a situation quite like this. There is no precedent, and because I need to put their qualifications to the test, I think the mutual presence of both applicants here will help that. Are you listening, Mr Quayle?'

Grace had been watching Mr Quayle sorting out his documents as the judge spoke, and he looked up now and said, 'Of course, your honour. I ask your pardon, but I am still trying to organise myself.'

'Then I suggest that you stop organising yourself for a moment and pay attention to what I am saying, because this will have some bearing on your applicant, if you are interested in hearing it.'

'Of course I am, your honour.'

'Very well. What I am saying is that in this case we have a boy who is not represented here in his own right. So it seems to me that what we have is a situation in which both sides will need a better qualification than their own claims to be the chosen one. That is why I have brought you all face to face so to speak. But I warn everybody present that this is a court, even though I have not had it formally constituted as a court. There will be no comment of any kind from anyone unless it is asked for by me or Mr Strapp or Mr Quayle. Any departure from this ruling or any attempt to comment without being asked will be dealt with by expulsion from the court. Have counsel warned their . . . their candidates of this?'

'Yes, your honour,' Mr Strapp said. 'It has been done.'

'Well, Mr Quayle?'

'In fact I didn't do so,' Edward Quayle said to the judge, 'because I thought it would be far more effective coming from you.'

'Thank you, Mr Quayle,' the judge said drily. 'Now this hearing will be informal. Statements can be asked for and the procedure will be relaxed. If I feel that someone has to be heard under oath, then I shall call for the oath to be administered. In other words if I don't believe you I shall have you swear to what you are saying.'

Taking a stub of pencil out of his waistcoat pocket Judge Laker pointed it first at Mr Quayle and then at Mr Strapp. 'Now, gentlemen, I know your capacity for rivalry as adversaries, nevertheless I am sure you will not treat this as a gladiatorial combat but as a means to giving this unfortunate orphan a decent home and a decent future.'

Grace, watching the judge, didn't like his way of showing them that he had absolute power over the life and limb of everybody in the chamber. In fact it seemed to Grace that he was relishing the idea of a struggle between Mr Strapp and Mr Quayle. 'A unique case,' he was saying again, and Grace was sure now that he had deliberately arranged it to be an adversarial contest.

'Your honour,' Edward Quayle said the moment the judge had finished his remarks. 'May I suggest, in view of the unhappy problems I have had in my preparation, that you hear the application of my honoured friend first . . .'

'Oh no . . .' Strapp didn't wait for Edward Quayle to finish. 'I think, your honour, that first or last in this case should be decided by some other reasoning. If I am to open the proceedings it will put me in the role of prosecutor, with Mr Quayle the defender, which is not the role I want in this.'

'If the court pleases,' Edward Quayle said. 'This is not a court for offenders, nor even a court for non-offenders. So my honourable friend seems unnecessarily worried about who goes first.'

'If you put me in first,' Strapp persisted, 'it will give Mr Quayle all the information he wants about our intentions – our case, so to speak. And it will also give him the last word.'

'I hadn't thought of that,' Mr Quayle said. 'So what does my friend suggest?'

'I don't know. Why not toss a coin . . .'

Judge Laker rapped his pencil on the table. 'There will be no decision by coin-tossing in my court,' he said. 'Mr Quayle's reasons seem sound enough to me, Mr Strapp, even though he cannot be given high marks for preparation. So perhaps you have the advantage anyway, Mr Strapp, and you may as well go ahead with it. In any case, I shall make sure that neither of you has the last word. I shall have it.'

But Grace, aware now of every turn and twist in what was happening, knew why Edward Quayle had been late and apparently disorganised. He obviously wanted Strapp to begin, and she was sure that he had done it deliberately.

'Well . . .' Mr Strapp began carefully. 'It is a strange case, your honour, and it has a strange history. Everybody in St Helen knows the boy concerned. He is a familiar figure in our streets, always barefoot, poorly dressed, always pulling a cart or carrying a little bag on his shoulder, always selling fish or crayfish. And he is well known too for his wild haunts along the river. In other words, from an early age, say six or seven, he has been something of a little vagabond around the town.'

Edward Quayle tapped the table with a squat finger and said, 'I really must protest, your honour, at this definition of the boy. To begin with . . .'

'To begin with,' Judge Laker said sharply, 'you are out of order. As Mr Strapp said, he is not the prosecutor and you are not the defender. If anyone has to defend the boy, I shall. And though certain court rules apply here, I am not going to allow interruptions or formal objections. You'll have your say later, Mr Quayle. Be content with that.'

'As you say, your honour. I accept your ruling.'

'You have no choice, Mr Quayle, so go ahead Mr Strapp.'

'The point I am making, your honour, is not derogatory of the boy. We are not blaming him for his abandoned condition. We are blaming the circumstances of his life which made a little beggar of him. And it is our contention, from the outset, that the only person in this town who, from the beginning, took an outside interest in the boy's welfare, and tried to do something about him, was Mrs Betty Arbuckle.'

'How old is the boy now?' Judge Laker said, and to answer his own question he looked at the application. 'Eleven. And when did Mrs Arbuckle begin to take an interest in him, Mr Strapp?'

'He must have been about six or seven, your honour. In any case it was almost from the first day he arrived in town with his grandfather and then lived with him in an old boiler down by the river.'

'A boiler?'

'Yes, your honour. That's where the two of them lived. The old man himself was already something of a gypsy around the town, a half-mad watchmaker who lived from hand to mouth by getting work from time to time. But he was well known to everyone in the town for his crazy shouting, his insulting behaviour, his midnight wanderings which sometimes frightened people in the town, and of course for the strong influence he had from the outset on his six-year-old grandson who learned early to copy his ways. Not only the old man's peculiarities – his shouting and his habit of wandering around the town – but all the rest of his primitive way of life in his fantastically painted boiler house, which looked more like something out of Dante's *Inferno* than a decent home for the child to be brought up in.'

'Is the boiler still there?' Judge Laker asked.

'No, your honour. I shall come to that later. It was burned down, probably when you were attending one of the other courts of the circuit. But almost from the first day that this five- or six-year-old joined his grandfather, Mrs Betty Arbuckle was down there trying to find out exactly what conditions the boy was living in, and trying publicly and vigorously to bring the boy's condition to the notice of the town, even to the police.'

'Did she succeed?' Judge Laker asked.

'I'll come to that too, in time. The point is that she was always met there with abuse and insults, and sometimes with physical violence from both the old man and the boy, who was usually egged on by the old man. There was a brief interregnum when, apparently from nowhere, the boy's mother joined them in the boiler house, a tragic figure who had been badly burned in a fire near Bendigo, in which her husband was killed – the father of the boy. Here too Mrs Arbuckle tried to help. She visited the boiler several times when the mother was there, offering her help, but the old man wouldn't let Mrs Arbuckle even talk to his daughter-in-law. Then, when the mother died, the boy's situation obviously worsened, because he became entirely dependent on the care of the old man whose approach to life had become a bitter hostility to everything around him. Every time Mrs Arbuckle went down there on her regular attempts to help the boy, the old man became more and more violent, and the boy too.'

'What about the boiler?' Judge Laker said as if Strapp's picture of it had caught his imagination.

'We come to that now. In one of his fits of madness the old man set fire to the extension he lived in, so that the whole place burned to the ground.'

'You mean the boiler too?' Judge Laker said.

'No, your honour. The metal shell of it was left, but the contents were burned out. Which, of course, left the boy homeless. And this time the old man was beyond saving. He died in hospital, completely insane. That is when Mrs Betty Arbuckle took the boy home, gave him a place to live, and tried also to give him some instruction in the Christian faith which the boy knew nothing about, because the old man had simply left the boy to his own devices. As a result, sir, our little vagabond has had no moral instruction from any church or Sunday school at all. He has been living the life of an African heathen. He has become a child desperately in need of saving, your honour, which Mr and Mrs Arbuckle took on as a personal responsibility.'

Grace had been watching Spit to see how he was taking this version of his life with his grandfather, but Spit was quite impassive, as if he was now expert in removing himself from anything that seemed likely to punish him or hurt him or disarray him.

'So the boy is now living with Mr and Mrs Arbuckle, is that right?' Judge Laker said.

'No, at the moment he is staying with Mrs Tree. When the old man died in hospital, the boy subsequently ran away. That is, he swam across the river and tried to live wild on Pental Island. But after causing considerable trouble and concern to Sergeant Collins and other volunteers who set off to find him, the boy was brought back to St Helen by Sergeant Collins. It was then that he was taken over by Mrs Tree who kept him in her house and refused to give him up to anybody. Since then he has been kept there, and despite Mrs Arbuckle's attempts to take the boy to her own home, Mrs Tree has refused to let the boy go, which brings us to the crucial issue of this application, your honour, the issue of matching ...'

'Ahh, I was wondering about that,' the Judge said.

'It's always a touchy subject, as you know, your honour, but there is a problem here which only the court can decide. Under the 1928 Adoption of Children Act, the issue of matching faith to faith is paramount, but what we have at the moment with Mrs Tree is a mix-matching, if that is the right word.'

'Mrs Tree is a Roman Catholic and Mrs Arbuckle is a Protestant, and so is the boy, that's what you are saying, Mr Strapp.'

'Yes.'

'Then say it. It will have to be a wide open issue sooner or later, so better to face it honestly rather than try to smother it in caution and hesitation.'

'Of course, your honour.'

'So?'

'The religion is, we consider, vital to the boy's present care. Mr and Mrs Tree are practising Catholics. If the court allows them to adopt the boy, they become the absolute parents and guardians of the boy, and as such will have a legal right to do what they wish with him. As adoptive parents, they will have the same rights as natural parents, and if they so wish it they can make a Roman Catholic of him. As adoptive parents, they would be perfectly within the law to do so. But this, of course, would become a denial of the boy's own rights, because constitutionally, and in law, Spit MacPhee has the right, even the requirement, to be brought up in the faith to which he was born.'

'Mr and Mrs Arbuckle . . .' the judge said, consulting the application again, 'are not Presbyterians. Their church is one of the evangelical sects, is it not?'

'Yes. But obviously their church falls clearly and firmly on the Protestant side of the fence, which is all that counts.'

'Do they intend to bring the boy up in their evangelical faith if they become the adoptive parents?'

'Only if the boy wishes. Otherwise they will insist that he take his religious instruction at the Presbyterian church. In any case a Protestant church, not a Catholic one.'

'I see. Is that your case, Mr Strapp?'

'Yes, your honour, except to say again that the boy is in need of care and protection, not simply for the clothes on his back and the food in his belly. He needs the care of someone who will rescue him from the gypsy life he was unfortunate enough to learn from his grandfather. He needs adoptive parents who are respectable and well liked, and well known in this town for their honesty and stability. And he needs the care of a family who have always been interested in the boy and his welfare. Above all, he needs the understanding and the help and protection of someone who will give him a Christian upbringing in the Protestant faith of his father and his forefathers, a profound and unshakable historical reality, sir, which this court dare not ignore.'

The judge threw up his hands in a mild gesture of protest as he said to Mr Strapp, 'When advocates tell the court that we dare not ignore something, Mr Strapp, I always have the feeling that, sitting in judgement, I am being blackmailed. Are you trying to blackmail me, sir?'

'There was no such intent, your honour.'

'Then in future do not tell the court what it dare or dare not do. The judgement of this court will be qualified only by the law, and by what is best for the boy. So Mr Quayle, we can now hear your proposition, and I hope that you will not stick pins into me in order to warn me that I am supposed to have blood in my veins as well as vinegar.'

'Nothing would be further from my mind, your honour,' Edward Quayle said, and he waited a full minute, as if he wanted all previous influences to disperse before he began. And Grace Tree, having listened closely and almost breathlessly to everything that Mr Strapp had said, wondered how Edward Quayle would be able to contest what seemed to her to be a perfect case. In a way everything Mr Strapp had said was true, even though she thought it was wrong.

'Spit MacPhee,' Mr Quayle began, looking up from his papers at Spit, sitting on the bench. 'Stand up will you, Spit MacPhee, so that Judge Laker can take a good look at you close up.'

Spit stood up promptly, boldly, defiantly, ready this time to shout at a moment's notice, 'You're not going to get me.'

'There he is, your honour, the boy we are arguing about, and if we want a model for the Australian boy, in perfecto, I can't imagine a better example than Spit MacPhee. A true native of the wide open spaces. A boy born and brought up to look after himself when necessity forgot him. A very bright lad who, in the deepest and best traditions of this new and pioneering country, has shown many adults in this town how best to utilise the country he was born in, how to enjoy it and make friends with it and, at the same time, merge into it like an autumn leaf. A vagabond? A gypsy? A wild thing? Absolute stuff and nonsense, your honour. Take a good look at him and make up your own mind.' As Judge Laker raised his stub of pencil ready to interrupt, Edward Quayle said sharply, 'Sit down, Spit MacPhee.'

But Spit hesitated a moment before he sat down and, sensing Spit's continuing resistance to all this turmoil over his head and around his ears, Edward Quayle said, 'It's all right, Spit. Nobody is going to harm you here, so sit down, boy. Just sit down.'

Spit obeyed, but he kept his eye on the judge who had been studying him with a rather puzzled expression. 'Mr Quayle,' he was saying. 'Why is he called Spit?'

'That's his nickname, your honour.'

'Does he spit?'

'The story is that in a contest at school, some years ago, he beat every other boy at the sport of spitting at passing bumblebees and flies and such. But though he doesn't spit any more, he is known affectionately, and I might even say respectfully, to everyone in this town as Spit MacPhee. But even if it is not a very salubrious nickname I am sure in the Australian tradition that your honour had one just as picturesque in his own youth.'

Judge Laker was startled for a moment. As a boy he had been called 'Lick' Laker because he always licked his pencil before using it, something he still did. 'I don't believe a word of your story, Mr Quayle,' he said. 'It's a little too good to be true. But never mind.'

'Well, your honour, as Mark Twain said: "If it isn't the gospel truth it's at least a possibility."'

'In the circumstances I should call it flim-flam, Mr Quayle. But I take your point about the boy if you really have to make the point.'

'Oh, I do, your honour, because this is not just "a boy". His grandfather was not, as my learned friend kept calling him, "the old man". He was Fyfe MacPhee, and this boy is Spit MacPhee and that is how we shall refer to them, because they must not be labelled and insulted here as nameless vagabonds and gypsies. They were not.'

'All right, Mr Quayle. You have established your characters, so get on with your plot.'

'Well, sir, the plot is really a simple appeal to the humanity and common sense of this court.'

Judge Laker groaned. 'Not again,' he complained. 'We have already been blackmailed with does and dares, and now you are messing me about with humanity and common sense. This is not Olympus, Mr Quayle, so get on with your story.'

Edward Quayle put his stubby fingers together and said, 'In fact it is really the story of a remarkable old man, who, by extraordinary courage and agonising self-control, was able to take care of a very young boy under very great difficulties when he himself was suffering the excruciating misery of pain and disorientation.'

'Is it important about the grandfather, Mr Quayle? Does it matter now?' the judge said.

'Yes, it does, your honour, because Fyfe MacPhee was not a

vagabond. He was an old soldier who fought with an Argyll regiment at Ypres and Lille, and suffered very severe head wounds in 1917. I was lucky enough to be able to trace some of his records from an old cap badge we found in the ashes of the boiler, and as far as I can make out he was invalided to Canada in 1917 and given a silver plate to cover the deep gash in his cranium, a very doubtful operation but the best they could do at the time to protect the exposed parts of his brain.'

Spit could take no more of it and he leapt to his feet and shouted, 'My grandfather wasn't mad, I don't care what you say.'

'Of course he wasn't mad,' Edward Quayle said sharply. 'Nobody is saying that he was mad, so sit still young man. Sit still, and we will do our best for him.'

As Spit sat down again he was blushing this time. He realised that he had spoken out of turn, and Judge Laker pointed his pencil at him and said, 'Any more out of you, Spit, and you'll leave the court.' The judge turned then to Edward Quayle and said in a wearied voice, 'I still ask you, Mr Quayle, is all this so important?'

'Let me finish, your honour. I assure you it is all relevant. The point is that Fyfe MacPhee had been a watch and clock repairer in Edinburgh before the war, and he at least had a trade when the war ended. Bringing his wife and son to Australia he lived in Melbourne for several years, where his wife died, and where his son also became a watch and clock repairer.'

'We know something of that from Mr Strapp,' Judge Laker said.

'Yes, but what you don't know is that when he walked into this town, fifteen years ago, the pressure of that silver plate on his brain was already so severe that it caused him to behave the way he did. He wasn't mad. He wasn't a vagabond. He was a perfectly sane man trying to discipline a damaged brain. And, as Doctor Stevens will confirm, he was always in frightful pain, which sometimes was so noisy in his head and so heavy on his rationality that only shouting and talking to himself, and even a degree of wild fantasy could help him to survive the noise or blot it out. That was the real reason for his peculiar behaviour. He was an old soldier suffering terribly from his wounds. But plenty of people in this town will confirm that he was the best watch repairer we had, and though the way he lived was an inevitable part of his suffering, he believed like an old soldier that he had to isolate himself to some extent so that he did not soak the rest of us with his unpredictable behaviour and his need for noisy, distorted relief.'

'Are you absolutely sure of all this, Mr Quayle?' the judge said, clearly troubled by the story. Judge Laker was an old soldier himself; and didn't old soldiers always bleed for other old soldiers suffering the agony of their terrible wounds?

'Yes, your honour. And if my learned friend opposite or his clients really had Spit MacPhee's interest at heart, they too would have tried to find out some of the reasons . . .'

'Oh for heaven's sake – isn't that going a bit too far, your honour?' Mr Strapp said.

'I agree, Mr Strapp,' the judge said. 'Stick to your own case, Mr Quayle and let Mr Strapp fail in his own way.'

'I'm only concerned with the truth, your honour, and in this boy's story it seems to be all suffering and tragedy, because his father was killed in a fire in Bendigo and his mother badly burned, and that is when Spit MacPhee first came to St Helen to live with his grandfather. That is when his grandfather built those extensions to the boiler and brought home Spit's mother, veiled as we all know from head to toe because her burns were so bad that she wanted to hide them.'

'Surely that is when she needed the help Mrs Arbuckle offered her,' Judge Laker said.

'No, sir. She did not want anyone to see her or help her. She was a tragic, dying woman, and though Mrs Betty Arbuckle did offer to help her, a kind act, Mrs Arbuckle showed little awareness of what this lady was suffering, and why she needed privacy. Mrs MacPhee simply needed to be left alone for the last few months of her life with her son . . .'

Grace, listening to the story as Edward Quayle was telling it felt pained and sickened by her own lack of interest in how horrible it must have been for Spit and his family. She looked across the room at Betty Arbuckle who had taken off her ugly hat and was now in tears. Betty, in distress, looked more beautiful than ever, but Grace didn't feel like tears. She felt angry. When Tom touched her arm gently and said, 'There's your husband,' she looked at the door and saw Jack sitting erect on a bench just inside it, soldierly and cold, as if he wanted to be as far removed from this as possible.

'How long has he been there?' she whispered to Tom.

'Since my father started talking,' Tom said.

'He heard everything?' she said.

'He must have,' Tom said.

There was a jug of water on the table near Edward Quayle and he poured some of it into a glass and took a sip before going on. 'You see, your honour, when young Mrs MacPhee died, Fyfe was already suffering so much from his head wound that, according to Doctor Stevens, he must have survived on sheer willpower in order to look after his grandson. And in living with his grandfather, Spit, who was six then seven and then eight and nine, shared the shouting and the apparent quarrelling and the wandering, and the river at the door. Far from vagabondage, it was an education in self-sufficiency that Spit MacPhee was getting from his grandfather because Fyfe MacPhee was never sure, from day to day, how long he could function with the agony and the pain and the terrible moments of his uncontrollable behaviour. Eventually it came to its end in the tragic affair of the fire. Fyfe MacPhee didn't know what he was doing, and later he tried to drown himself as the only solution left, fearing as he always did that in his moment of total mental loss he would do what he had just done – not harm his grandson but commit some foolish act that might seriously affect his life.'

'Where did he die, Mr Quayle?' the judge asked. 'I have forgotten.'

'In the local hospital, your honour. And I think it is safe to say that he died of exhaustion, trying desperately to keep alive for his grandson's sake.'

'But surely life in that boiler must have been rather hard on the boy?' the judge said.

'Not at all, sir. It was an admirable little house. Spit MacPhee had a room to himself, a comfortable bed, plenty to eat, and a devoted guardian to protect him. In fact Fyfe MacPhee was an orderly man by nature. He kept a fine garden, and though his house was painted in fantastic colours, no doubt as a reflection of his suffering, it was always neat and clean.'

Judge Laker held up his hand like a policeman as if that was the only way to stop Edward Quayle. 'Just a minute, Mr Quayle. Just a minute,' he said. 'Now, calmly, not in passion but in cold blood – can you justify that story of insults and attacks on Mrs Arbuckle? Weren't they true?'

'Yes, your honour. The lady made her approaches in good heart, but to Spit and his grandfather they were threats to their perfectly decent domestic life. It is well known to everybody in this town that Mrs Arbuckle had her mind set on sending Spit off to a Boys Home in Bendigo, even from the beginning. And that is what inspired such a violent response from both of them.'

'So there were some primitive imperfections in their behaviour after all,' the judge said, 'which, I might say, is putting it mildly.'

'There were many imperfections in that household by the river, just as there are imperfections in any household in this town,' Edward Quayle said angrily. 'But lack of affection and attention and care were not among them. If Fyfe MacPhee was loud and sometimes aggressive and negligent about his responsibilities, then his failure, for instance, to give the boy some Christian instruction was simply a reflection of his own condition rather than a slip in his morals. The proof is that Spit MacPhee is an honest boy. Everybody in this town knows that. He has never been accused of stealing or, in normal life, of insulting or hurting anybody. If he has had fights at school, they were usually to defend his grandfather against other boys who called him mad. And that is the true story of Spit MacPhee, your honour; not that farrago of ridiculous nonsense from Mr Strapp. The difference has to be understood if there is to be a fair judgement in this case.'

'You're at it again, Mr Quayle.'

'I know, your honour. But I mean no disrespect to yourself or the court.'

'All right. You have given us the background, you have told us a moving story of the boy and his grandfather, but you haven't yet made a case for your client, have you?'

'I was about to come to that.'

'Time is not on your side, Mr Quayle'

'I beg your pardon, your honour, but it is important . . .'

'In that case,' Judge Laker interrupted, 'I think we had better adjourn for five minutes so that you can catch your breath. But then we will deal with this matter speedily and objectively. In fact I need to remove myself for a few minutes from the influence of your presumptions, Mr Quayle.'

Judge Laker stood up and walked out, and as Edward Quayle leaned back and rubbed an eye thoughtfully, Grace asked Tom what it meant.

'It means,' Tom said, 'that Judge Laker has gone into the back room to have his morning tot of brandy.'

'That's enough, Tom,' Edward Quayle said sharply. He leaned forward. 'I want you to do something,' he said to his son. 'Go over to the bench at the back and tell Mr Tree that I need him up here for the boy's sake. And don't take No for an answer.'

'Do you want me to do it?' Grace said.

'No, no. He might resist you on principle. Moreover if there is to be any resentment it had better be against me rather than you. We shall need the semblance at least of a united family up here for what I am about to do. So tell him that if he resists and refuses to come up here I shall pack up and leave the court and abandon the case.'

'But he won't come, Mr Quayle,' Grace said quickly.

'I think he will, Mrs Tree. In any case, Tom, you tell him that I mean what I say.'

Grace watched Tom Quayle approach her husband. She saw Tom bend over and talk to him. She noticed the slight stiffening of Jack's back, and his face become set. And though she expected the worst, for some strange reason which she could not fathom Jack stood up and followed Tom.

'What on earth did you do to him, Mr Quayle?' Grace said quietly.

'Nothing,' Edward Quayle said, and added drily, 'Old soldiers, Mrs Tree. They are all old soldiers, and as you know, old soldiers never die.'

23

WHEN JUDGE LAKER RETURNED, EDWARD QUAYLE WAS QUICK to begin again. 'We now have Mr Tree with us so I shall proceed . . .'

'Your honour,' Mr Strapp said. 'It looks as if Mr Quayle is going to go on *ad-infinitum*. Surely there has to be a time limit to this?'

'So far,' Edward Quayle said, 'I have had to waste time correcting the false impression of Fyfe MacPhee and his grandson given in this court by my honourable friend, so I haven't had a chance yet to put our proper case.'

'That's one way of putting it,' the judge said. 'So do get on with it.'

'I shall be brief,' Edward Quayle said, 'even though more amplification would help. But I'll skip the rest and come to the point of our appeal. Mrs Tree is a Roman Catholic and Mrs Arbuckle is an Evangelical Protestant. That is an issue, I admit, but our case is based not on religion but on the difference between Mrs Arbuckle's idea of bringing up a boy and Mrs Tree's. No more nor less than that.'

'No more nor less, Mr Quayle?'

'Well, it seems to me, your honour, that in this case religion should have nothing to do with it. And even if it was crucial I would have to point out that there are Protestants and Protestants, and Catholics and Catholics. In other words, in both sects there is dogma and bigotry. There is hostility and hate. There are differences about what is good and what is evil, what is salvation and what is damnation. But what on earth has religious dogma and bigotry, or even the honest differences in faith got to do with fathering and mothering this boy? I refuse therefore, for the sake of this boy, to get involved in an insoluble historical argument which has been going on for four hundred years and may go on for another four hundred years.'

Judge Laker raised his hand again. 'Thank heaven for that,' he said. 'I was all prepared for you to give us a remarkable defence of the Catholic faith from your well known Berkleyian belief in the Reformation.'

'Sir,' Edward Quayle said, controlling his temper, 'I would gladly do that for you, but I am afraid it would be wasted here. Instead I turn to Mr and Mrs Tree as human beings, not as Catholics or Protestants. They are, like Mr and Mrs Arbuckle, a very respectable family in this town. Mr Tree is the Secretary of the Returned Soldiers' League and is an old soldier himself. The Trees have a ten-year-old daughter, Sadie, who is sitting there next to Spit MacPhee. Stand up Sadie,' Edward Quayle said.

Sadie stood up, head down, eyes down.

'Lift your head up, Sadie,' Edward Quayle said, 'and tell us what you think of your friend Spit MacPhee. It's quite important what you think of him because you are one of the nicest and cleverest girls in St Helen, and are highly thought of, so what do you say about Spit MacPhee?'

Sadie kept her head down. 'He's all right,' she said.

'It would be awful if this court took Spit away from you and your family, wouldn't it?'

Sadie nodded.

'So how would you feel about that, Sadie?'

'I'd be sick,' Sadie said, and lifting her head she said, 'It wouldn't be fair.'

'Oh, for heaven's sake, your honour,' Mr Strapp shouted. 'This is going a bit too far.'

'I quite agree,' Judge Laker said. 'So just make your statement, Mr Quayle, and leave the histrionics till later.'

Edward Quayle shrugged a little, waited a full minute again for the air to change, and then sighed and went on. 'What I was saying before these interruptions is that Spit MacPhee is already well established in the Tree household. He is happy there, and is now treated like a son and a brother. And the difference is this, your honour: Mrs Arbuckle in her faith and passion has already had Spit at her home and he ran away because he was frightened of her and unhappy with her. Why? Because she put heavy boots on his winged feet, confined him to quarters, forbade him the Australian life he knew best – the river – and tried to make a good Christian of him with the apostolic convention that he must above all be saved.'

'Is there anything wrong with that, Mr Quayle?' Betty Arbuckle cried out. 'Considering his condition and his wild behaviour. Is there anything wrong with trying to save him?'

'Nothing wrong with it at all, Mrs Arbuckle,' Edward Quayle said calmly, 'for thee and thine, so to speak. But your methods may not be good for everybody, and they were certainly not good for Spit MacPhee. What he wanted, a boy utterly alone at the age of eleven, was a home that asked nothing of him to begin with except his toleration. What he got in the household of Mrs Tree was not a religious or evangelical instruction in papism, which Mrs Arbuckle is so afraid of, but the understanding of a woman who realised what sort of a boy he is. A free spirit perhaps, but also a natural boy in a natural landscape; a boy living on a marvellous river; a boy with many unique talents; an Australian boy who asked absolutely nothing of anyone because he expected others to ask nothing of him. That was how he had been brought up by his grandfather.'

'But it's wrong, Mr Quayle,' Betty Arbuckle cried out again. 'It's not good for a boy to be like that.'

'Well, dear lady, you may be right. It's not the way I would bring up my own sons,' Edward Quayle said. 'But that is what he was. Not your son and not mine but Spit MacPhee, standing on his own two feet. And that is the boy Mr and Mrs Tree are willing to take up.'

'Oh, this is all nonsense, your honour,' Mr Strapp said angrily, wearily, half standing up and then sitting down again. 'We know for a fact that Mr Jack Tree wanted nothing to do with the adoption of the boy; that he was always reluctant. And far from being the united and happy household Mr Quayle portrays, it became a divided one because of the boy.'

The judge tapped his pencil once or twice on the table, to make sure that Edward Quayle was silenced before he could begin.

'Is that true, Mr Quayle? Is Mr Tree reluctant in this?'

'Why not ask him yourself your honour,' Edward Quayl said. 'He is right here.'

Grace got a grip on Jack's arm as she felt him stiffen wit resentment. She knew his responses; she knew what was goin to happen.

'Well, Mr Tree? Is what Mr Strapp says true?'

'Yes, sir, I was always reluctant.'

'Oh? Why?'

'I don't know. I thought he was a wild young devil in need o a good home, but not necessarily ours.'

'Didn't you like the boy?'

'I didn't like or dislike him, your honour. He seeme suddenly to come into my family, and I didn't want a strange in it.'

'Oh, Jack,' Grace Tree said miserably. 'You've spoile everything now.'

'I have to tell the truth, Grace,' Jack Tree said. 'I don't dislike the boy, your honour. He's got a lot of spunk an gumption. I agree with a lot that Mr Quayle says about him and I always felt sorry for him.'

'But not sorry enough to want him. Isn't that right?' M Strapp said.

Both Jack Tree and Grace Tree looked at Edward Quayl for help, but he was deliberately, obstinately silent.

'I'll tell you this, your honour,' Jack said. 'I didn't kno about old Fyfe until now when I heard Mr Quayle's story. didn't know he had been a soldier, and that it was his wound that had made him a bit crazy. I never thought of the old ma and the boy in that way. But I can say this, sir. Spit MacPhee i certainly no angel, but my wife and my daughter have becom very attached to him. And, if it comes to that, I will have th boy and do my best with him. He will certainly be much bette off with us than he would be with Mrs Arbuckle; and damned sight better off with us than he would be in a Boy Home in Bendigo. If he stays with us he will be given a goo home, and he and I will have to learn to get on togethe which, sitting here listening to all this, I can guarantee a goo try on my part. Allowing for all the usual faults of boys of hi age, I'm on his side in this.'

'Thank you, Mr Tree, for that very honest account of you

feelings,' Judge Laker said. 'Well, Mr Quayle, you have been rather silent all this time.'

'I simply wanted you to have an honest reply from an honest man, your honour. There was no deception in our case, only honesty. Our case is not perfect. There are many imperfections in the boy to be overcome, and in the family situation. But Mr and Mrs Tree are God-fearing, generous people, not narrow-minded bigots with salvation on their minds.'

'That's quite enough, Mr Quayle.'

'Your honour,' Edward Quayle almost snarled. 'What we need in this courtroom is some human discernment, not religious prejudice. Discernment has to count, sir, because Spit MacPhee's future depends on it – more than religion, and more than a pair of good black boots.'

'Is that the end, Mr Quayle?'

'Yes. I've got nothing more to say on the matter.'

Edward Quayle threw his glasses on the table as if he was finally finished with the whole business, and Judge Laker said to him, almost disappointed, 'Are you sure that is it, Mr Quayle? Nothing more?'

'Yes, your honour. That's it. Except that I suggest you ask Mrs Arbuckle why, after being so intent on sending Spit MacPhee to a Boys Home in Bendigo, she suddenly changed her mind and decided to adopt him instead.'

'Hmmm,' Judge Laker said, licking his pencil and writing something in a little notebook he kept in his waistcoat pocket. 'Well, Mrs Arbuckle? What do you have to say to that?'

'I always wanted him,' Betty said passionately.

'That's not true,' Grace cried out. 'It was only when I wanted to adopt him that Betty made an application herself.'

'Is that right, Mrs Arbuckle?' Judge Laker asked her again.

'Yes, that's right,' Betty said, 'because at first I thought he should be given a home with other boys his own age.'

'What sort of a home would that have been?' Grace said indignantly.

'Steady . . . steady.' Edward Quayle told her.

'Yes, Mrs Tree. Do be quiet. What changed your mind, Mrs Arbuckle? Why are you here now asking to adopt him?'

'When he came to live with us I tried to treat him like my

own son,' Betty Arbuckle said, her delicate skin already pink and lovely with a faint flush, her eyes glistening and her innocence so obvious that Grace knew why nobody could or should doubt her.

Edward Quayle put his spectacles on again. 'Your honour,' he said drily, 'what really changed her mind was her determination not to let the boy go to a Catholic family. Isn't that so, Mrs Arbuckle?'

'Yes, Mr Quayle,' she said and turned to the judge. 'I thought the best way to help save the boy, in his own faith, would be to adopt him for ourselves.'

'So what are your plans for him, Mrs Arbuckle?' the judge said. 'You want to make him a good, Protestant Christian? Is that right?'

'Yes,' Betty said,

'How?'

'He has to be saved,' Betty said in her quiet, determined way. 'Salvation to us is always a witness to the suffering of Jesus Christ, so that thereafter we can always serve him by word and deed; by day and by night.'

'Yes, yes,' Judge Laker said, 'but how does this apply to the boy?'

'But your honour,' Betty protested, 'you can see for yourself. He is like a little African heathen in need of guidance and help and prayer. That is how we bring up our own son and daughter, and how we would bring up Spit MacPhee. He would be one of us in the eyes of the Lord.'

'Thank you, Mrs Arbuckle,' Judge Laker said. 'You can sit down now.'

In her evocation, Betty had been standing up with her hands knotted tightly in front of her. She looked around her for a moment like a confused child and then said, 'All right. I'll sit down.'

'And Mrs Tree?' the judge said, 'What do you have to say about the boy's religion?'

'I'm not sure, your honour,' Betty said, troubled by the question. 'I don't know anything about salvation, if that's what you mean.'

'That isn't what I mean at all,' the judge said. 'Although as a Catholic you do believe in salvation, don't you?'

'I suppose I do, but only in the eyes of the church, and in accordance with the sacraments or the intercessions of the Holy Mother. That's all I know about it.'

'You would like the boy to be a Catholic, Mrs Tree?'

Grace looked at Edward Quayle who was leaning back staring at the ceiling as if he were miles away, generations away. 'Yes, your honour,' Grace said slowly. 'I have to admit I would like him to be a Catholic if he is to be my son. But he isn't a Catholic, is he?'

'But if he becomes your son, your son absolute so to speak, to do with him what you like? What then?'

'I would like him to be a Catholic. But if he isn't, then he isn't.'

'Is that possible? Is it possible for you to have a son who is a Protestant? Do you think your Church would tolerate that?'

'I don't know, your honour.'

'But I do,' Mr Strapp interrupted. 'I have already consulted Father O'Connel on that very point. I asked him what the church would expect of Mrs Tree if she adopted the boy, and he told me, unequivocally, that it would be absolutely incumbent on her as a Catholic to bring the boy up in the Catholic faith.'

'Do you accept that, Mrs Tree?' Judge Laker asked. 'Can you give me a simple answer to that question?'

Grace knew that she was now at her weakest, and she was already exhausted. She knew that her faith and her affection for Spit were now in opposition, and an answer now was beyond her. 'I don't know, your honour. I just don't know. But if I could, I would just leave him alone.'

'If you could . . .' Mr Strapp repeated menacingly. 'But can you, Mrs Tree? That is the question.'

'I don't know,' Grace said miserably.

The judge looked at Edward Quayle with a quizzical, amused expression. 'What have you to say to all this, Mr Quayle,' he said, 'since the question of religion is very important to the decision I must make.'

'Nothing at all,' Edward Quayle said. 'When it comes to the responsibilities and convictions of Mrs Tree and her faith I am not going to speak for her, or even advise her. She speaks well enough for herself. What we should count on here, your honour, is the boy himself, who, even in this situation, would be perfectly able to look after himself.'

'All right, let us ask the boy,' Judge Laker said. 'Stand up, Spit MacPhee, and see if you can help us solve some of this.'

'Do I have to stand up?' Spit demanded.

'Yes,' the judge told him.

'Well, all right,' Spit said and stood up.

'Thank you,' the judge said. 'Now: what religion are you?'

'Presbyterian,' Spit said.

'You don't have to shout,' the Judge told him. 'Just answer quietly. Do you think if you were adopted by Mrs Tree that you would be willing to become a Roman Catholic?'

'I'm a Presbyterian,' Spit said stubbornly.

'But if, as your mother, she insists. What then?'

'I don't know. I don't know what it's like.'

'May I interrupt, your honour,' Edward Quayle said.

'You usually do, Mr Quayle, but for heaven's sake keep it to the issue in hand. Our time is running out.'

'Let me ask you, Spit,' Edward Quayle said. 'If you were to be adopted by Mrs Betty Arbuckle, what would you do?'

'Run away,' Spit said loudly. 'They're not going to get me.'

'Oh dear,' Judge Laker said. 'This is all becoming a little too emotional, Mr Quayle,' He looked over his glasses at Ben Arbuckle and said, 'Who are you, young man?'

Ben stood up. 'Ben Arbuckle.'

'Well, you seem to be the only one here who hasn't had his say, so it's your turn. Do want Spit MacPhee to be your brother?'

'Yessir,' Ben said in his new loud voice. 'He's the best friend I've got.'

'Then that's about it,' Judge Laker said and made a point of closing his little note book. 'All right Mr Quayle, one last word from you, brief and to the point please.'

'I think the situation speaks for itself, your honour. Let me measure it *summum bonum* – by the highest good. We assign to men, or try to, the capacity for mental and physical enjoyment of their lives, and we must in all decency, adjust some of these privileges to our children. In this case there is a boy who has to be given the best we can offer him in an atmosphere of a family and a countryside that will give him what every child in this country needs. It is not a question of religion, it is a matter of common humanity. He is already living with a very fine family where he can be taught the simplest commandments of honesty and respect for others. What more can we ask of Mr and Mrs Tree than that, your honour?'

'Is that all, Mr Quayle?' Judge Laker said, obviously disappointed that he was not going to hear something a little more unreasonable.

'That's all,' Edward Quayle said.

'All right, Mr Strapp. But please keep it as brief as Mr Quayle.'

'Well, your honour, it must come back to the question of religion, no matter which way you look at it. How can we ignore it? Every man and woman in this country is born with a faith which is securely their own – historically as well as in daily life. It is strong, it is real, it is inescapable. The boy is a Protestant and should be brought up as a Protestant, even vigorously so in the evangelical way if necessary. The importance of religious matching is clear in the 1928 Adoption of Children Act. There has never been an exception to it. Any precedent here would create a situation that would go far beyond this courtroom. As for the decency and humanity of Mr and Mrs Arbuckle: here is their own son, a perfectly normal and happy boy who would welcome Spit as a brother. So, given the equal character and fitness of both families, given this equal respectability and decency, the weight of the decision must lie with a religious conjunction. At first it may be difficult for the boy to live with Mr and Mrs Arbuckle, but in the long run he would be as happy and contained and as bright as this boy here, Ben Arbuckle.'

There was a moment's silence. Then Mr Strapp raised his hands to indicate that he had finished, and there was a loud and heavy sigh from Betty Arbuckle. 'That's all, your honour,' Mr Strapp said. 'I have nothing more to say.'

'Gentlemen,' Judge Laker said, putting notebook and pencil into his waistcoat pocket. 'I thank you both for your quite remarkable presentations, and I shall give my decision tomorrow morning at ten o'clock in this chamber. This hearing is over, *casus foederis*, so to speak. But if the parents don't object I would like these two children, Ben Arbuckle and Sadie Tree, to come with me into the other room for a moment. Will you do it, Ben?'

'Yessir,' Ben said firmly.

'And Sadie . . . you are not frightened are you? It's for the good of your friend Spit, here. I just want to have a few words with you.'

'All right,' Sadie said, standing up and following the judge.

As Edward Quayle picked up the papers that were on the table before him (his self-made brief which he had not looked at) Grace waited a moment and then said, from what she felt was some far away place, 'What do you think, Mr Quayle? We haven't much hope, have we?'

'Only tomorrow will tell us that, Mrs Tree,' he said crisply and told Tom to come along.

Grace and Jack sat quietly, saying nothing and facing Betty and Frank Arbuckle across the empty room. And somewhere between them Spit MacPhee watched them all, swinging his legs, and waiting for Sadie to come back.

24

When they had returned home Grace told Sadie and Spit that they need not go back to school in the afternoon. 'I suppose if you've lost a morning,' she said to them, 'you wouldn't lose much in an afternoon.'

She was being a generous mother. She knew already that she was accepting defeat, sure now that this would probably be the last day that Spit and Sadie would enjoy together, so let them enjoy it.

She had tried to keep Spit close to her for a moment when they had arrived home by asking him to bring in more wood ('I filled the box this morning'), to put the cart away in the garden ('I did'), to see if there were one or two tomatoes left on the plants ('There weren't any left after the pickles'). It was her best attachment to Spit because she knew he would always do what he had to do: that had always been the closest response she could get out of him so that when she went out to the verandah where he slept to see if there might be something there to regret, she realised that apart from the bed he slept in there was almost nothing here to connect him to her. He owned nothing more than the school clothes he stood up in, an extra pair of trousers, two extra shirts, a toothbrush which she had persuaded him to use, and his school books.

'It's all so wrong,' she said bitterly to herself. 'It's so terribly wrong.' She heard Sadie calling out that they were going down to the river, and she called back in reply, 'Don't either of you go near the edge above the bend, because it crumbles away there now that the river is fast.' She had learned that from Spit himself.

'Don't worry,' Spit shouted.

'Off you go then,' she said, and she knew that she did not have to worry with Spit. He would look after Sadie.

The one thing that she could be grateful for, she decided, though it puzzled her, was Jack's change of heart. He had driven them home in the Dodge, silent and unquestioning, and after a silent lunch he had gone straight to his desk. She knew that he had a genuinely urgent problem with a dairy herd test that was going on, but she guessed that he really wanted to think. As she sat in the kitchen, preparing a batch of scones, he joined her and sat at the table for a moment without saying anything. She looked at his tight, disciplined face and felt sorry for him, and she asked him why he had changed his mind about Spit.

'I didn't change my mind,' he said stiffly. 'I didn't know anything about old Fyfe. I didn't know about the wound in his head. I didn't even know he'd been in the war. In fact I wonder why he never told anybody.'

'Tell who?' Grace said bitterly. 'Everybody thought he was mad.'

'He could have told the Returned Soldiers . . .'

'What for? If he was so terribly wounded and in pain, he probably wanted to forget the war, not remember it.'

'We could have helped him,' Jack said. 'He was in a bad way.'

'Why should being a soldier have made any difference? In any case I don't think he wanted your help. I think Mr Quayle was right. The only help he needed was to be left alone with Spit. It was probably the only way he could cope with everything, and with that awful pain. Anyway, the Returned Soldiers might have thought it best, like Betty Arbuckle, to help him by finding a place for Spit in some Boys Home,' she said.

'Why do you say that?' Jack said indignantly.

'Because . . . oh, it doesn't matter now. I'm sure we've lost him anyway.'

'Well if we have, don't for God's sake blame me for what happened,' Jack said.

'I'm not blaming you, Jack,' Grace said, and she took a good new look at her husband, because Jack defending himself was a new experience for her. Forgiving him was another one.

'You did all you could, and I suppose the only thing we can do now is wait.'

Jack got up to go and it seemed to Grace that he wanted to say something more, but the best he could manage was, 'Maybe you'll be surprised.' Which, she decided, was sufficient reparation for his resistance to Spit. In fact she loved her husband for those few conciliatory words, and she watched him walking up the back path to the Dodge as if she was watching a stranger, because she knew that if, by some miracle, she did get Spit, Jack would do his best for him as he had promised to do.

But it was still her own private problem, and she knew that somewhere along the river bank there were her two children, which was the only way she could think of them now. And, thinking of them, she watched her tears splashing noisily on the kitchen table as if they were the heavy raindrops which one always longed for as the heavenly relief to a hellish drought. It helped her, because she was normally too quiet to weep.

The children she was suffering for were themselves trying to find some method of constructing a small plank boat that would stay upright in the fast currents of the river. There had been heavy rains at the source of the big river, and the Water Board had opened up the weir on the little river to relieve the flow. It was now fast and full, so that Spit's little boats could not survive in it. But Sadie said she had seen in one of her father's magazines a picture of a south sea island catamaran which would survive anything, 'Even huge waves.'

'You build two arms on the boat, like that,' she said, spreading her arms and dropping her hands.

'What's the point?' Spit said.

'It stops the canoe tipping over one way or the other. Can't you do that, instead of trying to put a keel on the bottom? It just turns over anyway if it bumps something.'

Spit spread his own arms. 'It'll be too big,' he said. 'Too wide.'

'It doesn't matter if it's too wide.' Sadie insisted.

They were in the boiler where Spit's limited restorations had given him a place to work. 'All right,' he said. 'I'll give it a go.'

She watched him cutting, sawing, shaping, nailing, binding, and hammering, and she gave him advice until he had made a trimaran two feet long and, with outriggers, two feet wide. As he put the mast in the centre-piece he said, 'Where's the message?'

'I haven't written one,' Sadie said.

'I'll bet you forgot the pencil.'

'No I didn't. I've got an old red crayon.' Sadie had the crayon and a sheet of paper ready and she asked Spit what to write.

'Write . . .' Spit thought for a moment, 'Write . . . "*this boat belongs to Spit MacPhee and Sadie Tree. If found, please return to owners.*"'

'Return to owners where? You have to put an address.'

'Your place,' Spit said.

'All right. But you have to give a reason, otherwise people won't care. They'll just throw it away.'

'Say we are trying to find out how far it goes.'

'Do you think that'll work?'

'I don't know,' Spit said. 'But what else can you say?'

Sadie didn't know. The old days of piratical messages were over, they had grown out of their possibilities. So she wrote the message in red pencil and handed it to Spit.

'Wrap it around tight,' she said, 'and tie it on with string.'

Spit did as he was told, and as they walked up river to put the boat into the stream Spit asked Sadie, 'What did that old judge ask you?'

'All sorts of questions,' Sadie said.

'What about?'

'About you and your grandfather and what you did and things like that. What my father and mother did and what you and I did all the time. All sorts of questions like that.'

'What did he ask Ben?'

'Same thing,' Sadie said. 'Where are you going to put the boat in?' she asked him.

'Just above the bend,' he said.

'My mother said not to go near the edge there, Spit, because it crumbles.'

'She was telling that to you, so you'd better keep right back,' Spit said. 'She knows I won't fall in.'

But as Spit lay on the bank, pushing out the trimaran with a long piece of bamboo so that it could flow out into the fast current, the bank gave way and Spit went into the water with it. When Sadie saw his head emerge he was already being carried out to the middle of the river and downstream.

'Spit,' she screamed.

Spit was already in action, arms and feet working, but he lifted his head and spat out some water and shouted, 'I'm all right. I'll come in around the bend.' But then he disappeared again.

Sadie ran downstream to the bank around the bend, watching for Spit as he struggled to get free of the currents that swept him along in midstream. She knew that he wasn't going to make it, but then he put his head under, lashed out with his feet and arms in an Australian crawl and, as he was swept around the bend and reached a patch of dead water, he was momentarily free of the current. After another forceful plunge of arms and legs he reached the bank.

'Look at you,' Sadie said as he pulled himself up on the dry bank. 'You're sopping wet.' Sadie was not sure whether she was near to tears because of fright, or because she was angry with him for his mistake.

'What do you expect me to be?' Spit said as if he too had to make up his mind about momentary fright or his silly mistake.

'You shouldn't have done it,' she said to him.

'The whole bank must have been rotten,' Spit said indignantly, squelching in his sandals, shaking his legs to let the water run free from his trousers.

'Come on,' Sadie said. 'You'll have to get out of your clothes. And wait until my mother sees you.'

Spit, rarely shamefaced, had to keep his direct gaze averted when he presented himself at the kitchen door for Grace to see.

'He fell in,' Sadie said as she held open the door.

'You fell in!' Grace said. 'My God, look at your clothes.'

'They're wet,' Spit said firmly.

'How on earth did it happen?'

'I was pushing something in the water and I just fell in.'

'Where?'

'Above the bend,' Spit said loudly.

'I told you not to go near the edge up there,' Grace said angrily, already pulling off his jumper and shirt as he stood outside the door.

'I thought you meant Sadie,' Spit said,

'I meant you too,' she said. 'How on earth am I going to dry your clothes in this weather, and you haven't got another pair of shoes.'

'I don't need shoes,' Spit said.

'Yes you do,' she said, still furious with him. 'I don't know what to do with you, Spit. You should not have gone near the edge up there. Take your shoes and socks off and then go inside the bathroom and take your pants off and dry yourself, and I'll bring you what's left of your old clothes. I don't know how I am going to dry your jumper and trousers. And look at your sandals.'

'You can put them in the oven,' Spit said.

'And ruin them?' Grace said. 'You get yourself dry, and when you're dressed you can stoke up the fire. And Sadie, you should have known better.'

'She told me not to do it,' Spit said.

'Then thank heavens one of you listens to me,' Grace said.

She told Sadie to go and get the clothes horse to put before the fire, and as Spit walked barefoot into the bathroom Grace stood for a moment clutching the wet shirt and jumper and socks.

In the grip of what seemed to her to be the worst day in her life, she knew that in losing her temper with Spit she had broken the curious barrier that had always been there between them. After all, he was no more than a boy and she was an adult, and whatever had been equal in their companionship had suddenly been replaced by the response of a mother reprimanding a son. She felt it so deeply that once again, in her failure to keep him, she knew that she would have to go somewhere and have a quiet weep. But that, she decided, would not rinse and dry his clothes. It would not help Sadie, who was looking at her with a curious, worried expression, as if she too was upset, not by Spit's behaviour but by what was happening to her mother.

'I'm all right,' she said to Sadie. 'Go and get the clothes horse.'

'I'm going,' Sadie said, and Grace wondered how she was going to survive until ten o'clock next morning.

25

As they sat waiting for Judge Laker to appear like a materialising ghost through the door at the back of the chamber, Grace whispered to Tom, 'Do you know how much I'll owe you, Tom? I have the money.'

'You don't have to pay now, Mrs Tree,' Tom said. 'My father will send you a bill.'

'But I have the money.'

'He won't take it here,' Tom said. 'And anyway I don't think he's worked it out yet. It won't be much.'

'All right, but I wanted him to know that no matter what happens, I think he did his best. It won't be his fault if I don't get Spit.'

'I'll tell him,' Tom said, and as Judge Laker appeared so did Edward Quayle – head a little in the air as if he had everything else on his mind except the problem in hand.

'Good morning Mr and Mrs Tree,' he said in his English voice, and Grace was always a little frightened by that slight reserve. He sat down near her and thereafter ignored her and Jack too.

Like actors now, waiting for curtains to rise, the performers themselves were ready. Judge Laker cleared his throat and looked at each one of them as if they all needed to be closely inspected before being judged. A few appellate words from Laker, S.J., and the comedy would soon be over.

But Judge Laker took out his little notebook and looked at it carefully. Then he made another note before beginning. 'I have been looking at the 1928 Adoption of Children Act very carefully,' he said thoughtfully, 'and within the Act there are two quite different directions that, in judgement, I can take. There are very specific limitations about parental fitness that simply must be accepted. But on the other hand the Act gives me fairly wide discretionary powers. The applicants might not understand all this, but I have to put it on record, in view of my decision.

'Now then,' he went on, and Grace had the feeling that he was trying to be as gentle as he could, although he was not himself a gentle man. But he was trying. 'I have tried,' he said, 'to interpret the Act as a protective cover, both legal and humane, for an eleven-year-old boy in need of proper care and attention, as well as using the law to decide whether an applicant is a fit and proper person. In this case, I must decide which of two families can be judged as the better adoptive parents for a boy whom they both want. At the same time I have to think of the boy, not only as he is now, left quite alone, but his life in the future as he grows into manhood. So my decision here is based on both the immediate as well as the long-term needs of the boy. And, thinking about both applications, I find myself worrying more about the long term than the short term in this.'

Judge Laker bent forward a little as if he had suddenly noticed that both Sadie and Ben were sitting in their places on the bench.

'What are they doing here?' he asked. 'There is no need for them to be here this morning.'

'I thought you might need to question them further, your honour,' Mr Strapp said. 'That is, for our part.'

'I simply forgot to tell them they weren't needed, your honour,' Edward Quayle said. 'I apologise, although I suppose you might have needed them.'

'No. No. I have finished with them. They can go. They're better at school than they are sitting here.'

Spit, who felt that he had swallowed his silence long enough, suddenly stood up. 'I don't want to go to school, your honour. I'm not leaving here now.'

Judge Laker looked a little startled, and then he made a fragmented gesture with his pencil as if to recognise Spit as a factor in the case rather than an object of it. 'What do you want to stay here for, young man?' he said. 'You're not needed, you know. You don't have to stay.'

'What if I don't like what you're going to do to me?' Spit

said in his loudest voice.

'Mr Quayle,' the judge said, amused enough to allow himself a slight smile. 'Don't you want to say something?'

'No, your honour. If you'll permit it, the boy is doing rather well for himself.'

'Well, then,' Judge Laker said, leaning forward to look a little closer at Spit. 'What if you don't like what we decide? What will you do about it?'

Spit closed his mouth in a tight, stubborn grip, and it was Sadie who leapt up and said, 'He'll run away again, your honour. He won't do what you can't make him do . . .'

For a moment there was an almost passionate silence in the room. Everybody in the court looked at the two children; at Sadie who was blushing but who nonetheless had her head well up; and at Spit who was staring into the space he seemed to be aiming at.

'Is that true?' the judge asked Spit.

Spit still kept his mouth grimly shut, but he nodded as if words now meant nothing.

'Don't you trust us, Spit?' the judge said.

It looked as if Spit would persist with his threatening silence but then he burst out, 'Next time, your honour, they'll never catch me. I'll go so far . . .'

Edward Quayle raised a hand then and said, 'That's enough, Spit,' and he said to the judge, 'As you can see, your honour, the boy has spirit, and he already has a real if naive sense that his destiny is being decided here. So I suggest that you allow him to stay so that he can understand what we are trying to do for him, whatever the outcome. But I must point out too that he is warning us, sir, and I think the court must take him seriously. We don't want a tragedy . . .'

'Oh really, Mr Quayle,' Strapp interrupted. 'That is ridiculous.'

'Now really, Mr Strapp,' the judge said. 'Has this become a private argument between you and Mr Quayle?'

'Well, sir, let us not exaggerate,' Strapp said, his hands in the air.

'Speak for yourself, Mr Strapp,' the judge said. 'Personally I am in no fear of my own exaggerations. And I'm sure Mr Quayle isn't either, since he is a past master at it sometimes.'

Edward Quayle ignored the judge's easy jibe at him and said, 'Can I also suggest that Sadie Tree be allowed to stay if her parents don't object. The boy deserves the moral support he needs from this young lady, who is virtually his surrogate sister.'

'Mr Quayle,' the judge said sharply. 'Don't take advantage of everything that comes your way. Don't press your case all the time.' He turned to Spit and Sadie then, and he said, 'All right. You can both stay. But no more declarations of intent, please, from either of you.'

It was Ben then who stood up and said, 'Can I stay too, your honour?'

The judge looked down at Ben and sighed in despair. 'Oh dear. It's becoming a children's matinée. All right, Ben. If your parents don't object you might as well hear it out too. But sit down and don't wriggle.'

As Ben and Sadie and Spit sat down the judge swallowed in his dry throat as if he longed now for a short brandy to get him through the rest of this.

'Now for heaven's sake let us get on with it,' he said and looked carefully at his little note book. 'First of all,' he went on, 'I must make an important comment about the boy himself, because it may help both applicants to understand my decision. Spit MacPhee is obviously a very self-sufficient Australian boy, intelligent and, if a little turbulent, at least able to be guided by a firm hand if the firm hand is the right one. At the same time he seems to be very stubborn, and in his determination not to be restrained he could become a potential danger to himself and others, particularly if he is confused by conflicting interests, or resentful of restraint and discipline.'

He turned then to Betty and Frank Arbuckle. 'So let me take your application first, Mr and Mrs Arbuckle. You are obviously fine and respectable people, and I liked your son Ben and the way he spoke up for his friend Spit. He is the best advertisement you could have given me for your claim. I was always impressed too, with Mrs Arbuckle's deep convictions, and her belief in a faith that, in her severe devotion to it, could move mountains. But is Spit MacPhee a mountain? That was the question I had to ask myself, and I decided that he wasn't a mountain. Spit MacPhee is a small, rough, ready-made little boy who would certainly be unable to accept Mrs Arbuckle's faith as a guiding light, or even as a discipline. Not the way he is now. The boy himself is obviously determined not to be guided or disciplined by Mrs Arbuckle's evangelical methods. And I have to take very seriously his childish threats to abscond if he is forced upon them. I don't really believe he would do anything violent to them, but what his threats really mean is that a powerful resistance is at work which, if he is forced upon the Arbuckles, would almost certainly make a bitter rebel of him. As an adult he would probably become a man who would retain a deep and violent resentment as well as a bad memory of what had been done to him by this court. Inevitably that would lead him into serious trouble.'

Judge Laker took a glass of water and sipped it this time as if it was brandy or whisky – anything but Murray river water.

They waited on his lips, his wiped mouth, his slight sniff.

'So,' he went on, 'with this background to a difficult choice I must unfortunately reject the application of Mr and Mrs Arbuckle, much as I am sorry to do so . . .'

'But he would learn our ways, your honour,' Betty Arbuckle cried out. She was standing up, her hands over her breasts and her face on fire. 'And we would love him like a son.'

'I'm sure you would, Mrs Arbuckle,' Judge Laker said, 'but love is not enough. And in your case I don't think the justification of your Protestantism is enough. In your case it would, I'm afraid, become an impediment to this boy.'

'But please . . .' Betty Arbuckle cried out again.

'Sit down, Mrs Arbuckle,' the judge said sternly. 'It's done and you cannot change my decision. Your application is refused so please be quiet. Now . . . before giving my decision about Mr and Mrs Tree, I would like to tell both sides that, in order to be fair to both applicants, in order that I am not seen to be favouring one family or the other, or that I am making a simple choice of one against the other, I made it my business to look into the question of my discretionary powers on alternatives, such as adoption agencies and existing homes for boys like Spit MacPhee.'

'But your honour . . .' Betty Arbuckle tried again.

'Be quiet, Mrs Arbuckle. Otherwise I shall have to ask you to leave the court. I am already familiar with the two Boys Homes in Bendigo. I have had dealings with them for reasons of probation. So they don't frighten me as they might some people. Nor does the prospect of a boy like Spit MacPhee ending up there seem to me to be necessarily a bad thing, if it becomes necessary. Particularly for a boy like this one whose self-sufficiency would survive very well among a lot of other boys equally endowed. He would easily fit in and make his own way quite well. So I thought I must take that into consideration in all fairness, although I felt from the outset that a family home would be far more desirable than an institution. So I come now to Mr and Mrs Tree.'

Judge Laker pulled in his lips and looked down at Spit MacPhee with an almost puzzled air, as if judgement here was so difficult that he might still change his mind. Spit was wriggling, and as if a small postponement might help his decision, the judge asked Spit what he was wriggling for. 'You usually sit there as still as a statue,' he said.

'I think I'm still wet,' Spit said.

'What does that mean?'

'He fell in the river yesterday and got wet,' Grace said hurriedly. 'But it's his imagination. I dried and ironed his trousers thoroughly, your honour.'

'Then sit still, Spit,' Judge Laker said to him, 'otherwise you're a disturbance.' He then made a curious, resigned sort of gesture towards Edward Quayle, as if he wanted to attract his attention. But Edward Quayle looked so impassive and so still that he was obviously not going to be tempted to be anything else. 'So I come now to your clients, Mr Quayle,' the judge said.

'We are waiting, your honour.'

'You have made a very persuasive and sympathetic case for Mr and Mrs Tree, Mr Quayle. If the Arbuckles had been as flexible as your clients they would have had the boy without question. But Spit obviously prefers Mrs Tree, and I know from their daughter Sadie how well he has fitted in there, even if he has kept his own particular rules for his own particular behaviour. I note, too, that Sadie looks on him already as a brother. Is that right, Sadie?'

'Yessir,' Sadie said.

'So in all fairness,' Judge Laker went on, 'It has to be said that with Mr and Mrs Tree Spit MacPhee seems to have found something near his own environment. Everything sensible and possible, everything desirable, everything I could ask of adoptive parents is there. And yet . . . And yet . . .'

Judge Laker was so reluctant that Grace felt sick to hear those words.

'. . .And yet I have had to consider the problem of religion. I am not afraid of making an unusual decision in this. I am not afraid of setting a precedent. But I have to consider this question of legality in parentage; the legal rights of the adoptive parents, automatically, to have the right to do what they wish with a child within the limits of civil law. It is a very difficult obstacle to overcome.

'The 1928 Act makes it clear that in the long run the primary need is to match the faith of the child to the parents. I cannot ignore this. If I did, it would be a limitation on the boy's inalienable right to be what he was born to be. It would become a serious denial of this right if I hand him over to adoptive parents who would have a legal right then to do what they like with him. The right to a faith in our law is not simply a civil right. It is a constitutional and historical one, bound into our lives by hundreds of years of opposing concepts, bitterly fought over, and yet defined constitutionally into a human right. In the case of a child it is a right that has to be protected by the courts if his own protections are lost.

'So I am dealing here with something far more important than the faith of one small boy who could easily be thrown to the winds of fate. I am dealing with a vital heritage that in law I cannot and dare not alienate. It is not my choice. It is the law itself which, quite rightly, insists on safeguarding and protecting a child's right to the faith of his forefathers. So, with real regret . . .'

'Just a moment, your honour,' Edward Quayle said brusquely, standing up. It was surprising enough to be startling. 'Your honour . . .' he said again as the judge began to protest. 'If you please . . .'

'What on earth is it, Mr Quayle?' Judge Laker said. 'What are you interrupting me for?'

'Before you go any further, your honour,' Edward Quayle said in a calm voice, sitting down again, 'I wish to withdraw Mr and Mrs Tree's application for adoption before you pass any judgement on it.'

'You what?' Judge Laker said, astonished.

'I withdraw our application for adoption, your honour.'

'Now? At a minute before midnight? What is this, Mr Quayle? One of your tricks?'

'Certainly not,' Edward Quayle said, still calm. 'I am withdrawing the application for a very good reason.'

'It had better be good, Mr Quayle, and you had better explain yourself.'

Grace, staring at Edward Quayle in amazement, was trying to find in his English face an explanation of what he was doing. She could see nothing but the unshakable man she was used to and did not always understand. 'What on earth does he mean?' she whispered to Jack. 'What's he doing?'

'I don't know,' Jack said. 'I just don't know.'

'He's going to send me away to Bendigo,' Spit whispered to Sadie.

'No, he isn't.' Sadie whispered back. 'It must be something else.'

'Well, Mr Quayle?' the judge was saying. 'I'm waiting.'

'As I understand it, your honour, you did find Mr and Mrs Tree desirable applicants on the face of it.'

'Yes, I have said that.'

'And that if it were not for a legal impediment, concerning religion, they would get the boy.'

'Yes. Does it need explanation?'

'Not at all, your honour. I just want to establish that you are concerned here with the civil right as well as what you have called the birthright of Spit MacPhee to remain a Protestant; and that there must be some sort of guarantee to protect his rights.'

'That is correct.'

'You feel that in handing over to adoptive parents a right which they would have in law, to determine his religious faith, you would be handing over a right that you feel is beyond your legal powers to do so.'

'I wouldn't put it that way, Mr Quayle, but if you wish I shall simplify it again for you. A man and his faith is such a serious right that a court cannot hand over the choice of it, in circumstances like this, to another person or persons. It is not correct in law, particularly when there is a defenceless child involved. I cannot do it in law, and that is the truth of it. I cannot give away a constitutional or a statutory right, even though it may never be used. Mrs Tree may never exercise her right to make a Catholic of Spit, but I cannot give her that right. I repeat – it is wrong in law, Mr Quayle, as you well know.'

'Exactly, your honour,' Edward Quayle said. 'And that is why I have another suggestion to make. You were thinking, were you not, of your option to send the boy to a Home in Bendigo?'

'Yes, I was coming to that.'

'But there is another discretion open to you, sir, and I am applying to you now for an order in court, under the Neglected and Criminal Children's Acts of 1871, 1872 and 1884, and under the 1928 Adoption of Children's Act to appoint Mr and Mrs Tree the foster parents of Spit MacPhee . . .'

'Foster parents?'

'Yes, foster parents, not adoptive parents.'

'And how in God's name do you think that is going to help, Mr Quayle?'

'As foster parents, your honour, they will have no legal rights over the boy except to his care and attention. They will have no legal rights whatsoever outside the rights defined and even limited by this court. If you, sir, want to make a ruling that they can be judged as fit and proper foster parents only on condition that there will be no attempt to change his religion or to influence him in any way to change his religion, then you may do so. You can put any restraint on them that you like, in law, because in effect though they will be the foster parents in law, Spit MacPhee would remain a ward of the State of Victoria, and the court will be able to withdraw him at any time should it think fit. In every aspect of his upbringing, including the protection of his faith, Mr and Mrs Tree would have to answer to the Attorney General by regular assessments of the boy's condition, attested to by two assessors appointed by yourself . . .'

'I can't have this.' Strapp was on his feet. 'I really can't have it, your honour. I have to object in the strongest possible terms.'

'Just a moment, Mr Strapp.'

'But this is nonsense, your honour. Mr Quayle springs something like this on us without warning, without considering . . .'

'I said just a moment, Mr Strapp, and I mean it. You can have your say later. In any case this is not a litigation or a prosecution that needs one side or the other to be informed.'

'Even so, your honour. Even so . . . It is surely unprincipled.'

'Let us hear Mr Quayle out, Mr Strapp, and I will judge whether it is unprincipled or not.'

Incredulous, and watching these three men at their work, Grace knew that at this moment they each had an almost life-and-death grip on each other. She wasn't sure whether Judge Laker and Mr Quayle were now in mortal combat, or whether they were in some strange accord against Mr Strapp. But none of them seemed concerned now with Spit MacPhee. They had found something in law that was far more important and absorbing to them than the will-o'-the-wisp it was all about.

'What I would like to know, Mr Quayle,' Judge Laker was saying irritably, 'is why you did not make this your original application? Why on earth did you go through all this adoption charade if you were willing to ask for foster parentage in the first place?'

'But I was not willing to ask for foster parentage in the first place,' Edward Quayle said. 'I always preferred adoption. But what I wanted above all else was a fair hearing on the rival qualifications of the two parties, so that if it came to a different kind of choice, your own judgement could be clear. I wanted what you have so generously given to us, your honour – a chance to dispose of all other alternatives.'

'Then you shouldn't have caught me unawares, Mr Quayle.'

'I am sorry, your honour, but there was no other way.'

'So what do you want, Mr Quayle? Are you actually asking me to make a court order, here and now, on an application for

Mr and Mrs Tree to foster the boy?'

'It's perfectly straightforward in law, your honour. The requirements are more or less the same as for adoption, and we could easily complete the technicalities later on. There is a question of a small government grant which Mr and Mrs Tree will probably waive. And the court will have to decide later on what happens to certain monies that Fyfe MacPhee kept on deposit in two banks. But these are not problems we need settle here and now. The point is that, under the various acts, you are empowered if you so wish to make the order, simply on the evidence of fitness you have heard.'

'And what about the assessors to protect the boy, Mr Quayle? Do you have them up your sleeve too?'

'I have them ready and willing, your honour, which is a much better place to have them. I have spoken to Father O'Connel, our local Catholic priest, and the Reverend Duncan Mackenzie of the Presbyterian Church. They have both agreed to act as regular assessors if the court agrees. Together they will cover the two aspects required – the continuing fitness of the foster parents to keep the boy, and the protection of his birthright as a Protestant.'

'You mean they have actually agreed? You have persuaded them?'

'Yes, sir.' Edward Quayle allowed himself a thin, dry smile. 'In law it could be the ideal combination, your honour, and I thought it would appeal to you. On the one hand a protection for the boy's religion from the Reverend Mackenzie. And on the other hand some protection for the foster parents against false accusations from any outside source which I am sure Father O'Connel would see to. For the rest, your honour, I think we can leave it to the two prelates themselves to continue their historical debate, their old and bitter contention, as they walk up the slope from the Trees' household on their way back to their armigerous congregations. In any case they can settle or compact their differences in divine argument, but not with the body and soul of an eleven-year-old boy.'

'It is beyond belief; it is a travesty, your honour,' Mr Strapp shouted. 'If Mr Quayle can make an application on these . . on these flimsy grounds, so can Mr and Mrs Arbuckle. They are equally qualified and I hereby do so . . .'

'Your honour,' Edward Quayle interrupted. 'I waited until the very last moment of your summing up to make my application because I wanted to be sure that, given your own preference in judgement, apart from the impediment of religion, your choice would have gone naturally to my clients. Do I understand that to be the case?'

'Mr Quayle is right, Mr Strapp,' the judge said. 'The only impediment to choosing Mr and Mrs Tree was the religious one. Now Mr Quayle seems to have removed that.'

'It's not fair,' Betty Arbuckle cried. 'It's wicked.'

'Oh dear . . . Oh dear . . .' Judge Laker said wearily. 'Now it is wicked. But what is wicked? What is right? What is wrong? What is humane? Now, for heaven's sake, if I am to be a Solomon in this, then I must be allowed some qualification of my own. Do Mr and Mrs Tree agree to your proposition, Mr Quayle?' he asked.

'Yes, I can speak with certainty of that. Although they may want to say so themselves.'

'Mr and Mrs Tree?'

'Oh yes, your honour. We agree.' Grace said. 'We agree to everything Mr Quayle has said.'

'Then you have my good wishes,' Judge Laker said quickly. 'I can make the order now, appointing you foster parents to Master Spit MacPhee, but with all the various provisos that will be defined later, including the assessors and the method of reporting to the court, as well as the need for regular visits by the assessors as well as the financial arrangements of the grants, if any . . .'

'We don't want any money for it,' Grace Tree said.

'According to Mr Quayle there is some money available from funds left by Fyfe MacPhee, but use of that will have to be decided later by a court order. As far as this hearing is concerned, the matter is closed and you may all go home.'

Judge Laker let out his breath, stood up, shook his head a little, raised his eyes in wonder at the ceiling – at God above – and, followed by Miss Price the stenographer and Henry Fennel, he left the victims and the victors and the children to organise themselves into what was now the new shape of their things to come.

Betty Arbuckle was in such large tears that they were pouring down her lovely cheeks. In a moment's passion she rushed at Spit, who was standing up, and embraced him. 'You must be good,' she said. 'You must never give in.'

Spit, astonished, didn't pull away but waited for her breathless grip on him to exhaust itself. Betty squeezed him hard again and then reluctantly let him go. She took Ben by the hand and, with her husband walking invisibly behind her and Strapp in front, she left the chamber almost overcome by her distress.

'Somehow . . .' Grace said, unable to move but trying to get a grip on herself. 'Somehow I will have to find a way to thank you,' she said to Edward Quayle who had gathered up his papers which he had never bothered to look at. 'But I don't know how I can do it, Mr Quayle. I don't know how I can thank you.'

'Are you satisfied, Mrs Tree?' Edward Quayle said.

'Oh yes,' Grace said. 'Of course I am. I thought that . . .'

'And you, Mr Tree?' Edward Quayle interrupted, turning to Jack. 'Will you object to your house and home being inspected from time to time by Father O'Connel and the Reverend MacKenzie? Well, Mr Tree? Is that going to please you?'

'You might have asked us first,' Jack Tree said. 'But as far as I am concerned they can come any time they like.'

'And the boy? How will you treat him?'

'Don't worry. I'll look after him,' Jack said. 'You don't have to worry.'

'But I do have to worry because I am turning the responsibility for him over to you, and I have to be sure that I have done the right thing, because I can still ask the court to recall its decision.'

'I told you,' Jack said. 'I'll do my best with him. He'll be all right.'

'In that case,' Edward said, 'I shall bid you both good-day. You will have further details to settle later on, but you can do that with Tom.'

Edward Quayle left them without a glance or a gesture in Spit's direction. But Tom waited a moment, laughter in his blond, blue eyes. 'But are you really satisfied, Mrs Tree?' he said almost teasingly.

'Of course I am Tom. I can't tell you . . . And you have to thank your father again for me. I don't know what we'd have done without him. And never mind what Jack says about telling us. Just thank your father.'

'No good thanking my father,' Tom said. 'He'll say, "It's the law, Mrs Tree, the law." That's the way he sees it. If the law is there he will use it. Anyway, I'm glad for old Spit's sake,' he said, and he laughed again as he followed his father.

Grace and Jack were left with Spit and Sadie, bunched together like flowers in the field. When Grace, still a little bewildered, asked, 'What do we do now, Jack?' Spit said, 'Well, we don't have to go back to school anyway.'

'Oh, yes you do,' Jack said. 'Both of you.'

'But it's almost lunch time,' Sadie pointed out.

'I don't care what time it is. I'll take you up to school in the car,' Jack said. 'The holiday is over, so come on. The both of you.'

When the Dodge stopped outside the school gate – the silent school gate with a silent playground behind it and a low enclosure beyond it with children there, in learning, Grace said to Spit as he waited for Sadie to get out of the car from the other side, 'Do you want to say anything to me, Spit?' She too waited as Jack and Sadie joined them.

'I don't know,' Spit said, embarrassed now. 'Are you and Sadie's father supposed to be my father and mother now? Is that what the judge said?'

Grace hesitated, knowing that she must think carefully before she replied; realising too that she would have to think carefully before she answered many more questions that Spit would have to ask her in order to clarify himself – to find out who he was now and who he would become.

'No, Spit,' she said. 'You can only have one mother and father. We'll be what the judge said – foster parents, which is simply another way of saying that we will be responsible for you.'

Spit had to think about that word 'responsible'. He knew what it meant and what it could mean. 'You won't change anything, will you?' he asked her reluctantly.

Grace simply shook her head.

Jack Tree took a deep breath but said nothing, and Sadie stood carefully aside as if she knew that Spit and her mother had to settle something between them. She knew too how hard both of them were trying.

'What'll you do if I run away again?' Spit asked.

'I don't know, Spit,' Grace said. 'It'll depend on why you do it. If I think you're wrong I'll be very angry. If I think you're right I'll tell you so. But are you going to threaten me like that? Is that fair?'

Spit shook his head. 'But I'm not going to forget my grandfather,' he said aggressively. 'And if anyone laughs at him I'll only get into another fight.'

'I'm not going to stop you,' Grace said. 'Nor will Jack.'

'I'm not going to go to church either,' Spit said.

Grace restrained Jack who was about to say something, and she said, 'I don't know how we'll solve that one, Spit. I simply don't know.'

Grace also knew that Spit was trying to come to terms with her, lasting terms, not with promises but on some agreed possibility of mutual respect. And though she knew that Spit didn't exactly know what he was doing, it was obvious enough to her. It was obvious in the grip he had on the school gate, in his bold eyes which went down and then up again to meet hers – watching, waiting, testing.

'Come on, Spit,' Sadie said then. 'We'd better go.'

But Spit didn't move, as if for a moment he couldn't move; as if he knew that one life was about to come to an end here and another entirely different one was about to begin. In that grip he had on the school gate he was holding on to something for a lost moment, to everything that was about to disappear. The gate was the only thing at hand that he could hold on to, and it was Grace who gently undid his fingers from the gate and said to him with one of her gentle smiles, 'Yes. Go on, Spit. We can't stand here all day.'

'I know,' Spit said. 'I'm still wet though. I can feel it.'

'Nonsense,' Grace said, and she watched the two of them go reluctantly into the quiet school. Then, as Jack got into the car she said, 'I'll walk home, Jack.'

'Why? What for?'

'I don't know. I just want to walk a bit, that's all.'

'You're not going to let this business get the better of you, are you?' Jack said seriously, almost sternly.

'No. I have to think a bit, that's all.'

She left him, and as she heard the Dodge turn around and head into the hinterlands, where Jack did most of his work, she walked through the town wondering what it was that had made her take on this boy; where it was going to take her and what problems she would have to face. Because she knew, as all parents knew, that the topsy-turvy problems of children would always multiply and re-multiply as they grew older. And, with Spit, there was going to be a big multiplication in her life which would need all her patience and care, and she wondered how on earth she was ever going to do it. But the first thing she would have to do would be to cure Spit of those two bad habits – shouting and spitting – which would be a terrible burden on him in later life if she didn't make a point of putting a stop to them right away.

More titles in the **Plus** *series*

UNEASY MONEY

Robin F. Brancato

What would you do if you won a fortune? That's what happens when Mike Bronti buys a New Jersey lottery ticket to celebrate his eighteenth birthday. Suddenly, everything looks possible: gifts for his family, treats for his friends, a new car for himself – but things don't work out quite as Mike expects them to. A funny sensitive story about everyone's favourite fantasy.

THE TRICKSTERS

Margaret Mahy

The Hamiltons gather at their holiday house for their customary celebration of midsummer Christmas in New Zealand, but it is to be a Christmas they'll never forget. For the warm, chaotic family atmosphere is chilled by the unexpected arrival of three sinister brothers – the Tricksters.

THREE'S A CROWD

Jennifer Cole

How much fun can you have when your parents are away? No housework, no homework, a BIG party, and plenty of boys. Hey, who's throwing pizza around and where's Mollie disappeared to with that strange guy? (The first book in the *Sisters* trilogy.)

DEAD BIRDS SINGING

Marc Talbert

Mother gasped and slammed on the brakes. Matt was jerked further into the folds of the back seat. 'Oh, my God!'

Someone else's stupidity and a split-second of madness change Matt's life for ever. Kindness and concern from his friends keep him going but do nothing to cure the bitterness in his heart. Can he forgive? Should he forgive?

THE SHADOW IN THE NORTH

Philip Pullman

An elderly woman loses her money on an investment; a music-hall conjuror is pursued by thugs; and a clairvoyant in a trance mentions the names of the richest man in Europe and his mysterious company. Seemingly unconnected events set Sally Lockhart on the trail of an evil far more awful than she ever imagined.

MY SISTER SIF

Ruth Park

Erika's seventeen-year-old sister Sif has always been unhappy in Sydney and longs for the remote Pacific island where the girls were born. And so Erika plots their escape. On their return to the island paradise, however, Sif falls in love with Henry, a young marine biologist, and reveals her family's fantastic secret. But their love is tragically threatened by the pressures of an encroaching world on the seas around the island and the creatures living in them.

IT ALL BEGAN WITH *JANE EYRE*

Sheila Greenwald

For Franny Dillman reading is life. Her idea of heaven is an afternoon with *Jane Eyre* and a bag of crisps. But when she develops an unhealthy obsession for Mr Rochester, Franny's mother takes fright and supplies Franny with some 'modern teenage fiction'. And so the trouble begins . . .

FRANKIE'S HAT

Jan Mark

Three witty pungent stories. Unexpectedly free of her baby on her seventeenth birthday, Frankie goes crazy, or so it seems to her younger sister Sonia, in the title story. *Should* someone's mum be climbing on the parapets of bridges, wearing ridiculous hats and playing football?

CAN'T STOP US NOW

Fran Lantz

Can four girls make it in the music business? Reg Barthwaite, pop promoter and manager, knows he's on to a winner when he picks CC, Robin, Gail and Annette to form a new rock band. But soon they discover that making it in the music business isn't that easy, and as Reg becomes ever more insistent that they play on his terms, the girls are forced to question just what they want – fame at any price?

AT THE SIGN OF THE DOG AND ROCKET

Jan Mark

When her father slips a disc, school-leaver Lilian Goodwin realizes she's in for a frantic couple of weeks in charge of the family's pub – and the last thing she needs is a rude and condescending temporary bar help like Tom to train.

BASKETBALL GAME

Julius Lester

Allen is black and Rebecca is white, and in Nashville, Tennessee, in 1956 that means they must keep apart. They're interested in each other, but is that enough to survive the deeply rooted prejudice that surrounds them?

LOCKED IN TIME

Lois Duncan

When seventeen-year-old Nore arrives at the old Louisiana plantation home of her father and his new wife, she is prepared for unhappiness. She did not expect her new family to be so different, nor can she understand her own mixed-up feelings about them. Her new mother is exotically beautiful, yet Nore senses evil . . .

KILL-A-LOUSE WEEK AND OTHER STORIES

Susan Gregory

The new head arrives at Davenport Secondary just at the beginning of the 'Kill-a-Louse' campaign. Soon the whole school is in uproar . . .

YATESY'S RAP

Jon Blake

It was Ol's idea to play the Christmas concert. His second idea was to get a band together. A most unlikely band it turned out to be. Half of them couldn't play, most of them didn't like each other, and none of them had ever been on a stage. And then Yatesy arrived, with his reputation for being kicked out of several schools for fighting.

BREAKING GLASS

Brian Morse

When the Red Army drops its germ bomb on Leicester, the affected zone is sealed off permanently – with Darren and his sister Sally inside it. Immune to the disease which kills Sally, Darren must face alone the incomprehensible hatred of two of the few survivors trapped with him. And the haunting question is: why did Dad betray them?

THE MONEY SPIDER

Robin Waterfield and Wilfred Davies

Scotland Yard are calling you – you are T. S., the trouble-shooter. There is no apparent motive for the bomb, and no one has claimed responsibility. There is more to the crime than meets the eye. Was it merely a distraction while some bigger crime was committed? *The Money Spider* is part game, part book. The aim is to solve the crime. The rules are simple – you need the book, a pencil and eraser and, of course, all the wits of an ace detective.

THE WATER SPIDER

Robin Waterfield and Wildred Davies

A large consignment of gold has disappeared during a sea voyage between Cape Town and Southampton – worth £8.8 million. There are no obvious clues, no major suspects. And you, T.S. the trouble-shooter, are summoned to solve this web of intrigue.

THE WAVE

Morton Rhue

In only a few days Laurie's seen her classmates change from normal teenagers into chanting, saluting fanatics, caught up in a new organization called 'The Wave'. The Wave is sweeping through the entire school – and it's out of control. What can Laurie do?

A GIRL LIKE ABBY

Hadley Irwin

This isn't just another love story. Abby is trapped in her own nightmare world. Often she is 'absent' – not available – pulled far back inside herself in a world to which no one gains admittance. No one except Chip, who is let in just once and discovers her terrible secret . . . and he knows at once that he must do something to help her.

TULKU

Peter Dickinson

The Boxer rebellion reaches the once peaceful mission settlement in remote China. Theodore escapes and, after great danger, is drawn to a destiny beyond his imagining – in the mysterious gold-domed monastery of Dong Pe, high in the Tibetan mountains.

SUMMER OF MY GERMAN SOLDIER

Bette Greene

When Patty Bergen sells a red pencil-sharpener to the German prisoner in her father's store, a friendship is started which is to bring her much unhappiness but also the greatest joy she's ever known.

Tourism, Magic and Modernity

Cultivating the Human Garden

David Picard

berghahn
NEW YORK • OXFORD
www.berghahnbooks.com

First published in 2011 by

Berghahn Books

www.berghahnbooks.com

First paperback edition published in 2013

Library of Congress Cataloging-in-Publication Data

Picard, David.
Tourism, magic and modernity : cultivating the human garden / by David Picard.
p. cm. -- (New directions in anthropology)
Includes bibliographical references and index.
ISBN 978-0-85745-201-6 (hardback) -- ISBN 978-0-85745-202-3 (institutional ebook) --
ISBN 978-1-78238-321-5 (paperback) -- ISBN 978-1-78238-322-2 (retail ebook)
1. Tourism--Anthropological aspects. 2. Tourism--Social aspects. 3. Culture and tourism.
4. Magic--Social aspects. I. Title. II. Series.
G155.A1P517 2011
306.4'819--dc22

2010048095

British Library Cataloguing in Publication Data

A catalogue record for this book is available from the British Library
Printed in the United States on acid-free paper.

ISBN: 978-1-78238-321-5 paperback
ISBN: 978-1-78238-322-2 retail ebook

For the love
For my parents, Christa and Christof

Contents

FOREWORD

This is a remarkable volume, which pushes the limits of the ethnography of tourists and tourism. In part, this is the result of Picard's research methods, especially his long-term study of tourists and tourism, and of the sociopolitical scaffolding of the industry in Réunion. He used to good advantage his multi-year, almost continuous, residence in La Réunion where he studied tourism while engaged in a doctoral programme at the university there. Thus he was on the island not just as a researcher, but also as a student and as a resident engaged with other residents.

Picard employed the research strategy of participant observation – involving intimacy with both locals and tourists – to a greater degree than any other ethnographer of tourism so far. He was a participant in the lives of local people – at the university, as a resident, a neighbour, a friend or more, as well as a tour guide for two years. And he was far from being just an observer; he was active in people's lives, introducing people to each other, especially visitors and locals. In his close observations of the almost ritualistic behaviour of tourists at sites, he was sensitive to both their utterances and their silences. He was able to articulate their emotions, their senses of belonging and their shared experiences, though I chuckled on reading about the volcano as a 'peak experience', having myself recently visited the Azorean island of Pico, named after its own volcano!

Picard takes note of the tourists' discourse, with their emphasis on comparisons – of La Réunion with other holidays, with other places, and with 'home'. And he was able to tease out the liminal status of some, who were between life changes and using the tour as a self-imposed rite of passage (Frey 1998; Graburn 1983b; Hastings 1988). He was sensitive to their discoveries of local nature and of Creole culture, which they found interesting as a contrast to their home experiences – but the differences from home were not beyond comprehension (Graburn 1983b), not overwhelmingly challenging. What they came for and found on the island was like a huge stage – or garden in this case – with staged performances and role-playing, for displaying nature and culture and ultimately their moral dimensions.

Picard was a participant with and for the tourists: he was their tour guide and driver, and, being German like them, was also a friend; he understood and was empathetic to the former East German, Ernest, learning from him about the explosion of emotion he experienced as he overcame the restrictions of life under Communism, lamenting 'How could they [the authorities] have prevented us from seeing … [the glories of creation such as this tropical isle]' – a burning question in Ernest's life. Later he visited their homes back in Germany, where he was able to witness the integration of their memories and their souvenirs in their ordinary lives (see Frey 2004). There he found post-tour rationalisations, and the reflexive retelling of narratives, propped by their souvenirs and photographs – for many their living rooms were almost shrines to the magic of their holidays; as MacCannell (1976) pointed out, for modern people, their homes are museums of their lives. And after their visits to the tropical islands, they managed to hang on to some of the magic powers that lingered on from the 'unreal' vacation to their real world and everyday life.

The problems of undertaking the ethnography of tourists are emblematic of much of contemporary ethnography (cf. Graburn 2002): these are people on the move, people who are not necessarily beholden to the anthropologist's authority, who may be in a hurry, on a honeymoon, or in an altered state of consciousness. To study them, one can choose to move with them on the tour (Graburn 1995; Bruner 2005), or to remain as the tourists pass by a key node in their journeys (Van den Berghe1994), or one can wait for them to come 'back home' (Harrison 2003) and unravel their experiences in retrospect. Picard was able to undertake all three. Another common barrier to the ethnography of tourism is funding, as many scientific funding agencies do not take the subject of tourism seriously; indeed, this is a key joke in David Lodge's (1991) satirical novel *Paradise News*, where an anthropologist travels to Hawaii to observe the crowded beaches.

This is a very accessible book. The author notes that he self-consciously pitched his language at the level of 'long reportage', much as one might read in the *New Yorker*. This command of English, David's third language, is remarkable but the need for a degree of reflexivity in the choice of words and phrases may be an advantage, one that he shares with some other well-known tourism researchers, such as Pierre Van den Berghe, Erik Cohen, Tom Selänniemi and Ning Wang. Tourism as a topic is immediately comprehensible to most readers, it is something that they are familiar with in their own lives, much as they would be with films, television or popular sports. And yet this very mundane quality may be one reason why anthropologists, formerly known for their explication of the esoteric or the familiarisation of the exotic, have until recently found it difficult to get research funding for this field.

Yet, reading the book makes one aware of the author's intellectual eclecticism; his extensive footnoting allows one to see the depths of his argument and his exploration of many fundamental fields within and beyond anthropology, reinforcing the unpopular notion that tourism phenomena are intimately bound up with the central concerns of anthropology (Leite and Graburn 2009) and the other social sciences. His sources are both classical literature and contemporary Euro-American anthropology, and quite often the internet too; this is quite appropriate for the study of such topics as (a) tourism, (b) imaginaries and the media, and (c) today's politics of culture. Picard draws upon and contributes to the related topics of history, cultural studies, the 'economics of desire', the sociocultural anthropology of the postcolonial and 'racial' relations, and political ecology.

The central topic is magic, the magic of tropical isles – the interesting history of magic (from Magi) and of tropical isles (and paradise). Picard reinforces the presence of magic in modernism and peoples' need for magic to counter the discontents of modernism. Modernism was supposed to be 'logical', controllable and capable of improving the world – yet tourism/leisure is necessary as a balance to these hopes not being realised (cf. Rosenbloom 2010).[1] Magic is needed to 'do the impossible' of ameliorating modern lives, and tourism is a form of leisure outside the mundane workaday world, in a place where the usual 'rules don't apply'. This use of the concept of magic is a reversal of nineteenth-century progressivism, such as evolutionary sociocultural anthropology (Tylor 1865 and Frazer 1894) in which it was seen as alterity and hence literally 'backward', a survival of an earlier stage.

These ritual reversals (Graburn 1983, 2002) are sought to balance what is missing – which of course, varies from person to person and throughout life. The leisure is temporally outside and tourism by definition is also spatially removed from the ordinary work/home context. The spatial separation is made more powerful by going 'overseas' which is by definition required to visit any island, and for the majority of tourists from the rich temperate 'northern' civilisations, going to 'the tropics' is another marked experiential reversal, a symbolic passage (*rite de passage* [Van Gennep 1961]), crossing boundaries between one status and another. This passage is felt more strongly when going by ship, and may be invisible by plane until the tourists hear the announcement of their imminent arrival and excitedly raise their window shades to see their destination emerge from the sea.

Picard carefully delineates the ritual performances of the visitors and the locals as they meet. Each has reason to be suspicious of the motives of the other but they need each other for the tourists to have that magical experience and for the locals to earn a living and to preserve pride in their way of life. The local Creole characters Orom and his uncle Laslo perform every day on their garden-stage maintaining a back stage in the unvisited parts of the house. 'Strangerhood' is part of the magic, with the characters being 'larger than life' or from 'another life'; Ohnuki-Tierney (1993) showed that in ancient Japan, especially on islands, guests or strangers engendered an ambivalent gaze: the stranger, known as *marebito* (wandering person), might have good or evil powers, so one had to beware and take care not to offend and be punished, in the hopes that one might be rewarded by the 'stranger-God'.

In the postcolonialism garden of Réunion, Picard explains, the formerly pathologised children of the island (considered unworthy of the purity of '*la Mère Patrie*'), whose speech, culture and cuisine were looked down upon, have grown up to form the Creole, admired as beautiful adults, with a now admired cuisine and culture. This ethnicisation of culture (which reversed the colonial hierarchy) elevates the Creole as the ideal target for tourism. At the same time, France remains a mirror, represented by tourists and officials, in which the Creole learn to see themselves, according to the aesthetics of the outside world. Diversity, decentralisation, and cultural self-determination have come to be fetishised. So the Creole are now endowed, imbued with enchantment (Selwyn 2007), with the magic by which the visitors get re-charged as they partake in their re-creation. This powerful trope is celebrated by the locals themselves, for example, through festivals which celebrate the end of slavery and the emergence of a 'free Creole life'.

Picard has chosen the garden as a master metaphor for reflecting on tourism and island life. As Marie-Francoise Lanfant supposed, the garden is a perfect metaphor for the cultivated, yet natural stage on which life and inter-cultural contacts are played out on the island, and of which they become part: the garden is both natural, with its flora and fauna, and cultural, a product of human design and control. And nowadays the concept of garden extends to the marine world too, played out in the degradation and protection of coral reefs in the new Parc Marin, but on a larger scale, with the realisation that the oceans themselves are gardens to be managed and protected from the 'wild' excesses of fishing in 'the commons'. The garden, as we have seen in the tourist-local performative dramas, is a contested space, a struggle between the dangerously untrammelled and the sterilely over-controlled. And the garden is the perfect exemplar of 'sustainable development', which has become the central focus of today's discourse of tourism development, which in turn is a microcosm of the future of the whole world.

Gardens are closely related to other sites of struggle, both about nature and between humans. Parks are a larger form of enclosure, originally set off to protect the rights of the nobility to continue hunting over the rights of the peasants to cultivate and poach, and this struggle became worldwide with the establishment of national parks in African and Asian colonies and in the American West (Aerni 1972). The same class struggles can be seen in the regulation of fishing in the lagoons of Réunion, where even French tourists may exercise their 'antidote to civilisation' by showing solidarity with the cause of the rebellious artisan fishermen. Cultivating gardens is horticulture, as opposed to agriculture. The former is smaller scale, involving aesthetic arrangements, multiple species and the inclusion of remnant trees from prior wilderness; it is associated with hands-on care and constant experimenting with inter-planting, hybridisation, the individual tending of tied domestic animals, and children's first experiments with the world outside the dwelling. The garden is for men and women, as well as for all ages, and it is the immediate precursor to foods, storage and textiles, with close connections to that other great human realm of the culturalisation of nature, cooking, which is itself a key part of tourist consumption and sometimes education. As Berque showed for the Japanese (1986), the garden is that part of the region, of nature, of the country, indeed of the universe, which human beings control. It is a miniature version of the outside world, and lends itself, through the power of aesthetic manipulation and the application of sympathetic magic, to the efforts of humans to bring beauty and stability to the flux of life and society. As a metaphor for human society, humans are cultivated like flowers, and in the tropical garden of Réunion, the Creole are cultivated to bloom in the theatrical garden of contemporary tourism.

Nelson Graburn

PREFACE

This book has been written over a period of several years. Most of the ethnographic findings were initially part of a Ph.D. dissertation in anthropology defended at the University of La Réunion in 2001 (under the supervision of Bernard Cherubini). Since then, I have had the opportunity to discuss these findings with many colleagues, friends and family and to challenge them with different theoretical frameworks. In 2001, Marie-Francoise Lanfant introduced me to the Research Committee on the Sociology of International Tourism (RC50) of the International Sociological Association and, during a memorable conference in Liège, Belgium, I first presented my ideas about tourism and gardening to a wider academic audience (among them Mike Robinson and Scott McCabe, who later became my colleagues). In the same year, Emmanuel Fauroux sponsored me as a postdoctoral researcher at the French Institute for Development Research (IRD) in Toliara, Madagascar and introduced me, among many other things, to the field of political ecology and the study of deforestation in Southwest Madagascar. From 2002, employed as a researcher at the Centre for Tourism and Cultural Change (CTCC) at Sheffield Hallam University and, from 2007, at Leeds Metropolitan University in the United Kingdom, I became acquainted with the interdisciplinary approaches of the emerging field of tourism studies. Major outputs of my work there have been published in three books co-edited with Mike Robinson: *Emotion in Motion: Tourism, Awe and Inner Journeys* (Picard and Robinson 2012), *The Framed World: Tourism, Tourists and Photography* (Robinson and Picard 2009) and *Festivals, Tourism and Social Change* (Picard and Robinson 2006), and several conference proceedings. In the autumn term of 2006, Nelson Graburn sponsored me as a visiting researcher at the Department of Anthropology at the University of California at Berkeley where I had the occasion to present and discuss my work – and to reconnect to anthropological theory. In 2008, I decided that it was time to actually write this book. I was, at the same time, painfully reminded about what a terribly unsociable person I become when concentrating on my thoughts. I started to see gardens everywhere and was lucky to have kind people around me who took me walking in the fields or drinking at the pub. The first draft of this book was sent to Marion Berghahn in January 2009. In September of the same year, I moved to Lisbon, Portugal, to start a new job at the Centre for

Research in Anthropology (CRIA), at New University of Lisbon. The manuscript was accepted in January 2010.

Throughout this book, I have adopted a style of writing similar to the journalistic genre of long reportage, which may seem unusual for many anthropologists (one reviewer of an earlier draft found this style unacceptable for an ethnographic monograph), but which makes the text more accessible and engaging. The approach I have adopted focuses on individual social actors whose 'characters' evolve in various fields of tourism in the Indian Ocean island of La Réunion. The core of the ethnographic data was collected in this island between 1995 and 2002 while I was living and studying there, and complemented through fieldwork trips carried out in 2003, 2005, 2006 and 2007 (after starting work in the UK). To generate data, I have employed classical ethnographic methods (long-term participant observation and social immersion in the life of the social actors and contexts studied), semiotic and historical studies of various cultural productions (e.g. policies, planning strategies, built environments, museum displays, artworks, stories, gardens, landscapes, etc.) and life history methods based on repeated, open interviews, historical study, and biographical research.

This book is dedicated to my close family, Christa, Christof, Christine, Georg, Robert, Julian, Katrin, Leo, Valentin. I would also like to thank the many people whose thoughts, contradictions, and beauty inspired me, who gave constructive feedback, proofread my interpretations of the French and English language, offered me their friendship, solidarity and love, and joined in with the bad and silly jokes I made – in roughly historical order: Marie-Françoise, David, Jean, Marie-Reine, Sandrine, Jean-François and Raymonde Moutama, Michel Tixier, Peter Hody, Guillaume Samson, Laurent Niollet, Valerie Lilette, Patricia de Bollivier, Nicolas Theuma, Bernard Cherubini, Patrick Manoro, Marie La Pause, Gilles Pignon, George Lafable, Marie-Françoise Lanfant, Emmanuel Fauroux, Mike Robinson, Phil Long, Josef Ploner, Lia Philcox, Claire Dix, Carmen Pardo, Alessia Ruggiero, Nicolas Crouzet, Valerio and Hisako Simoni, Fabian Frenzel, Scott McCabe, Dorothea Meyer, Nelson Graburn, Sally Ness, Edward Bruner, Stephanie M. Hom, Naomi Leite, Alexis Bunten, Jenna Phillips, Christian Ghasarian, Pamila Gupta, Arianna Giovannini, Donata Marletta, Camila del Marmol, Simone Abram, Noel Salazar, Charlotte Terrapon, Sioned Pearce, Saskia Cousin, Jeanette Atkinson, Jackie Waldren, Marion Berghahn, Dean MacCannell, João de Pina-Cabral, Maria Cardeira da Silva, Anabel Roig, Dominik Metz and Catarina Moreira.

While this book has been written as an entirely new piece of academic work, earlier interpretations of the ethnographic data used have been presented to academic conferences or published as journal articles or book chapters. The key ideas of the Introduction have been presented at the EASA conference in Ljubljana, Slovenia in July 2008 and at a LAIOS/EHESS seminar in Paris, France in November 2008. Earlier interpretations of the data used in Chapter 1 have been presented at *Eyes Across the Water*, an Indian Ocean studies conference at the

University of the Witwatersrand, South-Africa in 2007 (Picard 2010a). An earlier version of Chapter 2 has been published as 'Through Magical Flowers' in S. Moorthy and A. Jamal's edited *Indian Ocean Studies: Cultural, Social, and Political Perspectives* (Picard 2009a). An earlier version of Chapter 4 has been published in French, as 'La relation à l'étranger à La Réunion' in Christian Ghasarian's edited *Anthropologies de La Réunion* (Picard 2008a). An earlier version of Chapter 5 has been presented to the ISA RC50 interim conference in Lesbos, Greece (Picard 2004) and a conference on tourism in French overseas territories at the University of La Réunion in 2005. It has also been published in Italian, as *Giardinaggio creolo: turismo e resistenza culturale nell'isola della riunione*, in Chiara Cipollari's edited *Scenari turistici. Sguardi antropologici sulle località turistiche* (Picard 2009b). Earlier versions of Chapter 6 have been published as 'La fable des coraux' (Picard 2005) in Bernard Cherubini's edited *Le Territoire littoral* and as an article, 'Coral Garden Economics', in *Etudes créoles* (Picard 2008b). Earlier versions of Chapter 8 have been published as 'Gardening the Past and Being in the World' in my and Mike Robinson's edited *Festivals, Tourism and Social Change* (Picard 2006). Finally, different earlier versions of Chapter 8 have been presented to the ISA Interim Conference in Liège, Belgium in 2001, the University of California, Berkeley's Tourism Studies Working Group conference, *Advances in Travel Theory*, in 2005 and the annual conference of the Association of Social Anthropologists of the United Kingdom and Commonwealth (ASA) in London, United Kingdom, in 2007 (Picard 2010b).

I will be happy to receive feedback on the ideas developed in this book and the style adopted. Please contact me through my website www.piccccc.com or through Berghahn Books.

Introduction
Penguins in the Paris Underground

Paris, France, March 2006. An early morning in an underground station. Odours of soap, perfume, cleaning products and old sweat were hanging in the air. The platform was filled with commuters in dark overcoats and greyish winter outfits. I had sat down in a plastic chair fixed to the wall and stared at a billboard on the opposite side, above the rails. A man was playing golf on top of a shoreline flooded in warm sunlight. There was a text that explained, in French, that 'there is an island where the sun remains faithful in every season'. It was an advertisement by the Cyprus Tourist Board. The train arrived and I rushed into the cabin. It accelerated abruptly. People were not talking, not even whispering. Some were reading magazines. I held on to a metal pole. The train's brakes made a squealing noise. A bodiless sound came out of somebody's earphones. My eyes were searching for familiar forms. They were caught by a small poster hanging from the cabin's ceiling. Three penguins were walking towards the lower edge of an ice-berg. The ice-berg was floating in turquoise waters under a bright blue sky, near a palm-tree fringed white sandy beach. The text was an invitation to 'Change the air!' (*Changez d'air!*). The penguins were about to leave their icy 'ship' to board a tropical island. It was a photo-montage advertising the World Tourism Salon that was to take place in Paris later that month. I reached the station where I had to change trains and got off. Caught up in the flow of people, I passed through different brightly lit tunnels and eventually arrived at another platform. I was almost alone. There was another billboard behind the blue plastic seats of the platform. It showed an aerial shot of a chain of arid mountain tops emerging from valleys filled with dark blue water. They looked like islands in a large sea. The image was superimposed with the words 'Snapshots of serenity' (*Instantané de sérénité*), printed in capital letters in the centre, and 'Croatia. The Mediterranean rediscovered' (*Croatie. La Méditerranée retrouvée*) in the lower right corner. It was an advertisement from the Croatian Tourist Board. I was standing there, freezing, thinking about why I have to be here when there are places out there of eternal sunshine, of serenity, with white sandy beaches fringed by turquoise water and a bright blue sky. While I did not think of myself in terms of a penguin, I must have looked very much like one.

This random sample of tourism advertisements in the Paris underground brings to the surface one of the most striking, yet, paradoxically, academically most obsessively ignored facets of modern culture: the idea that tourism can give access to a fantastic, somehow symbolically elevated realm out there. Many of the works developed in the relatively young field of tourism anthropology show that the aesthetics of such a realm also comes up in various other tourism advertisements and therefore seems to stem from a more generic underlying paradigm. Most texts used to advertise or otherwise visualise tourist destinations are, indeed, quite explicit about the idea that tourism is able to 'transform' tourists, to have an impact on their body, to allow them to reconnect to 'what really is important in their life', to rediscover 'nature' and search – and hopefully find – 'their soul'. If the people who create such texts mobilise a similar set of images that, in their understanding of the public to be addressed, best invoke the essence of tourism, then these may indicate the existence of what Roland Barthes (1957) called a 'significant consciousness'[1] among the audience addressed, e.g. mainly Western populations that represent by far the largest proportion of global island tourists. It may indicate that these images are able to appeal to an effectively shared 'collective' imaginary about, and desire for, places out there that are capable of changing the nature of life, of transforming the body, of rejuvenating the person, of 'recharging the batteries'. It may indicate that they are able to evoke what essentially is a form of 'magic'.

Approach

Here is a major paradox whose internal contradictions and – external – consequences I would like to explore in this book. While claiming a progress- and transparency-seeking rational as one of the guiding principles of modern life, Western society seems to institute firmly, at the same time, the idea of places-out-there imbued with quasi-magical qualities. In this sense, 'magic', which in Western society has long been considered to be the 'superstition' or the potentially dangerous supernatural power of others,[2] effectively seems to expose itself as a constitutive element of modernist thinking and the forms of social life it has shaped. Accessing such 'magic' by means of touristic travel seems crucial to maintain and renew that which legitimates the moral and political order of modern life. And this comes not only as an intellectual escapist fantasy by socially alienated literature students, but as one of the politically and socially most powerful institutions cultivated as part of modern culture and social life: tourism. How is such 'magic' being conceived, produced, maintained, renewed, exchanged, and made accessible, through tourism? What *is* 'magic' and how does it relate to the other grand paradigms of Western modernity, e.g. that of 'beauty', 'truth', 'goodness', 'liberty'? What roles and qualities does the projection of 'magic' confer to touristic 'destinations' and the people inhabiting them? How can it inform our understanding of the contemporary world and the forms of order through which it maintains itself? How does that work, when people and places become 'elevated' as tourist attractions, when what often has been considered as ugly or worthless in the past is aesthetically transfigured and elevated as a 'magical' realm and object of collective desire and aspiration?

In order to approach these broad questions in more depth, I focus my attention here on the particular case of one 'destination', the tropical island of La Réunion in the Western Indian Ocean. I arrived on this island in 1995, at first motivated by a paradigm of exoticism, adventure and discovery. Initially pursuing undergraduate studies in economics at the University of La Réunion in Saint-Denis, I later discovered anthropology and, subsequently, followed a postgraduate and then doctoral programme in this discipline. Eventually, I stayed on the island until 2002 and have, since then, regularly returned to see friends and update my data. As a result of the length of this stay, and my ongoing social immersion in various social milieus on the island, I achieved a deep degree of cultural intimacy, both privately and as part of organised ethnographic fieldwork. I was living in conditions similar to those of many people in La Réunion, fighting the same struggles, enjoying the same events, discussing the same politics, sitting in the same backyards, eating the same food, making the same jokes, enacting to a large degree the same social performances. At the same time, I remained an outsider, a *zoreil*, and I was reminded almost daily that this constitutes a particular, largely ambivalent role within local society. My family name, which by historical coincidence is very common among some of the rural populations in the interior of the island, often helped to overcome antagonisms; indeed many people approached me, not without humour, in terms of a distant cousin. Also, being German – and not French – helped me to escape the all-too-simple analogies made, within much of the local common sense, between the origins of people and what they are made to represent. In this sense, I was not, or was considered to a lesser degree, an 'arrogant' *métropolitain* (French mainlander) who was admired, on the one hand, as a model of reference and modernity, while on the other hand being rejected as an agent of the 'neo-colonial order'. Being there, living there, I was, of course, not a neutral observer but affected the social environments in which I lived and which I observed. I always believed that this form of agency worked to my advantage, as being part of the research setting allowed me, among others, to observe means and strategies directed towards myself as a particular type of stranger. At the same time, my permanence as a subjective and socially implicated observer generated a form of solid and relatively objective research frame; as a person talented with sensibility and a sense of aesthetic judgement, I became a kind of apparatus to observe, frame and judge reality.

Theoretical Aspirations

In this book, I wish to explore two main ideas. The first relates to the relationship between 'magic' and modernity, and how this manifests itself, in particular, in the field of tourism. The first chapter of the book takes up the challenge of this theoretical problem. Anthropology has, so far, neither explained how the personal experience of the touristic journey relates to public culture images and narratives of tourist attractions, in particular the quasi-omnipresent claim to 'magic', nor has it explained how tourism helps tourists to maintain and recreate themselves as modern subjects.[3] This first chapter is based on a systematic observation of tourists travelling through La Réunion. Taking on the role of tourist guide, I was able, as much as was logistically possible, to observe tourism as it happens on a daily base and in a normal setting. I developed relationships with many of the tourists I guided and revisited them back at their homes in Europe. Through ongoing exchanges and conversations, we dialogically worked towards the generation of an understanding about what tourism means to them and what it means at a more abstract level. This was a very enriching experience, both for me and – I do hope – also for my interlocutors. This first chapter is somehow distinguished from the rest of the book, which will focus on the transformations that tourism brings about in various social contexts in La Réunion. Yet it is important, as it will provide an epistemic anchor in that it suggests an explanation for how 'magic' relates to the grand paradigms of modernist thinking – beauty, truth, goodness, freedom, etc. – and the forms of social life shaped through tourism, in tropical islands in particular.

In the rest of the book, I will focus on the challenges presented by the modernist ontology of magic to the social lives and self-understanding of people living in the island of La Réunion. The case of this tropical island provides a good basis from which to study such challenges. Historically, for example, during the European Renaissance, representations of islands such as La Reunion have been formative of Western representations of paradise as a delightful tropical garden (Grove 1995). Merging various Golden Age myths described in ancient, classical and modern religious texts and the dream worlds depicted in Western Orientalist and Exoticist art, tropical islands became widely common tropes enabling tourists to indulge in ideas of original purity and authentic condition beyond time and history. Paradoxically, in a more recent context marked by the emergence of global tourism cultures, many tropical islands were being re-formatted in terms of the very representations they initially served as a model for. Through international development policy, the expansion of touristic infrastructures and spatial gentrification programmes, they were frequently re-'tropicalised' (Thompson 2006) and thus made to inhabit a generic Western model defining what a tropical island should look and feel like. In this sense, it may seem that the populations living inside such tropical islands had rather little agency over the form that their integration to the global tourism economy would take.

The second idea I would like to get at in this book is that of a 'global gardening state' (developed in the third part). The idea here is relatively simple once again. I will suggest that the long-standing and widely common practice of contemplative gardening – cultivating miniaturised models of the world, invoking and thus bringing into being ideas of a wider cosmos, working with mimetic or metonymic matter related to such a cosmos – has flowed into the realms of international policy making and tourism development in particular. I will argue that entire inhabited spaces – islands, regions, deserts, city centres, mountains – are 'gardened' through a post-national form of governance. They are gardened as living artworks within a global modernity, invoking and thus bringing to life the grand modernist paradigms of beauty, nature and time. In a context of agronomic crisis in which the colonial cash crop economies that hitherto defined the economic life of most of these islands can no longer provide sufficient subsistence, the latter are transformed into large contemplative gardens within a new realm of world society. They become cultivated as 'human gardens' within a tourism specific form of modern world system; a fair ground in which a global middle class meets, parties, resources itself and recreates the symbolic order of their worlds.

Through the focus on different social actors in La Réunion and the changing contexts in which their lives evolve, the core chapters of the book will explore how the models and logic of such a 'gardening state' are implemented on the island; how they create conflict by challenging cultural practices and the aesthetic of everyday life; how they generate new forms of exclusion and of inclusion; and how they integrate the island and its populations into the framework of a global modernity. I will show that, from the perspective of 'destinations' such as La Reunion, the touristic attribution of 'magic' does in no way constitute what Marcel Mauss (Karsenti and Mauss 1994) defined as a total social fact, but rather a messy field of contacts within a global ethnoscape,[4] with some clearly established shared symbols and carefully maintained boundaries.[5] I shall argue that embracing and indigenising the – initially exogenous – idea of 'magic' becomes a means for a variety of local social actors in La Réunion to claim participation in a wider 'modernity'. However, the social realms, whence such claims originate, remain for the most part separated. As I will show in the chapters in the second part of this book, they remain governed by a largely resilient logic of 'giving a good image' in public while attempting to create links with what people consider to be 'influential strangers'. Though at a very different scale, gardening plays here, once again, an important role, both in communicating an image of order and participation, and in enticing (touristic) strangers, which, in turn, become a means of social participation within the realms of local social life.

Tourism, Magic and Modernity

Moral categories of authenticity, beauty and nature (as presumably unconditional, somehow divine) often remain basic ontological premises upon which many religious but also social science approaches are build (existentialist quest for the real; search for symmetry and its associations with moral values; search into elementary principals of social life by the structuralists).[6] To recognise and theoretically engage with the omnipresence of claims of magic in tourism, we had to wait for the deconstruction of such notions. It seems today quite obvious that all politico-spiritual formations (including the 'established' religions, mysticist and other proto-religious movements) employ similar techniques in order to maintain and renew order and identity. They all appear to use invocation, mimesis, transfiguration and metonymy to enhance chance, effect reality, and maintain selfhood.[7] In many ways, such techniques have previously been considered either as 'religious', when employed by recognised 'religious' institutions such as the church, or stigmatised as 'magical' or 'heretic' when emanating from 'other' or alternative religious movements or practices. Recognising the, by and large, similitude of such techniques both in terms of their approach and their underlying ontology, magic can no longer define the 'superstition' of others and, corollary, the moral superiority of a self but, in a much more useful way, that what generates the very common propensity of humans to 'accord beings and things beyond their immediate community a definite place in its reproduction' (Sahlins 1994: 387). Many anthropologists and historians have observed that the attribution of magical qualities and powers usually emerges from the uncertainty that marks situations of social contact and distance. In this sense, magic is frequently attributed to a social other located beyond the immediate here and now of a person, place or community: a spirit, a stranger, a God, an alien object, a distanced place, a past or a future, a person of different gender or social status. Following this observation, the conception of 'magical' qualities seems related to the ontological work of creating and maintaining separations and distance between a relative self and other.[8] The general question underlying the study of 'magic', therefore, must be concerned with the way in which the 'authenticity' of distance and ontological difference is socially construed, and in which it is – convincingly – manipulated to maintain or transform specific forms of order and selfhood. In Marshall Sahlins' words (1994: 387), it must be concerned with the ways in which societies mobilise the attributes and qualities of divinities or enemies, ancestors or affines as a necessary condition of their own existence.

Acknowledging the fluid nature of the human condition and of those institutions formed to organise social life,[9] magic can thus be resurrected as an analytical category which finds its epistemological foundations in the social (and historical) phenomenology of perception developed in Edward Husserl's early work (1964) on formations of subjectivity and subjectively perceived life-worlds. It is not primarily important here to explain why certain practices – invocations of 'magic' through stories and images, collection of relics and other souvenir objects, material contact with attractions, etc. – do work for specific social actors, or to decry them as 'tricks', as many classical authors have previously done.[10] In line with classical phenomenology, the approach instead needs to adopt what has recently been defined as 'existential' (Jackson 1998) and also as 'reverse' (Kirsch 2006) anthropology. It needs to be interested in the political, demographic and ecological contexts from which – in this case – tourism and its underlying symbolic universes emerge, and within which they are maintained. It thus needs to be interested in the type of historical ethnography developed by authors such as Edward Said (1979), Marshall Sahlins (1994), Maurice Bloch (1986), Michael Jackson (1998) and David Graeber (2007), demonstrating how different social entities and collectively held subjectivities have been formed as a result of historical contact, cross-appropriations, and processes of innovation and fetishisation, and how these are reproduced, maintained or transformed in the contemporary context.

A historical anthropology of 'modernity' seems a rather 'gourmand' project. Yet, I believe it is not impossible if the focus is placed on some of the structural continuities that seem to underpin modernist thinking. In this context, despite widely diverging epistemic perspectives and aspirations,[11] most historians, sociologists and anthropologists seem to agree that the historic formations of modern societies stem from, or, at least, were accompanied by, the emergence of a specifically modernist aesthetic of the human condition which was to deeply penetrate the order and organisation of everyday life in the Western world. This aesthetic is usually considered to be based upon a symbolic separation between 'culture' and 'nature', both in terms of ontological and moral entities. According to this aesthetic, culture is thought of as growing out of an unconditional *ur*-nature.[12] It thus appears to be seen as conditional, in that it describes the consequences of a human choice to cultivate oneself in order to reach a higher state of enlightenment and to 'go towards perfection'.[13] This modernist aesthetic seems to take on cosmological qualities in that it provides an allegorical explanation for the origins of the world and a morally charged concept for reflecting on time, social separations and the future. It explains nature as a condition and realm that is detached from culture and that is, simultaneously, within culture, as an *ur*-condition of culture. The story of the 'initial' separation between culture and nature implies a morally charged aesthetic of time as 'history'. Theodor Lessing (1983 [1919]), whose writings were largely forgotten after he was killed by Nazi agents in 1933, stresses that 'history' is not about a positive truth, but about diverging political claims regarding the order of the present and the future. According to his observation, various political stakeholders, in attempting to 'make sense' of history, merely use past events to construct a 'historical' narrative whose underlying 'rational' is to approve specific political and philosophical claims about the human condition and the society of the future.[14] Yet, he concludes, despite the ideological differences underlying these different historical narratives, the idea that culture (in the present) grows out of a somehow more 'natural' *ur*-condition in the past remains as the overarching, widely hegemonic aesthetic of modernist conceptions of time. A wide range of authors have demonstrated how this specific model and its underpinning moral frameworks have been used to make sense of other separations marking modern society, e.g. the separation of the male from the female, of children from adults, of working classes from noble classes, of pasts from presents, of Europe from the rest of the world, of humans from gods. In each case, the separation between one and the other seems symbolically embedded in a relationship between an 'authentic' *ur*-condition and a 'historical' condition defined in terms of various historical 'logics', e.g. those of humanisation, progress and, also, disenchantment. 'Magic', as a way of affecting the 'normal' occurrence of reality (usually thought of in terms of cause-and-effect relationships), is here generally attributed to a relative 'other', mainly those described as 'being closer to', or 'in contact with', a presumed *ur*-condition of nature, e.g. women, children, Gods, spirits, priests, strangers, 'indigenous people', 'mad' artists, etc.

However, it seems to me that such ontological separations not only fashion and maintain boundaries enabling us to think about a relative 'self' and 'other' (as the cultural and postcolonial critics of the 1980s and 1990s have put it), but that they also constitute a phenomenon of mutual co-constitution. In Julia Kristeva's terms (1991), the uncanny qualities of the respective other do not only lead to the self, as Sigmund Freud (2003) suggested, but are actively cultivated and maintained as constitutive parts of the self. In this sense, the 'self' is sacralised through the embodiment of qualities and beings a priori situated outside an immediate here and now (Csordas 1997). As with the surreal figures developed in Jorge Luis Borghes' writings,[15] one and the other thus form a whole. They 'bewitch' (Cyrulnik 1997) each other, colonise and affect each other, possess and become part of each other, and cannot live without each other.[16] Roger Caillois (1950) and George Bataille (1988), and also some more recent commentators – for instance Victor Turner (1969), Maurice Bloch (1992), or Thomas Csordas (1997) – describe how such ontological differences and the political and moral order of selfhood, society and the cosmos they entail are maintained and renewed by means of festively embedded ritual transgressions. Through contact, invocation, the symbolic recreation of a presumed 'initial' condition and ceremonial re-enactments of the violence believed to have marked the 'initial' separations, such ritual transgressions appear to allow various social actors to reaffirm and maintain orders of social life. What legitimates order eventually always seems to relate to a power or 'force' stemming from an 'other' (Sahlins 1994), a past, a God, a distanced place. While this phenomenon has been abundantly observed in many societies studied by anthropologists, it has only recently been picked up by anthropologists studying modern society.[17] Tourism, travel, and hospitality provide here privileged social fields in which to study this phenomenon.

Dean MacCannell was one of the first authors to suggest a comprehensive theoretical study of tourism in terms of a modern social practice. In his still influential book, *The Tourist* (1976), he develops an approach of tourism in terms of a ritual, which he sees in its structure as being analogous to those observed by anthropologists in other contexts. For MacCannell (1999), modern tourism is motivated by a quest for 'authenticity' which is a classical concept that anthropologists had previously been observing, in various forms, in different contexts around the world (Frazer 1911; Malinowski 1992; Levi-Strauss 1966; Sahlins 1968; Fabian 1983; Delumeau 1992). MacCannell stresses that the concept of authenticity entails a particular moral order of modernity, specifically a particular relation to time and the idea of a 'lost' condition. According to MacCannell, tourism gives access to sites believed to have been 'preserved' from historical contact with the First World and thus being capable of bringing concepts of authenticity alive.[18] They function as attractions that, similar to the relic shrines venerated by Christian pilgrims (Turner and Turner 1978), bring alive and renew the moral foundations and cosmological order of modern society. For other authors working in the same vein, tourism is seen as having the capacity to connect the touring to the grand narratives and symbols of modernity, and to insert itself in the rhythms of production that mark modern social life (Urry 1990). For Nelson Graburn (1977), it constitutes a 'sacred journey' to a realm outside everyday life from which tourists come home 'recharged', renewed. For Christof Hennig (1999), tourism constitutes a festive time-space bringing tourists in contact with various 'sacred' realms of modernity, the 'arts', 'cultural heritage', 'nature', 'wild people'. Eric Cohen (2004a) and Tim Edensor (1998) nuance this proposal, describing various 'types' of tourists who, while being driven by different motivations and following different paths of tourism, remain 'moved' by similar types and sites of attraction. Stephanie Melia Hom (2004) explains this 'being moved' in terms of ephemeral 'tourist moments' during which tourists experience both psychologically and culturally embedded epiphanies; the deep emotion of 'connecting' to an 'authentic' realm, a 'common humanity', the 'beauty' of artworks, the 'forces' of nature, the 'magic' of famous places, the 'injustice' of difference, the 'loss' of youth, the 'magnificence' of the human condition.

These different approaches indicate that tourism has brought about widely shared cultural patterns that transcend individuals and have agency over them. And such patterns can be studied. At the same time, while tourism may seem a 'mass' phenomenon, most tourists do it in small groups or on their own. Anthropology has not yet explained here the tension between the attraction of public symbols and personal experiences in tourism, in particular the 'magic' certain places seem to exert on tourists before and during the journey and in the post-tourist context. Many authors seem content with the idea of tourism as a form of 'visual consumption', as if tourists, while on tour, were absorbing those images that initially were used to represent the places visited. As I will show, visual images may well attract or guide tourists to specific sites, yet they do not constitute attractions in themselves. Once on site, tourists are not moved by the pre-existing image, per se, in itself, but by the emotion triggered by the very site. The approach of tourism in terms of images may well explain the 'cartographic infrastructure' of their moving in and out of sites, but not the emotion generated by the material realms of the tour. Magic, approached from a phenomenological perspective, will provide here a better explanation of the emotions triggered by, and the forms of order mediated through, tourism. Before approaching the consequences of tourism in the specific context of La Réunion and the form of order it generates at a wider global scale, I, therefore, first suggest an approach to what actually happens when tourists 'do' tourism (Chapter 1).

Cultivating the Human Garden

Most of this study, then, will focus on La Réunion, an island in the South-Western Indian Ocean, first settled by French colons during the seventeenth century. During the nineteenth and twentieth centuries, La Réunion became an important cash crop colony marked by extensive sugar cane plantations and the settlement of colonials, forced labourers and contracted workers from Europe and the wider Indian Ocean region. It was transformed into a French overseas department (DOM) in 1946. During the Cold War, the French government and its local representatives institutionalised what Francoise Vergès (1999) calls a 'colonial family romance', metaphorically identifying the people of La Réunion as children of the French *mère-patrie*. According to this author, the rationale of this narrative implies that the Réunions were given the values of the French republic as a gift – leaving them in a condition of impossible reciprocity. France became a mythified white mother, whose goodness and pureness could never be achieved by its 'ugly' children, seen as degenerated as a result of endogamy and the mixing of races and cultures. The narrative was mobilised both inside the island to poeticise class divisions between *Grands Blancs* (mainly White land owners) and a large creolised proletariat, and between the island as a whole and the far away French 'motherland'. In this context, deviations from cultural ideals associated with the French republican model (related to kinship, gender roles, language, humour, arts, diseases, drug consumption, etc.) were actively pathologised by colonial agents and local elites, who, in turn, gained their political legitimacy by referring to these agents and 'France' as their model. A certain idea of France was consequently widely appropriated through forms of mimesis and metonymy. The relative 'magic' – a kind of 'reverse magic'[19] associated with the former coloniser – that seemed to stem from the wearing of French style clothes, the adapting of French style ways of talking, behaving and eating, the living in French style houses, the adopting of French leisure fashions, etc. became and, as we will see, largely remains today a powerful social means of establishing and legitimating political power and participating in the contemporary social worlds within the island.

The transformation of the island into a 'tropical island', willingly embraced by various social actors inside the island may be understood in these terms. As I will show throughout the remaining chapters of the book, 'being' a tropical island becomes seen as a means, at various social scales, of participating in modernity. Yet, the specific aesthetic of 'tropical islands' mobilised here to reconfigure the spaces and self-understanding of the islanders was not invented in La Réunion, but within the colonial and postcolonial realms of French and global modernity. According to Jean Delumeau (1992), this aesthetic finds its roots in pre-biblical idealisations of 'happy islands' ('*Iles Fortunées*'), which later merged with biblical visions of the Garden of Eden leading to the widespread belief in an earthly existence of paradisiacal islands. Throughout Western intellectual history, ideas of Eden or Eden-like islands, or islands that have been close to an 'original' Eden, have been cyclically revitalised through artworks, literature, pleasure gardens, TV series, tourism advertisements, fun parks, children toys, carnival costumes, nature conservation programmes and journeys through touristic island realms (Delumeau 1992; Crouch, Jackson and Thomson 2005). Nowadays, tropical islands remain one of the most cherished places-to-go in the pantheon of modern tourist destinations.[20] Their tourism-related aesthetic maintains a striking structural analogy with the initial descriptions of the Garden of Eden in *Genesis*, the first book of the Old Testament in the Bible. Similar to the biblical text, it evokes the idea of a time- and sorrow-less garden of blissful delight in which humankind endures in a condition of eternal spring, a garden walled off against the desert of the ocean, with a fountain forming rivers that bathe the land and produce fruits that are always ripe; an *ur*-garden guarded and gardened by a 'first' form of humankind. This tourism-specific model usually reduces tropical islands to a set of core signs, e.g. a 'lush', 'exuberant' and 'pure' nature, blooming flowers, clear water pools and rejuvenating sources, unspoiled white beaches and abundant platters of fruit and seafood that offer themselves for consumption, beautiful autochthones singing and dancing, or using rudimentary equipment to fish or work the ground. The observation of this analogy between the Christian myth of Eden and the widely generic model underlying modern island tourism indicates that tropical islands such as La Réunion are not just 'out there', as marginal cash crop providing peripheries of the modern world system, but have long been, and continue to be, formative of a global modernity within which they have been made to inhabit and act out a highly symbolic role.

Chapters two and three explore the processes of aesthetic transfigurations – social and moral processes by means of which the ugly becomes beautiful – that the island and islanders undergo in the tourism contact zone. Adapting a concept initially developed by Jacques Lacan (1966),[21] I will focus here on the triangular communicative logic of what I call a 'cultural' mirror stage triggered by the tourist gaze. Through the observations of a tourist guide and a museum project, I will show that this 'mirror stage' brings into play three types of social actors. Tourists and the tourist gaze seem to work here as a form of mirror in which local tourist agents candidly become aware of an island self-defined in terms of a 'beautiful', 'magical' place inhabited by 'beautiful', 'magical' people. This process of self-realisation takes place in the eyes of a wider island society, observing and reaffirming this newly discovered self. Performing 'magic' and 'beauty' for tourists thus becomes a way to 'give a good image' and to claim participation within the emerging public spheres of local society. In chapters three and four, I will deepen the understanding of these processes by focusing on the cultural logic and the often frictitious consequences of hospitality in La Réunion. Following the romantic relationship of a mixed couple, chapter four will observe the consequences of love in the context of inter-cultural contact – the struggles and challenges, and the new forms of social life it generates. Chapter five will explore a similar relationship, but at a wider institutional level; it will follow a tourist site development project led by a group of villagers who face the challenges of French environmental policy and spatial planning paradigms. Chapter six will further explore the issues emanating from this specific type of contact zone; it will focus on different paradigms of nature of, and the conflicts between, the different stakeholders involved in a project to transform the island's coral reef into a nature preserved area. 'Magical' and 'beautiful' in the eyes of the newly emerging middle classes and the institutional stakeholders of the French establishment, coral reefs remain an economic resource base for local fishing populations. In a context marked by an overwhelmingly dominant global environmentalist lobby and widely asymmetrical power relations in the local context, the fishing populations eventually get tagged as poachers. Chapter seven explores how such economic and social ruptures are socially negotiated. It follows a festive event in a former fishing village, showing how the theme of this event, the abolition of slavery, works as an allegory for these populations to make sense of, and express their feelings towards, these recent changes. Chapter eight will return to the initial premises of tropical island tourism and question what kind of society this type of tourism generates at the global scale. It will develop more fully the idea of a 'global gardening state' as a political form to govern and cultivate large inhabited spaces as 'human gardens'.

Part I

Aesthetic Transfigurations

Chapter 1
Tourism and Magic

Killing Ceausescu on a Volcanic Caldera

Tears were running down Ernest's cheek. He murmured: 'They would have let us die without allowing us to see all these treasures, this splendid nature.' After a brief pause he added, furiously, in a now louder, tear-stricken voice: 'We should have done what the Romanians did with Ceausescu.' His face was all red. He was short of breath and sweating. He looked at me without saying a word, then returned his gaze to the volcanic plain. He took two photographs and slowly went back to the bus. It was around half past eight. The morning sun was shining in a bright blue sky illuminating the land in warm golden colours. I had parked the bus on a ridge above a wide sandy plain, about two kilometres before arriving at the main site of the volcano. The tourists had gone out to gaze over the empty land. As with so many I had seen before, they had not talked much. A couple had held hands and exchanged a kiss. Others had taken photographs. All had seemed as usual. Yet, Ernest's reaction that day left me puzzled. While I had gotten used to the tourists' reactions, their silences, their 'ahs' and 'ohs', the awe in their eyes when confronted with certain sites, I did not understand how, in Ernest's case, the experience of being 'here' would trigger associations with memories of seemingly far-off events like those of the recent political history of Romania.[1] Back in the bus, while I was slowly driving down into the valley, Ernest asked, again and again, merely rhetorically, how anyone could prevent people from 'seeing such beauty?' I did not think that he expected an answer. The other tourists in the group remained silent, obviously irritated by his emotions. A woman who was travelling with him, a work colleague, gave him a paper tissue. Ernest wiped his face and became quiet. We soon arrived at the parking area of the site and disembarked.

That day, after arriving at our hotel in the evening, Ernest invited me to have a beer with him before dinner. We sat outside on a porch, beside the hotel's swimming pool and gazed at the sunset. He apologised for his 'emotional reaction' in the morning and explained that he did not want to 'embarrass' the other guests.

He told me that he was from Eastern Germany. During the day, he had talked a lot about how Eastern Germany was 'before' and 'after' the fall of the Berlin Wall (in 1989). He explained how much he regretted the 'loss of social cohesion' after the German reunification in 1991, the 'intrusion of capitalism' and 'brand marketing', the 'uncertainty' of 'whether people would keep their jobs', the 'generalised feeling of incertitude' that would 'now' (in 1999) define life. We finished the beer and ordered another one. His travel partner joined us. Ernest said that, 'however', he could not 'stand' people who 'glorify the past'. 'Despite some good things, it was terrible,' he said. He told me stories about the 'terror' that marked the former regime, how the East German state security service (*Staatssicherheitsdienst* or '*Stasi*') infiltrated groups of friends and work environments.

His travel partner was left behind as a child when her parents fled over the border to West Germany. She grew up in care homes and was not allowed to join or even contact her parents. She told me that when she grew older, she tried to get in touch with her parents anyway, was caught and spent time in prison. She was told she would never again see her own children, who were put in care homes. She was later given a flat in a tower block beside a highway crossing where she still lived. Ernest told me the *Stasi* was a 'state mafia' working for its own profit, using forms of psychological terror to alienate people that 'stood in its way'. As part of this terror, he explained, they used the threat of granting or not granting travel visas. The *Stasi* and their friends and clientele travelled to the Crimea and even Cuba. They had a saying in East Germany, he told me: 'seeing the Antilles once, and then die'. His face became furious again and he reiterated his reference to Ceausescu and what happened in Romania. He said, 'we should have killed them all.'

Ernest's emotional reaction challenges many assumptions made in recent tourism theory. It seems to indicate that tourists are not solemnly looking out for signs of specific attractions while on the tour, like a doctor would look for symptoms indicative of a disease, as John Urry phrased it in his influential book, *The Tourist Gaze* (1990). Images merely seem to lead tourists to an attraction, but they are not, in themselves, the attraction. Attractions, once tourists are on site, seem to exert their 'magic' independently from how they are represented in the pre- or post-tourism context, leaving tourists in a state of shock and awe. They seem to have a psychological impact that largely remains invisible to the outside observer, but that seems key to any understanding of what makes tourism such an important phenomenon of modern culture. We can certainly look at tourists who all appear much the same, and make jokes about them, as generations of researchers have done before us, without having an idea about the worlds that are crumbling behind their awe-filled eyes and silent faces. Yet, taking tourism seriously means overcoming our academic snobbery and trying to understand what is going on when people – and that includes us – go on a journey. Why are they in awe, and cannot escape being in awe, when facing certain places for the first time? How is this 'being in awe' socially construed, cultivated and maintained?

How does it lead to the formation of particular cultures of tourism and particular tourist attractions? How does it help tourists to maintain or renew the ontological groundings of selfhood and belonging, and the stories to live by inserting the personal body within a wider cosmological order? Once we understand the ontological work underpinning tourism, we can, with much more ease, explore the order underlying the social realities formed as a result of the institutionalisation of tourism on a global scale. In this chapter, I will follow the journeys of different tourists on the island of La Réunion and back at their homes in Europe, by taking on the role of the tour guide (the method is discussed in a subsection below).

Global Flows of Tropical Island Tourism

Ernest had saved for several years to 'offer' himself this ten-day tropical island holiday as a 'once in a lifetime experience', as he later said. While the experiences of his journey seemed to emerge from within a highly personal life context, he was not the only person in the world to dream of spending their holidays on a tropical island. According to the official tourist arrival figures for fifty-eight island-states or dependant island territories situated in the intertropical zone,[2] the worldwide number of tropical island tourists was just above 40 million (or around 27 million if larger 'island states' such as Australia, Indonesia, Malaysia, the Philippines, and Taiwan are excluded) in 2005. This represents five per cent of all international tourist arrivals in 2005 (or three per cent if the larger 'island states' are excluded). Within this global context, tropical islands in the Caribbean clearly attracted the largest number of tourist arrivals, at seventy per cent of the global total, followed by East Asia and the Pacific (twenty per cent), and the Indian Ocean (ten per cent). The islands with most tourist arrivals (again excluding the large island states) were the Dominican Republic (3.7m), the US Virgin Islands (0.6m), and Barbados (0.5m) in the Caribbean; Guam (1.2m), Fiji (0.6m), and the Northern Mariana Islands (0.5m) in East Asia and the Pacific; and Mauritius (0.8m) and Sri Lanka (0.5m) in the Indian Ocean. Tropical island holidays lasted on average between nine and twelve days. Almost half of all international tropical island tourists in 2005 lived in the Americas (mainly USA and Canada), and around one quarter respectively in Europe (mainly the United Kingdom, Germany, Italy, France) and in East Asia and the Pacific (mainly Australia, Japan, Indonesia). Tropical island tourists living in South Asia, the Middle East, or Africa represented less then one per cent of all international tropical island tourist arrivals in that year.

This broad statistical overview provides a general idea about the global structure of international tropical island tourist flows. It seems to indicate that this specific tourism phenomenon emanates almost entirely from some of the industrial and post-industrial societies of Europe, East Asia and the Americas. It appears that a specific holiday culture emanating from such centres has expanded into a global geographical sphere, and that it has generated a global economy of tourism flows integrating geographically marginal spaces such as islands into the realms of a global holiday culture. The analysis of tourist flows to tropical islands also seems to indicate that this form of tourism represents a (statistically) relatively marginal phenomenon, when compared with the global number of international tourist arrivals. In 2005, only one out of twenty international tourist journeys had a tropical island as a destination. Most international tourists travelled to the Mediterranean basin and spent their holidays near beaches in Spain and France. However, according to marketing research,[3] a large majority of people in Western Europe, North America and East Asia would be disposed to go on holiday in tropical islands, if they had the means and opportunity. From this point of analysis, tropical island tourism seems to imply a structured and well-established social phenomenon. While this statistical data can indicate the structural properties of this phenomenon, they cannot explain why people like Ernest actually go on holiday to tropical islands, spend vast amounts of money and become emotionally moved by the encounter of exotic landscapes. Neither can it explain how the personal journey of tourists relates to wider imaginaries and institutions related to tropical island tourism.

Ethnography of the Tourist Journey

If the ethnographic approach is to observe the general through the specific, within this research it will aim to study tourism as a form of modern culture through the observation of specific tourist practices, and will follow individual tourist journeys. This approach is marked by a number of logistic and epistemic difficulties. One of these is that observers cannot directly access what 'moves' their subjects and how this 'being moved' is articulated with the structural constraints that mark social life. They can only observe and analyse 'outer' articulations. Tourists talk. Tourists collect souvenirs. Tourists take photographs. They ask questions. They gaze at certain things. They do not gaze at other things. They consume food. They 'need' a drink. They are often silent. Tourists live in their own temporalities. It thus makes little sense for the observer to approach tourists only at one particular moment of the journey without being able to place the observations made during this moment within the wider context of the journey and the tourists' everyday life (Graburn 2002). Therefore, an ethnographic approach towards tourists ideally follows them from long before the departure until long after their return home. Another difficulty for ethnographers lies in the fact that tourism, like many 'modern' rituals, is profoundly personal and intimate. Even if they seem part of a large 'crowd', tourists usually travel in small groups, as couples or with friends. While ethnographers can get themselves accepted as fellow tourists / participant observers, such an approach remains ethically and socially ambivalent.[4] A honeymoon with an ethnographer as a constant companion may no longer be a honeymoon. Finally, possibly the greatest challenge of a comprehensive ethnography of tourism resides in the logistic and financial dimensions of a research design based on 'going on holiday'. Tropical island tourism is, relative to other forms of tourism, very expensive and it appears to be difficult to convince any research council to fund a vast amount of luxurious holiday trips to the Seychelles, Samoa or Bahamas, for the sake of ethnographic observations of what tourists do before, during and after being on holiday.

A pragmatic way to solve these dilemmas is to do participant observation by taking on the role of the tour guide.[5] This is what I have done. I gained employment as a guide for a tourism agency in La Réunion. Between 1998 and 2000, I guided twenty five-day round trips through the island. These always followed the same itinerary, stopped at the same hotels, passed through the same sites and included the same food. Because of the quasi-invariance of its context and time-space frame, this research achieved an almost experimental outlook. The groups were composed mainly of Germans who had booked their trip via a German tour operator. Their size varied between three and eight people. I stayed with these tourists all day long, sharing meals and drinks, driving the minibus, performing a guide discourse, engaging in often long informal conversations. I also spent the night at the same hotels. At the end of the round trips, I left the groups at the airport. However, I stayed in contact through correspondence and later revisited many of the tourists in their homes in Germany. This particular research approach allowed me to observe in great detail what actually happens when tourists 'do' tourism and, regrettably, to a less sophisticated degree, what happens when they return home. The principal limit of this approach is that it cannot study the processes of 'coming home', the journey home and the reintegration into the home environment, which seems to be a moment of crucial importance for any anthropological understanding of tourism.

Experience and Sense Making

The most striking observations made during these guided tours concern the consistent way in which the tourists – despite the differences of their travel motifs and social milieus[6] – experienced different sites, people, stories and environments encountered during the journey, and how they related these experiences to their personal lives and life-contexts back in Germany. Ernest, when facing the volcanic landscape started to cry and cursed the former German Democratic Republic (GDR) leaders. He seemed to be associating the emotions generated by the 'beauty' he appeared to be seeing in the volcanic landscape with the memory of a context of coercion marking life in the former GDR. He said he had not expected to ever be able to see such beauty. By gazing upon the landscape, he seemed to recognise a self he had been before the Berlin Wall came down, a self that was purposely prohibited by the GDR regime from seeing 'such beauty'. At the same time, he seemed to realise that he was no longer this self, that he was now free to travel and experience 'all these treasures and splendid nature'. The volcanic landscape seemed to work as a form of mirror, in which he recognised a persona he had once been; a persona whose desire to see beauty was repressed by a state apparatus. At the same time, he seemed to become conscious that he had been this person 'unnecessarily', that parts of his life had been determined by an authoritarian regime which prohibited travel, preventing him from living the moments of aesthetic joy that he fervently appeared to desire. During the rest of the journey he asked, again and again, merely rhetorically, how anyone could prevent others from seeing 'such beauty'. He explained that 'we would have all come back' (meaning he would not have fled East Germany to stay in the West). He 'liked' East Germany, he said. There were many other, usually less dramatic, moments during his journey, other encounters with people, places, objects and stories through which facets of his identity were brought back to him. Encountering children in the street made him talk about his own children, about his role as a father, about the problems children currently face in an uncertain economic environment. Listening to me talking about my studies, he started to remember his own studies, adventures long ago from when he was young, when he had to find ways of earning money. Visiting a cemetery and observing people praying made him talk about his parents and their illness, their eventual death; ways of dealing with the death of relatives.

Ernest, like the other tourists observed in this research, appeared to rationalise the emotions induced by these 'encounters' by embedding them into stories. These stories did not normally emerge spontaneously as consistent narratives, but were assembled, little by little, through the confrontation of different fragments of memory, by putting them into perspective, and by building more and more consistent wholes. The observations made in the specific cases of Ernest and most of the other tourists I guided therefore lead to a more general observation of what happens when tourists 'do' tourism. Most, if not all, went through a similar process of negotiation. In the first phase of this process, when facing a spectacular landscape or an extraordinary story, they were almost always speechless. They seemed to be in a state of shock and awe.[7] The apparent impossibility of finding the right words to express their emotions was verbally articulated by sighs and moans, by sounds such as 'ahh' and 'ohh'. The duration of this initial phase, as of the entire negotiation process, was extremely variable. Some tourists were actually very quick at finding their words; others took several minutes, sometimes even several hours or days before they started to talk. Some did not talk about these encounters at all. This does not mean, of course, that these encounters left them unaffected. Many tourists wrote about their appreciation or talked about it between friends or couples. When I later revisited some of the tourists back at their homes in Germany I was shown sometimes elaborate travel diaries which included detailed reflections about certain experiences. These were written down during the journey, often in several steps where subjects had repeatedly come back to an initial reflection. Most tourists sent postcards sharing some of their experiences with friends or relatives 'back home'. Almost all took photographs and collected souvenirs.

When facing a spectacular site or a strange story, it often seemed to me that the first words following this 'encounter' were merely pragmatic tools to 'say something', to objectify the experience. Tourists typically searched for referents to articulate their perceptions through analogies with aesthetic forms that already existed in their mind. This worked in visual and other sensory, as well as in verbal, encounters (when I told a story). The phrase 'It is like…' was most commonly used here. The volcanic landscape was 'like the moon' or 'like Lanzarote'. Flowers smelled 'like flowers in our garden'. Children looked 'like my nephews' or 'like my children when they were young'. Markets were 'like in Cuba' or 'unlike German' markets. Religious shrines were 'like religious shrines in Europe' or 'like shrines used by my parents'. Social movements and dynamics, religious practices that I explained were 'like what happens in East Germany now', or 'like life was a hundred years ago in Europe'. My explanations about current discussions in La Réunion about how to deal with the slavery heritage were 'like current discussions in Germany about how to deal with the heritage of the Holocaust'.

In the next phase of this negotiation process, tourists usually used an antithetic 'but' – 'but they are smaller'; 'but they smell stronger'; 'but it is cleaner'; 'but they are more beautiful'; 'but this is not good for the environment'; etc. – hence articulating the experience within a value system based both on personal references and wider moral ideals. This phase often seemed to induce reflections on personal memories or contexts related to the very references made: 'We were in Lanzarote last year'; 'Flowers here are much larger than in our garden'; 'We were travelling a lot together when we were young'; 'My parents used to go there before they became ill'; 'I am not as religious as my parents'; 'We are fine in Germany where we have our family and friends'; 'This would not be allowed in Germany'; 'We should have killed them all'; etc.

All significant tourist encounters seemed to induce a cognitive process through which tourists articulated the emotion of their in-situ experience through a chain of associations that eventually led most of them to talk about themselves, their lives, their relationships, their being in the world. The continuous confrontation with strange realms challenged them to recognise the familiar in the unfamiliar, and thus to engage with, and re-appropriate, stories, bodies and forms through which to think about themselves and participate in life. It challenged them to recreate order, to rebuild stories articulating their being in the world.

This story building, and the kind of being in the world it formulated, seemed to be articulated by the social contexts that marked the tourists' personal home environments. For instance, those tourists whose social life back home was made stressful by a tense work life frequently used the journey to remember, recreate and reaffirm stories of common belonging. This 'category' of tourists often comprised couples and groups of friends who had consciously booked the trip in order to 'find back together', to remember earlier times and do things together. This type of travel motivation commonly surfaced in the way in which encounters with the places visited would be negotiated. Couples often used sites as a trigger to actively engage a process of remembering, to retell and re-evoke their love stories. In a similar vein, groups of friends would often talk about former shared events, especially former holidays and festivities, and also shared references such as common friends, hobbies, or interests. A similar phenomenon could be observed among another category of tourists, often elderly or socially isolated people whose everyday life, back in Germany, was marked by solitude. For such tourists, the journey seemed to generate ephemeral moments of sociality shared with mainly unknown fellow tourists. Tourism in itself often became a common reference framework with its own topics, polemics and values. This type of tourist would often spend hours and hours discussing and comparing various previous travel experiences, places visited, guides met, different tour operators, hotels they stayed in, itineraries they had been on or where they wished to go. While for most tourists the encounters of the journey eventually led to the reaffirmation of a wider social and cosmological order that allowed them to continue their normal lives, in some rare cases, the journey appeared to be truly life changing. For a third category of tourists, the journey appeared to affect deeply how they thought about their being in the world. Some seemed so deeply affected that they changed jobs, reconnected to religious practices or moved on with their lives, accepting that they had entered a new cycle. A woman I had guided told me later that the trip had allowed her to 'digest' the separation with her husband. From this point of observation, tourist sites are not simply 'consumed', but have the ability to trigger powerful emotions among tourists. What makes these emotions? Maybe more intriguingly, what makes those similar patterns of sites generate emotions among a sample of tourists of rather radically different social backgrounds?

Aesthetic and Moral Ordering

When encountering a palm fringed white-sand beach or a clear lagoon, which aesthetically corresponded to the typical images of tropical islands used in tourism advertisements, the tourists observed in this study usually recognised these 'images', often by explicitly referring to them in terms of 'Oh! This is so beautiful [...] It looks like it does in the brochures [...]' (or: 'like in the movies'; 'like a postcard'; etc.). The brochure in itself became a reference, mobilised to talk about the experience of a site. However, it was very rare that tourists would engage in a conscious search of any form of determined 'gaze' (Urry 1990) associated with tropical islands.[8] In most cases, the aesthetic appreciation of the realm generated through the tourist journey seemed more passive and fluid. Tourists appeared sensitive to many different forms of visual, sensuous or verbal encounter. These included, most obviously, the visual elements of particular landscapes that emerged before their eyes: abrupt geographical formations such as mountain ridges, steep valleys or wide plains; the strong visual contrast and intensive colours of lagoons, clouds moving over a mountain, land covered in lush green rain forests; water violently rushing down in waterfalls or crashing into coastal rocks; the colours of flowers, trees, birds and the sunset over the horizon. Quasi-invariably, these also included specific types of humans and animals that tourists seemed to relate to, in many ways 'conventionalised forms' (Albers and James 1988) they were familiar with: women carrying babies, children playing in the street or going to school, teenagers walking up and down the beach promenade, old people sitting in chairs in front of their houses or working in the fields, cats sleeping lazily in the shade, cows grazing in meadows, birds courting each other or building nests, fish swimming in the sea, dying on market stalls or being eaten in restaurants. Throughout the journey, the tourists also encountered many non-visual sensuously perceptible forms they related to: odours; sounds and silence; the taste of food and drinks consumed; the sensations of the sunlight on the skin, of water, of the warm wind, of the cool and humid mountain air; sensations of their own body adapting more or less well to the tourism realm. Finally, they reacted to the stories I told them about the island or that they were otherwise confronted with at interpretation sites, in museums and at cultural memorials.

The apprehension of these different visual, sensual and narrative forms seemed to be based on a process that Alain Roger (1997) calls 'artialisation'. The tourists, confronted by the unfamiliar space through which they travelled, created order by searching for familiar forms. These were forms they had necessarily known through previous personal experiences or through their socialisation to specific aesthetic orders learnt in society. At this personal level, their vision was 'socially skilled' (Grasseni 2007) in that they contrasted what was perceptible to what remained imperceptible to their eye. Most spaces passed through during the journey did, indeed, remain imperceptible. Some of the spaces in which the tourists of this research spent a relatively long time (e.g. the hotel room, the minibus, the airport hall) generated little or no post-tourism memories at all. When I revisited them back in Germany, very few remembered what their hotel rooms looked like, what we had for breakfast or what kind of minibus we used. Nor did they remember that we spent a long time driving through 'dull' coastal land or got stuck in traffic jams in the island's urban peripheries. On the other hand, other spaces in which we had spent relatively little time (e.g. the volcano, certain viewpoints and interpretation sites) seemed to have generated disproportionally powerful memories. To a certain degree, the tourists thus seemed to 'share' their 'ways of seeing' (Berger 1979). To a certain degree, a collective dimension defined their individual vision. Accordingly, certain sites consistently appeared as the emotionally 'strong moments'[9] of the journey. The places that generated these moments provided the focus for most personal photographs and the most vivid memories in the post-tourism context. Eight photographs out of ten, among a sample of photographs of the journey sent to me in the post-tourism context,[10] showed panoramic shots of 'natural landscapes', in equal parts of the mountainous interior of the island and of the volcano. The volcano appeared to be particularly interesting. The tour had spent relatively little time here, no more than two hours, yet it generated a far higher number of souvenirs than any other site in the island.[11]

The largely collective aesthetic disposition among the tourists generated a specific aesthetic configuration of the island. Moreover, that which was perceptible to the tourist eye was also exposed to moral judgement. The touristic 'vision' often emphasised elements such as the 'wild' and 'pristine' nature of its interior, the 'beauty' and 'ingeniosity' of the Creole populations, and the 'endless sunshine' and 'clemency' of the tropical climate. Certainly, the touristic perception of various encounters, say a cat in the street or a woman with a child, was wide open to personal judgements. Some may have liked cats or pregnant women, others not. Yet, those sites that induced the most durable memories and stories after the journey seemed connected by a common moral order. They all implied the idea of 'nature' as a wild *ur*-condition, underpinning the human condition and the human struggles to uphold and refine humanity in the face of such a nature. The latter was thus clearly put in antipodal terms to the concept of modernity most tourists identified with as their social world. This was manifested, for instance, through touristic observations and discussions about what was in and what was out of place. Plastic packaging and other 'inorganic' things found in 'natural' sites (cars, radio antennas, concrete buildings, loudspeaker noise, etc.) were usually seen as 'polluting' elements.

According to this vision, 'natural' sites were ideally free of human traces, or at least free of traces of 'modernity'. On the other hand, where they related to 'local' populations, human traces were usually valorised. Here, two distinguished aesthetics of the 'local' emerged. One focused on the populations in the interior of the island, typically seen to be living either 'in harmony with nature', or struggling to uphold a form of humanity 'despite' nature. The figures of historical heroes, small-scale farmers, archaic life and decadent society supplied here metaphors through which to invoke different modern myths of time, e.g. the biblical evocation of a first humankind living in a happy countryside, the loss of this biblical heaven as a consequence of opposing the universal order of God, the beginning of history marked by the need to create a new garden on earth, by force of sweat and work, the struggles to achieve this by means of submitting to nature. The other dominant aesthetic element valorising the local focused on 'Creole' populations, which frequently supplied the tourists with images to talk about the 'historical struggles' of humankind or, at a more personal level, of the tourists' own struggles with life. The widely shared attraction for all things Creole among the tourists thus seemed to generate another level, this time, to enable reflection on the consequences of history.

As a result of the aesthetic and moral orderings that most of the tourists operated at on a personal level, a broadly generic 'public imagery' of the island emerged. Despite the important differences among these tourists, in terms of their social milieus and travel motivation, this 'public imagery' remained the overarching aesthetic frame of each personal journey. It also formed the resource base from which the local tour operator I was working for constructed the time-space of the round-trip product. Moreover, it ultimately supplied the visual elements used in creating advertisement campaigns by La Réunion's tourist board. As a result of these multiple collinear forces, the island became visible through a tourism specific form of geographical structure and semiosphere. The 'purity' and 'authenticity' of a 'wild' 'natural' interior was connected, through concentric circles, metaphorically following the rivers from their source in this interior, to an urbanised coastline inhabited by 'Creole' populations. The dialectic of inside and outside projected onto the populations and the land they inhabited therefore provided a powerful allegory about time and history. The island appeared as a large stage making visible, and thus bringing alive, both the ideas of an *ur*-nature (located in its interior), and of 'culture' growing out of such an *ur*-nature (located on the coast). Interestingly, most tourists seemed to consider 'culture' in terms of a dynamic and widely directionless experience rather than a progression towards any form of pre-determined state of moral and aesthetic perfection, as many religious and philosophical currents would have it. This may be indicative of an epistemological break in the public, everyday aesthetic of culture and nature, implying a new way of seeing history, no longer as a directed process towards a morally higher 'end', but as an ongoing process of contact and changes. It may also be indicative for my own power, as the tour guide, to convince the tourists observed here about the fluid nature of the human condition…

The 'Magic' of Souvenirs

In the post-tourism context, the stories built upon the in-situ experiences of the tourist journey usually became more 'solid'. Most of the tourists, who I revisited between three and six months after their holiday in La Réunion, had 'cooked down' their memories of the journey to a good handful of souvenirs, a set of 'solid' stories related to some of the sites or atmospheres, some events that happened or encounters they remembered, some funny, stupid or intelligent things I might have said. The tourist journey seemed closed. Its souvenirs had become part of the ex-tourists' everyday life. They had been organised into classification systems, in 'folders' dedicated to the particular field of holiday. In most cases, these souvenirs had been contained in different forms of material culture. The photographs of the trip to La Réunion were treated in the same way as the photographs of previous trips. Some had developed elaborate photograph albums; others had left the photographic prints in their envelope stored in the same drawer as all the other envelopes with holiday prints. In some other cases, I found prints of photographs taken during the journey framed and put on the walls of hallways and toilets. One couple did not bother developing their photographs at all. They had no one to show them to, they explained. With the widespread use of personal computers and digital photography, just starting to become popular in the early 2000s, this phenomenon did not change in its nature, but only its support with photographs being stored on hard discs, in special holiday folders with sub-folders for each journey. The very diverse material objects collected or otherwise acquired during the journey were usually integrated into wider collections of tourism objects. In many houses, I found them arranged in some sort of 'living room shrines', personal collections of natural matter, stones, shells, artisan objects, and framed photographs taken during diverse journeys. These were often displayed on a special shelf, sometimes arranged on the TV or top of a drawer. On some rare occasions I found living rooms so full of objects that I could hardly pass through. Other objects had been given away to friends and relatives, or been used and consumed.

Trying to understand the significance that the ex-tourists attached to these objects and displays, I engaged in long informal conversations, in some cases continued by an ongoing exchange of letters and, later, emails. This approach proved fruitful and provided a number of answers. Firstly, it became clear that the highly self-reflective realm of the journey had been closed at some point during or after their return home. In the post-tourism context, in which my visits took place, they wanted to talk about something else; about their lives, their jobs, their friends, their next holidays. The trip to La Réunion had become a souvenir among other holiday souvenirs; its significance was not up for debate. Secondly, the diverse material souvenirs were integrated into the realm of their everyday lives. Their significance seemed to be largely separated from the emotionally heightened context and experience of the journey. People seemed to use these objects to assemble a materialised allegory of their selves. 'This is me, this is my life', I was sometimes told. The object collections thus seemed to work as a personal museum, a double, a mirror, a self put on display, a self-display. Thirdly, while these 'personal museums' seemed to remain for most of the time 'silent' living room décors, they could be 'activated' in at least two different ways. On the one hand, the objects allowed them to evoke and share their holiday stories with friends, relatives, work colleagues and other people (and certainly also to communicate the social prestige associated with long haul travel).

They allowed a form of social participation and exchange within the everyday life context. On the other hand, many of the subjects explained to me how they used some of the material holiday souvenirs for personal evocations. Some told me that, for instance, on occasions when they felt miserable, alienated or stressed by their jobs or partners, or when the weather was cold and grey in winter, they sometimes looked at their holiday photograph albums, touched souvenir objects or used cooking or spa ingredients bought while on holiday. They said that gazing at photographs, smelling the odour of vanilla or essential geranium oil, tasting curcuma or red pepper, or touching stones, handicraft objects or even photographic prints brought back to life memories from the journey and helped them to feel better. These objects seemed imbued with a quality or power that perpetuated the material realm of this island within the home context.

This last observation seems crucial for the understanding of souvenir making in tourism and the wider meanings of the ontological order underlying, and maintained by, tourism. It indicates a way of thinking about material souvenirs as being able to capture, or evoke, a kind of 'power' or 'spirit' associated with the island and to transport this back home. This usually remains latent, but can be 'activated' in specific moments. Why and how do people, in this case tourists, associate such a quality with their souvenirs and, by extension, with the holiday spaces these souvenirs relate to? While on holiday, they collected natural matter like stones or shells, took photographs and bought handicraft objects in souvenir shops. They also talked about these acts, usually emphasising stories related to the bargaining process, not being cheated, or the artistic quality or beauty of objects. They showed their acquisitions to each other, sometimes indicating what would happen with these. However, it seemed that the 'magic' associated with these material objects was only generated, or only became visible and effective, through the act of separating them from the actual space of the journey. Within La Réunion, these objects remained ontologically part of the island; they were 'just objects' with no specific quality. Yet, once transported home and integrated into the tourists' domestic spaces, they appeared to perpetuate a material presence of the island in the home environment. Similarly, the body of the tourists, through the physical contact, gastronomic consumption, exposure to weather, and exchanges with people, became somehow imbued with the island's quality. When the tourists returned home, it seemed that this could persist, at least for a while. They had sunshine in their eyes, some said. Others told me that they felt strong and powerful – as if the physical presence in the island had allowed them to load the body with a specific charge, to operate a kind of ontological handshake that would transfer the 'energy' of the island into their bodies.

The 'magic' of objects taken home, of the 'recharged' tourist body, seems to originate in the very idea of distance and ontological separation that defines the relationship between the quotidian space of the tourists and the places of the journey. A prerogative of generating such 'magic' seems to lie in the separation of objects, entities or bodies into different ontological realms. This implies a double act. The first, of a poetic nature, consists in the creation and poetic enchantment of the separation and distance between – here – the island and the home environment (which then become seen as ontologically distinguished realms); the second, of a ritualistic nature, consists in social practices overcoming this separation and distance by means of the touristic journey. Material tourist souvenirs taken home or the 'recharged' tourist body seem able to perpetuate a 'sympathetic' power associated with the island within the home environment. They seem to work as metonyms whose power lies less in their symbolic ability to represent the holiday experience, than in their material quality to uphold an 'authentic link' (Steward 1993) with the place of the journey. This explanation could equally elucidate the rather peculiar practice of tourism photography. Photographs imply, of course, different semiotic layers. However, their critical principle seems to lie in their materiality and the act of the tourists actually being there and taking the photograph. The later print only becomes authenticated (and thus imbued with the power or 'aura' of the photographed original) through the 'physical' contact between the photographed object and the photographic print. Through its optical technology and chemical (later digital) recording, the camera frames and captures light, somehow thought of as being able to transport the quality of the photographed object onto the plate. In an analogy with Renaissance techniques of capturing the magical power of religious relics via mirrors, the photographic camera hence seems to work as a 'transmaterialisation' device (Gell 2005). It allows the preservation and reproduction of the original's 'aura' or 'magic' through its photographic copy.

In many cases, especially in the process of time, this 'power', 'aura' or 'magic' can fade. People change lives and develop new selves, inhabit new jobs, make new friendships, find new places to live, or simply get older. In some cases, they feel that these new selves are no longer a reflection of who they were before. These changes and coming-of-age phenomena are often directly reflected in their souvenir collections. Sometimes objects are put into boxes and disappear for many years in an attic. On rare occasions, these objects are simply thrown away, considered as 'garbage of a past life', nothing anybody would be interested in, an old couple told me. Other objects are re-elevated and re-signified; they may no longer be holiday souvenirs per se, but souvenirs of an epoch of personal life, a place, a relationship, or a person that has vanished.

Maintaining Modernity

The observations made in this study seem to indicate that tourism, while fundamentally personal in terms of the experiences made, relates to larger shared forms of ontological, aesthetic and moral order. Despite very different social and contextual backgrounds, the German tourists observed here during their journey through La Réunion enjoyed sites and attractions defined by significantly similar patterns. Almost without exception, all were left in speechless awe when confronting certain sites of 'wild nature', mountain panoramas or abrupt volcanic landscapes – or when enjoying a drink at the beach during the sunset. The journey to and through these spaces seemed to generate a specifically touristic realm, a 'liminal'[12] time and space challenging the tourists to recreate order and reflect upon the social and cosmological foundations of their social lives.

The study demonstrates how the touristic disposition towards reality changed according to the different phases of the journey. Before the journey, the island was not much more than a representation of a desired space, aspired to in a very diffuse, uncertain way, yet eventually leading the (future) tourists towards a certain form of practice. After careful preparation, the consideration of economical and various practical issues, the soon-to-be tourists eventually went on a tour to and through La Réunion. Once there, the holiday-anticipating representational realm of the island all but disappeared. Rare were the cases where tourists walked around consciously looking out for those signs upon which the idea of tropical islands was construed in the pre-journey context. While on holiday, reality was perceived in a much more direct, unorganised way. The tourists had to undertake the journey and the ontological work provoked by the unfamiliar grounds they encountered on their own, only helped by their travel buddies, travel guides and technical tools which enabled them to capture and make sense of their experiences. While the processes of touristic cognition can be best understood from a psychological perspective, they remain a highly interesting topic for anthropological study in that they appear to be based on largely 'shared' aesthetic dispositions towards reality. While these aesthetic dispositions were of course part of the cognitive apparatus of individual people, they seemed to be framed or 'governed' here, among a large sample of German tourists, by a shared culture of 'seeing the world'. The most likely explanation for this may be provided through studies of the historical processes of learning and disciplining, and the institutionalisation of certain aesthetic forms in society, here in Germany. I must admit, it is far from clear to me how such processes worked out in detail, what made those 'Germans' of such varied social backgrounds seem to share such a homogenous aesthetic of nature, culture and their being in the world.

During the journey, the representational realms of tropical islands, so dominant in the pre-tourism context, chiefly re-appeared only when tourists entered a reflexive mode. The immediate experience of places and encounters was negotiated and made meaningful; it was familiarised by associating it with references to pre-existing familiar forms, and embedded in narratives. The widely generic model of tropical islands underlying much tourism advertisement became one possible form to create familiarity among others. From this point of observation it can be said that this model may well have directed the tourists to a particular place, the island of La Réunion, but once there, it did not govern their experiences. The island 'really looked like it did in the brochures', but it also looked like other places the tourists had seen before, 'like Lanzarote' or 'like Sri Lanka'. The tourists did not consume a pre-fabricated 'representation', but merely used this representation in a reflective fashion to make sense of the enticing effect certain sites had over them. In many cases, typical images of tropical islands provided the best 'summaries' of such experiences. Yet, these emerged only as the result of a cognitive process that was started immediately after the experience and was usually carried into the back-home context. During the journey, tourists mainly had to deal with many small events and a multitude of very personal histories. The various facets of everyday life in La Réunion worked like a mirror in which they recognised various facets of their own everyday life in Germany. During the trip the tourists spent far more time talking about cats, children, partners, parents, jobs, cooking recipes, hobbies, cars, football, the German economy and politics, and love than about any topic directly related to La Réunion.

Paradoxically, in the post-tourism context, most souvenirs of the trip were encapsulated in largely common visual memories about specific sites within the island. Despite their social differences, the group of German tourists seemed to share a fascination with the 'forces of nature' found in the interior of the island, the human heroism shown in opposing nature and submitting it to their will. Another strong theme among the tourists was that of the 'beauty of the Creole people', which may be seen as symbolic for an optimistic vision of the present and future, of cultural contact leading to a better world, a world in creolisation. Attractions which embodied this idea were mainly located in sites on the outside of the island. They created a spatial structure marked by a dialectic of inside and outside. The island tourism realm emerged as a particular semiosphere, purposely fabricated and dramatised by tour operators; a living landscape cultivating miniaturised images of the world; a garden staging the ideas of cosmic time and unconditional nature, and of the human relation to such an *ur*-nature, the ongoing struggles to oppose, and separate from, a state of unconditionality and to think of humanity in term of free-willing individuals.

Eventually the tourists had to go home. Through their physical immersion in the material space of the island they had, to a certain degree at least, become part of it. Contact with local places and people, the immersion in the local nature, water, air, cities, the ingestion of local food, fruits, waters, the absorption of the sun, seemed to have worked here like an 'ontological handshake', equalising charges between an ontologically separated here and there, in some cases in quite an electrifying manner where the tourists were left in a state of shock and awe. When they returned home, their body and the material matter acquired or collected during the trip seemed able to maintain the ontological quality of the island in this context back in Germany – be it only for a limited time. They felt their bodies were 'recharged', while material souvenirs, analogous to religious relics, appeared able to pertain to a sympathetic quality of the island.

These qualities, associated with the material realm of the island, seemed to be thought of in terms of a tension growing out of an underlying ontological difference. A good model which helps us to visualise this way of thinking may be provided by the concept of cathotic tension developed in electrophysics. Cathotic tension appears when two physically separated metal plates are loaded with different electric charges. Bringing the two plates in contact would equalise the charge and nullify the tension between them. Bringing a third much smaller metal object in contact first with one, then with the other, and then again with the first plate would trigger, respectively, a small electric discharge. The small metal object and the plates it would have been brought in contact with would, respectively, in each phase of the experiment, equalise their charge. Similarly, through physical contact, tourists absorb the 'power' of a foreign and distanced realm, which, once carried to their home context, allows them to reconstitute their self. In classical anthropology, this 'power' stemming from an alien realm, the sympathetic quality embodied in metonymic matter, was generally defined as 'magic'. This study shows how tourist souvenirs appear able to pertain to such sympathetic qualities; they can be activated, they provide betterment in situations of distress.

Such 'magic' associated with the material space of the journey is also invoked through narratives and metaphors. Indeed, those representations of tropical islands used in tourism advertisement are frequently identical to those the tourists would use in the post-tourist context to remember their travel experience. Yet, it would be too quick an assumption and a poor vision of humanity to presume from this that tourism merely consists of a 'visual consumption'. Public images of tropical islands direct tourists to the kind of experience that they actually propose – a 'magical' experience – and they also allow them to summarise and tell the story of their experience in the post-tourist context. Yet, the idea of a hermeneutics of public representations, of personal experiences leading to the appropriation of public symbols, is incomplete. Tourists have their experiences on their own and merely use public representations and models as a language to articulate, objectify and communicate these experiences. Hence the post-touristic affirmation made by so many tourists back home: 'You have to go there to experience it yourself; it is not just an advertisement slogan, it is truly magical!'

The structuralist approaches to tourism and tourist attractions by Victor Turner (1973), Dean MacCannell (1976), and Nelson Graburn (1977) provide a good explanation for the wider frame within which tourism happens. This study shows how this structural level is articulated at the level of personal experience. Representations of nature, culture or, in this case, tropical islands lead tourists to attractions, but they are not attractions in themselves. The attractiveness emanates from the sites, the worlds and moral orders they are able to evoke and bring to life. Representations of sites become 'public discourses' which are used by tourists to make sense of their experiences. They thus provide a socially very successful illusion of public culture, of an apparently coherent understanding among a group of people about what certain spaces mean. In many cases, it is hard for tourists to express what they feel when encountering a site. The language they use always seems insufficient to make sense of their emotions. They necessarily return to the 'best' words or concepts they are offered, and talk about the 'magic' of the sites. While the study cannot explain the collective dimension of individual experience observed here (which certainly would require a more sophisticated historical study of the instrumentalisation and institutionalisation of German romanticism and ideas of time and nature), it can state the facts. Tourists 'technically' personalise public images and representations of tropical islands, more as a result than as an active process; as an outcome. In the post-tourist context, they turn to the public imagery as the 'best way' to summarise the experience of specific sites. As a result of the poverty of concepts or words to describe their individual experience, and the disciplining effect of language as a tool to communicate, they thus reaffirm these public representations.

The relationship between 'magic' and tourism is, therefore, defined by two different realms. One relates to the psychological 'material' experience of specific sites that seem to have a seductive power over tourists. The other relates to representations of the 'magic' of tropical islands, which are merely texts used to create social aspirations associated with certain places or make sense of experiences in such places. In Western culture, these representations seem highly resilient as a result of a hermeneutics of experience, where the actual experience of places with 'magical' qualities is rationalised through the very representations of such places as 'magical'. In a hermeneutic cycle, one and the other perpetuate themselves, with representations both anticipating experience and allowing it to be put into images or words. However, it seems important to stress the difference between these two realms, because one can explain the other, but representation alone cannot explain the historical resilience of this model of tropical islands and their 'magic'. In the rest of this book, I will 'change sides', and study the transformations brought about by, and the modalities of inhabiting, this model within the tropical island of La Réunion.

Chapter 2
Creole Beautiful

Camellias

Orom made us halt in front of a camellia tree. He was wearing his tour-guide uniform, a straw hat, khaki shorts, a white T-shirt, heavy hiking boots and a black mountaineering backpack. The group of tourists formed a half circle around him, waiting to see what would happen. He started telling a story about a woman who disliked the odour of flowers. She would not use perfume and the only flowers cultivated in her garden were camellias. Why only camellias? He asked the people surrounding him. There was a moment of silence. The tourists guessed at different reasons. They were all wrong. Because camellias are odourless, he said and smiled. And they are also beautiful. This is why the lady was called the *Dame aux Camélias*. He picked a couple of flowers and passed them around. The people raised the flowers to their noses trying to grasp the absence of a scent. They looked at each other, smiling and affirming that the flowers effectively had no, or only a very slight, odour. Orom announced that he would tell them about 'proper' Creole ways of using camellias. During processions, he explained, people would throw the flower's petals onto the path before people passed. However, he added, possibly the most interesting use of the flowers, especially of the white ones, was simply as soap. The tourists looked doubtful, facing him with a questioning gaze. He picked a large white camellia flower and started rubbing it between his hands. After a certain period of time, a white soapy mousse appeared between his fingers. Ah! The tourists seemed astonished. He smiled, happy with the effect of his demonstration. Two of the tourists themselves started to repeat the experiment and, just like Orom, generated soapy foam. Before, Orom explained, everything was used. Today we constantly pass by flowers and plants that previously had multiple uses. Some people still know about these flowers and plants, but they are no longer in use. He did not want to make children – his children – use them, he added, but he concluded that it is important for children to know about these flowers and plants and how these had been used in the past. So, the white camellias were used for washing cloth. Efficient! He had finished his explanation and the tour was ready to continue.

Postcolonial Development Dilemmas

I first met Orom during the late 1990s. He was then around forty. He had grown up in Hell-Bourg, a village deep inside the valley of Salazie – the village we had just left as part of his guided tour. His parents had not owned land and so had worked for local farmers. These had mainly small farms, with narrow patches of land and small herds of cattle. The surplus of the local produce was usually sold to the markets and the large domains outside the valley. During the 1960s, the period that followed La Réunion's transformation into a *département d'outre-mer* (DOM) (in 1946), most of these small-scale family-run agricultural enterprises faced increasingly fierce competition from imported goods. In 1963, Michel Debré, French prime minister under President de Gaulle and a fervent defender of France's overseas colonial interests, was elected a member of the French parliament (thanks to massive vote-rigging, according to various independent sources), representing the first circumscription of La Réunion. During his mandate, he engaged in an eager struggle against the Communist Party of La Réunion, a movement led by Paul Vergès to fight for the island's autonomy (Gauvin 1996). To counter the political influence of the Communist Party, Michel Debré often used the colonial rhetoric of France as a motherly *Mère-Patrie* (Vergès 1999). He distributed free milk to the newly created school canteens and initiated a wide-ranging economic and social development programme for the island. A new college was founded in the south of the island and the island's economy was opened to imports from the French mainland. The French welfare state was introduced, giving the population previously unknown access to consumables, especially the women who received family allocations for their children. It often left the men in a socially and symbolically ambivalent role, as disempowered heads of families, incapable of retaining their position as the main income provider.

At the same time, the translation of the republican *Mère-Patrie* rhetoric in the context of social welfare redistributions systematised a post-colonial form of dependency which left the island's population incapable of reciprocating (Vergès 1999), quasi-powerless to create an autonomous island identity. In this context, Michel Debré organised the migration of young Réunions to the French mainland (along with the forced migration of more than a thousand children who were taken away from their parents in La Réunion to repopulate deserted areas in France). The optimism of the dominant economic development doctrines of the 1960s reached Salazie and other rural areas of the island at the same time. To make the agricultural sector in these areas more productive, hamlets were regrouped into villages, new access routes were built and land reform was initiated to increase the size of agricultural exploitations. People without land, like Orom's parents, were left with little to do and often had to leave for the urban centres at the island's coast or, via one of Debré's emigration programmes, to the French mainland in far-away Europe. It was in this context of rural decline that Orom had left the valley and moved to Saint-Denis, the largest town on the island's coast. In the years that followed, he had worked as a musician for private parties and as a waiter in different restaurants.

In 1996, Orom was approached by local development agents who were about to establish a training programme for local tourist guides. The training was accompanied by a study bursary. Orom was offered a place and accepted. From 1996, he spent a year of classroom teaching and study, with modules in enterprise management, heritage communication and project development. As part of this training, he had to undertake a professional internship and develop a professional project, a tourism product that he could run independently after completing the course. Orom did his internship with a mountain hiking company then new to Salazie. He also collaborated with the Salazie Ecomuseum, a new museum initiated by local development agents and university researchers that was then preparing its very first exhibition. Tutored by the director of this new museum, a French anthropologist, Orom developed an ethno-botanical guided tour. Since meeting Orom, I had observed the different aspects that had emerged through this tour for several months. Orom normally introduced me as his assistant, which allowed me to participate as a silent observer. At the same time, we became friends and often spent time doing things together. This insider perspective allowed me to situate the observations of the tour within the wider scope of his family, the village and the island development and conservation programmes.

Locating the Island's 'Soul'

Orom's professional re-education must be seen within the wider dynamic of the local redevelopment policies that emerged in La Réunion during the 1990s. Tourism was to play a central role, both as economic sector and as a mediator in the reformulation of collective identities on the island. By the mid-1990s, the vast majority of tourist activities and accommodation facilities were situated along the island's west coast beaches. Paradoxically, despite these rather unequivocal qualitative and quantitative realities of tourism, a widely proclaimed common knowledge among local populations, journalists, academics and political stakeholders in the island located La Réunion's principal tourism resources and development potentials chiefly in its mountainous interior. In a context in which the largest part of the island's formerly rural population had moved to the newly established towns on the coast, one of the most powerful visions for La Réunion seemed to advocate its future as lying in its steep valleys and high plains, in the 'traditions' and 'heritage' of its vanished or vanishing rural populations. It is here where the island's soul is located, insisted the 1995 Regional Development Scheme (Région Réunion 1995). The 'integrated development' of this space became a principal policy priority during the 1990s.

The specific dynamic of this redevelopment appears related to a wider context of structural and contextual changes that occurred during the early 1990s. With the end of the global Cold War, the political and ideological tensions between republican and autonomist movements inside the island slowly vanished or metamorphosed into new ideological battle grounds. Through continued capital transfers from France in the form of public sector wages, social allocations and investments in the transport, health and education systems, and through the integration of La Réunion into the European Union's structural funding schemes, the island achieved by far the highest GDP per capita in the Indian Ocean region. At the same time, despite higher incomes and high educational levels, the population continued its rapid growth. The artificially created economy was unable to absorb the ever-increasing numbers of job seekers, leaving almost forty per cent of the active population unemployed. Unlike other islands of the South Western Indian Ocean (e.g. Mauritius, Seychelles, Zanzibar), which developed agriculture, textile, tourism, IT and financial service industries, La Réunion was not successful in diversifying its economy and creating export-driven sectors. Tourism in particular remained for a long time a highly contested development option. Most of the ambitious tourism development plans of the early 1960s were never implemented and the little tourism development that did happen was not integrated into a wider spatial planning strategy, sometimes with dramatic consequences for the environment.

The absence of planned tourism development on the island can be linked to the powerful movement of resistance by different political action and lobby groups that had emerged since the late 1970s. These groups grew out of various contexts and represented a broad range of anti-colonial, ecological, conservationist and institutional and local development interests. During the 1970s and 1980s, they found a common agenda in the assertion not to 'sell off the best beaches of the island to foreigners' (Serviable 1983). During the 1980s and 1990s, the creation of environmental protection agencies at national and local government level further reinforced the anti-tourism discourse underlying this claim. Tourism, especially 'mass tourism', was widely seen as 'destroying' or 'polluting' 'local culture', landscapes and environments. During the 1990s, at a rhetoric level, if tourism was to be developed at all, it had to be 'integrated' into the island's social, natural and cultural environments. Tourists, it was often claimed, had to be educated.

In 1996, the *Commissariat à l'Aménagement des Hauts* (CAH), a government agency created twenty years earlier to coordinate the reorganisation of the rural economies of the islands' valleys, launched the first training programme for local tourist guides (*Guides de Pays*), already mentioned earlier. This programme led to a recognised professional diploma, the BAPAAT.[1] According to an internal strategy paper, the initiative was based on the assumption that 'youthful human resources in the rural areas, with often limited professional qualifications, had an intimate knowledge of the environment and were willing to communicate this to (tourist) visitors' (DATAR 1996: 1-4, translation by the author). The objective of the programme was to structure small-scale tourism products within a new type of tourism market based on 'the discovery of a territory through its cultural, natural and economic heritage' (ibid.), with the aim of increasing the number of tourist nights spent in the rural areas of the island. Orom started to guide tourists on a more or less regular basis from 1997.

Laslo, a Popular Heritage Celebrity

That day, having left the camellia tree behind, Orom led the group into a forest. Following a rather well established script of explanations and performances (I will come back to this at a later stage in this chapter), he introduced different plants and the ways these had been used 'before'. The group then left the forest and followed a road for a couple of hundred metres. It eventually reached Laslo's garden plot. Laslo was Orom's maternal uncle. Around sixty-five years old at the end of the 1990s, he was a former forest labourer and dockworker in the harbour of La Réunion. Since his retirement, he had spent most of his days in his garden plot, maintaining the courtyard, the kitchen and a small wooden house, looking after the fruit trees and vegetables, and receiving friends for a talk and a coffee. He had also started selling fruit and vegetables that he put on a table by the road. The garden plot had previously belonged to his parents and he had been brought up there. Some members of his immediate family still lived in small houses next to his. Laslo had shortly before moved to a purpose built house in a nearby village called Mare-à-Poule-d'Eau and only came back to his garden during the day. I first met Laslo through his sister in whose house I was renting a room. Both treated me like a member of their extended family. Lalso, when I met him, therefore kissed me on the cheeks, a sign of social intimacy (as opposed to the more common handshake).

Following his local guide training, Orom was temporarily employed by the Salazie Ecomuseum to help with a new exhibition with the theme of 'The nature of know-how' (*La nature des savoir-faire*) inaugurated in 1998. Along with ethnographers from the University of La Réunion, he participated in the collection of objects and in the erecting of exhibition displays. Laslo, who by then had just moved out of his old house, wanted to demolish the old wooden buildings in order to expand the garden. Orom convinced him to keep these and to transform the plot into a 'heritage site'. To make the garden more accessible, Orom and Laslo built a ramp between the road and the pathway leading to the old wooden house. With the financial and technical help of the Salazie Ecomuseum and the ethnologists of the University of La Réunion, Orom and Laslo added a straw hut to the existing structures, using traditional building materials and techniques. The building of this straw hut was visually documented by a team of university ethnologists (Pandolfi and Quezin 1998). From 1997, Laslo became a privileged informant for the ethnologists working for the Salazie Ecomuseum. Repeatedly interviewed, observed, photographed and filmed, he progressively transformed into an enigmatic figure representing and embodying the essence of an immediate past, of a popular culture that had just been 'lost'. Various fragments of his life, especially those related to 'traditional life', were widely represented at the 1998 Ecomuseum exhibition. He also appeared in academic articles published in the journal of the National Museum for Popular Arts and Traditions (MNATP, 1999) and in numerous journalistic photo-reportages about Salazie and its 'popular traditions' in international and local media. Since 1998, local tour operators programmed visits of Laslo's garden as a tourist site. International travel journalists invited by La Réunion's tourist board were taken to Salazie to visit – and write about – his garden.

While Laslo was transformed into a kind of popular heritage celebrity at the local level, he seemed little concerned about this new public persona. In private, in the presence of his friends and family, he usually avoided talking about it. Only once did he show me a collection of French and US-American travel magazines in which he appeared. These he had put out of sight, in a toolbox in his kitchen. Otherwise, he seemed to have continued life as before. In the morning, he usually started his day by sweeping the courtyard of his garden plot and the floor of the wooden house. As with most people in La Réunion, he wanted to have his courtyard and house 'clean', free of dust. He then built a fire in the kitchen to boil water and make coffee. The doors of the kitchen were usually wide open and a radio was playing. He fed his cats and then spent the rest of the morning looking after his plants. At lunchtime, he usually ate a meal that he had brought with him to the garden and then slept for a while in the kitchen and, later, in the newly built straw hut.

This daily routine was slightly altered when tourist groups were expected for a visit. In most cases it was Orom who would bring these groups to the garden, but sometimes other guides working for tour operators based on the coast would come. The relationship with these guides was always personal; Laslo knew them individually and the guides knew they had to call him before paying a visit. As a sort of entrance fee (Laslo would not call it this), Laslo received 5 French francs per visitor (approximately 1 Euro). Sometimes tourists also left tips. Tourist groups usually arrived between 10 and 11 am and the site visit took about one hour. When such groups were expected, Laslo, after sweeping and cleaning the courtyard and the house, and after lighting the fire and making coffee, usually went into his garden to pick a selection of fruits and vegetables – according to the season, bananas, passion fruits, tree tomatoes, lychees, mangoes, pineapple, etc. These he placed on a table in the wooden house. He also placed a christophene (*chouchou*) on a rock in the courtyard between the house and the kitchen. He rearranged the fire so it would not smoke too much. Orom had told him to do so, Laslo once explained me. And he turned off the radio and hid it under a pillow. When the time of the visit approached, he usually got nervous – like an actor before going on stage. He repeatedly went back and forth between the kitchen and the house for a last check, picking up leaves fallen in the courtyard, stroking the cat. During this time, he would hide behind bushes and trees, not to be seen, watching out for signs that would announce the arrival of the tourist group. Once he spotted the tourists through the woods, he would jump into his kitchen and hide behind the half-closed kitchen door. Sometimes, I was hiding with him and, especially at the beginning of my fieldwork, he explained to me what would happen next. The tourist guide, usually Orom, or one of the tourists would ask, in a loud voice, if someone is home ('*Il y a quelqu'un?*'). Once this sentence had been uttered, he would open the kitchen door, slowly step down into the court yard and walk down the path towards the street, to welcome the visitors.

Orom and Laslo at Play

Orom had gathered the tourist group at the entrance to Laslo's garden plot. In the Creole garden, he explained, there is no entry gate. However, there is an invisible boundary that visitors should not trespass without being invited by the owner of the plot. A specific type of plant marks this boundary. The group halted and Orom explained that there were three questions one can ask in order to be granted licence to enter a house. The group chose among these options and, all shouting together, loudly enquired if 'someone is home' ('*Il y a quelqu'un?*'). After a short while, an elderly man appeared on the path under the trees, smiling and inviting them to come in. Orom presented the man as Laslo, his uncle. Laslo and the tourists shook hands and then entered the garden plot. Orom took the group to the courtyard between the kitchen and the wooden house. What followed was a relatively sophisticated performance acted out between Orom, Laslo and the tourists. Orom usually started by announcing that he had 'his own way of seeing things', but that he also respected the way his parents understood and still understand the world. He picked up different plants in the garden and explained how they had been used by his parents. Laslo intervened at specific moments, when Orom – seemingly spontaneously – asked him to develop or confirm one of his stories or explanations. Orom spoke in French, with a slight Creole accent, and Laslo in Creole. When Orom addressed Laslo, he talked to him in Creole and then explained to the tourists, in French, what he had asked him or what Laslo had answered. In most cases, this 'translation' was not strictly necessary as Laslo's Creole was pretty much understandable for French-language speakers. Orom and Laslo largely followed a script, which seemed to have emerged from the frequent repetition of the visit. They played different roles, Orom the mediator between 'tradition and modernity' and Laslo the living representative of a lost past. Orom talked about contemporary issues, about scientific proofs for the naturalist knowledge of his parents, about economic, social and environmental problems. Laslo talked about his parents, about how life was before, about how to use certain objects, about the medical use of plants. Laslo confirmed Orom's explanations by adding stories of his childhood, his own past. The same set of stories was told, again and again, during this standard itinerary. They were often based on objects, plants, fruits or buildings 'found', as if by coincidence, along this itinerary. Many of these were props which had been purposefully placed in specific locations.

After his introduction to the front yard, Orom asked the group to enter the wooden house. Laslo no longer lives here, he explained. He lives in the village down the road. However, he is here everyday, whether there be cyclones, volcanic eruptions, earthquakes or landslides, because, he explained, Laslo loves this kind of life. It is fantastic that he has kept this kind of traditional life while everything around him has changed. This is why, Orom said, two years ago he had the idea to show this place to visitors, so its memory would not be lost. He explained various aspects of the architecture of the house and Laslo pointed out where exactly he, his brothers and sisters, and his parents had slept before. Orom explained the building technique of the house, the wood used, the 'intelligent' aeration system, the beliefs related to the position of the door and the windows. Laslo added short anecdotes. The visit to the house was concluded with an invitation for the tourists to try some of the fruits put on the table. The group then left the house and entered the kitchen, a wooden construction around an open fireplace, covered by a straw roof. The kitchen used to be the place for people to meet, a social space, Orom explained. It was here that people received visitors, where the family came together to eat, where important decisions were made, he added. The house, on the contrary, was only used for sleeping. It was always kept clean and nicely decorated, so people who passed by could look inside. His parents rarely received visitors in the house; it was far more convivial to receive people in the kitchen. This, he concluded, is proper Creole hospitality.

The tourists sat down on wooden benches around the fire. Orom talked about different objects in the kitchen, how these were used in former times. Laslo talked about how the family came together here, how they were not allowed to talk while taking their meals, how his father used to punish him and his brothers, how his mother was compassionate with them when they were punished. Orom's stories about 'how the world has changed so quickly in recent years' often triggered more generic conversations, typically[2] about 'how globalisation has left the world empty of values', 'how young people cannot connect to the world and have become violent', 'how hard it is for people to find jobs', 'how the Americans have imposed their values on the world'. Orom usually took a specific 'position' within these conversations. He explained that his motivation for guiding tourists was so that he could bring people from different locations together, he could bring alive a commonly lived Creole moment. He often explained that his past, the traditions he grew up with, were disappearing as well. After these 'kitchen conversations', he usually got out his guitar and suggested singing a song, normally *Mon Ile*, a popular song about La Réunion. Although this suggestion appeared spontaneous, it was part of the standard visit programme. The song's lyrics were about the singular beauty of the island, a declaration of love by the singer for the place in which he grew up. Through the emotion in Orom's voice, the ambience of the fireplace in the dark and smoky kitchen and the mood created by the conversations about some lost condition, this song generally generated an emotionally very moving moment. It was not rare that some of the tourists started crying, hiding their faces with their hands. Even I, who had many times participated in this almost ceremonially choreographed moment, had the shivers.

When the song was finished, Orom stood up and invited the tourists to go back into the garden. He led them to the old-style straw-hut that he and Laslo had built close to the kitchen. The tourists entered and it was mainly Laslo's role then to explain that people 'really lived in this kind of house before'. Orom usually watched through the window and started to explain, smiling, that the bed doesn't 'run'. It was fixed to the wall so it can't 'run'. And before, as it was often raining and people like Laslo's parents had no TV, it was important that the bed didn't 'run'. He smiled again. It explains, he said, the large number of children in the Creole families. The tourists smiled as well. They understood Orom's underlying suggestion that a bed that 'didn't run', a bed solidly fixed to the wall, allowed for very frequent love-making. Laslo usually added, seriously, that even during a cyclone, the bed didn't 'run'. Orom, again with a wry smile, repeated 'even during a cyclone' (implying the double sense 'even during making love like a cyclone'). The juxtaposition of Laslo's serious demeanour and Orom's double-meaning of 'during a cyclone' amplified the comic nature of this situation. So, the bed doesn't run, Orom concluded, again with a smile. For the rest of the day, sentences about things that 'don't run' became running jokes among the tourists. The joke almost always worked.

Allegorical Flowers

Like many other tourist guides, Orom had learnt to interact with tourists. He had observed their reactions, understood how to anticipate expectations, how to throw rhetoric hooks, build tension and then nullify it through forms of comedy or tragedy. Orom constantly flirted with social, gender, phenotype, time, space and moral boundaries. He projected tourists into a kaleidoscope of possible roles and existences, of selves in which tourists could recognise their own histories and desires of being and belonging. Through the quick juxtaposition of such potential roles and existences, through the editing of images of poverty against images of progress, of cruelty against happiness, of order against chaos, he frequently took them on an emotional rollercoaster ride. In one moment, they could identify with Orom's implicit critique of modernity, his pessimism toward a disarticulated social life, the loss of beauty and social solidarity of an idealised past. Orom repeatedly talked about the rich naturalist knowledge of the generation of his parents, a knowledge that he explained was now being forgotten. People no longer know how to use plants, he repeatedly explained. In the next moment, he had changed this nostalgic narrative to an optimistic one of social progress. He talked about his children who could now go to school for free, who had access to modern medicine, to the mass media, to travel. He talked about himself, being of black phenotype, born into a family with no land ownership, who was now able to look after his children, who had become part of modernity at a time when the striking poverty of the past, the cruel times of slavery and social injustice, of severe punishment, were over. In the next moment, he often once again juxtaposed this optimistic narrative of social progress against a narrative of social complexity, of social fragmentation – where people belong to a variety of different, usually non-articulated contexts; where they are lost; where they search for roots.

A set of rhetoric and non-verbal performances appeared in all his guided tours. They formed a kind of core register of narrative possibilities, of scripts that were acted out through his guide's performance. These were usually based on the opposition between an immediate here-and-now, and different types of alien worlds: the past, Western modernity, female gender, wilderness, etc. The tourists were habitually made to identify with roles related to these alien worlds. In many ways, they were identified with strangers, representatives of a global modernity, or of the former coloniser (France). Orom projected himself into the role of the castaway, the runaway slave who escaped the cruelty of a society dominated by the French coloniser. He thus created a situation which was usually uncomfortable for the mainly French tourists who, at least implicitly, were identified with the role of the former coloniser. In some cases, by addressing the tourists with terms like 'your ancestors did that…', Orom made this role attribution quite explicit. Yet, he had a particular talent for dissolving these uncomfortable situations through forms of comedy or tragedy. He joked, for instance, about the difficulty runaway slaves had when they tried to run away with thorns in their feet. The violent story of slavery and hardship was dissolved; it became a comedy that Orom and the tourists could laugh about. They 'could' laugh about the past because Orom (who identified his ancestors as slaves) laughed about the past. The rhetorically built ontological difference between the self-victim and the other-colonial exploiter (implicitly projected onto the local-tourist relationship) was nullified. In the end, everyone was at the same level – a member of a common contemporary humanity. Orom often dissolved his stories about social progress in a similar way, by using a form of tragedy. He talked about a commonly experienced loss of authenticity and disenchantment brought about by the modernisation of the world. Here again, he merged the initially ontologically separate entities of tourists and La Réunion into a collective condition. Everyone was caught up in the same types of contradictions marked by, on the one hand, the desire for social progress leading to better chances and equality and, on the other hand, the fear of dissolving forms of order and traditional forms of solidarity.

Through his experience as a tourist guide, Orom could anticipate how tourists would react to these stories and their endings; how they projected their own contradictions of life into the narratives he used to structure his stories. He could anticipate quite well that tourists perceived the tragedy of his life to be an allegory for their own tragedy of life. Orom was a brilliant performer, able to spontaneously re-arrange scripts and interpret them in ways that would surprise. His performance was marked by changing rhythms and the staccato of dramaturgic turning points, by a juxtaposition of moments that created deep aesthetic emotions, feelings of heartbreaking sadness, thrills of erotic temptation, joyful happiness and profound sensations of existential human connectivity. Particular situational contexts generated further possibilities to refine the role-play. Sometimes, it suddenly started raining and Orom spontaneously improvised his rhetoric in this specific context. He would use the rain to talk about modernity and the progress brought about by 'good roofs'; to evoke nostalgic images of the past, of being a child walking through the warm summer rain. Or, if there were particularly pretty girls among the tourists, he would simply develop a juicy, sexualised metaphor about the effect of rain on flowers, or the effect of La Réunion on organic matter imported to the island. The tourists often threw images back to him and the dialogue that developed from this sometimes reached hilarious climaxes. In such contexts, Orom variably mobilised explanations, grimaces or jokes, out of a pre-existing personal register, which he configured with regard to the situational context. Sometimes, new jokes or stories emerged through the contact with tourists. Sometimes, tourists made spirited or funny jokes or connections that Orom would later re-adapt and, if these proved successful, integrate into his register.

Creole Magic

Through his guide performances, Orom persistently related his personal existence to a form of belonging to La Réunion – excluding the tourists as members of a world outside, usually the European French mainland. The separation between these worlds was discursively marked by the ascription of respective attributes and qualities. La Réunion was depicted as a place full of juices, colours and flavours, luscious odours, monstrously magnified vegetables and plants, flowers that look like sexual organs. It appeared imbued with qualities capable of transforming imported things, of awakening the vitality of ordinary European garden flowers, of sexualising people, plants and objects, of making things bigger, more tasteful, and juicier. Orom constructed the island as a magical realm able to liquefy categorical boundaries between people and things, to dissolve ontological difference, to reinstate the reign of an idealised essential nature of all things. To define the product of this specific quality of the island, Orom constantly returned to the term 'Creole'. This term was made to signify a form of solidarity between flowers in Laslo's garden, populations in La Réunion, humans and nature, male and female gender, of La Réunion and the world outside. 'Creole' became a way of being in the world, a romanticised ethno-method to living contradictory relationships. It became a way to package the accidents and complexity of social history in models and stories, a kind of remedy to make sense of oppositions and boundaries other than through racial or class categories. It was a narrative that suggested an alternative cosmos based on forms of solidarity and interfluidity, an idealised world of harmony, a utopia come-real within a here-and-now. Tourists could make sense of this narrative; they could identify with this Creole world, with La Réunion as an island that had managed to enable peace and intercultural understanding. By emphasising his belonging to the island, his being Creole, Orom constituted himself as one of the island's products, a Creole ontologically linked to and imbued with its 'magical' qualities. Through his tourism performance, he constituted himself as part of the island's nature; as a man with an intimate connection to this nature; a man talented with the spiritual and sexual power of this nature. At the same time, through other references (e.g. his narratives about social progress and nostalgia), he portrayed himself as a self-conscious and cultivated person, as a man who speaks the language of humanistic culture, who defends humanistic values.

Giving a Good Image

When the tourists had left that day, he asked me if I wanted to join him for a drink at his house. We walked up the street from the central square of the village and talked about one of the girls that was part of the group. Talking about girls was one of the themes of interest we shared; it was an easy start for a conversation. Then we talked about things that had happened in the village, the preparations for the village festivities that would take place two months later. The memory of the visit guided during the morning quickly seemed to fade. When we arrived at his house and met his wife and children, the emotional theatre of the morning, the songs, the stories and the tears, seemed to have vanished. They seemed only significant in terms of a job Orom had done, as his profession. They were not discussed any further than that. Orom's son brought each of us a bottle of beer and we drank together. A complicity and friendship had developed between us since we had spent many months in the same village, and many hours on guided tours. I had met his family, been invited to some of his Sunday family picnics.

We had some private parties in my house and often went to Laslo's garden plot to fix things or just for a coffee.

Orom knew that Orom-the-Creole-hero was a successful plot. It was his job and it was this job that legitimated his participation in the social life of the village. It was the performance of 'being Creole' for tourists that constituted him as a social persona within the context of his immediate social environment. One day, a couple of weeks earlier, after finishing a guided tour, Orom had started a conversation about his job. He had asked me not to think badly of him, but explained that he would 'normally not work everyday'. I had not understood what he wanted to tell me. He explained that other people in the village guided tourists every day, even on Sundays, that they often even had several groups a day. In these cases, the contact with tourists becomes very industrial, he said. It is like slavery, he added: you do the same thing over and over, and you lose its essence. When I had met him early on in the village, he told me how important it was to him to 'preserve' and 'value' (*valorise*) Creole traditions, a discourse not very different from the one he usually performed for tourists, local development agents or the ethnologists of the Salazie Ecomuseum. It was he who had invited me to accompany him during his tours. It was only later that he realised that I would be staying in the village for quite a few months. He told me that his wife had asked him to go to work while I was around, to 'give a good image' both of his family and the village. During my fieldwork in other contexts in La Réunion, I had repeatedly come across the term of 'giving a good image'. It seemed to indicate a communicative dimension to individual acts where the finality of doing things seemed to lie less in the immediate transformation of a reality or the re-establishment of a kind of order, than in the public display of the very act of doing things. In this sense, acts like gardening or going shopping frequently seemed to be associated with social significations that went far beyond their presumable immediate utility. They seemed to be social performances of 'giving a good image', which meant projecting a certain image of the self into a local social realm. In this sense, going shopping or gardening could be seen as scenes of a social theatre, scenes for a local audience that allow assumption of certain roles and images associated with these roles. People would often take a shower, dress up and clean the car before going shopping, as a preparation for the dramaturgic act of shopping in the realm of an intersubjective space created between the social performer and the eye of the neighbourhood or other audiences watching (or imagined to be watching) the act of shopping.

Similarly, within the village context, the publicly performed act of guiding tourists seemed to legitimate a social role for Orom. This role was almost ritually reaffirmed during village festivals and public ceremonies. During these events, Orom would dress up in his usual tourist guide uniform and perform 'Creole traditions'. Wearing khaki shorts, a white T-shirt with 'Tour Guide' for a logo, hiking boots, and a straw hat on his head, he would sing Creole songs before a local audience. In the eyes of this local audience, he would look precisely like a tourist guide. People did not dress like this in La Réunion. His dress code belonged strictly to the realm of tourism. Straw hats were for elderly men living in rural areas. 'Modern men' in La Réunion did not wear hiking boots or hats. The songs Orom performed during these local events were pretty much the same ones he performed for tourists. Through this kind of performance, Orom dramatised himself as a professional performer for tourists, as a tourist guide. Just as local farmers would use these festive events to 'perform' their attachment to the earth and the fruits they gain from it, Orom 'performed' his attachment to 'Creole traditions' as core values of his tourism activity. At least, this was how many people in the village initially saw it and accepted it.

Transformations

During the late 1990s and early 2000s, tourism became economically more important in the village and a process of objectifying 'local Creole traditions' took place within its wider public realms. During this epoch, with the help of public subsidies, the active involvement of neo-rural villagers and the technical advice of public sector 'experts', houses were repainted (according to colour-schemes developed by the governmental agency for architecture and heritage, SDAP, reflecting an 'authentic system' of 'Creole aesthetics' – probably based on total nonsense as shown by Laurent Niollet's (1999) ethno-historic work on local architecture), wooden facades repaired, a central square built, heritage highlights made visible through signposts. In La Réunion's Regional Development Plan (SAR), the village was proposed as an 'authentic Creole village' (Région Réunion 1995). The economy of the valley began to shift from an initially agricultural to a more 'horticultural' logic of gardening. Performing 'Creole traditions' or a 'Creole lifestyle' became the new means of social participation. Orom's activity was hardly sustainable because it was not what he wanted to do eight hours a day, every day. However, he was present whenever local TV crews filmed reports about the village, whenever travel journalists or agents visited the valley, or whenever local or national politicians were shown the 'successes' of local development programmes in Salazie. Often, I was not sure whether his job had a commercial economic end to it at all, whether the remuneration he gained from it was more than a symbolic sanction re-affirming that he was actually doing a job.

While there is no positive logic in historical events and their consequences, they still happen and condition specific contexts of social life. They set frames within or along which individual lives emerge and develop. In La Réunion, these frames have been shifting rather radically within the past forty years. The political economy of the colonial society, based on the production and export of sugar and the exploitation of cheap labour introduced as slaves and contract workers, has progressively dissolved. From the 1960s, the origin of wealth was no longer associated with the fertility of cash crop land or cheap labour, but with French and European Union cash flows arriving in the island in the form of subsidies, public sector wages and public infrastructure investments. The formerly agricultural populations were, to a large extent, resettled in urban coastal areas. Many of them remained jobless and received social welfare allocations. Others managed to get public sector jobs or worked in the quickly emerging building and service sector industries, nourished by the population's newly acquired purchasing power. Through the floral allegories of his 'guide discourse', Orom talked about this historical rupture. He talked about the end of an era, the end of the plantation society that had left his parents and himself without a clear idea of the future, that had dissolved a moral order of social life and projected him into the uncertainties of a new era. The longer I observed him, the more I gained the impression that the sense of tragedy he developed through his friendly metaphors was his own tragedy. It translated his ambiguous feelings about his newly found social freedom and the simultaneous loss of the life he had grown up with. At the same time, he turned the rhetoric employed during the postcolonial context of the Cold War on its head. The Creole, hitherto visualised as a culturally and racially degenerated child, never good enough with regard to its idealised mother, France, the centre of reference, the *Mère-Patrie* (Verges 1999), became elevated as a new ideal, a public persona 'threatened' by the polluting effects of a form of modernity emanating precisely from this *Mère-Patrie* (by then renamed the *métropole*). The Creole, no longer the unworthy child of a colonial mother, metamorphosed into a global ideal, a model to think about the social realities of the world in terms of contact, exchanges and transformation (instead of 'pure cultures') gained prominence. Tourism to places like La Réunion made this idea tangible. At the same time, it implies the transformation of La Réunion into a new form of social theatre, a large contemplateive garden cultivating ideas of and aspiration to society. Local populations became part of the stage, a sort of human flower embodying ideas of time and Creoleness through their bodies, life and productions. The next chapter will focus on the modalities and underlying models of this new form of 'garden culture'.

Chapter 3
Cultivating Society as a Human Garden

The Time of a Space...

Crouzet Richard[1] was too young, too inexperienced; he did not have the appearance of an Alexandre Delarge, the eloquence and long hair of a Parisian intellectual. He did not have the aura of a Raphael Folio, the white hair and the authority of the colonial noble, or the nerve of a Jean-Ives Loufox (pseudonym), the confidence of the local entrepreneur to maintain a public face while arranging profitable deals with his clientele in hidden backrooms. The people in the village I had become friends with over the previous months had widely agreed that Crouzet Richard only got his job because he was from the *métropole* (from France mainland), because he was a *métroplitain*, a *zoreil*, because he was supported by other *zoreils* working in the public sector of the island. They also seemed to agree that he would not be able to take the project anywhere. They would eventually receive support from the newly elected regional policy makers, La Réunion's Communist Party. Crouzet Richard would become one of the first high-profile victims of 'regional preference', an informal, officially illegal practice of employing 'locals' instead of people from the French mainland.

I first met Crouzet Richard during a conference at the University of La Réunion in 1999. I was about to start fieldwork for my doctoral research and was interested in a project that the research centre I was then associated with, the *Centre Interdisciplinaire de Recherche sur la Construction Identitaire* (CIRCI), had been heavily involved with: the development of an 'ecomuseum' inside Salazie, one of the three main valleys of the island. The overarching aim of this project was to generate new livelihoods and revitalise social life in this valley by means of conserving traditional rural practices and life-styles and transforming them into a tourist product. The concept of the ecomuseum included the development of thirteen sites, where 'locals' would show traditional handicraft techniques and sell their products to tourists. Permanent exhibition sites with changing exhibitions were to be established in the three largest villages of the valley. Only one road leads into the valley, through a tidal gorge, with a waterfall and a bridge, and a house beside the bridge was to act as a kind of entrance door. The role of public art was to add meaning to the natural landscape and create village centres. The connection of the two cul-de-sac villages by a road was intended to make the valley a circuit. The implication of the project was a designed territory that, ideally, was to insert itself into the patterns of the valley's everyday life. It was to be a conservation of an authentic form, the 'real life', made visible to tourists. The valley was to be transformed into a large garden with the population somehow being part of the cultivated matter and made visible to the tourists' eye. The model underlying this new territory appeared to be located within a longer tradition of garden theory and practice. It seemed to be based on a broader model of landscape garden, a 'human garden', where 'locals' become part of wider images of a certain rural authenticity.

In 1999, Crouzet Richard was employed to run this new ecomuseum. He had been selected for the post in 1998, after responding to a job advertisement in a national French newspaper and following several rounds of interviews. He was a trained anthropologist who had been working as an associate researcher for the French National Scientific Research Centre (CNRS), in a programme focusing on the material culture of food. When he arrived in La Réunion in early 1999 to take up his job, he found himself caught up in the power struggles that followed the regional council elections that had taken place two weeks earlier, with a radical shift of votes in favour of La Réunion's Communist Party. Paul Vergès, one of the enigmatic figures of the island's 1960s and 1970s autonomy struggles, had been elected as the island's new regional president. Crouzet Richard, wanting to touch base with his interlocutors in the local and regional administrations. He explained me that he was told 'to go back home', that he could no longer assume that he had this job. He went to see the French governmental labour inspection agency (whose role it is to insure the application of labour law), where he was told that his work contract had been signed for a long time and the test period had run out. His contract was therefore legal and he could not be fired. With this information in hand, he announced that he would go to the labour court and claim 200,000 French francs (approximately €40,0000) in compensation if his work contract was unlawfully terminated. He told me that during a confidential meeting with regional and departmental leaders of La Réunion, he finally accepted that his three-year contract should be reduced to eighteen months while his monthly wage was increased by 5,000 French francs (around €1000).

During these eighteen months employment, the collaboration with the local and regional governance bodies remained difficult. He focused his principal attention on the preparation of an exhibition staged in one of the permanent exhibition sites of the Ecomuseum in Hell-Bourg. Its theme, decided before his arrival, entailed a certain irony: 'Time of a Space, Space of a Time' (*L'espace d'un temps, le temps d'un espace*). Officially, it was about the social history of the valley of Salazie. At a more subtle level, it was also about Crouzet Richard's journey through the disarray and conflicts in and between French post-colonial administrations and cultural policy makers. The exhibition was inaugurated in December 1999, on the day of Crouzet Richard's departure. The re-advertisement of the director's job clearly indicated the qualities of the person to be employed; it stated that the candidate should have 'an excellent knowledge of the Réunion field and culture' and should be able to 'master the Creole language both orally and in writing'.

Crouzet Richard's unexpected transformation into a *persona non grata* and his violent rejection for not being 'local' indicates wider issues related to the mobilisation of the 'local' as a criterion to establish inclusion or exclusion. Paradoxically, the very category of the local was first introduced to La Réunion by colonial administrators and nineteenth-century romantic artists, and later picked up by ethnographers, curators, journalists and tourism developers. It was to constitute the ontological and moral foundation for the redesign of the valley of Salazie in terms of what I suggest could be called a 'human garden'. Equally paradoxically, this category was subsequently appropriated by stakeholders in the island as a way of fashioning a 'local' self, as an auto-ethnographic trope providing a widely consensual category to discriminate between what is considered as local and what is not, eventually to expell those elements – plants, objects and people – considered to be exotic. In this chapter, I will use the case of the Salazie Ecomuseum to show the dialectical process underlying this double paradox and the cultural and political forces behind it. The approach is based on data collected through ethnographic observations between 1999 and 2001, and the study of policy documents and meeting notes found, mainly, in the archives of the Salazie Ecomuseum.

Grounding of the Island's Romantic Landscape

The geomorphology of La Réunion is defined by two volcanic formations joined by a high plain. The older of these volcanic formations, situated in the island's north, is marked by three steep valleys formed around a central peak, the *Piton des Neiges*, more than 3000 metres high. One of these valleys is Salazie. It is situated in the north-eastern part of the island, also called 'under the wind' as north-eastern Alize winds bring regular, often heavy, rains, which envelop the mountains in cascading waterfalls and contribute to a lush green vegetation. The valley was first populated by maroons, runaway slaves, who, during the eighteenth century, fled the plantations on the island's coasts. During the nineteenth century, the progressive colonisation of La Réunion under the reign of the French East India Company led to an increasing rarity of good agricultural land along the island's coast, and new land concessions were created in its less accessible areas

– the high plains and the three northern valleys. In 1830, a group of white settlers from the north-east coast obtained temporary land concessions inside the valley of Salazie and founded a village besides a small lake, the Mare-à-Poule-d'Eau. The group developed small vegetables, tobacco, tea, coffee and christophene exploitations and, by introducing agricultural labourers and slaves, progressively grew larger and subsequently obtained larger permanent land concessions. By 1858, the population of the valley had grown to 7500 inhabitants.

In 1831, thermal sources were discovered deep inside the valley, and their exploitation for therapeutic purposes began in 1850. During the second half of the nineteenth and the beginning of the twentieth century, the newly founded village of Hell-Bourg became an important societal centre for the agricultural and political noblesse of the island. The feudal system of the plantation society, especially the principle of *colonage*,[2] developed on the island during the nineteenth century and this largely freed the local sugar cane bourgeoisie from the need to work. Following spa fashions that had emerged on the European continent since the late eighteenth century, this bourgeoisie consequently formed a local leisure class who would spend the hot summer months in the freshness of the mountains, to 'change the air', while the cooler winters were spent at houses built along the beaches of the island's west coast. The effervescence of the Salazie spa, from the second half of the nineteenth century, is confirmed by the construction of more than fifty villas, a casino, three hotels, a military hospital and a cemetery, and by the vivid memories of some of the elders, interviewed in 1999, who remembered the urban chic of Hell-Bourg – there were pavements and benches to enjoy the landscape – and the extravagant balls hosted by the governor. Daily life in this eclectic holiday village was marked by social and leisure activities. People entertained invitees in splendid gardens and porches, took the waters, gambled at the casino, practiced fine arts and poetry, cultivated the body through sports and spa treatments, and organised leisure and hunting excursions.

At the same time, the valley of Salazie, the spatial and aesthetic backdrop to these activities, was poetically enchanted as a landscape. Poets, travel writers and painters close to the La Réunion's colonial bourgeoisie, educated in the nineteenth-century European centres of intellectual and artistic life, namely in Paris, adopted different aesthetic tropes of nature then fashionable and projected these onto the island's mountainscape. Most of these artists and writers were born to colonial families on the island and had moved to Paris at an early age for further studies. Some returned – at least temporarily – to the island, while most settled permanently on the European mainland. Possibly most famous among these 'local' artists is Charles Marie René Leconte de Lisle (1818–1894), who took over the French Academy chair of Victor Hugo after the latter passed away. Others include Antoine Bertin (1752–1790), Eugène Dayot (1810–1852) and Evariste de Parny (1753–1814), but also Auguste Lacaussade (1815–1897), Léon Dierx (1839–1912) and Jean d'Esme (1893–1966). The work of these writers and poets generated a whole new vision of the island as a romantic heaven. They transformed the valleys, formerly perceived as dangerous, poor and aesthetically bland, into rough and wild natural landscapes. The abrupt valleys became visible and perceptible through dark romantic ideas of nature as a super-force absorbing the human into its spells. They lauded the beauty and heroism of the island's maroons, slaves who had fled the sugar cane plantations and found a more or less fragile freedom in the island's mountainous wilderness. They often juxtaposed these gothic romantic images of nature and noble savages with a militant realist aesthetic of rural poverty, and hence projected the nineteenth-century European bourgeois fashion of a humanistic critique of modernity, of the exploitation of labourers, of slavery, into the social-poetic realm of La Réunion – while comfortably indulging in a leisure environment made possible by the very injustices and exploitations of the colonial feudal system that their texts and artworks decried (Vergès 1999, 2001). Picking up 'native' names of places and projecting noble savage themes onto the physical landscapes of the island's mountains and valleys, they generated a new type of map (that would eventually, to a large degree, flow into the official maps of the island), which transformed the island into a material support for stories and myths; an allegorical territory that allowed the bourgeois classes to reflect on a specific history and order of social life, and to experience the erotic temptation of wilderness as an imagined *ur*-condition, without getting dirty. While reformulating the island's geography and lacking the foundations of the imaginary structures of what would later become its tourism industry, these new spatial tropes and forms of landscape 'artialisation' (Roger 1997) seemed to have had little contact with, or impact on, the island's large proletariat. The writings that accompanied the post-Second World War autonomy movement of the 1960s and 1970s and the post-Cold War local development policies of the 1990s and 2000s would play a central role in their wider vulgarisation.

The Poetics of Rural Renaissance Policy

The building of the Suez Canal at the end of the nineteenth century decreased the logistic importance of La Réunion as a supply harbour on the sea route between India and Europe (Doumenge 1984). The economic downturn caused by this event was further amplified by steadily falling world market prices for sugar since the late nineteenth century, partly due to the invention of cheaper production processes based on sugar beet planted on the European continent. Trade embargos during the two World Wars further worsened the situation of the island's economy. In 1946, La Réunion, hitherto a French colony, became a *Département*, with initially little effect on its precarious economic situation. In this context, facing an uncertain future, many members of the island's bourgeois classes emigrated to other French colonies or to the French mainland in Europe.

The effect was clearly visible in the spa town of Hell-Bourg, largely abandoned by the island's previous leisure class by the early 1960s. To a certain degree, the bourgeois landowner class that had settled in Salazie since the early nineteenth century also started to leave. The hotels were closed and the spa site, devastated by a cyclone, became unusable. Some of the abandoned bourgeois villas were sold to members of La Réunion's newly emerging middle class who in many ways imitated the lifestyle of the former island bourgeoisies. Others were abandoned and started to decay.

The 1960s were marked by the neo-colonial struggle by the French government against the Réunion Communist Party-led autonomy movement. This was accompanied by the initiation of economic development programmes and the progressive introduction of the French welfare state. Facing increased economic competition from imports and more productive agricultural sectors on the island's coast, the large agricultural population of Salazie struggled to survive. Most agricultural exploitations were too small and unproductive to gain sufficient income that would allow their owners to keep pace with the quickly modernising society. To address these problems, a French government programme initiated a spatial reform based on the regrouping of the many hamlets and isolated exploitations of the valley into three major villages. It also proceeded to build new types of houses, using metal sheet and concrete, equipped with fresh and waste water systems, replacing the straw huts of the agricultural population. Despite these efforts, the continued economic crisis led many, especially those not owning any land, to leave the valley to find jobs on the coast or on the French mainland in Europe. In the early 1970s, facing the rapid rural exodus of the island's valleys and the consequent hyper-urbanisation of its coastal towns, the French government started a new initiative aimed at the rural development of the island's interior. This re-development was based on the modernisation of agricultural activities and the development of tourism as a new form of livelihood (Benoist 1983). By defining the spatial boundaries of its political action, the newly created *Plan d'Aménagement des Hauts* (Highland Development Plan), implemented by a governmental agency, the *Commissariat à l'Aménagement des Hauts* (Highland Development Commissariat), introduced an official understanding of the island's interior, eighty per cent of its total surface, as a separated territory.

The idea of using tourism as a development tool was not new. It had already been suggested by a spatial planner, Jean-Claude Allaire, commissioned to define the direction of Salazie's development plan in 1964. Allaire (1964: 51) suggested that Hell-Bourg should 'become the departure point for numerous mountain circuits', a new tourism hub that would eventually replace its former vocation as a climate station. The model behind this idea was taken up and pushed further by the 1995 *Schéma d'Aménagement Régional* (Regional Development Scheme; SAR), the island's principal official spatial planning tool. Section 2.3.3 of this scheme defined as an overarching aim the 'perpetuation of agricultural traditions in La Réunion'. The objectives were to generate new livelihoods, to defend forms of rural solidarity and 'to preserve environments, natural heritage and traditions that constituted the foundations of La Réunion's society [...] essential to ensuring the development of tourism activities' (Région Réunion 1995: 60). While the SAR recognised capital-intensive agriculture as the principal development option in the fertile and flat rural zones of the island's coastal areas, it proposed a rather ambiguous development option for the island's highlands. In its introductory chapter, it defined these highlands as 'a space that [had] managed to ally modernity and tradition – modernity through the development of infrastructures, service sectors, an intensified and diversified agriculture; tradition by successfully preserving and symbolising the "Reunion soul" through its lifestyles, architecture and landscapes' (Région Réunion 1995:13). The type of social life formed in the inside spaces of the island (as a result of development policy in particular) was part of a wider realm of modernity in the island: like a stage (or human garden), their modernity lay in their capacity to perform and embody symbolic values (of authenticity, a rural realm lost) adding sense to a wider La Reunion identity. Its proposed economic and social vocation appeared to be a garden, which was cultivated, preserved and made visible, through various artefacts and folkloric practices, in order to be considered as the island's 'soul'.

Cultivating the Valley as a Human Garden

In the late 1980s and throughout the 1990s, while Salazie's demographic exodus peaked, a new type of settler, mainly of French continental origin, moved into the valley to work in public sector jobs, to retire or to launch tourism enterprises. Facing the material decay of Hell-Bourg's colonial buildings, these newly arrived people created a not-for-profit association for the 'safeguard and renaissance' of the village. Supported by the then newly created *Service Départemental d'Architecture* (Departmental Service for Architecture; SDA), the association began to carry out different renovation and repainting projects and succeeded in getting several bourgeois houses and architectural elements put on the official list of preserved historic heritage. This meant that any construction within 300m of such classified sites needed the official approval of the SDA. The association hence managed *de facto* to 'protect' the built environment of the entire village, much to the dismay of the rural population, who aspired to knock down the half-rotten bourgeois wooden villas and replace them with 'modern' concrete houses. Various studies carried out during the 1990s explained the symbolic depreciation of building materials such as wood or metal sheet, seen as a synonym for poverty among large parts of the rural population (Ecomuseum Salazie and Université de La Reunion 1998: 2; Niollet 1999). In 1988, the CAH and the Departmental Council of La Réunion suggested the creation of a *Pays d'Accueil Touristique* (a

'Touristic Host Country') in Salazie, in order to better 'valorise the architectural heritage' of the valley, to create tourism infrastructures and to integrate the rural population into the development of a local tourism sector (Benoit 1988). According to an official report produced by the CAH in 1995, the objective of such a *Pays d'Accueil Touristique* was to 'develop countryside tourism integrated to the local economy and respectful of the environment' (CAH 1995: 2). Finally, four Touristic Host Countries – governed by the Charta of the French National Federation of Touristic Host Countries (*Fédération Nationale des Pays d'Accueil Touristiques*) – were created in the island, one of them in Salazie.

To realise the double objective of 'making the authenticity' of the valley 'emerge' and 'promoting the local economy through the creation of a new range of products' (CAH 1995: 1), the Departmental Service for Architecture (SDA) sponsored the first president of the Salazie Host Country on a visit to different ecomuseums on the French mainland. Returning from this trip, the association's president seemed convinced that this option was the right institutional framework with which to develop the valley's cultural economy. In 1995, a not-for-profit association called Ecomuseum Salazie was founded as a joint venture involving different government agencies and local, departmental and regional governance services. The University of La Réunion and the National Museum of Popular Arts and Traditions (MNATP) became scientific partners in 1998. The initial plan of the museum suggested the creation of thirteen 'heritage islands' distributed throughout the valley, each highlighting a specific heritage aspect of Salazie. These 'heritage islands' were to be linked within a tourist itinerary by following the valley's main roads. This itinerary was to start at the 'entrance' of the valley, defined by a tidal canyon and the passage of a waterfall cascading on the road. Tourists were to be welcomed here at a visitor kiosk which would also provide information about sites and possible visits. Following the main road into the valley, visitors would arrive at Salazie village, where they would visit a permanent exhibition site. After this village, the main road separated into two, leading respectively to the villages of Grand-Ilet and Hell-Bourg. The Ecomuseum project was to promote the idea of building a new road that would link these two villages in order to create a circuit; tourists would no longer need to turn around once they had arrived in the villages, but could follow a circular itinerary.[3] Different 'traditional' activities were to be developed and exhibited in tourist sites along the road, including hat-making, bee-keeping, knitting, etc. In both Hell-Bourg and Grand-Ilet, permanent exhibition sites were to be developed. From the inception of the project, one of the overarching objectives was to use the different sites to address both tourist and local audiences. In 1990, a report commissioned by the Regional Delegation of Commerce, Artisan and Tourism stressed the pedagogical function of the newly developed heritage sites for local populations. The report recommended that 'the new heritage centre will need to accomplish a mission of sensitising the public and local population to the necessary safeguarding of the environment and of making them the guardians regarding the authenticity of local cultural practices' (Huchet 1990: 89).

The various local development initiatives planned for Salazie since the 1960s seemed to come together in a largely shared design model. Salazie seemed to be thought of in terms of a large garden, which cultivated what was seen as not only the heritage of this rural valley, but also of the wider island nation. It was to become a place about the island's rural history, but was somehow outside history; an ideal location that was able to evoke and bring to life (or keep alive) stories and symbols of an imagined local primordialism. It was to be transformed into an allegorical territory making visible the essence of the island's being both for local and touristic audiences. Through all these development initiatives, the valley was progressively transformed into a large hospitality venue designed for a range of visiting outsiders. The models underpinning most of these initiatives, especially those adhering to the doctrine of sustainable development adopted on the island during the late 1990s, seem to propose a different concept of time, unlike the dominant thinking of the time in terms of linearity and progress. During a local development workshop organised by academics and governmental development agents in Hell-Bourg in 2000, the principle of this alternative model was illustrated by a diagram of a linear vector of 'time' being put orthogonally to a circular vector of 'progress'. If this model suggests that an idea of 'progress' can be seen as independent of 'time', it would imply an end-of-history idea of timelessness; an idea that nothing new would ever happen, only transformations within an eternal present.

The inhabitants of Salazie were to become part of this new social configuration, this new type of social theatre; their role was to perform 'authentic' traditional life-styles and activities, to cultivate an idealised idea of their own rural poverty as a means of participating in the realm of the island's modernity. As I will show later, people at different levels of social and political life did eventually start to take the rules of this play seriously. They would mobilise the notion of local heritage in the formation of auto-ethnographic stories and concepts of social life which would eventually legitimate the exclusion of the very inceptors of the notions at the base of these stories, the French agents who had planned the development and conservation of local social worlds from the social realms that they planned and implemented. Before discussing this, however, I wish to explore the stories that unfolded within the realm of the Salazie Ecomuseum and Host Country programmes.

Making Museum Displays

The first three exhibitions staged at the permanent site of the Salazie Ecomuseum in Hell-Bourg explored themes related to different sites that were about to be developed along the wider tourist itinerary through Salazie. They concerned people from the valley, among others, Orom (cf. chapter 2). I had driven up to

Hell-Bourg a couple of times before moving there permanently for six months, as part of my ethnographic fieldwork. I identified the demographic structure of the village and the insertion of social hierarchies and family and sociability networks in its physical spaces. I also identified the network of people that had formed as a result of the initiatives of the Salazie Ecomuseum. Crouzet Richard had just arrived and we socialised and became friends. He was an associate researcher at my research centre at the University of La Réunion and gave me access to the museum's archives and internal documents. He lived on the coast and usually drove up to the museum's office every day. We often had lunch together and I followed him during the different phases of the design and programming of the exhibition he was about to stage. The title of this exhibition was 'Time of a Space, the Space of a Time', and was part of the centenary celebrations of the commune of Salazie, as mentioned above. The scientific committee of the museum, headed by an anthropologist from the University of La Réunion – the director of my PhD studies – suggested three themes to be developed through this exhibition. These included the technologies and know-how of the rural and agricultural professions, the religious heritage of the valley, and the ethno-history and social life of the nineteenth-century spa society in Hell-Bourg. The collaboration with the National Museum of Popular Arts and Traditions (MNATP) allowed several ethnological studies – on popular housing, the religious markings of space, the historic phenomenon of marooning – to be financed and carried out by graduate students of the University of La Réunion. I had known most of these students as my classroom fellows and was in fact observing how some of my best friends and the director of my PhD studies mobilised ethnological practice and rhetoric to stage a museum display. They knew about my approach and we often made jokes about the ambivalence of this situation.

The organisation of the exhibition, overseen by Crouzet Richard, also included a private company specialising in the production of displays for museums, theatres, events and shop windows. The exhibition site had four rooms of equal size. To create a spatial narrative linking these four rooms into a coherent exhibition story, the idea that emerged, during an initial brainstorming session involving Crouzet Richard and the designer of the display production company, was to attribute to each room a dominant element, a historic focus and a generic theme. The dominant elements were to be 'earth', 'water', 'fire' and 'air'; visitors would move from an 'earth room' to an 'air room', passing through a 'water' and a 'fire room'. The historical foci were the first and second halves of the nineteenth century, treated in chronological order by passing from one room into the next. Finally, the 'generic themes' approached in the different rooms were, in order, the 'history of the valley's colonisation', the 'social history of Hell-Bourg', 'people in their environment', and 'memorable events'. These three over-layered thematic sequences – realised through the spatial configuration of the exhibition – seemed to be based on a specific narrative logic. Crouzet Richard explained to me that the visitors should first feel the anxiety of moving into the valley, the steep mountainous walls 'threatening the stability of individual existence'. The first room was also to communicate the uncertainty and anxiety of the valley's first settlers in the early nineteenth century – maroons and colonials from the coast – who were 'hoping to create a better future'. Panels on the wall, which reproduced texts and illustrations from nineteenth-century novels and lithographs by some of the 'local' artists mentioned before, would communicate 'how life was represented during the period of the first settlement of the valley', according to Crouzet Richard.[4] The panels were organised in three sub-sections, focusing respectively on marooning, the colonisation of the valley and the early developments of the spa business. The story of marooning was illustrated by a sequence of images and accompanying texts taken from *Les marrons*, a novel by Louis Timagene Houat (first published in Paris in 1844). The first of these images showed 'slaves in the plantation', the second 'the moment of marooning' (e.g. of fleeing the plantation), the third 'life in a cavern', the fourth 'the ambush and capture of the maroons by slave hunters', the sixth and seventh their condemnation and execution. The second theme, the colonisation of the valley, was illustrated by reproductions of historic land concession documents, cadastral plans and inventories of goods belonging to the colonial families of the valley (including references to the number of slaves they owned). The third theme, the development of spa and leisure activities in Hell-Bourg, was illustrated by the reproduction of twelve lithographs and texts taken from Louis Antoine Roussin's and Charles Merme's *Promenade à Salazie* (first published in 1851).

Following their introduction to the valley, visitors to the exhibition should then, in the second room, 'experience a transition into a different world and historic period'. This transition was symbolised by different installations, a large mirror with water flowing over its surface and a small wooden bridge. The mirror was to symbolise a water cascade called 'piss in the air' (*pisse en l'air*); this, together with a bridge, was situated at the entrance to the valley. According to Crouzet Richard, both installations were also intended to mark the transition from the pioneering theme staged in the first room and the leisure society theme of the second. Reproductions of black-and-white photographs on the walls were to show different scenes of social life within this leisure society. The third room was to show how the settlers and the agricultural population had coped with the 'rough' environment of the valley and managed to develop agricultural and rural activities. Different building materials – metal sheet, dressed wooden panels, concrete and solid wood – covered the walls, in order 'to serve as a support for talking about the values the rural populations attached to different building styles'. Next to a wooden bridge that the exhibition's visitors would have to pass, the figurine of a virgin was placed in a small shrine. Crouzet Richard explained that it referred to the religious marking of the territory by the rural populations. Virgin shrines were commonly found besides rivers and passages, to invoke protection for the passerby. An argument had broken out during one of the meetings of the museum's local user committee when Crouzet Richard presented his initial idea to use a Saint-Expedite figurine, which was seen as somewhat unusual by outside visitors. Such figurines were commonly used to invoke the spirit of Saint-Expedite both to seek protection against evil and to engage in malicious practices. The Saint-Expedite cult was poorly regarded by the powerful Catholic Church in La Réunion and so was usually practiced in secret. The first director of the Salazie Ecomuseum had once repaired a Saint-Expedite figure that he had found broken in a courtyard. Ignoring the common practice of knocking off the head of this figure if Saint-Expedite did not fulfil the wishes addressed to him, the director glued the broken head back into place. The naivety underlying his act subsequently became a major topic within the local gossip and was later repeatedly used, in conversations I had, to argue that 'all these foreigners' actually know little about local life. Following the concerns raised by the local user committee, Crouzet Richard accepted the use of a Virgin figurine as what he called the politically correct solution. The fire theme was eventually dropped as a topic for this room. The aim of the fourth room was to introduce – or 'recall' – the 'collective memories of the valley'. Newspaper clippings of curious events from the beginning of the twentieth century were stuck on one wall. Images and short biographies of eight people who, according to Crouzet Richard, had marked the memory of the people of Salazie, were placed behind glass on the other wall. Three of these people were members of the island's bourgeoisie who had spent time in the village of Hell-Bourg; three were clerics who had founded churches or schools; and two were mythical figures of the island's colonial history, the maroon Anchaing and the bandit Zitte.

These museographic displays were political in that they employed powerful rhetoric techniques to allow a selection of historical facts to be embedded in the form of a story.[5] They employed techniques of montage where meaning was generated through the juxtaposition of images and the generation of sequences. In the first room of this exhibition, the dark romantic story of marooning ending with the execution of slaves was juxtaposed with the story of the valley's colonisation and a set of poeticising images of Hell-Bourg's leisure and spa society. All three stories were underpinned by a similar plot of leaving or fleeing the coast, of establishing a form of life inside the valley, and ultimately of having to leave the valley forever. This plot generated a specific spatial semiotic based on the dialectic of inside and outside. The visitor to the exhibition was given the role of an outsider who progressively moved deeper inside the valley to discover it as a utopian world of various historical periods – a heaven where slaves found freedom, where impoverished colonials found new fertile grounds, and where the island's bourgeoisie found a place of leisure. Just like the runaway slaves, the colonials and the bourgeois society in the exhibition's stories, the visitors would ultimately have to leave the valley. The exhibition thus could be seen as a miniature of a wider time-space model situating the valley in relation to the rest of the island; the model of a liminal space of happiness that would ultimately not last; an ephemeral Garden of Eden found, enjoyed and lost. It was a story that captured a specific idea of time as an eternal cycle.

To develop this underlying plot, the storytelling mobilised different references and contexts. It was never really clear which of these references related to fiction and which to historical facts. It was possibly not that important as long as, through their interplay, they managed to capture and convince the audience. Academic arguments were woven into specific formats of story and historiography, in particular the narrative logic of the idea of Eden and Eden lost. These academic arguments seemed able to naturalise the subjective nature of the story and make it appear as positive scientific knowledge about time and place. They seemed imbued with a quasi-magical quality, which may be related to the symbolic power of the institution of academia in modern society or, within the specific postcolonial context of La Réunion, to the symbolic assimilation of academia and 'modernity'. The three-part structure of the story lent itself for the projection of a particular history of La Réunion in this island's space. The poetics of the exhibition and of the wider museographic project of the Salazie Ecomuseum and Salazie Host Country brought about a largely dominant development logic; Salazie was to become what can be seen as a 'living museum', a 'human garden' that was to nurture and cultivate a romantically framed vision of the Réunion's collective self. As I have shown above, this vision initially emerged through the romantic writings and landscape practices of the island's nineteenth-century bourgeoisie; it seemed to remain widely hegemonic within recent development conceptions by policy makers, curators and spatial planners.

Transculturation and Auto-Ethnography

While the display of the 1999 exhibition and the wider territorial symbolism projected by the Salazie Ecomuseum onto the island's space seemed to imply a specific communicative logic, its reception by visitors and mediators proved highly variable. Whatever the initial intentions of the museum producers or political planners might have been, the site, once opened to the public, became a place of multi-vocality where individuals and groups reconfigured the different signs and forms presented to them in personalised forms of stories and allegories. By following different guides mediating the exhibition to visitor audiences, I observed various forms of divergence from the 'ideal story' by the curator, but also the persistence of specific formal aspects implied in this ideal story, in particular the dialectic of an inside and an outside that appeared in the stories by these guides. The exhibition was inaugurated in December 1999. It employed two 'cultural mediators' to guide visitors through the different rooms. During the first weeks that followed the exhibition's opening, I repeatedly recorded the discourses of these mediators, and also of Crouzet Richard during the inauguration night.

Focusing specifically on the first room, I started with an analysis of the contents explored by these discourses. All mediators structured their talks around the three main topics developed through the display of the first room: marooning, colonisation and Hell-Bourg's leisure society. However, the weight given to each of these topics within the respective discourses varied largely. While Crouzet Richard employed respectively approximately the same time and number of words to talk about each of the topics, the two mediators clearly made the marooning theme the main story of this room (respectively eighty-two per cent and sixty-three per cent of the words used in their discourses focused on this theme). Furthermore, the different mediators let this specific story unfold in quite different ways. Crouzet Richard repeatedly told visitors that the scarcity of traces left by the marooning slaves made it difficult to carry out a scientific investigation into this historic phenomenon. Yet, in the next part of his speech he explained what he called the 'classical journey' of a marooning slave. Using the reproductions of images and texts from Louis Timagene Houat's 1844 novel *Les marrons* as a support, he explained the conditions of life of slaves in the coastal plantations, the act of fleeting and finding freedom inside the valley, the use the maroons made of an apparently sympathetic nature, the ultimate downfall when they were discovered by slave hunters and taken back to the coast to be judged and executed. Crouzet Richard specified that the visual support of his story had been taken from a novel. Yet, he said, it was 'realistic because the author of this novel was a freed slave'.

The discourse by one of the 'mediators', a twenty-year-old man from the village, began from a different departure point. He explained that the first inhabitants of the valley were maroons who had fled from the brutal world of slavery situated on the island's coast, 'on the other side of the river'. He developed his story by adopting a perspective from within the valley which he depicted as a heaven of freedom, happiness and harmony between people of different races. Following his discourse, this 'happy valley' was consistently threatened by an uncertain, always brutal outside world, personified in particular by the figure of the slave hunter who moved up the river to capture maroons and bring them back to the coast. He also introduced a different ending to the story. 'The maroons were too strong and proud to be captured', he said, 'they were only discovered as a result of treatise', and 'even then they preferred to die rather than to return to a condition of slavery'. He told the story of Anchaing, a maroon who lived on top of a hill inside the valley; once discovered by Bronchard, the famous slave hunter, Anchaing threw himself from the edge of a cliff, and while he fell he transformed into a buzzard. 'It is a legend', the mediator then said. He told the visitors that he had been shocked when he learnt about a case where a freed slave immediately procured slaves himself, 'to work for him'. 'They had their own values at the time', he concluded, 'the more slaves one owned, the richer one was'. The second mediator, a twenty-three-year-old woman from a different village in the valley developed her story of marooning from a similar 'insider' perspective. She used the same spatial structure, constrasting the cruel coastal area with the peaceful heaven of the valley. She further reinforced the differences between these two worlds by developing a story about a child separated from her slave mother and sold. She asked how people could be so cruel and explained that inside the valley such a thing was unimaginable; the valley was a 'world of love'.

The spatial dialectic underlying these and similar stories was generally very 'successful' with a range of different people. They became largely hegemonic wherever it came to talking about the island's space, people or history. They had been picked up not only by local development agencies, European tourists, the local mediators of the Salazie Ecomuseum, and Crouzet Richard, but also by local artists, supermarkets advertisement campaigns, international journalists developing features about the island and organisers of local sport and folkloric events and festivals. The success of these stories seemed to stem from their allegorical power to evoke the culturally widespread dialectic between a potentially dangerous outside world and a peaceful, harmony-seeking inside world, and to articulate this dialectic through the journey of a hero, the maroon. While this dialectic of the inside and the outside is a common cultural phenomenon that may originate from the way in which humans perceive their being in the world and shape their world views accordingly (Bachelard 1994a [1958]), it became subject to a contextually specific interpretation in La Réunion. The island's space became intelligible, for a variety of people, in terms of this widely understood dialectic and the specific spatial semiotic it generated. From this point of view, Salazie became an allegorical territory that, for many people, seemed to encapsulate the idea of a preserved rural space, a kind of ideal garden inhabited by people firmly grounded in the land they live in, thereby generating a stable reference within a rapidly transforming, disoriented contemporary society.

The first politically relevant appropriation of these allegorical tropes took place during the 1960s when La Réunion's autonomy movements began to mobilise some of the romanticised hero stories and the related symbolism of the island's mountainous wilderness to formulate a rhetoric in favour of the island's cultural and historical self-determination (Lilette 1999). The story of a heroic maroon opposing the violent condition of slavery and oppression imposed by the European coloniser and finding freedom in an almost motherly nature seemed to provide a pertinent allegory to help to make sense of feelings of neo-colonial oppression by the French state during the 1960s, and the claim for auto-determination that was at the heart of the island's autonomy movement. In this sense, the nineteenth-century bourgeois tropes of wilderness and anti-modernity were used in what Mary-Louise Pratt (1992) calls an 'auto-ethnographic' fashion; they were reconfigured in terms of stories that seemed to make sense of postcolonial struggle within a locally specific political context. Thus, the set of tropes originally projected onto the island by an aesthetic fashionable in the nineteenth-century metropolitan centres was subjected to a process of 'transculturation' (Pratt 1992),[6] a process whereby alien elements are given new signification and appropriated into the terms of locally significant practices, aesthetics and patterns of signification.

Colonial Mimesis and the 'Magic' of Locality

At the same time, the reference to the former coloniser seemed to remain the chief symbolic tool to legitimate these auto-ethnographic discourses. Their power seemed to stem from an act of mimesis of aesthetic models and forms associated with this former coloniser. In this sense, the use of concepts such as 'heritage' or 'locality' found their legitimacy in the dominant culture of French policy makers. They allowed some of the architects of the autonomy movement to advocate the formalisation and then preservation and protection of 'autochthon' and 'local' culture against the 'threat of cultural homogenisation' brought about by the colonial empires during the Cold War and the acceleration of the globalisation phenomenon since the 1980s. This process of transculturation hence generated a paradoxical situation where localised political action in favour of the island's autonomy had been empowered by the adoption of the colonial (and touristic) aesthetic of La Réunion as a pure and authentic island locality. It subsequently legitimated a claim of 'purification' of this very locality among others via the expulsion of the coloniser as a form of colonial mimesis, the foreign notion of locality becomes an emic category in La Reunion; in its original context (in France, among French anthropologists, developers and curators), this notion is based on an ideal of the 'purity' of local culture and claims to conserving/purifying local culture. Once locally appropriated, it allows populations in La Reunion to expulse those people who have taught them this notion (The French, the former coloniser). As I will show in this section, the colonisers were finally expelled – 'regurgitated' – by their own creations.

In order to be recognised by the French ministry of culture, the Salazie Ecomuseum had to represent its collections according to the museographic norms defined by the French national museum legislation. To help the new museum to implement these norms, the scientific committee of the Salazie Ecomuseum had formed a collaboration with a French national museum, the National Museum for Popular Culture and Traditions (MNATP), in 1998. The preamble of the Memorandum of Understanding signed with the MNATP stated that 'the ethnological heritage of La Reunion was poorly known and threatened'; that 'La Reunion's rural culture has produced poor quality artefacts and that the climatic conditions and the lack of representation regarding the knowledgeable notion of heritage among the population accentuated the phenomenon of degradation and loss of this ethnological heritage'. It explained that 'there is an urgency to collect' (MNATP and Salazie Ecomuseum 1998: 2). The first objective of this memorandum indicated that the MNATP wished to constitute a collection of objects in order to have La Réunion represented in the national ethnological collections. At the end of his first mission to La Réunion in 1998, the representative of the MNATP wrote in his report that 'the presence of a La Réunion collection within the MNATP is a necessary tool for the knowledge and recognition of the history and society of La Réunion in the *métropole*' [commonly used word to designate the French mainland]. 'Furthermore', he specified, 'it was not normal that the 200,000 Réunions living in the *métropole* did not see their culture represented within this national institution'. He emphasised that 'the constitution of a collection respecting the lines of the *Memorandum of Understanding* related to the same movement as the efforts by the Réunions to make themselves known through the development of cultural tourism and the exportation of music and the arts in all their forms and gastronomy'. 'The collection', he stated, 'was to contribute to the integration of La Réunion in a global cultural policy respectful of specificities' (Martin 1998: 1-3). In this sense, it seems that the dominant understanding within the French cultural policy *milieu* was that a locally specific cultural heritage was to be integrated into a wider national heritage matrix. Locality, materialised in specific cultural heritage objects and practices, seemed to be employed here as the common format to represent and rethink the constitutive parts of the nation's body. The category of locality consequently emerged as a somehow soft cooked set of signs of cultural differentiation within a far more rigid structural framework of national heritage policy.

The implementation of this doctrine through multi-levelled cultural policies in La Réunion – in particular, the development of the Salazie Ecomuseum – had a paradoxical and sociologically complex effect. According to the official minutes taken during a meeting of the island's chiefs of cultural equipment on 14 July 1998, a leading figure of the cultural service of the departmental council of La Réunion, Mr M., 'recalled the problems caused by the attitude of the civil servants from the MNATP'. He said that 'it seemed that the latter had organised a collection of objects. Both the Departmental Council and the Regional Council of La Réunion [the two principal locally elected chambers with limited responsibilities for the island's development and governance] were against this type of exploitation'. He asked everyone present at the meeting to be 'vigilant' and 'to stop any form of collaboration with people who used to pillage the regions in order to centralise everything in Paris' (DPCS 1998). Ten days later, on 24 July 1998, Crouzet Richard met the regional director of cultural affairs at the offices of the regional council. According to his account, he wanted to clarify the financial situation of the Salazie Ecomuseum, especially with regard to promised financial commitments that both local chambers had not respected. According to the official minutes taken during this meeting, he was told that 'informally (*officieusement*), the departmental council followed the regional council, blocking the earmarked budget transfers for 1997 and 1998'. The minutes quote Crouzet Richard as asking 'why the financial situation was blocked'; the regional director for cultural affairs, Mr B., 'explained the point of view of the Regional Council with regard to the Salazie Ecomuseum project: it did not agree with the memorandum of understanding between Salazie Ecomuseum and the NMATP and the fieldwork of a NMATP researcher pillaging La Reunion's heritage for the profit of the *métropole*'. 'Crouzet Richard explained that this memorandum of understanding was an important act for Salazie Ecomuseum, allowing it to form a core collection of objects, in collaboration with the NMATP, that in the long-term was to be recognised by the national Direction of Museums of France (DMF) in order to allow Salazie Ecomuseum to become a museum controlled by the national government and co-financed at 40% by the French ministry of culture'. 'The memorandum', he continued, 'implied that all objects were to be collected in duplicate, with all unicats remaining in La Reunion'.[7] 'Mr B. responded by explaining that the Regional Council had no interest in seeing Salazie Ecomuseum becoming a museum controlled by the national government. While the government financed Salazie Ecomuseum at 40%, it contributed little to the actual functioning budget of the museum, which remained an important financial weight for the Regional Council' (Conseil Régional 1998: 1).

It seems to me that the hesitation of the local councils to continue their collaboration with the museum project was neither – as they claimed – about a financial issue, nor about the 'pillage of the local heritage'. Rather, it was concerned with the ownership of local heritage, the question of who was allowed to exhibit local heritage artefacts in public displays. Adopting a rhetoric of locality allowed local policy makers to mobilise the inside-outside dialectic against the interference of governmental agencies such as the MNATP, seen as belonging to the outside. The category of the local – imbued with the relative 'magic' that stems from the postcolonial *métropole* – hence generated a new meta-narrative at the local level. It allowed people here to think of and justify social discrimination in terms of their local belongings. In this sense, the dominant model of Salazie as a human garden, a living heritage and anti-image of modernity, allowing people to indulge in the nostalgia of a lost paradise to be preserved for future generations, was mobilised against the very governmental development agencies that had developed this model from the 1960s and especially the 1990s. The model of the human garden was striking back, evicting its very creators – architects, planners, curators, landscape gardeners – from its office of command, under the mainly approving eyes of naïve tourist audiences. After his departure from the Salazie Ecomuseum, Crouzet Richard worked as an independent consultant. Together with the researcher who carried out the initial fieldwork for the MNATP, he co-founded a not-for profit association whose official aim was the knowledge, transmission and promotion of the cultural, natural and ethnological heritage of

La Réunion, the Indian Ocean and the fringing countries of the zone. During the following years, he was commissioned to create various exhibitions in town halls and local museum sites, and to organise cultural workshops and events. In 2008, he was appointed as the new director of cultural affairs of the commune that he had been living in since his arrival on the island ten years earlier.

Epilogue on the 'Reunion Miracle'

In 1999, Paul Vergès, then newly elected president of the island's Regional Council, announced the creation of a new, far more ambitious museum, the Maison des Civilisations et de l'Unité Réunionnaise (House of the Civilisations and Reunion Unity). In the preamble of the project outline (MCUR 2008), he asked the rhetorical question: 'How can we, Reunions, a small people who have always been encouraged to imitate the West, promote, enrich, understand and explore what some call their "roots", yet retain the basis of our own cultural differences?' 'If we can demonstrate,' he explained, 'that our cultural diversity strengthens our society instead of pulling it apart, that it is a binding force for dialogue and cohesion, that we respect others as equals and acknowledge the originality of each respective contribution, then we can talk of a Reunion miracle: we will have managed to creolise all the incoming values without being assimilated by any one of them, whereas the general tendency is to try to assimilate groups different from one's own and make them fit into one's own cultural values. I think that this is Reunion Island's contribution to the world.' He further explained 'that all the ancestors of groups which came from various continents and belonged to diverse civilisations, be they from Africa, Madagascar, Europe, Dravidian and Moslem India, with all the cultural aspects attached to them will be given recognition'. He concluded that 'by referring to the notion of "heritage", we enhance the value of those civilisations while situating them all on an equal footing'.

Paul Vergès' discourse seemed to be guided by a rhetoric of 'unity in diversity' that has been emanating from the political and cultural centres of the Western world since the 1960s. What exactly does this rhetoric entail? If there is unity in diversity, then both concepts are situated at different levels. The integration of cultural differences within a common framework, a form of human unity, may be achieved through forms of what Claude Levi-Strauss (1966) called symbolic digestion; the soft-boiling of cultural difference that becomes a signifier of 'cultural differentiation' (Baudrillard 1972) at a different level of society; a sign-object exchanged within a wider cultural economy that emerges within the global landscape of a newly emerging transnational social theatre. In performing the dramas and tragedies of modern being, these theatres play out the idea of diversity and transform it into a new hegemony, of a dominant global taste for all things Creole.

Paul Vergès seemed to push the rationale further and argued that the museum was ultimately to be about 'unity'. 'Faced with the impending conflicts that the Indian Ocean region will witness tomorrow', he writes, 'unity is our most precious asset'. From this point of view, he described the island's capacity to demonstrate 'unity' as a value that would define the future terms of the island's participation in a wider world society. Through this rhetoric, the idea of the human garden seems to be projected on the entire island space. La Réunion was to become a model for the world; a world 'that had not reached unity; that was struggling more than ever to manage its demographic and environmental crisis'. Paul Vergès had already raised this idea several years earlier (1993) and, although today it seems to continue to underpin the approach of the new museum project,[8] it should probably be considered within the historic context of the early 1990s marked by the end of the Cold War and the widespread, optimistic belief in what Francis Fukuyama formulated as the 'end of history' (1992), 'the end point of mankind's ideological evolution and the universalisation of Western liberal democracy as the final form of human government'.

However unrealistic Francis Fukuyama's idea may have been, it gave rise to an appealing model and, according to Paul Vergès, La Réunion's society was to serve as the ground in which to cultivate it. His words hence promoted the classical utopia of an ideal society, of a garden of earthly delights in the here and now. He suggested it as a mode of social participation within a world society. His project implied ambivalences, in particular with regard to the island as a place in history, a place where people actually live and possibly contest the idealised vision of 'unity in diversity' – or unity in creolisation – that is projected upon them. On the other hand, the perpetual repetition of a specific utopian model of society by different mediators – schools, media, development programmes, leisure activities, etc. – may lead to the formation of normative frameworks in the island's society where the performance of a utopian existence and everyday life practices acting out something that could be recognised, by external observers, as an utopian existence, become undistinguishable from one another: social performance in a tourist setting becomes indistinguishable from social practice; self-conscious performance becomes social practice. From such a point of view, defended among others by Karl Marx (Arendt 1977), the instrumentalisation and interiorisation of a utopian model of society would have led to its normalisation. The initially fluid nature of social performances would have led to largely naturalised, unself-conscious cultural practices within a new global cultural economy.

Hanna Arendt (1977) highlighted the dilemmas of Karl Marx's political approach to history, which was based on the idea that the normalisation of a specific moral would lead to a state where morals would no longer need to be policed in and by society. Like many other places of utopian projection, La Réunion is not, or at least not for everyone, a place of earthly delights. At the end of the 1990s, almost forty per cent of the active population were unemployed while at the same time seeking to participate in the emerging realm of a local 'modernity', especially through mass consumption. In this context, it appears difficult to convince most Réunions to find personal pride and identity in a role which consists in being happy doing nothing under a tree. It also seems hard to convince them that their precarious lifestyle is part of a wider project and culture which offers a model of unity for the world. Life and love continuously disrupt people's ideal cycles; they do not care much for ideologies, but evolve, in Jorge Luis Borges' words (2004: 20), in an eternal present.

Part II

The Hospitality of the Garden

Chapter 4
Hospitality and Love

Eating Strangers in the Garden[1]

After leaving the motorway, the yellow coach from Saint-Denis slowed down and stopped besides the road. Adamsky saw Eve-Marie waiting. He waved through the window. She recognised him and made a welcome gesture with her right arm. She smiled. Adamsky and his two friends got off and went over to meet her. They kissed in greeting, and then she led them along the road into a residential quarter. They passed through lush garden plots with small brightly painted houses built of metal-sheet and wood facing the street. They were talking about their trip. Eve-Marie picked up a small rock from besides the road and threw it at a couple of dogs that had started to bark at them. The dogs made an abrupt screaming sound, as if they had been hit, and retreated, their tail between their legs. After a couple of hundred metres they arrived at a wide garden plot with a fence totally overgrown with bushes, flowers and several trees. Through this floral façade, Adamsky could see a metal-sheet house painted in white, with green wooden shutters and a red roof. Marie-Eve led them inside the garden and along the house towards a table laid for a meal under a large mango tree. She introduced them to her younger siblings and to her mother.

Adamsky and Eve-Marie had met several months earlier at the student restaurant at the university campus of Saint-Denis. Adamsky had then just arrived on the island and was living in a small room at one of the on-campus student residences. He had been waiting for the student restaurant to open and saw a girl standing next to him. It was Eve-Marie. He had noticed her long black hair, her dark skin, and her eyes looking at him. She had been wearing blue jeans, a blue top and flipflops. She was slim and relatively tall. He found her pretty. He asked her if she knew when the restaurant would open. A brief conversation developed and they ate dinner together. Adamsky invited her to a student party in his room that was to happen some days later. She did not turn up. She later explained that she actually went to the residence, but hesitated to enter Adamsky's room when she 'heard the voices of so many strangers'. Both had met again about a week later. They had talked for a long time about their lives and their aspirations. Marie-Eve had told Adamsky about the poverty she had known as a child when her father died. Adamsky had told her about his upbringing in central Europe, about his dreams of living close to the sea and his study aspirations. One night they had kissed and over the following months, they had become a couple. Some weeks before Christmas, Eve-Marie had asked him, together with two of his friends, to join her for Sunday lunch at her mother's house. He had been happy and curious about this invitation, without however giving it any further consideration.

That day, Eve-Marie's younger siblings and her mother, Claudette, had been preparing the Sunday lunch since the early morning. Her brother had cut and raked the lawn and burnt the rubbish. Claudette had gone to the supermarket to buy meat, also a white paper cloth for the table, colourful paper dishes and cups, and plastic cutlery. After finishing these basic preparations, they had taken a shower and put on freshly ironed clothes. The table was carried from behind the house to a place in the shade under the mango tree and laid with the paper tablecloth and the colourful paper and plastic dishes, cups and cutlery. As aperitifs, they had put peanuts and crisps in small dishes placed in the middle of the table, together with a carafe of water and two 2-litre bottles of Coca Cola.

After her introduction to Adamsky and his friends, Claudette asked them to sit down in the shade and offered them a drink, a glass of rum punch. The sun was shining under a bright blue sky. It was dry and hot. They willingly accepted. Marie-Eve's two younger sisters brought two pots of curry from behind the house, together with a big cup full of white beans and a large pot of white cooked rice. One of the curries was made of lamb, the other of chicken cut into small pieces. Claudette started to serve everybody, first Adamsky and his friends. For the latter, eating the chicken curry proved to be quite difficult as small sharp fragments of chicken bone had been left in the food and the plastic cutlery did not seem to be the most appropriate tool for eating the dish. Eve-Marie was visibly amused when she noticed her invitees' difficulties. She ate with bare hands and explained that the *Malbars* (Réunions of Indian Tamil origin; cf. below) eat with their hands (It was an ethnic self-irony. She usually ate with fork and knife). Luc, her younger brother, equally amused by the foreigners' difficulties in using the plastic cutlery asked his mother if he could also eat with his hands. Claudette severely denied his request, saying that he should behave well at table (*il faut bien se tenir à table*), that he was not a savage. Luc replied immediately, laughing, that he was a savage (*sauvage même*). Everybody laughed and finished eating their dishes with their hands. After the meal, Claudette offered her guests a dish of camembert. Her partner, Bernard, a fifty-five-year-old man originally from the French mainland, was the only one to take cheese. Eve-Marie then went inside the house, returning with a colourful fruitcake and, to the astonishment of Adamsky and his friends, with a bottle of champagne. Claudette explained that, 'Yes, one should not live in misery every day; when we are together we should be together well' (*Eh non, il faut pas vivre la misère tous les jours, quand on est ensemble, il faut bien être ensemble!*). The conversations at table touched upon different themes: the importance and difficulties of university studies, a trip through Madagascar that Adamsky and his two friends were planning to undertake over Christmas. When one of Adamsky's friends asked if he could use the toilet, Eve-Marie looked at her mother, both seemingly embarrassed. Claudette said, 'You know, we are not rich; we do what we do with what we have'. Eve-Marie explained that the toilets were inside the house, 'behind the red curtain'. In the early evening, Eve-Marie, Adamsky and his friends had to return to the university campus in Saint-Denis. Claudette gave them a set of large cups that she had placed in a basket, filled with the rest of the curry, and Bernard drove them back to their student residence.

The Cultural Logic of Hospitality in La Réunion[2]

Two months later, Adamsky was again invited for a Sunday lunch at Claudette's. The occasion was the birthday of one of Eve-Marie's brothers. The context and form of the hospitality were similar to those he had experienced previously. He began to like Claudette, her garden and what he saw as her 'happy poverty'. He knew she was not rich, yet admired the way she engaged in what, he thought, was really important to life: a beautiful garden, abundant family meals, a lot of free time to be with friends and a deep empathy with her children. He felt he had found in her what he had been looking for on arrival in La Réunion: a kind of simple life focusing on the essence of happiness, the beauty of love, and unconditional affection for people she was close to. His idealisation of Claudette's life was shattered some weeks later. He had been on the west coast of the island and passed near Claudette's house. He decided to say hello, also hoping to get a good meal, as he had not eaten since the morning. To his surprise, he found the fridge almost empty. There was a cup of dried rice, a bottle of tap water, two almost empty tubes of ketchup and mustard, half a camembert, some white beans and spicy tomato sauce. He met Eve-Marie in the evening and asked her about the empty fridge. She explained that her mother was not rich; that essentially she lived off family allowance from the French welfare institutions. Moreover, Bernard, her partner, did not work regularly, so often the family only ate rice with beans and spicy sauce. Adamsky realised the naivety of his ideas about Claudette's life and became increasingly intrigued by Claudette's generous hospitality towards her guests.

During the years that followed, he spent many more Sundays at Claudette's house. He observed, and eventually participated in, the preparation and staging of a Sunday lunch. The meals were usually based on meat curries. The choice of meat, as well as the type of table decoration and the location of the table within the garden, were usually a function of the importance and status attributed to the guests and to the occasion. More expensive curries, based on lamb or seafood, were usually reserved for important guests or occasions such as Christmas, Easter and family celebrations such as christenings or weddings. Less expensive curries, based on chicken, pork or vegetables, were prepared when more familiar guests – Claudette's family, Adamsky and Eve-Marie – were present, or during specific ceremonial occasions prohibiting the consumption of meat. The structure of the Sunday lunches remained largely consistent. In contrast with weekday eating practices (with a simple dish of curry, rice with beans and spicy sauce), the Sunday lunches adopted the structure of a French meal, with aperitif, amuse-gueule, starter, main dish, cheese, dessert and coffee. Table decoration – almost always accompanied by colourful plastic cutlery, paper cups and dishes, and paper napkins – was bought only for important occasions. On less important occasions, Claudette used her normal tableware and cutlery. For more important occasions, Claudette and her children would always take a shower in the morning and wear freshly ironed clothes. The house and garden were meticulously swept before the arrival of the guests, and the sandy areas were watered to keep the dust down. Special attention was given to the cleaning of the front rooms open to the street and to the bathroom behind the house. To avoid getting dust inside the house, Claudette forbade her children to enter until the guests had arrived. On some occasions of extraordinary importance, e.g. Christmas, the invitation of Adamsky's parents several years later, etc., the house was freshly repainted and new sunshades installed. Later, when Claudette received more money from the social welfare institutions,[3] she undertook major renovation works at her house; significantly, one of the first projects was the installation of a wall and doors separating the bathroom from the living room area. Thus, she explained, she was able 'to correctly accommodate her invitees'. Throughout my fieldwork, I have regularly come across this phenomenon, usually with the same explanation. In some cases, people had built sophisticated bathrooms in rather modest metal sheet houses.

Adamsky started to appreciate Claudette's hospitality both as a game to enchant her guests and as a set of, in his eyes, pretty tedious performances whose meaning he did not understand. However, he knew the effect it had on European guests. About a year after he had first met Claudette, he started to work as a tour guide. One day he worked for a team of European TV journalists. He got on well with them and suggested that Claudette invite them for Sunday lunch. Claudette accepted. He gave her part of his wages to buy drinks and meat. The journalists were impressed by the friendliness of their hosts, the quality and abundance of the food and the beauty of Claudette's garden. The cameraman let Eve-Marie's younger brother film with his big TV camera. He also filmed during the meal. After the journalists had left, everyone came together behind the house to talk about the event. Claudette asked Adamsky whether she had 'given a good image'. One of Eve-Marie's sisters commented that 'they' had very much enjoyed the curries, as they had helped themselves three times. Her other sister laughingly added that they had also enjoyed the wine and summarised how many glasses each of them had drunk. Listening to these conversations, Adamsky realised to what degree the guests had been subjected to a meticulous observation by their hosts who then evaluated the efficiency of their strategy to charm the guests and 'give a good image'.

The meaning of 'giving a good image' appears to be a central issue for an anthropological understanding of hospitality in La Réunion. It implies two different aspects relating to what a good image represents in terms of Claudette's understanding, and to whom it is being given. According to Jacques Simonin, Michel Watin and Eliane Wolff (1993), the social act of 'giving a good image' is part of the communication system of the *kartié*, which, according to these authors, traditionally organised the way of living together at the micro-local level of the rural and post-rural communities of the island. Following Michel Watin (1991), the *kartié* represents a micro-local public sphere that emerged from a sociability of 'interconnaisance' based on shared kinship and everyday life relations within the residential quarter. For Watin and Wolff, the – literal – gaze of the *kartié* represented here a powerful institution of social control (Watin and Wolff 1995), associating an important communicative function with everyday life practices. From this perspective, social acts such as cleaning the house, gardening, going shopping, receiving guests or buying a newspaper at the local corner shop – banal in Adamsky's eyes – can be analysed as communicative actions performed in the eye of the *kartié*. By conforming to, but also by subtly contesting, social codes and aesthetic norms prescribed within the *kartié*, they allowed social actors like Claudette to participate socially and symbolically position herself within the residential quarter. The importance associated with 'giving a good image' demonstrates the omnipresent concerns of these social actors to avoid the shame and disgrace of public mockery (*ladilafe*) within the traditional sociability networks of the residential quarter, but also within the new sociability networks emerging in the new public spheres created by the media, public sector institutions such as schools and administrations, sports clubs, medical cabinets, supermarkets, cinemas, nightclubs, beaches and picnic grounds (Idelson 2002). The staging of public 'facades' allowed these social actors to actively enchant the spectators of their social performances, to anticipate the mockery within their sociability networks, to minimise its impact or, by staging a specific image, to lure it in a particular direction.

The hospitality shown towards strangers such as Adamsky and his friends, or the European TV crew invited into Claudette's garden, appears to emerge within the wider context of the cultural logic of the *kartié* and the models of behaviour and thinking about the world that it has brought about. These models were present in the very physical grounds and cultures of the domestic space. The aesthetic order underlying Claudette's house and garden plot seemed to repeat a widely common pattern that ethnologists had observed throughout the island (Barat 1978; Ghasarian 1988; Watin 1991; Zitte and du Vignaux 1993; Niollet 1999). This pattern is usually based upon a bipolar spatial structure with a front space which is visible from the street and a back space which is reserved for members of the closer sociability network of the house occupants. The front space has often been interpreted as a 'façade' staged for the public eye of the quarter. As in Claudette's case, it is usually comprised of densely arranged floral and arboreal displays in the front garden, meticulously cleaned pathways and the equally meticulously cleaned front rooms of the house made accessible to external view by having their doors wide opened. It often also includes other, more recent, elements that seem to have been incorporated into its spatial logic, such as cars parked in front of the house. According to most ethnological writings on traditional domestic space in La Réunion, these façades mark both a physical and social limit between the local public sphere of the residential quarter and the social intimacy of the house. Sensitive spaces that could be subjected to public mockery, sorcery or spells, e.g. the toilets or cooking area, are normally found in the backyards, often further protected by magical objects believed to turn aside the evil eye of neighbours or other potential intruders.

The front garden and front rooms of the house seem to represent an intermediate space that allowed certain visitors – deemed as particularly important, uncertain or potentially dangerous – to be accommodated. When Adamsky had nowhere to stay a year after his arrival in La Réunion, Claudette invited him to lodge in her house. He was given the front room, as if this was the natural thing to do. When Adamsky's parents were to visit several years later, and Adamsky and Claudette discussed the modalities of their accommodation, Claudette suggested that he welcome them in the living room in the front of the house. Adamsky, who by then understood the symbolic logic of the domestic space, rejected this idea and suggested that Claudette host them in the back yard. 'They are no strangers', he explained.

I observed similar ambiguities related to the spaces in which to host strangers, both in commercial outlets and private accommodation settings throughout the island. In most cases, the spatial structure of the Creole house seemed particularly adapted to the accommodation of tourists who were almost always accommodated in the front rooms. Additional bungalows were usually built in the front garden. *Table d'hôte* style dinners normally took place in specially arranged dining rooms, usually also in the front of the house. Some commercial guesthouse owners had initially invited their clients into their private kitchens, to share dinner within this intimate space. In all cases, these initial approaches were ultimately abandoned and clear spatial separations re-establishing the division between front space and backspace were introduced. 'We had to preserve our intimacy', they usually explained. In some more recently built 'modern' guesthouses, constructed according to different architectural models (e.g. with the kitchen or toilet to the front, living rooms to the back, etc.), the generalised tendency to re-establish the widely shared spatial model of the Creole house led to sometimes difficult situations, with signposts inside the ontologically uncertain spaces of the house – spaces that were neither clearly back space, nor front space – to restore the divisions between front and back space. In these cases, the communicative function of the front space to 'give a good image' to the outsider often got lost, to the deep frustration of the hosts. According to Eliane Wolff's (1991) work on the sociability networks emerging in one of La Réunion's major social housing estates, formerly agrarian populations aimed to re-establish, often with similar difficulty, the symbolic logic of this specific spatial culture within the new type of collective living. They faced similar difficulties in other contexts where the cultural logic of the *kartié* clashed with that of newly emerging public spheres that had often been brought about by institutions imported from the French mainland.[4]

I believe that the observations of the hospitality forms and practices observed in Claudette's house and garden can be related to wider social issues concerning the accommodation of strangers on different social levels of the island. Claudette seemed to conceive of the contact with Adamsky and his friends in terms of the cultural logic of the *kartié*. As students from Europe, the latter appeared to constitute a new type of stranger invoking a new type of hospitality realm. This realm remained governed by the interplay between the subtly arranged performances of Claudette's garden and lunch display and the naïve eye of these strangers who were easily charmed. Despite the cultural and personal differences between hosts and guests, this hospitality was – initially – largely successful. The guests were almost always enchanted by the display and ambience of Claudette's Sunday lunch. They subsequently validated the specific display of social identity and being in the world that Claudette made them see. They fulfilled their role as guests. Moreover, they became part of another, simultaneous, stage setting that evolved within the traditional context of the residential area. Their accommodation as 'important strangers' was made visible to the public eye of the *kartié*. While lunch was usually taken in the more intimate backyard, ostentatious Sunday lunches which involved important guests were frequently brought closer to the front space of the house. When Adamsky and his friends were first invited to Claudette's house, the table was set out under a mango tree close to the street, visible from the street. While Adamsky and his friends had easily fallen under the charms of their hosts, they had also unexpectedly become part of the garden display and the deeper lying cultural logic of the *kartié*. They had become a special type of ornamental flower cultivated in Claudette's garden, watered with Coca-Cola, wine and chicken curry.

The widespread success of Claudette's Sunday lunches with European visitors may be related to the specific historicity of hospitality cultures in La Réunion. It may be related to historic processes that have led to the normalisation of specific practices and models prescribing how to accommodate strangers 'correctly'. It is likely that these hospitality cultures have emerged within the contexts of the plantation society, marked by strong social hierarchies, clientelism and powerful paternalistic relationships between social classes. The European bourgeois model of hospitality cultivated by the island's elites, who were mainly of European origin, may have defined here a model for popular hospitality practices. From a broader phenomenological perspective, it could also be argued that the spatial division between front and back was a pragmatic solution that emerged from the specific social circumstances marking plantation society; that it could have developed independently, not as a form of cultural acculturation but of cultural 'bricolage' by populations for whom the stage managing of their public image had become an essential element in their social mobility strategies (see Ottino 1999, discussed below). Further historical research on the Creole garden would certainly provide data contributing to a better knowledge of processes of cultural adaptation in the long term.

Social Mobility Strategies and Expectations of Reciprocity

During the first months of their romantic liaison, Eve-Marie and Adamsky often talked about their youth and their different upbringings. Eve-Marie told anecdotes about her life at school, about how she and her friends had not taken their lessons seriously. At the same time, she explained to him how much her mother, Claudette, had insisted that she succeed at school – that she 'did not hang out on the street' (*qu'elle ne traîne dans la rue*). After passing the *baccalauréat* (the diploma that in France enables students to enter university), she registered as a student at the university of La Réunion. That was one year before meeting Adamsky. She failed her first year of studies and had to retake it. At that time, the French student welfare system automatically offered financial aid to students from economically modest backgrounds. However, these aids were only paid for regular study years, not for the years that students had to repeat after failing. Consequently, while Eve-Marie had benefited from a bursary during her first year of studies, she was left with no public financial aid when she attempted to retake her first year. She lived off an irregular allowance that she received from various sources, including her maternal uncle, her mother and the social services internal to the university. She met Adamsky in the beginning of her 'second tour'. A year later, she once again failed her exams. When her mother, Claudette, learnt about this news, she became furious. She asked Adamsky, who she had invited to stay at her house a week earlier because he had to leave his room at the student residence in Saint-Denis, to leave. Adamsky told her that he and Eve-Marie had decided to leave together and to go to Europe. They wanted to continue their studies on the French mainland, he explained. It was a plan both had had for a while. Claudette told him in clear words that her daughter would remain under her surveillance, that she would never let her go 'like this', with a man who 'has nothing', a man who is 'not serious' and 'hangs out on the street' (*traîne dans la rue*). According to Adamsky's memories, the conversation then became very loud with both actors throwing increasingly crude insults at each other.

Eve-Marie finally stayed with her mother and Adamsky left the house alone. He found somewhere to stay for a couple of nights and thought about returning to

Europe and giving up his relationship with Eve-Marie. Some days later he met her by chance on the campus. (Mobile phones and the internet had not reached the island at that time.) She was about to register for another first year. She told him to do what he felt was best for his life, that she would survive the separation. Both decided to stay together and fight for the life and love they wanted to live. She did not return to her mother that night and Adamsky gave up his plans to move back to Europe. With hardly any money, they lived for several months in the house of a friend of theirs, and then moved into a cheap apartment that they shared with other students. Both found part-time jobs and, they explained to me, for the first time in their lives they felt independent of their parents and the world. At Easter of the following year, more than six months after the fight between Claudette and Adamsky, after Eve-Marie's not returning to her mother's house, Claudette invited them once again to her house. During all this time, they had not seen each other and the only contact had been established by Eve-Marie's younger siblings who her mother had sent to Saint-Denis to see if she was fine. They made peace and, from then on, Eve-Marie and Adamsky spent most of the weekends at Claudette's house. Adamsky was even allowed to stay the night, though in a different room. In September of that same year, Eve-Marie finally succeeded in her exams and moved on to the second year of undergraduate studies. She did not fail any further study years and left the university with a master's degree three years later.

The recital of these events may appear extraordinary, reminiscent of Hollywood in its ending. At the same time, it is indicative of a set of expectations associated in this specific case with the hospitality of the stranger. In a way, Adamsky was expected to reciprocate the hospitality he had been offered. Claudette's silent acceptance of her daughter's intimate pre-conjugal relationship with Adamsky seemed nourished, at least in part, by the hope that this would help her succeed at university. It seemed indicative of a deeper-lying strategy of social mobility. According to Paul Ottino (1999), social mobility strategies in La Réunion can be understood in terms of the historical 'thirst for land' that had marked the social and economic strategies of the proletarian populations of the plantation society. The principle underlying this idea is that the essential means to make social mobility happen, within this context, was to access land ownership. Ottino outlines different strategies – kinship and friendship alliances and the integration of clientelist networks – that people had employed to achieve this access to land ownership, often over several generations. In the recent past, Ottino argues, this logic had not disappeared but had transformed into the post-agrarian contexts of the newly emerging urban society. Public sector jobs in particular, he stresses, offered a similar degree of independence and social status to that offered by land ownership within the former context. The historical 'thirst for land' remained the principal motive of personal economic and social strategies. However, it had been refocused on ways to access public sector jobs, especially on education and the establishment of clientelist networks with and within public administrations.

In this context of change, the powerful social position of the lord mayor in many ways substituted for the historical role of the paternalistic landowner, dominating social relations within the context of the plantation society (Cambefort 1988). Furthermore, the generalised access to public education was considered, in certain milieus, as a means to secure public sector jobs (Chane-Kune 1996; Simonin and Wolff 1996). However, for the social milieu most alienated from the technologies, cultures and networks of the island's recently emerging modernity – the majority of the island's former rural population – social mobility strategies based on education were usually complicated by a widespread incomprehension of the values and language taught at school, and a consequent lack of support within the families (Simonin and Wolff 1996).

After the death of her husband during the 1980s, Claudette had been left with little or no social networks that she could call on to help her children get a job. In her understanding, the education of her children was the only means for them to find a better life (*pour qu'ils s'en sortent*). Yet, dyslexic and with only a very basic school education, she encountered huge difficulties in supporting the educational projects of her children. Her apparent willingness to accept, maybe even subtly to encourage, the relationship between Eve-Marie and Adamsky can possibly be seen in the light of this ambiguous situation and the social mobility projects she had for her children. Eve-Marie was the only person of her local age group to go to university and leave with a diploma. While this type of 'success story' is not unique in La Réunion, it remains the exception. The reasons for this seem linked, once again, to the cultural logic of the *kartié* and the challenges faced on the micro-local scale by those who invite strangers into their houses. Once it became obvious that Claudette had accepted Adamsky into her house (very visibly, he left his car in the street overnight), she and her family became the subject of often violent mockery within her residential quarter, sometimes with open insults thrown in her face. She anticipated and sat through these verbal and social violences. It was not the first time she had to endure them. Indeed, after the death of her husband, she had started to see a man of European origin. She became pregnant and while giving birth at the local hospital, the sister of her dead husband employed men (*gros bras*) to destroy her courtyard, tableware and water tubs, and to steal the chickens she kept in her backyard. According to Eve-Marie, who witnessed the scene – she was then twelve years old – her aunt was screaming loud insults at her mother. Several people of the residential area witnessed this sinister spectacle, without intervening. The *gendarmes* arrived late (their base was located less than 500m from Claudette's house) and, according to Eve-Marie's memory, explained that the conflict needed to be solved privately, without their involvement. During my fieldwork studies, I heard many similar stories, often equally violent, where young unmarried women who became pregnant were rejected by their own families. The motive behind this violent behaviour seemed to be related to the fear of public disgrace in the eye of the *kartié*, the mockery and exclusion that the family risked when not conforming to values and norms prescribed by the collective gaze. Claudette was clearly able to anticipate the reactions that her acceptance of Adamsky would provoke. In her socially marginal situation, it seemed that she had few alternatives. The aim of social mobility for her daughter seemed to take presidence over the fear of mockery she would be subjected to. Once Adamsky proved he was a 'serious guy' (he found a flat; Eve-Marie succeeded her exams), he became an almost permanent member of her family.

No social phenomenon is simple or monolayered. If I had previously explained the hospitality shown towards European strangers – Adamsky, in particular – in terms of a cultural logic inscribed in the social and economic strategies of social mobility in La Réunion, I may have seemed overly analytical or reductive. To convince the reader, maybe to convince myself, I may have focused on only one layer of a socially complex phenomenon that does not explain its totality. While I believe that my approach provides a good theoretical model, I 'feel' that the specific layer it focused upon was superimposed by something else, maybe more crucial, that made the main characters of this ethnographic account act. Through their shared experiences, enchantments, struggles, collaborations, illusions and delusions, through their common journey, Adamsky and Eve-Marie developed a deep feeling of 'love'. It was this love that allowed them to break out, at least temporarily, of the structural constraints of their immediate social environments, to generate a new social context, and eventually, to sustainably transform the cultural norms and frameworks dominant in their respective social milieus. It was also that love that transformed them as persons.

Love

Several years later, having successfully completed her studies and left university, Eve-Marie started to look for a job. Every morning, she went to the government job centres to look out for new offers. She applied for a variety of jobs corresponding to her level of studies. At that time, La Réunion had a high unemployment rate, approximating forty per cent of the active workforce, and even higher among young people. After several weeks, Eve-Marie had not found a job, and had not even been invited to a job interview. Together with Adamsky, she had moved into a studio flat in Saint-Denis measuring eighteen square metres. Adamsky was about to write up a Ph.D. dissertation. He usually worked from home. After going to the job centre in the morning, Eve-Marie normally returned to their studio flat and stayed there for the rest of the day. Adamsky complained that he could not concentrate on his writing while she was in the room. Frustrated by this situation, they had arguments on an almost daily basis. Some weeks later, Eve-Marie could not put up with this situation any longer and decided to move back to her mother's house. Adamsky, left alone, spent most of his days in front of his computer, went out only to buy food and more or less stopped seeing his friends. He often forgot to eat, smoked a lot and lost weight. He saw Eve-Marie irregularly, spending some weekends with her at her mother's house. After a couple of months, he became so physically and mentally tired, he said, he could not write any more. He decided to take a holiday at his parents' home in Europe and only returned six weeks later. He had then gained a lot of weight. It was summer in the southern hemisphere and he and Eve-Marie went to the beach. She did not want to be close to him because, she said, he looked like a 'big white hairy potato' (*une grosse patate blanche poilue*). Both laughed about this image, but the humour had a more serious undertone. She was ashamed of his looks – cheese white with a belly – and did not want to be seen together with him in the public sphere of the beach. The couple were about to split up. Eve-Marie started to search for a studio flat to live in on her own.

During the same period, Eve-Marie's mother, Claudette, had begun to participate again in a series of *services malbars* to help her find a job. According to Christian Ghasarian (1991) such *services malbars* are based on the principles of a Dravidian Hinduism traditionally practiced in the rural milieu of South India. This particular form of the religion had been practiced on the island since the second half of the nineteenth century when an important Indian labour force immigrated to work in the local sugar cane industry. Locally, this form of the religion is commonly called *religion malbar* ('Malbar religion' – a reference to the Indian coast of Malabar). While pertaining to certain structural and aesthetic elements of its Dravidian origins, the *religion malbar* is a result of a creolisation process, having incorporated liturgical elements and forms from European, Malagasy and East African belief systems (Barat 1989; Benoist 1998). Claudette was born into a largely creolised family with mainly Malagasy and Indian ancestors. Since her early childhood, she had been following both the Catholic catechism and the annual festival cycle of the *religion malbar*. Her husband, Eve-Marie's father, was born into a family of strictly Indian ancestorship. The ethnic and phenotypical 'purity gap' (Ghasarian 1991) between him and Claudette was heavily disapproved of by his family and had led to constant tensions between the two families. These tensions seem to have further increased after the death of Claudette's husband (he died of blood poisoning, a consequence of his alcoholism) and climaxed in the violence described above, after Claudette gave birth to a child by another man. Following these incidences, Claudette decided to abandon the world of Malabar religion and to educate her children within the Catholic religion: 'less vicious', according to her, 'not made to hurt your relatives and neighbours'. However, she continued to 'consult' Malabar priests regularly, usually in a hidden way to obtain treatments for her children's diseases, and to participate in private ceremonies organised by her brothers. It was much later, several years after Adamsky had arrived within her family space, that she decided to 'return' openly to the Malabar religion and to participate in ceremonies organised in both public and family temples. Her openly celebrated return would cause another major clash with Adamsky.

It was a Sunday afternoon, several weeks after Adamsky's return to La Réunion. After the meal and some glasses of red wine, Adamsky and one of Eve-Marie's sisters were sitting under a tree, relaxing. She told him that she and her mother had recently participated in a Malabar ceremony. She explained that the priest had told them that a Hindu god was 'against' the family because they had abandoned the religion for many years. He had said, she recalled, that 'as long as Eve-Marie went out with a non-believer' – Adamsky – 'all the paths in their life and in the life of the other family members' would remain 'blocked'. They would not find jobs, nor have children. Learning this 'news', Adamsky became furious and started to insult the Malabar priest (who was not present) loudly, calling him a manipulator, racist and profiteer. Claudette, who was inside the house, heard these insults. She came out and heatedly asked Adamsky to 'respect the religion of others' and to 'start believing in something'. Adamsky became angry and, in an even louder voice, repeated his words about the priest. Eve-Marie, also present in the garden, remained silent during this dispute. For many years, she explained later, she had had severe doubts about the possibility of a link between divine obedience and the chance one had in life. She particularly disliked the persona of the priest – whatever his or her confession – who she saw as a manipulator telling stories that kept the poor happy to be poor. Her university studies, heavily influenced by the teachings of French Cartesian philosophy, and her frequent discussions with Adamsky had further reinforced her doubts about a supernatural logic of chance and religious redemption.

The dispute between Adamsky and Claudette ended with Adamsky and Eve-Marie precipitately returning to their studio in Saint-Denis. The pressure put on Adamsky by the newly recovered religious milieu of Eve-Marie's mother brought the couple back together. Eve-Marie moved back into the studio flat and both, once again, seemed to feel closer to each other. The seemingly utilitarian logic of Claudette's social mobility strategy, described in the first part of this chapter, was here disrupted by Eve-Marie's solidarity and 'deep feeling of love', in her words, with her boyfriend rather than with her mother. It was this disruption that generated a new social context beyond the established formats of social life. It violently imposed new values and a new way of life where the infant generation appears to be less subjected to the will of parent generations and their social milieu.

Social Dyspepsia

The personal conflict between Adamsky and Claudette seems indicative of a wider societal rupture that marked La Réunion at the beginning of the 1990s. In this context, the rapid adoption and local adaptation of 'modern' values, practices and technologies by many of the younger generations led to an ambiguous situation, leaving a large part of the elderly, less educated and urbanly marginalised population excluded. At the same time, many fields of social life – social rites, household budgets, personal identity, liability for individual acts – began to escape from the traditional authority of the family and the micro-local milieu (Ghasarian 1991, 2002; Live 1999; Poirier 1999; Medea 2002). The dynamic of these changes appears related to the symbolic and political asymmetries that define the relation between La Réunion and its former colonial centre. For instance, the project of the island's modernisation had always been managed in the terms and conditions defined by institutions on the French mainland. Formally, it was implemented through the integration of La Réunion into the national territory and institutional apparatus of the French state. Pragmatically, it was operated through the creation of new forms of revenue redistribution and the installation of the welfare state, the introduction of legal institutions and the individualisation of civil responsibility, the intensification and industrialisation of production processes and mass communication, and the generalised access to public education, health services, transport, mass consumption and paid holidays.

These changes challenged the forms of social and symbolic order – values, meta-narratives and taxonomic systems – established within the contexts of the plantation society (Live 1999). During the 1990s, the emergence of new forms and borders to define the individual and collective belonging were observed. These variably engaged with previous categories of social identity, in particular the symbolic correlation, prevalent during the plantation society (Benoist 1983), between ethnic, social and local forms of belonging and phenotypical appearances. This led, in some cases, to a polarisation of ethnic representations related to phenotypical stereotypes, reinforcing the historical amalgam between 'race and class' (Labache 1996; Medea 2003, 2005). Laurent Medea, for instance, describes the continuous systematic exclusion of people of 'black' phenotype who he finds at the bottom of the island's societal ladder, both in economic and symbolic terms (Medea 2005). In other cases, a new form of social fluidity seemed to emerge, manifesting itself through new forms and types of social identity, namely within the context of new urban cultures based on common professional, sportive or artistic interests (Gilbert 1993; Cherubini 1996a; Maillot 2002; Carret 2002; de Bollivier 2005).

The observation of this antagonistic dynamic in La Réunion, defined by processes of both social polarisation and fluidification, cannot be dissociated from similar observations made in places with no direct connection (Picard and Robinson 2006). The acceleration of the globalisation of exchanges since the 1980s and the popularisation of the Internet since the late 1990s have raised a new awareness of the historicity of cultural flows between different social spheres and their role in constituting ethnicities and localities. They have raised a new awareness about the fact that most spaces have always been socially and culturally heterogeneous and that creolisation was the norm rather than an exception (Hannerz 1996).

The emergence of new social milieus in La Réunion thus repeated a phenomenon that had marked the island's demography since its first colonisation. People and ideas arrived from outside and formed new forms of sociability. Within the postcolonial context of the last forty years, these new forms of sociability were dominated, in large part,[5] by the arrival of European emigrants, mainly from France, and Réunion immigrants who returned to the island. Those who were part of these new sociabilities were usually much better qualified than the people in La Réunion (in terms of education and work experience) and integrated into different, often more powerful, political, economic and social networks in the island. These 'local strangers' consequently found it relatively easy to occupy key positions in the private, public and associative sectors of the island. They thus had a predominantly powerful influence on the formulation of public policies and spatial development plans, public education strategies, fashions and the interpretation of local history and identities. They represented powerful social actors in the 'contact zone' (Pratt 1992) between this newly emerging modernity and the social life of the rest of the population, capable of transforming established economic, political and social structures at the level of the island. They became representative of a new model that found in French metropolitan fashions, styles, and ideologies a common reference. Their adoption of a taste for heritage, nature, the arts and ethnographic things – initially associated with the former coloniser – can be seen in terms of a mimetic strategy. The 'power' associated with the former coloniser is invoked through the formal adoption of their style and political agendas. At the same time, these appropriations can be understood in terms of a process of 'transculturation' (Pratt 1992), where certain symbols, values and practices of the presumably powerful are resignified within the local context. Performance of such mimetic behaviour could thus be seen as a particular manifestation of the wider social practice of 'giving a good image' within a particular public sphere of the island. In other words, mimicking and publicly performing a widely idealised postcolonial Frenchness becomes a means to perpetuate the culture of the *kartié* and its underlying aspiration of social mobility. However, as the case of Eve-Marie and Adamsky has demonstrated, this appropriation is often full of ambiguities and can have unexpected effects. Examples typically quoted here include the urban violence in La Réunion which is often directed at immigrants from Europe and other islands of the Indian Ocean, sometimes at the very symbols of the emerging local modernity, its leisure spaces, its beaches and publicly advertised fashions. The contact with strangers thus commonly provokes a collective stomach-ache, a chronic dyspepsia without any certain remedy. From this point of view, the love between Eve-Marie and Adamsky can also be read as an allegory for the relationship between La Réunion and the French mainland; a love marked by often contradictory forces, desires and fears, collaborations and oppositions, integrations and violent rejections.

Chapter 5
Bougainvilleas at the Riverside

Down by the Riverside

The group of young men were standing in front of a metal shipping container. We shook hands and said hello. One looked at his watch and said it was nine. The others also looked at their watches and confirmed. 'We have to start,' one of them, Simoni,[1] said. He opened the doors of the container, went inside and came out with large bush knives (*sabres*) and a roll of large plastic bags which he passed around. The group formed teams of two. Each of them took a knife and a plastic bag. We started to walk down the path and arrived at an open water canal which we followed until we reached a tunnel. The landscape got progressively steeper and the vegetation more humid and verdant. We walked carefully, one after the other, so as not to slip and fall into the valley on our right. The young men picked up rubbish they found along the way and put it into the plastic bags. The conversations that had been started earlier were picked up again. At the tunnel, we took off our flip-flops, rolled up the legs of our trousers above the knee and carefully slid into the canal. The water was clear and cold. We moved inside the tunnel careful not to fall over on the slippery ground of the canal bottom or to hit our head against the low ceiling. It was pitch dark and the water reached up to our knees. Some of the young men started to scream and sing. Some imitated animal noises.

After a minute or two we reached the other end of the tunnel and continued our way along the canal. The rubbish bags were hardly filled at all when we reached a flat area in the valley forming a natural dam. We could hear waterfalls rushing down from the end of this plain into a vast cauldron inside the valley. The dry savannah of the place where the cars were parked had given way to lush green and moist vegetation under high shade provided by tamarind trees. We passed a small path through the bush and reached the edge of the bassin bleu, a large blue water pool that had formed inside the valley, with several waterfalls cascading down from the surrounding cliffs. The different teams went straight to a number of places around this pool and collected the rubbish they found hidden behind several big flat rocks, a rock cave, and a couple of large trees and around a lawn area next to the water. The rubbish mainly consisted of remains from family picnics that had taken place here the day before: plastic bags with food waste, polystyrene boxes, plastic and glass bottles, tins, etc.

The rubbish bags were quickly filled and, as we still had two hours until the lunch break was to start, we moved up onto the concrete roof of a former water pumping station besides the pool. We sat down and the conversations were once again taken up. We talked about what we did during the previous weekend. Some of the men had gone clubbing, 'not in Saint-Gilles', which, they said, was 'too racist', and where, they said, some bars did not allow Black people to enter. Ploner told me that the Creoles preferred to go to parties organised by their village committees. They liked to drink rum priced at two francs at the boutique, he said, rather than spend a lot of money in a French style bar. The conversation eventually turned to one of the men's favourite topic: the tuning of their cars. They talked about the sound systems they had installed, the different types and specifications of amplifiers and loudspeakers they used, the volume these provided and how best to fix them. They made jokes about each other's car's performance and how their own car was, respectively, more powerful and, therefore, more prone to attract each other's girlfriends. They made jokes about my car, an old VW Polo, and asked how I managed to pull a girl with this car. This triggered another favourite topic: why Creole girls liked to go out with *Zoreils*. (I had told them before that I was going out with a Creole girl.) Simoni explained that 'the Creoles don't like to work'. Ploner contradicted, ironically, saying that 'actually the work does not like the Creoles'. They laughed. Simoni explained that the *Revenu Minimu d'Insertion* (RMI) – a minimum allowance paid to the unemployed – was the problem; people preferred to sit in front of their houses and cash in on the social help, rather than go to work. Frenzel, who had listened to our conversation, added that the Creoles never undertook big projects, but were happy with a small job and wage. Simoni added that enterprises always preferred to employ a *Zoreil* rather than a Creole, 'because the Creoles are lazy'. He later explained, with an ironic smile, that 'you need ten Creoles to make up one brain'. Self irony was one of the many means they used to make themselves laugh.

Two men, employees of the communal water service, arrived and asked how it was going. 'As good as it can go on a Monday', Ploner replied. We continued to sit and lie on the concrete platform, in the shade of a large tamarind tree, until a quarter past twelve. We then walked back to the cars. The plastic bags were put in a corner of the parking and the tools stored inside the container. We stood around in a circle looking at our watches. When it was *exactly* half past twelve, everybody went to his car and drove home. We had to be back an hour later, at half past one, for the afternoon shift.

Gardening the Riverside

Two years earlier, in 1998, Lionel Jospin, then French prime minister, had passed the so-called Young Employment law (*dispositif des emplois jeunes*) to foster the creation of jobs for young unemployed people in associative and administrative institutions. In practical terms, this law allowed the French government to sponsor eighty per cent of wages for such newly created jobs over a period of five years. As part of the French national territory, La Réunion saw the implementation of this law within the same year. It allowed the community association of Grand-Fond, a village on the island's west coast, to create ten new jobs. The rationale justifying the creation of these publicly sponsored jobs was to 'embellish and develop the tourist site of the Saint-Gilles river' (CADOQ 1998). This site referred to a series of water pools inside a valley situated at around 2km from the village. The contrast these pools formed with the arid savannah of the island's west coast had made them a major attraction for international tourists and domestic visitors throughout the 1990s (CTR/GB2 1998). They had also become a popular place for local families to spend their Sundays picnicking.

I followed the work and the working of this association and its riverside development project over several months in 1999 and 2000. I was intrigued by two aspects of this project. The first related to the idea that a group of young men with little or no officially sanctioned ecological or landscape knowledge should conceive of and develop a tourist site. The contemporary French landscape architect, Gilles Clément, had written about gardening as an 'involuntary art' (Clément 1997), revealing underlying aesthetic orders and moral references which can be analysed through its material productions. How, I wondered, would these young men realise this tourist site? What plants would they use and how would they arrange them? Would they have a theory about their selections and creations? Or a model? The second aspect I was interested in related to the contact between these young men and their landscape gardening art and the aesthetic and ecological principles that govern public policy and scientific approaches to landscape development in La Réunion. When submitting their proposal for the ten young employment jobs, the association attached a concept for the projected development work to be undertaken at the tourist site. After only a couple of months, they had learnt that their proposal was successful, with the condition that a reassessment of the site development concept be undertaken by the island's environmental services and with the obligation of formal training of the young men in landscape theory and practice. The modifications mainly concerned the nature of building materials to be used and the selection of plants to be introduced and cultivated at the site.

The group of young men effectively started their work in 1999 and I joined them, on a daily basis, in early 2000. Suspecting me to be an inspector working for the public services, they were initially rather tense and formal. However, after working together on the site for a couple of days, the contact became less and less formal, and I started to form friendships with some of them.

Creole Gardening

The concept the ten young men had developed for their initial proposal included detailed maps and descriptions of how the riverside space was to be developed, which plants were to be used, which material structures were to be built and what activities would define their daily work. The proposal included a general map of the site structured by separated sub-spaces. Within the widest frame, a line separated the space of the parking and the actual site. Other lines framed the entrance to the pathway on its two sides. Along both types of lines, ornamental flowers and fruit trees were to be planted in three juxtaposed lines, with geranium and hortensias in the first line, bougainvilleas, hibiscus and banana trees in the second, and mango, carambole and litchi trees in the third. These plantations were to become sparser the more one penetrated into the valley. They were to disappear completely about halfway where the dry savannah had given way to dense vegetation. The path that led through several sub-paths to the different water pools was to be filled with concrete, which, the proposal explained, would provide a 'better cleanness' of the site. It would also allow the elimination of all 'bad weeds' and 'bushes' in the immediate environs of the access paths. The proposal foresaw the installation of drinking water taps, picnic areas and plastic rubbish bins along the paths. It also suggested the building of small wooden huts around the pools, benches and barbecues made of concrete and small bridges facilitating the crossing of the open water canals. At the entrance of the site, besides the car park, the proposal suggested the building of a small hut where the young men could sell drinks and souvenirs. The concept also included a management plan defining the milestones to be achieved – different phases defined by the building of the heavier infrastructures – and the daily activities to be carried out at the site: sweeping the concrete paths, watering and nurturing the plants, cleaning the site in the morning, building infrastructures and planting new vegetation in the afternoon.

While the spatial structure devised for the future tourist site indicated a clear underlying pattern, none of the young men could provide an explanation or a 'theory' for this. I repeatedly interviewed the project leaders about their development concept. The answers were significantly brief, as they seemed to take care not to give away any motives or information regarding the project. Later, when I was more familiar with the group, I was told that, during these first interviews, they were scared to say something 'wrong' that would compromise the success of their proposal. Even during the many weeks I spent working with them at the site, it was rare that our conversations or discussions would focus on the meaning of their landscape creation. While I learnt much about the importance of car tuning, nightclubs, drugs, social exclusion, job qualifications and, most importantly, girls, I gained little understanding about the specific spatial configurations, the selection of plants or building materials planned for the site.

I later asked them if I could interview them again. The confidence that had developed between us provoked a totally different response. I used a video camera which gave this interview a more formal outlook and asked them about the different spaces within the map of their initial project. They responded freely, explaining that the flowers and plants were to introduce a nice facade, to mark off the site from the dust and dirt of the street. They talked about the waterfalls and pools as a space that was 'fresh', 'wild', 'genuine', 'calm', 'pure', 'clean', and 'free'. At the same time, the space surrounding this site – the street, the arid savannah and the heavily urbanised coast of the island – were associated with attributes including 'hot', 'dry', 'dirty', 'polluted', 'noisy' and 'salty' (the sea water). The function of the floral façade between these two spaces, they explained, was to 'give a good image' of the site. The same argument – to 'give a good image – justified the use of concrete on the paths and the planned daily sweeping, 'to keep it always free of dust and bad herbs'. 'Tourists who come to La Reunion', they explained, 'usually like to taste local fruits like mangos and litchis'. This is why they wanted to include these and other fruit trees at the site – so tourists could 'taste different fruits that grow in the island'. The project of developing barbecue areas and huts around the pools was related to the idea that people could then come together there and enjoy the place 'correctly'. 'Correctly', they explained, meant that people could make a fire and sit down during their family picnic, but also that tourists had places where they could get changed after swimming in the pools. They told me that tourists, especially Germans, regularly got changed in public. 'The Creoles do not like this', they said, 'they would not hesitate to engage in a physical fight'. They explained that 'it may be normal for the tourists to go naked in their countries, but in La Réunion it generated big problems', 'especially when there are parents with their children around'.

The conception of the space devised for the future tourist site development thus implied a structure which seemed to emerge from a specific aesthetic and symbolic appreciation underlying the work to be carried out at the site. This appreciation seemed based, fundamentally, on the opposition between an outside and an inside space. The interstitial interspatial zone between these two spaces was to be marked off by a sophisticated floral façade and different material infrastructures. According to this conception, the more one moved inside the site and towards the water pools, the more the heat and impurity associated with the outside space would give way to a pure and serene space embodied not only in the clear cold water of the pools and the exuberant vegetation surrounding them, but also the meticulously cleaned paths leading there. For the young men, the concept of the short walk to the pools seemed to symbolise a deeper metaphorical journey, a dialectical journey from the impure to the pure. Following the discourse of the young men, the dichotomy of pure–impure used to make sense of the spatial discontinuities that structured this space was linked to other dichotomies used to define the same spatial opposition. A paradigmatic relationship hence seemed to emerge from concepts such as purity, freshness, wilderness, authenticity, calmness, cleanliness, and freedom to signify the inside of the site. On the other hand, a similar relationship seemed to emerge from concepts such as heat, dryness, dirt, pollution and noise to signify the outside of the site. The walk to the pools also seemed to be conceived of as a metaphorical journey from an inhospitable, loud and polluted condition of civilisation to a genuine and calm condition of nature. The site was to become a place where families and friends could go to get away from the burdens of everyday life and temporarily reconnect to a form of 'lost' freedom and reality.

Tourism and the Culture of the *Kartié*

The young men consistently emphasised that the aim of their work at the site was to project 'a good image' of La Réunion to visiting tourists, and explained the good image this would consequently reflect well upon their own residential quarter. The act of working on the site, visible to tourists and local audiences, therefore seemed to be underpinned by a communicative function similar to the one implicit to the culture of the *kartié* (explained in the previous chapter). The morning programme of activity normally consisted of the cleaning of the site and the nurturing of plants, while the afternoons were mostly used for the building of heavier infrastructures, including anti-erosion measures along the paths, benches made of bamboo poles, etc. All these activities were performed in view of the many tourists and local visitors that made their way to the pools. Tourists often engaged the men in conversations, telling them how much they appreciated the beauty of the site and sometimes asking for more details. The men were rather shy about these interactions; in many cases they asked me to explain to the tourists what they were doing at the site. They said they let their gardening work talk for them. While only rarely directly engaging with the site's visitors, they often commented on them once they had left. They talked about their bodies, especially those of the girls, but also of particularly corpulent or sunburned tourists; 'they like to eat a lot in their country' or 'his wife must be a good cook' were common comments. When young girls and women passed by, the men would invariably follow them with their eyes while loudly inhaling. Once the girls had gone, the men normally looked at each other, acknowledging the 'beauty' of these girls. For several weeks, while they were waiting for the building materials for certain infrastructures to be delivered, the young men did not know what to do. They spent most afternoons down by another pool, the one most popular with tourists, talking, sleeping, picking fruits, watching the girls and making comments.

The site can be seen as a large social stage which different actors entered and where, whether they wanted it or not, they became part of the settings and interactions that unfolded. From the perspective of the young men, tourists were acknowledged here as welcome outsiders, as important visitors who needed to be treated well, who needed to be enchanted by the site. The rationale of this enchantment strategy seemed initially quite straightforward; 'we try to do something for the tourists, because tourism brings money into La Réunion', Ploner explained. Tourism seemed to be thought of in terms of an economic sector that enabled the creation of jobs and wealth in the island. At the same time, tourists acknowledged the efforts made at the site, by publicly praising the work carried out by the young men. Simoni explained that 'when the tourists come here, they say: "Oh, it is so beautiful!" and we are happy then. The more beautiful it is, the more everyone gains from it'. Ploner specified that 'many tourists who come here say we do a good job. They thank us a lot. This gives us a big push'. From this point of view, the exchange of looks between young men and tourists created a new form of transnational participation: a transnational social theatre that seemed to translate the culture of the *kartié* at the scale of the tourist site. By developing floral façades and a material culture familiar to their domestic gardens, the young men seemed to think of tourism development in terms of the culture of social relations that they knew from their own residential quarter. They seemed to project this culture on an island-wide scale and its relations to the outside world. Accommodating tourists and enchanting them within certain tourist spaces on the island seemed to be thought of in similar terms as accommodating important visitors and enchanting them in the domestic garden. Tourism in La Réunion and the new type of contact zone that it brought about hence became structured in terms of the cultural logic of the domestic space. The riverside developed by the young men was to become a clean, floral façade 'giving a good image' of La Réunion to the world outside.

As I explained in the previous chapter, the culture of the *kartié* is based on the exchange of a gaze and forms of mockery; on the perception of the *kartié* that works as an institution of social control. While concerned about 'giving a good image' to outside tourists, the young men were equally, if not more, anxious about giving a good image of their residential quarter. Simoni explained that 'our work aims to develop and restructure the site, to give a good impression of La Réunion to the tourists and for ourselves, to give a good image of our quarter as it is situated close to the site – to have a clean site'. Ploner added that 'we do this a bit like at our place, nice and clean'. Simoni concluded that 'many see that there is a great difference from how the site looked before. Before, it was disgusting, the pools and the path. This will be classified as an official tourist site. But we want people to know that these were folks from Grand-Fond who did all this. There is a lot of work in the project, and it is very beautiful after all'. Just as Claudette wanted to have her courtyard clean, to avoid mockery and 'give a good image', the young men want their site to be clean, to give a good image of their own quarter. The social theatre described above therefore appears more complex, involving a second layer of gazes and social relations. The eyes of the *kartié* seemed to be projected within a wider social sphere, where the riverside development appeared to be symbolically assimilated to the residential quarter of the young men, and was thought of in terms of a 'large domestic space' kept clean in the eyes of the wider island society. The young men thus seemed to use the culture of the *kartié* to make sense of relationships between them as a collective, as representatives of their quarter, and as diverse social and professional actors from within La Réunion. 'Giving a good image' of La Réunion to tourists hence seemed to be thought of in terms of a strategy of giving a 'good image' of their quarter to the rest of the island. The young men wanted their site beautification project to be recognised as a collective action of Grand-Fond, their residential quarter. The social space of the residential quarter hence seemed to be projected onto the scale of the island. Planting beautiful flowers and fruit trees and keeping the site clean and tidy for the external visitors allowed them to 'give a good image' of the quarter of Grand-Fond within a new regional public sphere. Tourists were attributed the role of external observers or guests whose role was to judge, morally and aesthetically, the quality and the beauty of the site and, allegorically, the quality and the beauty of La Réunion.

Flowers as Allegories

At the end of 1998, the regional government committee drafted a letter notifying the association that their bid had been successful. However, the project leaders were asked to readapt the initial site development concept. During the two months that followed the official recruitment of the young men, the latter had to meet with the engineers and technicians of the National Botanic Conservatory, the environmental service of the county of Saint-Paul, the Regional Environmental Direction (DIREN), the National Forestry Office (ONF) and the Departmental Architecture and Heritage Service (SDAP). During these meetings, a series of modifications was introduced to the initial concept. These concerned in particular the selection of plants, building materials and installations. Specifically, the flowers and fruit trees planted around the parking and along the access path were substituted with a selection of endemic and local agricultural plants. The new plant selection included vetiver, sugar cane and aloes because, according to the engineer of the National Botanic Conservatory, these 'stand' for the agricultural history of La Réunion. Lava stone walls and wooden structures were to be built on the uphill side of the access path to prevent erosion. Other plants and trees including tobacco, benjoin, indigo wood and tamarinds were to be grown along the paths. The use of concrete for the construction of the path and the barbecue plots was prohibited. The argument was that here they should keep the 'sandy aspect' of the access paths, according to a DIREN technician. The rubbish bins were to be made not of plastic, but of wood. The rubbish would not be burned and buried, as initially foreseen, but collected and put in plastic bags. The projected construction of various infrastructures, including barbecue sites, banks and cabins for getting changed, was removed from the plan.

These modifications appeared to reveal a different development philosophy for the site and a different landscape art and ideology. Through a selection of endemic plants and the use of organic building materials such as wood and stone, this new approach, imposed by the public institutions, aimed to reinvent what one technician called an 'authentic nature', a form of landscape that looked like La Réunion before human settlement started in the seventeenth century. On the other hand, through the selection of agricultural plants including vetiver, sugar cane and aloes – 'plants that played a central role in the island's history' according to another senior technician – the aim was to use the horticultural displays developed at the site as a means to communicate nature as a historically 'manoeuvred' realm. The juxtaposition of these two selections of plants, and the stories of both an endemic nature and a social-historic past of La Réunion stories they were to stage, generated a different vision of what the 'garden' was to be about. It implied two meta-narratives, one of a 'primordial' and 'authentic' Réunion, and one of a 'historic' humanly transformed Réunion. I had already earlier come across these narratives in public policy actions, in particular their use in making sense of spatial discontinuities and legitimate specific forms of development within the island's rural interior (Chapter 3). They seemed to be variations of classical tropes of a timeless paradise garden and of the loss of this garden and the beginning of time. In this sense, the public policy project for the riverside seemed to stem from models less concerned with the social dimensions of the site as a garden, and more with its allegorical power to make sense of a specific conception of time, which was deeply anchored in Western imagination.

Syncretism and Non-Gardens

The model which was finally implemented relied heavily on the modified development concept, imposed by the public policy and scientific institutions. The young men largely ignored the rationale underlying the symbolic choice of new building materials and plant selection. 'It has been explained that this is a protected natural space and that it is forbidden to plant flowers or to use concrete', one of them explained. 'This really is a pity because now we cannot sweep the paths. It would have been much cleaner had we used concrete', he added. During the operational phase of the project, the quotidian work of the young men was largely dominated by the uncertainty over what they were 'allowed' to plant and what they were not. As a result of this, the young men concentrated most their activities on the collection of waste. The only ornamental garden flowers they introduced were bougainvilleas, an exotic yet largely common plant in the Creole garden. Several bushes were planted at the entrance of the site. 'Everyone in La Réunion has bougainvilleas in the garden, so it cannot be forbidden to plant just two trees here', the men explained.

They also used the new selection of agricultural plants to recreate the floral façade they had originally envisioned to mark the limits between the parking and the site area. In addition, they arranged sugar cane, vetiver and aloe plants along the access path leading to the pools, instead of the fruit trees and flowers proposed in their initial project. 'The interest in these plants, we have been told, is that they come from La Réunion and people have been planting them for many generations', Simoni explained half-heartedly. 'In fact, it is to recreate the old context. It is because these things are old', another of the young men added. In this sense, staging 'old things' was given a similar value as planting beautiful flowers or fruit trees, as was initially planned in the site development concept. The young men thus somehow managed to translate the new set of communicative elements (e.g. endemic plants, agricultural plants) into their own concepts and art of gardening. Despite contradicting the symbolic values they attached to certain ornamental floral species, these new elements allowed them somehow to recreate a culture of the *kartié* within the enlarged social spaces of the tourism contact zone. Planting old things for tourists became a new means within a largely resilient cultural pattern of gardening. It allowed the young men to communicate a 'good image' of the residential quarter of Grand-Fond and hence to participate within the wider social contexts of La Réunion. Yet, it constantly needed mediation, especially when locals passed by. The young men then often felt an urgent need to explain why they had planted such 'ugly flowers', that these were actually 'top notch' in the eyes of tourists and the scientific institutions on the island. They were not always were convincing.

The intervention of public policy and scientific actors in this project did not only lead to the frustration of the young men who were prohibited from creating a meaningful form of garden, but it has contributed to the hegemony of a global landscape model always based on the same set of stories: a reactionary non-garden[2] staging a Western conception of time and being through the inventions of an endemic nature as opposed to a colonised nature; a format now underlying the landscape development strategies in almost any tropical country of the world. Through the legal and political power of these actors, much land, formerly considered as worthless because it was not appropriate for agricultural use, has consequently been reformulated as 'exceptional landscapes' (Follea and Gauthier 1994) and defined as 'local heritage' (Région Réunion 1995). The violence exerted here through public policies may well lead to the modification of the aesthetic appearance of a place and the objects through which it communicates. Yet, the cultural logic of gardening, here related to the culture of the *kartié*, appears to be resilient. Their underlying communication systems are not defined by the object of their message but by the way in which it is uttered, a point stressed by Roland Barthes many years earlier (1957: 193). A different situation exists where architectural structures, in particular, make the recreation of particular symbolic and communication systems impossible, where modified spatial patterns deny individuals the possibility of performing meaningful practices. In one case I encountered some years later, an innovative architect had the idea of turning the aspect of a Creole house in order to make it better fit the grounds. The front of the house, usually visible from the street with its implicit communicative role, consequently faced a lateral wall, whereas a lateral wall opened up parts of the backyard intimacy of the house to the public gaze. The family moving in the house, however, tried to recreate the usual domestic space pattern by changing the use of certain rooms. Among others, their living room was moved into the garage.

Chapter 6
Poachers in the Coral Garden

The Lagoon Fishing Crisis

A day at the end of January 1999. During the morning rush hour, a group of approximately a hundred people had started a sit-in on the main road of La Réunion's west coast. Long traffic jams immediately formed on both sides, hindering commuters on their way to work and parents taking their children to school. The protesters were mostly fishermen from the nearby villages of La Saline-les-bains and La Saline-les-hauts. In the early hours of the same day, some of the fishermen had been intercepted by the nature brigade, a police force attached to the island's Regional Environmental Agency (DIREN), while fishing in the lagoon without fishing permits. Their equipment had been confiscated and they were fined. This move came after the sub-prefect of La Réunion's western circumscription, Anne Gras, had advised a strict application of fishing rules in the lagoon. Her action followed the lobbying by La Réunion's newly created marine park association who stressed that illegal fishing in the lagoon contributed, for a large part, to the degradation of the island's coral reefs. During the demonstration, the fishermen and their families and friends insisted they would not stop the street blockade unless their fishing equipment was returned and their fines were waived. They wanted to talk to Anne Gras to explain their point. Despite fierce negotiations with different mediators and the police, the road remained blocked for several hours. Just after noon, an anti-riot squadron from the national gendarmerie arrived and dispersed the crowd using tear gas grenades (Floch 1999). In the days that followed this event, both the ham-fisted handling of its ending by the gendarmerie – the protesters included many women and children – and the wider backdrop of the nature brigade's early-morning intervention were much discussed in the local media. Some journalists defended the fishermen in the name of 'ancestral fishing traditions', while others treated them as marginalised brigands and poachers threatening a fragile marine environment.

The divergence of opinions expressed through this reporting made visible one of the most striking sociocultural schisms dividing La Réunion's society since the late 1980s. It is, superficially, about the use of the island's shores, especially the lagoon and fringing coral reefs on the West coast. Throughout the 1990s and 2000s, this relatively small zone, covering an area of not more than 25 square km, became a major symbolic and ideological battleground between what are essentially different types of conservationist forces. These included, on the one hand, environmental lobby groups, who wanted to conserve the lagoon as an almost divine place of natural beauty and, on the other hand, fishing associations wanting to conserve it as a fishing ground. The friction between these forces was amplified and politicised as a result of the clear social class divide marking the respective lobby groups. The environmental lobby groups and those who largely shared their quasi-spiritual vision of the lagoon were initially driven by a group of European immigrants and members of the island's educated classes. The pro-fishing lobby groups, in contrast, were initially formed around family and friendship networks of fishermen who were part of the island's traditionally stigmatised coastal proletariat (Loupy 2001). In the months and years that followed the conflict described above, lagoon fishing became one of the most prominent battlegrounds within the island's local and national political arenas. It was taken on by all political parties in their attempts to capture the popular vote, often as part of a subtle polemic against the French central government and its local representations. The political and social polarisation created by this issue – which in actual figures concerned only a relatively small number of people, not more than 200 – consequently became a powerful social marker dividing La Réunion's society. At different levels of social life, it became important for people to position themselves with regard to the lagoon fishing issue and, in a much more general way, with regard to the modernisation of social life in the island. It generated a new set of roles of social participation and identity: people could choose between being a poacher or a philanthropic naturalist – both identities holding certain attractions for them, both providing income and social esteem.

In this chapter, I will explore the wider historical and social backdrop of the lagoon fishing crises and trace the cultural and political dimensions of the conflicts between fishermen and environmental lobby groups. I wish to show the connections between the social dynamics of environmentalism in La Réunion, translated especially through efforts to create a local marine park and to reformulate the lagoon as a 'heritage', and the powerful global forces that have led to international normative actions and the establishment of legal instruments on a global scale. The chapter will conclude with key questions that emerged from the ethnographic study: the relationship between the socially and politically powerful idea of natural beauty and the establishment of legal frameworks to protect forms of natural beauty; the role of sciences, especially marine sciences and environmental economics to supply arguments for the preservation and management of marine environments; how a research question concerned with an aesthetic issue can instead become an economic concern; and how arguments for a deeper underlying motive can, little by little, become mixed up with the motive, or become the motive itself.

Contested Seashores

Until the 1960s, La Réunion's coastal economy was based mainly on supply industries for the sugar cane plantation sectors, especially the production of chalk and foodstuff. The populations that used to live in the coastal areas were widely stigmatised within the plantation society which was dominated by agricultural activities. Fish was considered the food of the poor. The social centres of the plantation society were situated around the domains and sugar cane mills built in the centre of the most fertile and productive land, situated in the island's North-East, West and South-West, at an altitude of up to 800m. The less fertile lands – the hot western littoral, the mountainous interior and the rainy east coast – were populated by a marginalised, often proletarian population (Defos du Rau 1960; Benoist 1983). The sandy dunes of the west coast hosted a couple of villages whose unfortunate inhabitants survived on small farming, fishing and occasional agricultural or other manual work. For most of the island's proletariat the sea represented an area filled with diverse dangers – in any case it was no place for leisure (Serviable 1983; Roos, Bertrand and Tessier 1998).

Since the early nineteenth century, the local aristocracies in La Réunion had adopted European bathing and holiday fashions and established winter residences along the white sandy beaches of the west coast. They initiated a dynamic that eventually entirely transformed the island's west coast into a vast leisure space. This transformation was accelerated during the second half of the twentieth century when the involution of the plantation economy and its use of more capital intensive production processes led to more large-scale exploitations and the widespread use of machines. It also led to the expulsion of many agrarian populations from the rural areas and to their resettlement in villages. The rapid development of secondary and tertiary sectors since the 1960s progressively replaced the agricultural logic that had up till then characterised the coastal areas. At the same time, the arid and sandy littoral of the island's west coast, formerly unvalued for being too hot and covered in dust, was transformed into a new centre of social life for La Réunion's then emerging middle classes. This was characterised in particular by the development of European style residential areas, beach resorts and tourism infrastructures along the coast, and the exponential growth of property prices, today by far the highest in the island. This spatial transformation was further amplified by a significant immigration from the French mainland that settled, to a large part, in these coastal areas and popularised leisure fashions relating to the beach and the sea.

As a result, the coastal area of La Réunion's west coast became marked by the rather uneasy cohabitation of quite different types of populations, the island's poorest and richest living next to each other. This cohabitation was defined by radically different lifestyles, professions and income levels, and also by highly diverging visions and usages of the seashore. For the new middle classes, the sea shore became a space to spend free time, to lie on the beach, have picnics and get tanned, to play, swim and surf in the water, to admire the beauty of fish and corals in the lagoon, to sit on the terrace of restaurants and private houses and look over the water, to enjoy the sunset over the horizon. For the fishing populations, it was primarily a space to go fishing, to gain food for the family and sometimes to engage in commercial activities. During the weekends, the uneasiness of this cohabitation heightened by an important flow of people – both European migrants and Réunions – who spent their days on the beaches and their nights in bars and nightclubs on the west coast. Here again, the social divide was clearly marked by the choice of beaches and bars, with the principal open water beaches of the west coast – Boucan Carnot and Roches Noires – almost entirely appropriated by local residents originally from the French mainland and the forests behind the beaches of the lagoon populated with Réunion middle-class families meeting for picnics. During the late 1990s, the social polarisation of spatial practices largely persisted, with the continued exclusion and stigmatisation of the local fishing populations and the gentrification of the shores as a leisure space for the newly implanted society. The increasing land property prices and often uncertain land ownership situation further accentuated this polarisation, with many fishing populations being relocated from the shores to villages several kilometres within the island's interior.

One defining issue in this spatial transformation process was the very complex question of land ownership. In most situations, fishing populations had squatted on coastal land that was officially the property of the French state or that was part of vast private land concessions dating back to the early nineteenth century. Because the island had become part of the French national territory (in 1546), informal squatter rights that had governed land ownership within the context of the former plantation society were no longer recognised by the judges of the French civil and administrative courts. In this postcolonial environment, the French civil and administrative law was applied throughout the island. As a consequence, many families who had long occupied land, often 'given' to them by land owners in exchange for services, had difficulty in legitimating claims to this land. In many cases, amicable solutions were found in collaboration with communal services, governmental land agencies and the private land management companies of the former sugar industries, solutions sometimes facilitated by the pressure exerted by political movements, namely La Réunion's Communist Party (PCR). Furthermore, the legal instrument of the *prescription trentenaire* ('30-year prescription'), recognised by French civil law, allowed many families to generate land property where they could prove that they had occupied a piece of land for at least thirty years and the legitimate owner had not made any official claim on the land during this period (Picard 1999).

Another principle of French land law, dating back to the time of French monarchy, implied that a stretch of land along seafronts and rivers belonged to the public domain and was policed by the departmental services of the French central government (Mirault 2004).[1] This legal principle was not systematically enforced in La Réunion where both public and private buildings, especially hotels, bars and private residences used by the powerful new middle classes, occupied parts of the public domain and its public access paths. The non-application of the law resulted from a widespread *laissez-faire* attitude on the part of the public administrations, and administrative competence struggles in particular between communal services, who continued to support their local clientele, and national government services. During the 1990s the establishment of a spatial planning scheme at regional level and the approval of spatial occupation plans at communal levels began a complex and often highly contested process of regularisation of various customised spatial usages. The regional spatial planning scheme included a specific development plan for the shore and its valorisation for different economic and leisure activities, the SMVM. It thus legally determined specific practices and boundaries by means of establishing legal texts which, from then on, were to govern the usages and ownership of the seashore. It replaced the formerly fluid social relations established within the paternalistic networks and clientele of the plantation society with new modes of spatial governance. The politics and aesthetics of these new modes of governance appeared to be clearly dominated by those who had the power to make laws, or to lobby for the implementation of laws: the social elite of the newly established middle classes whose power seemed to stem from the permanent reference made to France and French cultural models. One of these models – which was largely hegemonic among Europeans in the island, myself included, and transcended leisure and tourism practices, local development policies and the lobby work carried out by environmental protection groups – implied that coral reefs, or experiences of coral reefs, were somehow 'magical'. This model appeared to stem from a transnational aesthetic culture that progressively imposed itself on the island. Tourism played a central role in this process.

Coral Reefs and Their 'Magic' in Western Culture

Some weeks after first arriving in La Réunion, in October 1995, I found myself at the beach in Boucan Canot on La Réunion's west coast. I was with a group of international students, mainly British and German. One of them had brought a diving mask, a snorkel and fins, which he lent me. It was the first time I had used such equipment and I was amazed. I could breathe under water! I was slowly swimming under the surface observing the bottom of the sea and the fish swimming. The sea was open and quickly became five to ten metres deep. Two of my friends and I challenged ourselves to dive to the bottom and bring up stones or shells. On one of the following weekends, I went to another beach, at L'Hermitage-les-bains, a few kilometres further south. I had then bought my own goggles, snorkel and fins. It was a hot and sunny day under a clear blue sky. I put on the equipment and swam into the sea. The water was shallow, less than a metre deep and the sea formed a large lagoon protected by a fringing reef around 300 metres from the shore. I swam towards the reef barrier and, after some ten metres or so I reached what I perceived to be underwater buildings that came in various forms, colours and organic shapes. Some looked like petrified plants with branches, others like giant mushrooms or miniature forests inhabited by different multicoloured fish. The whole 'scene' was flooded in bright sunlight, refracted on the rapidly changing surface of the water. Swimming under water was at first disorienting; the modes of perception and behaviour were totally different from being on land. The buoyancy of my body generated the sensation that gravity had been abolished. I felt like a bird slowly hovering over a bizarre world that was emerging before my eyes.

The way the human eye perceives the immediate environment is altered when under water; its angle of vision and its depth of field are expanded. The underwater space hence appears more distanced, larger and wider. At the same time, objects at different distances are 'in focus' within the same frame of vision – similar to the effect achieved in photography by using a high aperture. The visual experience of the underwater world was further reinforced by other sensory perceptions. When under water, ears perceive sound differently than in air; sound appears more distanced and amplified, and it is often difficult for divers to judge where it is coming from. The heat of the sunshine combined with the coolness of the water to create what I thought of as a lemonade effect on the skin; like the combination of extreme sweetness and sourness in lemonade, the extreme heat of the sun and the coolness of the water created a delightful medium experience – neither too hot, nor too cold. The unusual bodily experience of being under water, the combined effect of heat and coolness, the disorienting underwater soundscape, the strangely altered visual perception of my eyes, and the eccentric organic forms of the coral colonies and their population of colourful fish made me feel as if I had been abducted into a magical, weird and wonderful exotic world. Two years later, I started scuba diving, which allowed me to go a step further. I was no longer only hovering at the surface of this exotic world, but felt that I was temporarily immersed in it, becoming part of it. I loved to slowly swim into families of fish, to float seemingly weightlessly, seeing nothing other than fish surrounding me, looking at the slow motion of large gorgonians, the multicoloured spectacle of the underwater world.

I am not describing these personal encounters and impressions for the sake of telling the reader about how wonderful my life used to be, but because I recognised that I shared these impressions with many other people. The way in which I perceived this underwater world and the 'magic' I spontaneously associated with the experience appeared to be largely collective. To study further this seemingly shared appreciation of the underwater world, I subsequently participated in a scuba diving course. I also worked at a hotel beach hut handing out snorkels, goggles and fins to tourists and engaging in informal conversations about their experiences in the lagoon. Moreover, I interviewed the professional divers of La Réunion's marine park and, more recently, I had long informal dialogues with mainly Western marine biologists and students about their experience of the underwater world (as part of a research project on coral reef conservation programmes in Zanzibar and Madagascar). The core of the stories and descriptions remained widely consistent throughout this heterogeneous sample of people. They were largely interchangeable with my own descriptions given above. The majority described a colourful exotic world apart, compared to forests or picturesque plants; a world sometimes seen as fundamentally different from the world of organised social existence, a 'last space of real wilderness' where 'you can feel your body, you feel your physicality'. For more experienced divers, the practice of diving was frequently seen as an act of creating distance, of creating 'an external vision of the ordinary world', to 'reconnect to where we came from'. These more experienced divers often seemed to attribute a quasi-spiritual dimension to the underwater world, which was seen as an existential place that established them as humans. Paradoxically, this primordial space could only be accessed by a trick, by a technology overcoming the physical constraints of the human condition: the invention of scuba diving equipment.

In Madagascar and Zanzibar, I had the opportunity to interview villagers who had been trained as divers, mainly to assist research programmes or to work as tourist dive assistants. It appeared that the Malagasy divers seemed far less interested in the colours and forms of corals or fish, or the effect of floating in gravity-less space, than, in their words, in 'the way fish move'. They were fishermen and their principal experience of fish was as a dying animal, being taken to the surface of the sea. Their aesthetic appreciation of the underwater world hence seemed far less focused on the perceived strangeness and colourfulness of 'plant-like' corals and fish, than on forms they could relate to. The specific perception of beauty in nature that I seemed to share with so many Western tourists, marine scientists and professional divers hence seemed, to a large degree, culturally bound. While many non-Western societies have developed culturally specific appreciations of coral reefs, the specific form of 'magic' that many of these Western people associated with coral reefs and the underwater world seemed to stem from a specific Western history.

In Europe and the Eastern Mediterranean, the attribution of 'magical' qualities to corals is not a new phenomenon. Historically, such an idea appears to have been present at least since the Hellenistic epoch. According to Greek mythology, corals are blood drops that fell into the sea and petrified after Perseus cut off the head of the Gorgon, a mythical figure that turned humans into stone (Hansmann and Kriss-Rettenbeck 1966: 41). Up until the late European Renaissance, red corals were traded from the Eastern Mediterranean into Central and Western Europe, widely used in ornamental, sacred and therapeutic practices and objects; amulets, sculptures and medicines supposed to protect against the evil eye and magical spells. However, there is not necessarily a link between these historical imaginings associated with coral as a material object and the more recent Western fascination with coral reefs as experienced as part of touristic underwater sports. With the technical evolution of the visual media, especially photography, during the nineteenth century, images of corals in their original geographical context started to gain a wider distribution (Saville-Kent 1893, quoted by Pockock 2004). While scientific study journeys exploring the nature of coral reefs were organised from the early twentieth century, the first touristic advertisements for coral reef related tourist activities only appeared during the late 1960s. The 1968 *Holidays Overseas* catalogue by the British tour operator Thomas Cook[2] included one of the first ever mentions of coral reefs in a commercial travel catalogue. A private advertisement for Hayman Island inserted in this catalogue described the experience of Australia's Great Barrier Reef as 'nature's greatest ocean fantasy, where you can view the coral gardens in all their close-up glory from glass-bottomed boats or fossick among the reef's marine wonders at low tide' (Thomas Cook 1968: 66).

In 1975, the *Cunard Caribbean* catalogue by the same tour operator mentioned a Barbados hotel with a 'water sports shop on the beach where you can book sailing and fishing or hire snorkelling equipment' (Thomas Cook 1975a: 20). In the same year, the Thomas Cook *Far and away* catalogue explained in its Seychelles section that 'the only crowds you're likely to see are the kaleidoscopic shoals of fish that swarm the coral reefs' (Thomas Cook 1975b: 34). At that time, snorkelling with goggles, initially invented for military purposes during the Second World War, started to become more widespread as a leisure activity offered to tourists. Scuba diving – also developed initially for the military, allowing divers to breathe under water with the help of air tanks – became an increasingly popular leisure activity, with the number of new adepts increasing from 3226 in 1967 to almost 70,000 in 1977 and around 315,000 in 1987.[3] The first Thomas Cook catalogue offering scuba diving as a tourist activity was the 1986 *Activity Holidays* catalogue. Promoting a resort in Cyprus, it explained, together with a lot of technical details about diving, that 'you will be fascinated by the tameness of the fish – from the reef dwellers such as parrot fish, soldier and damsel fish, to the bigger wrasse and groupers. If you are lucky you may see one of the turtles … or disturb a moray eel or slipper lobster' (Thomas Cook 1968: 12). The invention of underwater photo and film cameras by pioneers such as Hans Hass, Jean-Jacques Cousteau, and the late Leni Riefenstahl allowed the production of colour motion and still photography of coral reefs and the underwater world which have had a broad distribution among a wider Western and global audience (mainly USA, Western Europe and Japan).

In La Réunion, the first leisure dive clubs appeared during the early 1980s, run by migrants from the French mainland. While initially mainly attracting a local audience of leisure practitioners who were part of the island's newly emerging middle classes, they integrated the local tourism industry during the 1990s, offering regular dive trips. The beach huts of the west coast hotels started to lend beach equipment such as goggles, fins and snorkels to their guests. They also put up small posters with images of different fishes. When the tourists returned from their snorkelling adventures, they frequently used these posters as the material focal point for discussions about what they had seen and how they had experienced the dive.

During the 1990s, scuba diving became a mass leisure activity among global tourists visiting tropical and subtropical places. In 1997, 750,000 people became certified divers, and in 2000 there were an estimated total of 10 million certified divers worldwide. Australia, Thailand, the Egyptian Red Sea, the Bahamas, the Maldives, Mauritius, Costa Rica, and Belize became the most important new destinations for dive holidays. The 1995 *Worldwide Faraway* catalogue by Thomas Cook included for the first time an extensive section dedicated to 'The Pleasures and Treasures of Diving': 'there are coral gardens of unimagined colour as little as three metres below the surface, and there are sub-sea sanctuaries where the "locals" are as inquisitive as their visitors. In short there are as many reasons to dive as there are fish on the reefs. Much more than simply a sport, scuba diving opens a new window on the world, revealing treasures seen by only a few' (Thomas Cook 1995: 12).

During the late 1990s, Thomas Cook bought the holiday tour operator, Neilson, specialist in the marketing and production of dive holidays around the world. The phenomenon of scuba diving has since continued to grow, reaching ever more tourists. While initially seen among tourists and tour operators as a hazardous environment, prone to injury, cuts and bruises, during the 1980s and 1990s coral reefs seemed to have been elevated as a new space where tourists can engage with a mysterious and beautiful nature. Engaging with the perceived magic and beauty of the underwater world has become a defining pattern of modern tourism culture in tropical places. It seems to have added a new layer to traditional beach activities such as tanning, playing volleyball or swimming in the sea. The admiration – the veneration – of the beauty of nature within the distanced realm of the underwater world seems to have generated a new space for self-reflection and existential engagement. Paradoxically, the emergence of this new tourism phenomenon, and the subsequent commoditisation of coral reefs as a tourist product, went hand in hand with the emancipation of coral reef sciences and the reinforcement of global efforts to conserve coral reefs, especially after wide-scale coral reef bleaching events had been observed during the 1980s and especially during the late 1990s and mid-2000s.

Coral Reef Conservation Politics

During the early 1980s, marine biologists in La Réunion observed that large parts of the corals populating the fringing reefs of the island's west coast had 'bleached' (Conand 2002). Corals are small marine organisms with a small cylindrical body and tentacles which are used to capture food.[4] Some corals live in colonies and build communal skeletons of calcium carbonate. Over a very long period, on the geological timescale, these skeletons, and their periodic destruction and erosion caused by natural events such as tropical cyclones, are responsible for the formation of coral reefs. Reef-building – or 'hermatypic' – corals generally require well-tempered, clean and nutrient-poor marine environments. They usually have little resistance to short-term environmental stress due to changed levels of water salinity, ocean acidity, nutrients, solar irradiance, sedimentation or sea surface temperature (Dove and Hoegh-Guldberg 2006). Corals live in a symbiotic relationship with photosynthesising unicellular algae – the 'zooxanthellae' – that live within their tissues and give them their specific coloration. In situations of environmental stress, they tend to expel the zooxanthellae they live with and, if the stress is maintained, they often die. Their remaining skeletons look 'bleached'. While many of the corals in La Réunion seemed able to recover partly during the 1980s and 1990s, new major bleaching events took place in 1998 and 2006, ultimately leading to the death of up to fifty per cent of the island's corals (Spalding, Ravilious and Green 2001: 207). The reasons for these events were attributed to the significant, temporary increase of sea surface temperatures during the summer months of 1982 and 1998 (Wilkinson 1998) and, more recently, in 2006. Further factors identified as having contributed to the bleaching of the island's reef were physical damage caused by tropical cyclones, higher levels of sedimentation following heavy rain, augmented water pollution and nutrient levels caused by agricultural activities and untreated waste water discharged into the lagoon, and the trampling of corals by fishers, swimmers and divers.

The bleaching of La Réunion's relatively small coral reef did not represent an isolated event, but was indicative of a more general global environmental phenomenon. In the same years, major coral reef bleaching events were reported from most other tropical islands and shores of the world (Hoegh-Guldberg 1999). The Intergovernmental Panel on Climate Change in its Fourth Assessment (IPCC 2007: 52) suggested that coral reefs are 'likely' (which means with a probability above sixty-six per cent) to be especially affected by climate change. The report specifies that 'increases in sea surface temperature of about 1 to 3°C are projected to result in more frequent coral bleaching events and widespread mortality, unless there is thermal adaptation or acclimatisation by corals' (IPCC 2007: 65). Basing its findings on data collected between 1980 and 1999, it warned that global average annual temperature changes of 1°C would result in 'increased coral bleaching', while changes of 2°C would leave most corals bleached and 3°C lead to 'widespread coral mortality' (IPCC 2007: 51). The report further stressed that 'while there is increasing evidence of climate change impacts on coral reefs, separating the impacts of climate-related stresses from other stresses (e.g. overfishing and pollution) is difficult' (IPCC 2007: 33). As a major newly identified threat, it mentioned in particular the progressive acidification of oceans 'expected to have negative impacts on marine shell-forming organisms (e.g. corals) and their dependent species' (IPCC 2007: 52). This threat arises from the fact that increased carbon dioxide levels in the surface waters of the world's oceans seem to lead to increasing acidity levels in the oceans which reduces the ability of corals to produce calcium carbonate skeletons and even threatens to 'dissolve' these skeletons entirely (Gattuso, Frankignoulle, Bourge et. al. 1998) – just as acidic components are used in household products to dissolve calcium, or acidic soft drinks erode teeth. Both phenomena – global warming and increased ocean acidity – can be seen as directly related to increasing atmospheric carbon dioxide levels caused by anthropogenic carbon dioxide emissions especially by industrial and industrialising countries. Many marine scientists agree that if the current dynamic of coral reef destruction, brought about by global warming, is not reversed within the next few years, up to fifty per cent of all corals will have disappeared by 2030 (Norlander 2003).

The global factors of coral reef bleaching described above are usually seen as being amplified by a series of local environmental impacts. These include, on one hand, 'natural factors' such as cyclones, tsunamis, high tidal waves, heavy rains and epidemics that destroy coral skeletons or infect corals with diseases. On the other hand, they include 'anthropogenic factors' related to the urbanisation of shores and badly managed waste water systems, intensified inland agricultural activities which use fertilisers that increase the level of nutrients in the water, the deforestation of land which causes soil erosion and increased levels of sedimentation in the lagoons, over fishing leading to a decrease of zooxanthellae, and the increased trampling of the reefs provoked by the development of coastal fishery and tourism industries. The local consequences of coral reef destruction are often dramatic, especially in poorer countries where coral reefs are the principal livelihood resource base for coastal populations. Coral reefs are the most densely inhabited ecosystem that exist and provide a breeding ground and secure kindergarten for many fish and marine species. In many countries of the western Indian Ocean, their destruction has led to a rarefaction of coastal and reef fish resources and to the impoverishment of coastal populations. It has also led to the increasing adoption of more destructive coastal fishing techniques (e.g. net fishing, spear gun fishing, dynamite fishing, scuba fishing, poison fishing) and hitherto rare and economically unviable practices of juvenile fishing. Moreover, the fragile health of corals, combined with rising sea water levels, has led to the increased erosion of many fringing and barrier reefs, leaving beaches and shores exposed to the eroding effects of storms and strong tidal waves.

The global threats of coral bleaching and the destruction of coral reefs was first addressed by the World Commission on Environment and Development (1987) and the ensuing United Nations Conference on Environment and Development in Rio de Janeiro, Brazil in 1992. The principal outcome of this conference was the ratification of the Rio Declaration on Environment and Development (UNCED 1992) and its attached global policy programme, Agenda 21 (UNEP 2003). Reaffirming the goals of UNCLOS (1982), it recognised the limit of current approaches to marine and coastal resource management, leading to rapid degradation and erosion of coastal resources and environments (Gray Davidson 2002: 529). Chapter 17 of Agenda 21 defined the implementation of integrated management models to protect such environments as one of its strategic objectives. Several paragraphs of this chapter dealt with the protection and preservation of rare or fragile ecosystems such as coral reefs and mangroves. Paragraph 30.a.V. stipulated that states should assess the need for additional measures to address the degradation of such marine environments by both human and natural sources. In 1994, an international organisation, the International Coral Reef Initiative (ICRI) was founded with the aim of implementing Chapter 17 of Agenda 21 and other international conventions and agreements for the benefit of coral reefs and related ecosystems (UNEP and WWF 2003: 10). The first ICRI workshop was held in the Philippines in 1995, resulting in the formulation of both a Call for Action and a Framework for Action. The ICRI and its approach to the environment reaffirmed the largely functional and utilitarian discourse already observed in Agenda 21. Paragraph 73 of the latter stated that coral reefs and mangroves 'often serve important ecological functions, provide coastal protection, and are critical resources for food, energy, tourism and economic development' (UNEP 2003). Similarly, in the foreword of a brochure UNEP presented during the Rio+10 World Summit on Sustainable Development in Johannesburg, South Africa in 2002, Klaus Töpfer, then executive director of UNEP, explained that 'due to their complexity and diversity, coral reefs can provide food and livelihood opportunities to millions of people. They are vital for small-scale and artisanal fisheries, producing 10 per cent of the world's fishing harvest. Further, they are hosts to a wide range of organisms that may hold the key to future medical advances. They also provide services such as shoreline protection and recreational opportunities' (UNEP and WWF 2003). While Klaus Töpfer further claimed that all the various uses of coral reefs make 'their importance for the economies of coastal communities and entire nations immeasurable', it became the principal endeavour of the newly emerging academic disciplines of environmental economics to measure the positive economic value of coral reefs or the economic impact of their destruction. Throughout the 1990s, academics, initially from Anglo-Saxon countries, especially Australia and the USA, later also France, adopted a neo-classical approach to the value and management of coral reefs. From the perspective of environmental economics, natural space was seen as a profit generating capital (Serageldin 1997). Through complex calculations, coral reefs were given a commercial capital value which could be entered into national and regional environmental accountancy systems. Similarly utilitarian approaches to the environment were discussed during the ICRI conferences throughout the 1990s and 2000s and they seemed to have developed into a global standard environmental management model (Ryland 1982; Pendleton 1995; Hatziolos *et al.* 1998; Colwell 1999; Cesar 2001; Carr and Mendelsohn 2003). A 2008 report published by Conservation International (CI) estimates the total economic surplus – the 'net benefit value' – generated by the world's coral reefs, mangroves and seagrasses at $29.8 billion, with respectively just above thirty per cent ($9.6 billion and $9.0 billion) generated by tourism and recreational activities and coastal protection services, and around fifteen per cent respectively by fisheries and the reproduction of biodiversity (CI 2008: i-ii, 1).

Rhetorically reduced to an economic resource, coral reefs were to generate benefits. In this context, environmental policy makers seemed to have rediscovered tourism, especially under its softer sounding name, 'ecotourism', as a provider of revenues and alternative livelihoods for coastal populations.[5] The ugly mass tourism had long supplied a stereotyped character for cheap and acceptable xenophobia among social elites; similarly to many anthropologists who saw tourists entering their sacred gardens, marine biologists often seemed to have considered tourists as ignorant environmental polluters who were best locked away in holiday ghettos far from the vulnerable marine environments they had made their personal and spiritual centres. In La Réunion, tourism development provided a rather paradoxical argument for the conservation of the lagoon; only an intact marine environment represents a viable resource for tourism, militants began to claim during the 1990s, so in order to develop tourism, one needed to conserve this environment (Mespoulhe, Troadec and Martin 1994). Tourism seemed to be no longer considered as necessarily having a 'negative impact' – the paradigm dominant during the 1970s and 1980s – but as providing a powerful argument to protect the coral reef and gain economic benefits from their exploitation.

However, the rhetoric of economic utility often appeared to hide a deeper meaning. Many publications on coral reef conservation stress, usually in their forewords or conclusions, the beauty and magic of coral reef environments, 'one of the world's most spectacular ecosystems', 'packed with the highest densities of animals to be found anywhere on the planet' (Spalding, Ravilious and Green 2001). Furthermore, a detailed reading of the 1992 Rio Declaration enables an allegorical understanding of this legal text, which seeks to protect nature in general, and corals in particular. While the first of this declaration's principles stressed that 'human beings are at the centre of concerns for sustainable development' and that 'they are entitled to a healthy and productive life in harmony with nature' (UNEP 2003), the third specified that 'the right to development must be fulfilled so as to equitably meet developmental and environmental needs of present and future generations'. Both principles relate to a discourse which defines humanity in relation to a non-human nature on the one hand, and to human generations of the future, on the other. They imply a specific ontological and temporal framework. This here and now is constituted through the relationship between a human and a non-human world, and the way in which this relationship will be judged by future generations. The future therefore becomes symbolically integrated into a holistic conception of the present world. This seems to represent a break with the linear eschatology of neo-classical thinking and the capitalist logic of accumulation and growth. The anticipation of the needs of future generations implies an intergenerational exchange: contemporary action is to be judged by the future generations who hence become a powerful social institution reaffirming the individuality of present generations beyond time and death. On an individual level, acting in accordance with the needs of future generations and, in particular, preserving natural environments become the means of prolonging one's individuality beyond one's own time. Practices of engaging with and managing natural environments become morally charged and subjected to political processes of normalisation.

This dimension – which makes the utilitarian approach to coral reef management appear to be a rhetorical trick – reveals a form of deeper almost spiritual engagement whose semantics were openly announced in international texts until well into the 1990s. UNESCO's 1972 Convention Concerning the Protection of the World Cultural and Natural Heritage, and its preliminary 1962 Recommendation concerning the Safeguarding of the Beauty and Character of Landscapes and Sites, stemmed from a strictly political-aesthetic approach to the world and world governance, especially the official UNESCO project to create lasting peace. The institutionalisation of world heritage sites appears here to be nothing more than a projection of heritage concepts used by European nation-states throughout the nineteenth and twentieth century. What is new is that the concept of nation is projected onto a world scale; world heritage is to embody and mediate a global nation, a global national identity (whose modalities were to be governed by Western philosophies of time, history and being [di Giovine 2008]). From this point, the motives underlying the politics of environmental conservation and the constitution of natural heritage are often unclear. Initially, scientific and leisure practices can be said to have shared very much the same root and departure point. The initial motive of both practices is – and often largely remains – aesthetic, the consequence of an 'enchantment'. Yet, thanks to the scientific approach, the discoveries made ensure that the motive becomes something else; that it leads to a better theoretical understanding of nature, and also to the development of pragmatic economic management models that allow the initially enchanted grounds to be preserved and valued.

The Coral Reef as 'Local Heritage'

From the 1990s, different French governmental institutions began to introduce the frameworks underlying these international programmes at the national and regional level of the French territory. A new French legislation commonly called 'littoral law' (*loi littoral*), passed in January 1986, gave these frameworks a legal status and a legitimate power. As a part of this law, national and local political institutions in La Réunion were asked to develop a Maritime Zone Valuation Scheme (SMVM) which integrated the needs and usages of the littoral into a unique plan. The SMVM consequently became part of the Regional Development Scheme (Région Réunion 1995), the principal legal spatial planning tool at the regional scale.

Local environmental lobby groups and stakeholders suggested that policy makers should adopt a marine park model for the regional context, with the idea of generating marine-protected areas and no-take zones around the most productive reefs that would then allow the damaged reefs to rejuvenate. The idea was taken up after several years of studies and negotiations and, in 1997, La Réunion Marine Park, a not-for profit association involving several governmental, regional, departmental and communal institutions, local associations and university institutes, was created. The official aim of this new institution was to manage and protect the maritime and littoral zones of the island's south and west coast, and to generate a social dynamic towards a concerted and integrated management of the island's most vulnerable marine spaces, in particular its coral reefs (Parc Marin 1999a, 1999b). One of the main activities of this association was to educate the different users of the coastal zone, including fishermen, tourists, bar owners, hotel managers, and school classes. This activity used a number of texts about coral ecology and conservation in its pedagogical tools which were invariably presented by the association's employees and eco-guards during community meetings, green school classes, seafront festivals, stakeholder meetings and educational documentary films. These texts were made available in the form of printed documents, especially a poster widely distributed in the public spaces of the coastal zone – copies were permanently placed in the pathways through which different users of the marine space accessed the beaches and the lagoon and were circulated to local tourism offices, hotels, schools, community centres and sports clubs – and a small educational brochure, *Le monde merveilleux du récif corallien* (The Marvellous World of the Coral Reef) (Gabrié 1999), distributed to school classes, fishing communities and hotel beach recreation staff.

The poster was composed of a large drawing, a transversal cut of the lagoon, and various text and image inserts. It bore a title separated into two parts, inserted respectively in the upper and lower part of the poster. It said, 'Le récif c'est un monde à part … Mais un monde fragile que nous devons préserver' ('The coral reef, that's a world on its own… But a fragile world that we must preserve'). The focal point of the large lagoon image – between the sky and the sea – placed the viewer as standing upright in the middle of the lagoon. The central motif in the centre of the visual composition was constituted by a heteroclite symphony of colourful corals, sand and various coloured fish. On the second plane of the image, slightly blurred people and beach umbrellas were visible on the beach, on the left of the image, while other equally blurred people were snorkelling on the water surface, on the right. The image thus seemed to reproduce the conventionalised visual language classically used in European painting (Roger 1997: 66f); however the traditional sacred element – figures of saints and later monarchs in the centre of the image – was replaced by the representation of an underwater natural space. The underwater world was elevated as the sacred centrepiece of the image while the humans pictured in its second plane became part of its decor. In the upper part of the poster, short texts and small picture inserts described the particular function of different organisms living in the lagoon while a series of texts in the lower part explained the biological value of the reef ('highly diversified ecosystems'), different human and natural reasons for its degradation ('pollution of water through the use of pesticides in agriculture', 'trampling on the reef', 'fishing outside the allowed fishing periods') and the imperative to protect it ('The coral reef is our heritage. Each of us is hence beholden to preserve it. All together, let us protect our reefs.'). The presentation of these different texts and images – first magnifying the wonder of the underwater world, then locating the culpability for its destruction in certain human activities, and finally suggesting a deliverance in the form of a specific code of behaviour – highlight the centrality of the underwater world as the figured element of this image. Both the visual language of the image and the morality implied in its textual elements appeared to formulate what could be described as an underwater liturgy.

The text printed in the brochure[6] seems to confirm this observation. It developed a story about the living world of corals and the history of coral reef environments. By adopting the perspective of the polyp – the organism building the coral skeleton – it fashioned the latter as a narrative that audiences could identify with. Through the analogies used in the story, the polyp was made to take on different roles. It was first represented as a sort of foetus (it has a baggy body shape, is of minuscule size and initial softness, and slowly develops a skeleton), then as a good and pure soul (it creates twins and lives in large families; it is hospitable and sociable; it needs light and pure water to survive; it does not harm anyone) and finally as a reliable worker and somehow magical gardener (it never stops building despite the risk of being swept away by the current; it constructs an oasis in the desert of the ocean). Through such analogies, the story situated its hero's living world in a specific type of social environment. On one hand, the coral reef was seen as an urban space marked by the buildings of the coral colonies and the chaotic interactions of a multitude of different beings that took place between them. On the other hand, it was seen as an 'oasis in the desert of the ocean', in other words a garden of thriving life within a vast inhospitable wasteland.

The story told through the brochure text and the visual narrative of the poster situated the here and now of the coral reef within a specific temporality. It had emerged within a very long term, geological timescale; it was a quasi-prehistoric monument that was still alive. The reef thus allowed a connection between an almost infinitive past and the present. It was elevated as some kind of a-historic dinosaur that had not been affected by the heaviness of time and being. It provided continuity, infinitude, in a world marked by discontinuity and death. The hero of the story would always be there; and if we made this hero ours, if we would become this hero, we might always be there too, even if we are no longer around. The coral allowed the audience to think about time and, by becoming part of us – of our heritage – to overcome the identity crisis caused by changes in the living world, ultimately by their death. Maybe because of all the qualities associated with the polyp and the wonderful underwater world it has created, it could be seen as fragile. While it was said to survive easily in a natural environment, it could not defend itself against humans and the impact of human activities. Humans were allocated the role of potential anti-heroes within the story of the polyp. They constantly threatened to destroy the environment that was essential to the polyp's wonderful life. The liturgy of the underwater world suggested a series of solutions. Humans had to chose their camp: either be poachers and destroy 'in a second' what had taken centuries to grow, spoiling the fragile environment of the coral reef through illegal hunting and polluting modern lifestyles, or become good gardeners and preserve and adore the reef as local heritage. The analogy with the biblical story of Eden is striking here. The moral framework underlying the story of the coral prescribed a set of rules – preserving the reef – and promised as a reward an enchanting garden of earthly delight. It also implied the need for a disciplining scheme for those who would not comply with these rules, who would become socially outlawed and alienated poachers, or who would no longer be granted access to the delights of the coral gardens. A divine paradise, rediscovered in the form of the underwater world of the island's reef, would once again be lost.

Poachers, Gardeners and Social Participation

The story of the coral used by La Réunion Marine Park subtly projected its underlying roles – hero and villain – onto the local social context of the island. Although this was not explicitly stated, it required little intelligence to understand that the local fishing populations, as well as the stakeholders and politicians responsible for the pollution of the lagoon especially through the discharge of waste water, were seen as potential villains. For these and others, including school children, tourist operators, tourists, etc., to be seen as a 'good' person and to 'give a good image' within the new social space generated by coral reef conservation, they had to identify with the hero of the story and submit to its rules. As a result of the continuous public repetition, throughout the 1990s and 2000s, of this story and its underlying moral not only by La Réunion Marine Park but also by the local media, school teachers, local politicians and public events, protecting the reef became a highly symbolic act through which people began to situate themselves in relation to the island's local modernity. It seemed to generate what Roland Barthes (1957) called a 'significant consciousness': a collective understanding of the lagoon as a 'local heritage' whose preservation became a social performance in the public eye of the island. By generating a new form of symbolic economy and new forms of social participation and exclusion, it seemed to translate the culture of the *kartié* into a new social ground.

In 1997, La Réunion Marine Park and various local authorities asked the fishermen who used the lagoon as their resource base to organise themselves and set up associations, so that they could be represented within the marine park association and participate in the programme of developing marine protected areas. Six associations were consequently created. However, as Stéphane Loupy (2001) explained in her ethnographic study of the fishing milieu of La Réunion's west coast, none of these newly created associations included members of the old fishing families. She argued that the historic stigmatisation of these old families, and the social exclusion they had been subjected to, was reproduced in the context of the marine park project. With low levels of education, limited French-language skills (like most Réunions they spoke Creole), and a negative self-image ('fish does not feed a family', was a saying among them), these fishermen seemed unable to make themselves heard or, quite literally, understood by the authorities running this park project. All the texts used by the association were written in French. Moreover, the discussions that took place during the stakeholder meetings were held in French, often using the technical vocabulary of the marine sciences, spatial planning and park management. Unable to write letters or to engage in verbal dialogues, the fishermen often preferred to avoid interaction with the marine park authorities rather than to engage with them. Stéphane Loupy (2001: 140) reported a case where a fisherman considered getting drunk before a stakeholder meeting at the marine park, in order to have the courage to speak to the director and scientific committee. The difficulty of entering into a dialogue with the park authorities ultimately led to the roadblock described at the beginning of this chapter.

While these old fishing families remained largely excluded from the decision-making processes regarding the future of the lagoon, a group of 'new' fishermen emerged during the 1990s who were better equipped and better educated, and some had invested in offshore fishing gear. These 'new' fishermen, often with no family background in fishing, had a largely positive self-image and managed to make their activity economically viable. They consequently came to represent the interests of what was rhetorically redefined as the 'traditional' or 'ancestral' fishing practices of the island's coastal populations (Loupy 2001). The polarisation and politicisation of the lagoon fishing issue, especially following the violent end to the road block in 1999, did little to help the old fishing families who preferred to remain invisible to the public eye, or otherwise encourage their children to find different jobs. For the 'new' fishermen, however, it became an opportunity to gain public support for their activities; several of the new associations designated charismatic spokespersons to represent their interests in the numerous stakeholder meetings that continued to take place during the early 2000s. At the same time, illegal lagoon fishing came to be seen, in certain social milieu, as an act of public defiance against the political authority of the French state in the island. Also, in a more generic way, it sometimes became romanticised as an act of defiance against what was seen as the occidentalisation of the island and the acceleration of globalisation. Some of the new fishing associations employed a rhetoric claiming the ocean as a 'place of wilderness' that needed to be defended against modernity, that needed to remain open as a fishing ground. During fieldwork carried out in some of the west coast hotels, I observed several cases where tourists from the French mainland accompanied local fishermen going harpoon hunting in the lagoon during the early morning hours. They explained their behaviour in terms of their 'solidarity with the island's working classes', as their contribution to the struggle against state oppression and the capitalist system.

Despite the violence and the long-successful resistance by some of the fishermen, the global logic of the preservation of the reefs ultimately imposed itself. With the help of the legislative power of the French government and its representatives in the overseas department, the prefect, the policing power attributed to the state authorities and the persuasive sensitisation strategy of the marine park association, a legally recognised national marine natural reserve was created in February 2007, substituting the not-for-profit association of La Réunion Marine Park. Some children of the former fishermen had by then been employed as eco-guards, while others created a not-for-profit association, *Les Jardiniers du Lagon* (the Gardeners of the Lagoon), whose aim was the preservation and amelioration of the coral reef and its validation through tourist activities. The story is ongoing.

Part III

Cultivating the Human Garden

Chapter 7
History as an Aesthetics of Everyday Life

Meeting the Lulas

It was an early evening in December 1999. I met Mrs Lula[1] under a tree in front of the community hall. The sun was about to go down over the lagoon, shimmering in golden flashes through the pine trees. I was saying hello. I had called her some days earlier, after the girl from Saint-Paul City Council had given me her number, in order to explain my research interests in the activities of the Hermitage Village Committee. Mrs Lula invited me to participate in a meeting they were going to have to prepare the celebrations to commemorate the abolition of slavery. Mrs Lula was the president of the Hermitage Village Committee, an umbrella group which united other associations in the area. She and the other members of this association had already organised the abolition of slavery commemorations in the two previous years. A dozen people, men and women, were present. They introduced themselves as members and volunteers of various sports and cultural associations domiciled in the quarter of L'Hermitage-les-bains. I explained my research topic and my specific interest in their festival. We spoke in French and Creole.

Mrs Lula explained that the *Belle Jeunesse* dance group that she was a member of and whom she was representing wished to perform a dance depicting the abolition of slavery. They had spent several months preparing this dance, she said. She added that the climax of the festival would be a street procession through the neighbourhood of their residential quarter. The central act of this procession was to be a group of 'chained slaves' and a 'white master'. Somebody suggested that Mrs Jeannette's husband, Alessio, should play the role of the master as he was the only *Zoreil* among the group. He declined, saying that he should not have to take on the role simply because he was *Zoreil*. 'Why not Fred, he's white as well?' he proposed. Fred, a red-haired man of clear skin colour, originally from the village, looked askance. 'No, Fred can't play the master because he's Creole', was the others' prompt response.

The discussion dragged on for a while. It grew dark and people wanted to go home. Daniel, the father-in-law of Mrs Lula's daughter Emilie, took over the discussion and established the preparation schedule for the festival. He suggested the construction of three straw huts and a podium, and a bar where sandwiches, cakes, and alcohol would be sold. He noted that musical groups were needed and his son, François, suggested leading on this. Within a few minutes, the remaining issues – related to the building of the festival site, the transport of material and the construction of mock straw huts – were settled. Mrs Lula and her husband Alessio invited me to their house to talk and have a drink. I lived near to the quarter and during the following months I would often be around there and meet the rest of her family. The next meeting of Hermitage Village Committee was set for a Saturday at the home of Mrs Lula's brother Claude.

Societal Life Crisis and Long Festivity Cycles

From the mid-1990s, most villages and urban quarters in La Réunion began to initiate or revitalise festivals, often themed around former pastoral activities, products or plants. In addition, a large number of what were commonly known as 'ethnic' festivals were created or were made visible to a wider public audience, discursively emphasising for various reasons either the 'cultural distinctiveness' of particular 'communities' (usually defined by a combination of religious, phenotype and origin criteria - cf. Labache 1996) or the cultural creolisation of La Réunion's population. Moreover, almost at the same time, an important number of sport festivals appeared or were re-profiled to become regional or international events, usually focusing on so-called 'outdoor' or 'natural space' activities. In this chapter, I will examine the abolition of slavery celebrations organised by the Hermitage Village Committee in order to understand this sudden increase in the number of publicly celebrated, local folkloristic, ethnic or sportive festivals (Cherubini 1996a, 1996b). I am particularly interested here in the way in which the recent structural changes in the island's economy and territorial organisation were symbolically articulated and made meaningful through festive performances and the aesthetics of the festival space.

Like most of these festivals, the celebration of the abolition of slavery was publicly instituted in the island from the late 1980s and became an official festival during the mid-1990s (Eve 2003). The celebration of the abolition of slavery has often been the subject of public debate in La Réunion and regularly engendered political controversy, crystallised in particular in debates about the festival's official title, which ranged from *fête kaf* (*kaf* being the Creole term for persons of African descent, *fête* being French for 'festival') or *fet kaf* to *fête du 20 décembre* (referring to the actual date of abolition, 20 December 1848), *La fête de la libération*, (The Liberation Festival), or *La fête de la liberté réunionnaise* (The Réunion Freedom Festival). Throughout the 1990s, the theme of abolition became widely appropriated by local village committees who started to stage their own celebrations. I will argue that the emergence of this new festival and of the recent festival boom in general can be understood with regard to a societal 'life crisis'[2] caused by the structural changes in the island over the last twenty years of the twentieth century.

The village of L'Hermitage-les-bains represents a significant case for this study, as this former fishing village had recently been affected by major spatial and economic transformations. It used to be one of three settlements on La Réunion's west coast, previously known as the 'second' village – the two others were the 'first' and the 'third' villages (Maestri 1998). Since the 1970s, the former 'second village' began to be surrounded by new middle-class residential areas and several international seaside resorts. Former economic activities, including lagoon fishing, were challenged by new leisure usages of the seashore and the newly created La Réunion Marine Park. Furthermore, the substitution of the plantation economy by modern capital intensive agriculture had left many of the villages' inhabitants unemployed and dependent on the social welfare allocations given by the French state. At the same time, property prices increased by up to 3000 per cent between 1980 and 2002. Former patterns of spatial and social organisation, historically linked to a large extent to the economic functions of the sugar cane industry, were clearly shifting (Benoist and Bonniol 1994; Ottino 1999). The rapid urbanisation of the coastal areas resulted in the closure or disappearance of many paths to the beach or to other nearby villages. Many landmarks – various sugar mills, a small lake, etc. – which represented shared references for the collective being and memory of the coastal populations were transformed, demolished or made inaccessible. In this context, what has set the Lula family, Mrs Lula and her brothers, apart is the way in which they have coped with these changes and somehow managed to transform them into opportunities for social mobility. They said they managed to 'get out of the poverty' (*s'en sortir*). As was the case with Claudette (chapter 4), Mrs Lula ensured, by various means, that her children succeeded in school and went to university. Her brothers created a building society and, little by little, generated a new livelihood. In this chapter, I will describe not only the way in which the festival celebrations allowed this family and the wider village community to appropriate, reformulate and perform different images and stories associated with slavery and the abolition of slavery to make sense of more immediate social and symbolic ruptures and separations, but also the new connections that marked their social life. An earlier version of this text bore the title 'Gardening the past' (Picard 2006), referring to the staging of a flower and agricultural garden as the spatial and thematic frame of the event. I suggest that to study this form of garden, is a way of cultivating, embodying and performing a vision of the world by selective and spatial arrangements of flowers, artefacts and plants.

Mock Straw Huts in the Festive Ground

On the Saturday following my initial meeting with the Hermitage Village Committee, I went to the house of Claude, Mrs Lula's brother. I arrived at around 9.30 in the morning and saw a Peugeot 406 parked at the entrance. Daniel and another man were unloading straw gathered at the house of a relative living at L'Hermitage-les-hauts, a village some kilometres inland (les *hauts* was the name given to the mountainous inner region of the island). About an hour later, more men arrived, and we began to fabricate a set of three mock straw huts that would be used to decorate the festival space. Pierre, another brother of Mrs Lula, and Daniel showed us what to do. Pierre explained that he had been familiar with straw huts as a child. He told us how to put up the wire so we could attach the straw. We worked in groups of two or three. Bamboo and aloe branches were attached to wire to create squares measuring two metres by two metres. The straw was sewn on top, 'not too densely because it's just decoration,' as Daniel put it. At the end of two hour's work we had six panels completed. Claude sent one of his sons to bring us cold beers, which went down nicely. Some people drank Coca-Cola. Claude had arrived with his wife shortly before. He commented on our work with a smile: 'But they didn't have wire back then.' 'Anyway, you should build with concrete, it's stronger,' he added and laughed cheerfully at his joke. Around midday friends of Claude – two women from the village, both with *Métropolitan* husbands – arrived. They commented on the work and the beer we were drinking. 'The dodo [name of an extinct bird and the local beer] didn't exist then,' they said. One of the men pointed to one of Mrs Lula's brothers saying, 'so they're having a festival for you Monday.' The brother explained that he had a pointed nose and therefore was not *Kaf* but *Indian*. Everyone laughed. The men set a meeting for the next evening to build the podium. The next day, they agreed, they would pick up pallets and support frames from a building site run by the Lula brothers' construction company.

The festival took place on a Monday. Early in the morning the entrance to the car park, normally used by visitors to the beach, was closed off with a red and white banner. The set-up of the festival space began with the installation of various structures and the planting of a selection of vegetation. Two straw panels respectively formed, in all, three mock straw huts installed in the corners of the space in which the festival was organised. A fourth hut, constructed of palm leaves, housed the *boutik karner*, where the village's bowls club sold sodas, beer, rum and sandwiches. 'Karner was the name of an old Chinese man who owned a shop in the village,' Pierre explained. A sign announced the price of drinks, written first in French by one of Mrs Lula's brothers, and then in Creole by Alessio, Mrs Lula's (*Métropolitan*) husband. Rum bottles were placed under the bar and their content abundantly sampled. The entire festival ground was decorated with flowers and plants taken from participants' gardens, with cut banana trees, sugar cane, palm leaves, flowering plants, agaves, and corn stalks being 'replanted' (they no longer had roots) in the ground and watered. Palm, coconut palm, and *vacoa* leaves were tied to the podium and the bar. 'We used to work in the sugar cane fields,' Pierre explained to his children and outside visitors that were passing by. Daniel dug a hole in front of the podium to create a *boucan*, an open fire for cooking in a suspended pot. Three trunks served as benches. A *tramail* (a net for lagoon fishing) was hung between wooden sticks, placed near the entrance. 'We put the *tramail* there because in our quarter, there are fishermen', Daniel explained. The preparations of the festival were carried out by different groups defined, to a large degree, by criteria of gender and generation. While the men conceptualised and constructed the material space of the festival, the women, partly aided by their daughters and granddaughters, made cakes and contributed 'old-time' household items – an iron, a coffee grinder, two corn grinders, and a *gregue* (coffee pot) – which they placed on a small chest of drawers in front of the straw huts. Mrs Lula told a woman that she used one of the carbon irons until the 1980s and that her 'unfortunate' (i.e. 'poor') mother did not have the means to purchase a coffee grinder. A platter with fruits that, according to one woman, 'we no longer know' was set in front of the hut to the left of the podium, where the women sold their cake. A gas stove was installed behind the podium, under the roof of the community centre, and a *cari volaille* (a dish consisting of rice and chicken) was cooked at midday. Behind the podium, in the shade of a large tree, the sound equipment and the compere's post were placed. Two large speakers were put on the podium. The space behind and on the podium was arranged by two young men, nephews of Mrs Lula, belonging to the *'Maloya Traditionnel'* association. Throughout the festival, the gender and generation groups continued to occupy specific spaces. The podium constituted the centre of the festival ground. The young adults later grouped behind this podium, around the sound system and the DJ, whereas the space to the left was mainly occupied by women and children, and to the right by men.

By the end of the morning, at around eleven, the festival space had been set up. Mrs Lula asked the children to leave the grounds. She, her husband, Pierre, Daniel, Fred, and other helpers then went home. A quarter of an hour later, they reappeared, wearing what they called 'old-time' clothes. Mrs Lula was in a floral dress and had a scarf around her head. Pierre and Fred had put on suits, 'good' shoes, and hats. Daniel wore torn trousers and a shirt with red flowers. Daniel and Mrs Lula sat down beside the *boucan* and lit a fire beneath the cauldron. Daniel peeled bananas and manioc for cooking. This proved amusing to the other men who had gathered around the *boutik karner* to talk and drink rum. It was unusual in La Réunion to cook bananas, and this was thus a very individual contribution that Daniel, from Martinique, brought to the festival. When I asked if I could film them cooking, Mrs Lula asked me to wait for her to take off her sandals and dispose of a little bottle of gas used to light the fire. 'Because they didn't have those back then,' she explained and both Mrs Lula and Daniel had to laugh. From half past eleven, women with children, adolescents, and men arrived in small groups to look around the grounds and then to assemble, the women with the other women who were selling cake and the men with the other men who continued drinking rum at the *boutik*. They joked around, wishing to all people of African phenotype a 'Happy festival, *Kaf*! Today's our day.' This banter continued all day. Tourists with cameras and people visiting the beach passed through, some stopping a moment to look or talk, before leaving. The children and teenagers were found mostly near the cake stand or on or behind the podium. Some of them jumped about and danced to the music. A little before noon, Mrs Lula asked them to get off of the podium. Daniel came up and took the microphone to welcome everyone. The public was invited to visit the grounds, eat, drink and watch the performances. It was midday and quite hot. The space gradually deserted. Most people went back to their homes, a couple of hundred metres away from the festival ground, to eat and rest.

The festival ground remained empty until the early afternoon. At around half past two, people started to arrive in far larger numbers than during the morning. They included elderly men and women surrounded by children and adults, groups of teenagers, men and women, and *Métropolitan* families who walked around the grounds, looking at the straw huts, drinking, eating cake and talking. Mrs Lula invited her daughter and grandchildren inside one of the mock huts and explained the 'old ways of life'. 'Even in full sunlight, the air stays cool under the straw,' she said, 'it is better adapted to the tropical climate than houses made of concrete.' She also showed them how to use various household objects. Another woman explained where to find and how to eat some of the 'forgotten' fruits she was displaying on a platter. Pierre joined in, explaining that the planters of the village used to grind their corn at the home of one of the few men in the area who owned a corn grinder. 'And the pestle serves to crush chilli peppers and to make *rougail* [a spicy sauce]. Sometimes, to punish a child, my parents made me stand outside in the sun with a pestle on my head,' he added. For others, the visual encounter with *agave* plants triggered memories of working on the *moulin kader*, a mill which transformed the stalks of this species of aloe for the fabrication of rope. The encounter with these fruits, by then rare or little known, led to conversations about common childhood memories, the 'freedom of strolls' through land not yet developed, where everyone knew when and where the harvest took place. All the stories associated with these objects and fruits brought back snippets of memories, and were told with nostalgia, with laughter, and, sometimes, with eyes on the verge of tears.

In front of the podium, family clusters were grouped around several elderly people, seated comfortably in chairs they had brought. Several tourists, easily recognised by their clothes, their cameras, and the whiteness (or redness) of their skin, mixed with the crowd. They watched, photographed and filmed the performances that followed. These visitors did not go unnoticed: Mrs Lula later proudly observed that 'they filmed it, so they liked it, didn't they?' The performances on the podium began with children dancing to a popular international pop song, *Ibiza*, followed by three teenage girls in tank tops and black trousers who had choreographed a dance accompanied by *ragga* music. Next were three girls in *pareos* who danced a *maloya*. The tension gradually rose. The last two acts were sexually provocative: the female bodies stirred, men whistled, and the public became enthusiastic and applauded. Next, about ten people, among them some of the festival organisers, got up on the podium to sing and dance bits of a *maloya*. The crowd, now quite large, around 200 people, looked on and applauded. At the end of this musical act, the women of the *Belle Jeunesse* group performed their abolition of slavery dance which culminated in a collective dance involving the public. The festival came to a sudden end when they learned that a resident of the quarter had just died. Daniel made the announcement, apologised, and thanked everyone. The festival audiences dispersed rapidly. The festival grounds had to be quickly deconstructed. 'You can't have a festival when someone's just died,' Mrs Lula told me.

The Abolition Dance

Using a small video-camera, I filmed the Abolition Dance performed by the *Belle Jeunesse* dance group, which proved helpful later in transcribing the observations in more detail. The act had a multipartite structure. It was begun by seven women lying on the ground, barefoot, in dresses and straw hats. One of them 'woke up', looked about, got up on her knees, and touched the others, who then 'woke up' as well. The women joined hands, and then raised their arms to the sky. This opening lasted about two minutes and ended as it began: women stretched out along the ground. Next, a group of five women in dresses, cloth in hair and barefoot, 'worked' the manioc then walked, 'with difficulty', towards the centre of the stage. They then made movements representing the cutting of sugar cane, and after that joined the other women still on the ground. After this, two 'bourgeois' women entered, wearing light dresses, 'good' shoes and holding Chinese parasols, who went towards the women grouped on the ground. One said, 'Look how dirty you are!', then shouted at them, 'Come, you must work!'. The women on the ground cried, 'pity!'. One of the 'bourgeois' women closed her parasol and used it to hit one of the women on the ground. The audience laughed. The two 'bourgeois' women then left. The other women took care of their 'wounded' companion. Another woman appeared, barefoot, wearing a dress and straw hat, and went towards the women stretched on the ground. She said in Creole: 'We all live in this miserable state; we get up in the morning, rain or shine, because we must work.... The day will come when we can teach others how much pain the whip causes. Come then, you must rise…' A *maloya* song was played and she started to dance, and touched the shoulders of the other women, one by one, who then stood up. The scene terminated in a collective dance and the frenetic applause of the audience.

In the following scene, a woman stirred a cauldron. Others 'worked the earth' and 'drank rum'. One of them went towards the centre stage and said (in Creole), 'So many years of painful stories, one never forgets the whip.' She called the others, who then gathered around her. One woman said, 'I'm tired. My back hurts.' The first woman asked, 'Children of the islands, where are our roots?' The other women responded, '…close your eyes!' They started clapping their hands to the rhythm of another *maloya* song and formed two lines. They chanted, 'ah-ah-ah-ah-ah' and raised their arms towards the sky. They then lowered their arms and dispersed, going off to imitate household tasks again. This 'work' scene ended in the 'death from fatigue' of one of the women. While she lay on the ground, the others were dancing around her, screaming and crying, and then carried her off-stage. They shouted, 'alive, alive, alive...' A woman on the podium started to read a poem (in French) about the Anchaing (a popular maroon figure; cf. chapter 3), the heroism of his actions, the liberty he found on the island. The poem ended with 'I am free!', which the other women, still below the podium, repeated, 'free, free...' Then, at the podium, Mrs. Lula started to read another text (in French), 'The Secretary of State, Victor Schoelcher, presided over the commission that wrote the declaration of emancipation of all slaves on French territory, on 7 April 1848. It was not until eight months later when Sarda Garriga, Commissioner of State, announced the abolition of slavery on the island.' The women cried now even stronger, 'free, free...', while clapping their hands. Accompanied by another *maloya* song, they began to dance and invited the public, especially the men and women from their village, to join them. At the end of this song, women dressed in black spandex, dresses and tee-shirts, wearing masks of coloured feathers, assembled in front of the podium. Imitating the flight of birds with their arms, they began to dance. The crowd applauded. Other women, now in brightly coloured floral dresses, got on stage and invited the audience to dance. Most men and women hesitated at first, but finally many joined in with a collective dance.

Identity, Social Belonging and Festive Roles

The festival made visible and allowed participants to recreate different sets of social belonging and identity fundamental to the organisation of social life within the village. On one hand, the organisers – Mrs Lula, her husband Alessio, her brother and neighbour Pierre, her brother Claude (living fifty metres away from her house), her daughter Emilie, her nephew François, Daniel, father of François, Fred – were linked by kin and neighbourhood relationships. They were all born in or had long been living in the village, and most were linked to the wider Lula family. During the festival, the core audiences were composed of other neighbours and members of Mrs Lula's family that do not, or no longer live in the village. However, the festival also involved a concerted effort to address an outside public, beyond the immediate kin and neighbourhood community of the village. By voluntarily staging the festival ground and performances in the contact zone between the village and the public space of the highly frequented beach and seafront, the festival organisers deliberately attempted to tie the village into a broader social-symbolic space. This strategy of literally carrying the *kartié* into a public sphere was also manifested through the distributing of press releases by Mrs Lula, to achieve, as she put it, 'recognition of the village and all the work we have done'. In a way, the festival organisers therefore projected the culture of the *kartié* (cf. chapters 4 and 5) and the communicative logic of the domestic garden onto the wider public sphere of the island. Indeed, other more intimate or family celebrations (sports club, baptisms, marriages, bereavements, etc.), that I have been able to participate in, were usually organised at a small place within the village, in its 'private' space. Hence, the festival allowed its organisers to put their village on show, 'to give a good image' of their village within the wider social sphere. They saw it as it would be seen by an outside world, represented here by local journalists and external tourists.

On the other hand, on a more intrinsic and individual social level, the festival allowed participants to reaffirm gender and age related roles, and identities based on phenotype. Accordingly, the majority of the elder women occupied the space to the left of the stage. They had baked cakes with their daughters, which they then sold, and they exhibited old-time household items. They were mostly members of the *Belle Jeunesse* ('Beautiful Youth') association and usually met three evenings a week to do gymnastics and to choreograph dances that they would perform during this and other festivals. The elderly men occupied the space to the right of the stage where they were selling and drinking sodas and rum. Most of them were members of the *Club de boules du lagon* (Lagoon Bowls Club) and usually met in the evening around five o'clock, to play bowls. Some of them also regularly met each other at the *Kap Zamo* association, which brought together farmers who grew vegetables in plots close to the village, and a fishing team that regularly went to fish capuchin in the lagoon. The teenagers and young adults, male and female, were members of different friendship and activity groups. Some of the younger girls were friends and regularly met in the afternoons, among other things to choreograph dances such as the ones they performed during the festival. Some of the older teenagers were organised in the *Maloya Traditionnel* (Traditional Maloya) association. They usually met each other several times a week, during the evenings, to socialise and make music. During this and other festivals organised in the village, they were usually responsible for the musical entertainment. They also performed dances on stage. Through the socially differentiated logistical tasks, attributed roles, on-stage performances and occupation of spaces within the festival ground, the festival allowed each of these sub-groups to act out and reaffirm the affective and symbolic groundings of their respective sociability. They allowed them to do things together and thus to reaffirm and deepen friendships and sociability networks, and the moral and aesthetic order of – in this case – gender and age categories that these networks were based upon.

While reaffirming such gender and age defined social networks, the actual official occasion of the festival – the celebration of the abolition of slavery – gave rise to another form of discrimination that seemed to be based on phenotype criteria, which diverse social actors participating in the festival attributed to specific geographical origins. This is based on a series of observations. Firstly, among the organisers of the festival, very minute differences of opinion were expressed concerning the title of the festival; everyone – except Alessio, Mrs Lula's husband – seemed to agree on *fet kaf* and on the positive relationship between certain phenotype and origin criteria and the roles that people were given in the festival performance space. After my first meeting with Mrs Lula, at her home, she explained to me that 'the festival commemorates the abolition of the enslavement of black people'. In a later context, provoked by the sentence 'So they're having a festival for you on Monday,' one of Mrs Lula's brothers responded by pointing to his 'Indian' nose, to say that he was not '*kaf*' (meaning 'of African descent'). The joke during the festival of wishing people considered of 'African' phenotype a 'happy *fet kaf*' – or 'Happy *fet, kaf*!' – further reaffirmed the positive association made between certain phenotype criteria (considered as 'African') and the attribution of slave ancestry, seen as the topic of the festival. Secondly, the role of the masters seemed to be positively attributed to a criteria of recent European origin. For the scene in which several slaves were to be led by a master, the choice of actor to play the master fell, as if it were only natural, on Alessio, Mrs Lula's *Métropolitan* husband. He defended himself by instead suggesting Fred, a 'white Creole', which was turned down because, according to the other participants in this meeting, 'Fred is Creole'. In this sense, the role of the master was positively attributed to individuals who had recently emigrated from the French mainland. This observation was further confirmed by the choice of actors for the roles in the abolition dance. The role of the 'bourgeois ladies' was attributed to two *Métropolitan* women who were part of the *Belle Jeunesse* Association. Both forms of festive role attributions – of slaves and masters – given respectively to people with specific phenotype and origin criteria, did not prevent the festival participants being friends or cultivating close kin and sociability relationships. Several 'mixed' couples were involved in the event and formed part of the village's core social community. From this point of view, phenotype or origin criteria were not necessarily, or only in specific contexts, indicative of specific social identities and the formation of segregated social groups. Within the social realm of the village no fixed meaning was attributed to them. They remained widely uncertain, always subjected to negotiations, especially through forms of humour. Within the realm of the festival, these criteria and the people chosen to act out the festive roles they were associated with – slaves and masters – seemed able to enact a specific metaphorical world through which participants made sense, in an allegorical way, of contemporary contexts of changing social, temporal and spatial relations. The performed opposition between slaves and masters as part of the festival hence appears as a means of making sense of the symbolic underpinning of current relations between La Réunion and the French mainland ('*la métropole*'), but also between a largely idealised recent past and a present often perceived as ambivalent, marked by the desire for progress and social mobility but also a feeling of nostalgia; a present spatially and socially defined by new models of society and leisure-based coastal space practices, seen as emanating from the French mainland.

The Past as an Allegory for the Present

Through the plants, objects and performances used in the festival ground, many participants rediscovered experiences, tastes and smells they associated with their childhood. They remembered moments of their past, talked about fragments of memories and shared these with their friends, but also with the younger generation and the wider festival audience. These encounters frequently initiated the telling of longer stories and the poetic reconstruction of childhood memories, institutions of traditional social life and life histories. This was witnessed through stories told around household objects such as coffee pots or sweet corn grinders. In the context of the former agrarian society, both objects had played an important role in the establishment of social and economic relations within the village. They had enabled their owners to invite guests – and offer them coffee – and to produce corn flour and animal food. Both were objects of value not always accessible to all agricultural households in times past; symbols of participation in social life, objects of desire and fear, objects ritually given on the occasion of a wedding. At the same time, these embodied encounters with the 'past' – initially a collection of individual memories – allowed participants to construct a collective story; the past became a collective reference point adding meaning to a more immediate here and now. Hitherto considered mainly in terms of a space of misery and poverty, the past thus became something else, a departure point symbolically grounding the contemporary social life of the village. This was illustrated through Mrs Lula's idealising discourse on the straw hut, which, according to her, was 'better than modern constructions to protect against the heat'. Until the 1960s, straw huts were the principal form of housing for the island's agricultural proletariat. With the introduction of new materials, most notably sheet metal and concrete, they quickly disappeared. Natural building materials such as straw and wood consequently experienced a heavy decline in use amongst a large part of La Réunion's population, who considered them to be synonymous with misery and economic poverty (Niollet 1999). In the late 1990s, except for some very marginal cases, there were no more people living in straw huts in La Réunion. From this point, the empirical history of the straw hut no longer had an effect on the contemporary world, which seemed to be the requirement for it to gain it a new meaning. According to Mrs Lula, they were no longer a symbol of poverty and exclusion, but of a collective past, a collective story linking the conditions of the present to the memory of a common past.

The discovery of the past as an allegorical space also brought about the dramaturgy of the abolition dance staged by the *Belle Jeunesse* Association. It was structured in two parts with a pivotal turning point symbolised by the act of the abolition of slavery in 1848. The first part of the dance depicted life 'before the abolition of slavery', with two parallel worlds projected onto the island's space: a 'slavery world' on the coasts and a 'maroons' world' in the mountainous interior. Both worlds were linked by the figure of the maroon who, in a heroic act, fled the plantations and found freedom in the inner sanctum of the island. The first part of the dance, in the way in which it mobilised different spaces of the island and linked them through the story, therefore generated a metaphorical and morally underpinned spatiality. The mountainous inside – where most of the festival organisers had never actually been – came to be seen as a space of escape and new found happiness. It became a highly symbolic space that seemed to allow its performers – or some of its performers – to articulate and make sense of desires for such a space of escape and newly found freedom. It may be interpreted as a metaphorical space where it is possible to think and articulate feelings of lost freedom, probably much more apt in a contemporary context than in a far-away past that no longer has a direct influence on the present. In this sense, the world of the pre-abolition past depicted in the first part of the performance may be seen as an allegory articulating and making sense of more immediate feelings of loss, of a transformed social context, of no longer being able to 'go freely through the fields and pick fruits'.

The main turning point of the story performed through the dance was the re-enactment of the declaration of abolition of slavery, in 1848, by a French administrator played by Mrs Lula. This turning point initiated a 'new world' of colour, light and social inclusion, symbolised by floral and brightly coloured 'pretty' dresses and the final collective dance. The emphasis placed on the French administrator who enforced the abolition of slavery through a legal act can again be interpreted as a metaphorical means of making sense of contemporary contexts. In L'Hermitage-les-bains, and also in many other places on the island, many people believe that, within the context of recent changes in the coastal zone, a few people – usually identified as local politicians, lord mayors and entrepreneurs – have gained a lot of money by speculating on land property, by manipulating spatial development plans and by corrupting political decision-making processes. In this sense, the association of the act of abolition with an outside figure who was able legally to enforce the abolition of slavery in the island may be seen as a way of making manifest a feeling of deep distrust in local political and economic stakeholders, and the expectation that legality and freedom in the island were guaranteed by French governmental institutions. This interpretation only seems to apply to the performances observed in this particular context, marked by an important fluidity of social and phenotype boundaries and a certain social integration of people from the French mainland. It can certainly not be generalised for the entire island. Moreover, it must be seen within the polarising political contexts at the regional and local levels of the island, that have long experienced the political polemics of both the autonomy movement led by the La Réunion's communist party and the island's pro-republican movement (cf. chapter 2 and 3).

Conclusions

The objective of this chapter was to analyse how locally organised festivals allow social actors to mediate the contexts of rapid social, spatial and economic change that La Réunion has seen over the past thirty years or so. I have focused in particular on the celebration of the abolition of slavery staged by a group of inhabitants of L'Hermitage-les-bains. This case seemed particularly interesting as this former fishing village had recently been surrounded and to a certain extent invaded by newly constructed middle-class residential areas and international tourism resorts. The festival allowed a tight network of social actors grouped around one family, the Lulas, to reaffirm different social roles and identities. Accordingly, through their involvement in the festival's preparations and logistics, the building and decoration of its space, different on-stage performances and the sociability that emerged during the festival, these social actors created forms of sociality based essentially on gender and age criteria, but also on friendship and kinship networks within the village. Furthermore, by staging the festival in the highly visible space of the back beach, one of the principal social playgrounds for the island's new middle classes, the festival organisers generated a temporary space of hospitality that included the outside audience as part of the festival sociability. This space of hospitality seemed to be conceived of in terms of the culture of the *kartié*, in order to 'give a good image' to an outside gaze, embodied here by tourists and journalists. It can be said that the social pattern underpinning the organisation of the festival at these different levels was largely independent from its official theme, the abolition of slavery.

However, the latter was clearly evoked through humoristic comments about people with certain phenotypic characters, considered by the festival organisers and participants as being 'of African origin' and through the symbolism underlying several of the on-stage performances. A widely accepted consensus seemed to exist here that, within the festive performances, the slaves should be played by actors considered to be of 'African' phenotype (based on nose, hair and skin colour criteria) while the masters should be played by actors of French mainland origin. The symbolic slave-master opposition was also mobilised to generate different metaphorical spaces which allowed at least some of the festival organisers to rearticulate the ruptures that marked their current social environment and being in the world. The performance of a mythical past seemed to generate here a meaningful allegory allowing a consideration of these ruptures and a way of relating the collective here and now to a common symbolic reference point. At the same time, these stories of the past, and their embodiment in objects and dance performances, seemed to become detached from the actual past. For instance, the abolition dance performed during this event did not seem primarily concerned with the empiric history of slavery, its abolition or its consequences, but with the mobilisation of a particular type of story that enabled the village community to articulate a collective identity and make sense of recent changes.

From this point of view, this festival was not about remembering a far-away violent past, but rather offered a stage and a set of familiar aesthetic signs, story plots and heroes to enable reflection on and a social re-enactment of the social separations that defined the contemporary social existence of the village. The idea of history as the relation between a past and a present was thus ultimately adopted in an auto-ethnographic fashion, as a matrix through which the actors of the festival could tell their own story and feelings about time and being. Initially a disvalued space, symbol of poverty and exclusion, images of the past were thus elevated to what Arjun Appadurai (1981) once called a 'scarce resource'. In the intersubjective space that defined the culture of the *kartié* in La Réunion, and its translation onto the wider social scale of the island, the ability to formulate one's past and relate one's history seemed to emerge as a condition for social participation in the contemporary social world of La Réunion, a publicly performed sign of the 'modern' (Dirks 1990). The cultural logic of such a performance implies as a consequence a widespread re-appropriation, re-vitalisation and re-invention of traditions (Hobsbawn and Ranger 1983), the production and exchange of cultural signs of the past as a shared cultural economy that goes beyond the strict spaces of touristic production and consumption (Featherstone 1990). In this context, the past as an element of the island's 'destination culture' (Kirshenblatt-Gimblett 1998), initially generated within the global tourism- and media-scapes, is subjected to a process of transculturation. It becomes part of an auto-ethnographic story of the past and present which is governed by local actors like the Lulas, but which remains framed by the widely hegemonic aesthetic of history as a means of ordering and making sense of everyday life. The modern separation between an a-historical *ur*-condition (found in 'nature') and history as a process initiated through self-conscious human action seems to find here a structural analogy and thematic variation in the stories of marooning and abolition, both representing symbolic turning points leading humanity from an initial condition of archaic dependency to one of freedom and historicity. At this structural level, it seems to constitute the ideological underpinning of an emerging local modernity cultivated within La Réunion. The narrative logic of history has come to frame a new aesthetic of everyday life. Time becomes here a moral category within a particular 'modern' form of cosmological order in which social life appears directed towards a particular future, defined by the past.

Chapter 8
Towards a Global Gardening State

Thinking Through Gardening

A faintly perceptible breeze emanated from the small fountain in the pool. We were sitting on a bench under a bamboo tree, in the 'Zen' part of the *Jardin d'Eden*, a landscape garden just south of Saint-Gilles-les-bains on La Réunion's west coast. Though it was already the end of May – the beginning of the austral winter — temperatures remained well above 25 degrees Celsius. Marie-Françoise Lanfant[1] was to return to Paris the following day, and after a week of driving her around the different sites of my fieldwork, I wanted to wrap up the conversations we had had. We were talking about the German tourists I had been guiding over the previous two years, Orom and the transformation of Salazie into what I saw as a living museum, the young men who were gardening the riverside, the politics of the coral reef conservation programme, and the processes that had led to the elevation and celebration of certain practices, concepts and material cultures as 'heritage'. Marie-Françoise Lanfant was glancing at a flyer we had been given at the entrance of the garden; it included some text about the philosophy of gardening and the 'magic' of the gardener that she read out loud. She suddenly turned towards me and said: 'And what about thinking of La Réunion as a large garden?' We talked about her idea and realised its intellectual consequences.

The idea appeared to imply that, as a result of the enchantments the island had been subjected to since the nineteenth century, various spatial planning and development programmes since the 1960s, and more recent museum and heritage interpretation initiatives, the island had been reformulated in such a way as to bring alive different tropes, utopias, ideals and desired qualities which were projected into its social and spatial realms. It had been transformed into a 'garden' – not only in terms of a particular aesthetics associated with its space or populations, but as a deeper underlying mode of social production and being in the world. From this perspective, cultivating the island as a 'garden', a 'human garden' whose populations were part of that which was cultivated and made visible, ultimately 'being' a garden, may have become a new form of social participation within a broader transnationalised world society, within a tourism-specific form of sign-economy evolving within what Arjun Appadurai (2003b) defined as a global ethnoscape. In this sense, the ancient culture of gardening may have flowed into a new form of post-national cultural economy and the political realms of global governance, in particular cultural and environmental policy making. It may have brought about what I suggest could be called a 'global gardening state',[2] a new world order based on the production of places whose natural, cultural and human 'furnishings' are cultivated in a specific way so as to allow the invocation of an imagined authentic condition – an allegorical Eden – which appears to constitute the moral and aesthetic grounding for many modernist ideas of nature, time and being.

In the following chapter, I will try to situate the making of tropical islands within the historical fabric of diverse gardening cultures and demonstrate their interconnectedness and global expansion into different social and political realms. I will then articulate this historical approach, detailing the principal outcomes of the ethnographic approach developed throughout the chapters of this book, in particular the relation between tourism and magical thinking as part of the cultural logic of modernity; the idea of quasi-religious liturgies underpinning the making of international cultural and environmental policy doctrines; the idea of the transformation of tropical islands into 'human gardens' as a result of the implementation of these doctrines and the development of tourism specific infrastructures; and the idea that 'being a garden' can constitute a new form of social identity and mode of participation within the local social realms of tropical islands.

Anthropological Studies of Gardening

During the days that followed Marie-Françoise Lanfant's departure, I started reading what was a mainly French body of anthropological and art-historic literature on gardening.[3] Anthropological texts about gardening – Bronislaw Malinowski's (1935) study of gardening among the Trobriand islanders is possibly the most famous one – usually emphasise the symbolic aspects of what Arjun Appadurai (1996) pointedly summarised as 'working the ground'. To all appearances, gardening is about the organised cultivation of plants, but also other commodities such as salt, fish, or domesticated animals within an enclosed space. Most garden theorists distinguish between utilitarian and contemplative gardens (Mosser and Teyssot 1991; Assunto 1988; Milani 2005). The aim of 'utilitarian' gardens usually was and still is to produce agricultural outputs, in other words to put seeds into the earth, nurture plants by giving them water, nutrients, sunlight and by keeping flower beds clear of 'bad herbs', hungry birds and other plant eating creatures.

Gardeners work with 'natural' matter and usually generate theories about why this matter grows under certain circumstances – why a single seed can multiply into multiple seeds. This mystery of growth is heightened by the hazardous circumstances in which gardening is practiced. Indeed, the success of gardening depends on the interplay of various 'natural' conditions, e.g. propitious weather, abundance of water, absence of parasites, etc. Under any circumstance, the outcome of gardening remains uncertain until the time that the harvest is brought in. Malinowski and commentators who have studied garden cultures elsewhere note that, in most cases, the different phases of gardening are therefore accompanied by invocations; magical spells and rites intended to increase or tame chance, to avoid accidents, produce favourable weather conditions and generate rich harvests (Gell 1988). Besides their strictly utilitarian function, gardens are thus also places to engage with, and to bring into being, the supernatural world, the 'forces of nature', the gods and the spirits whose invocation is believed efficient to generate favourable conditions.

Most garden historians situate the oldest forms of gardening in Egypt and Mesopotamia. From the thirtieth century BC, sedentary populations in Egypt created utilitarian gardens that they watered through complex irrigation systems using water from the Nile. While these early utilitarian gardens were principally focused on an efficient use of water, during the same epoch, the country's sovereigns built early contemplative gardens that used the scare resource of water in a rather ostentatious way. Michel Baridon (1998: 96), author of a comprehensive history of gardens and gardeners, relates the case of King Snefou who, in the twenty-sixth century BC, had a large water room fabricated to accommodate a ship on which he would row in the company of twenty women dressed in nothing more than nets. Based on this and other such observations, the second type of 'contemplative' gardening – the one that seems most relevant to this study – has often been seen as a governance device; a political tool to display wealth (especially through the ostentatious dissipation of scarce resources), legitimate specific forms of political and cosmological order, and make social asymmetries look 'normal' or 'natural. The aesthetic objective of many contemplative gardens was to generate a materialised model of abstract ideas relating in particular to the nation, the world of the gods, enchanted islands, etc. Michel Baridon (1998: 350–1), describes how, in the third century BC, the Chinese emperor Qin Shi Huang Di created his gardens in a way that would make visible the extension and design of his empire and the political power of his persona. He brought wild animals from all provinces and constructed lakes with small islands to evoke – and by the same act to appropriate and make his 'own' – the imaginary 'happy islands', divine places believed to be located in the Chinese sea. Throughout all later ages, contemplative gardens would appeal to similarly imaginary spaces whose evocation and control usually represented a key to political power.

Accordingly, the early Islamic gardens that emerged during the seventh century AD in Syria evoked the image of the oasis as a walled space built around a water spring, a highly metaphorical space built around the sign-image of water as life giving, a place for the human caravan to rest, reflect and recreate. As a result of colonial expansion, the distinctive traits of this garden – its symmetrical pattern, the symbolism of water, its use as a place of contemplation – were diffused over three continents, among them Europe (Baridon 1998: 201–12). With the expansion of the Greek, and later Roman empires, legends about these early forms of contemplative garden would be the basis for new garden cultures in the Eastern Mediterranean. The Greek garden was in a way an early form of 'public garden'. Located within the agora, it was less a personal display of wealth and power than a place that reflected the democratic values and maxims of human cultivation that governed the city of Athens (Baridon 1998: 125). Inspired by these Greek gardens, early Roman gardens, during the first century BC, initially evoked the heroic period at the beginning of the Republic and later became places where one could live in opulence, ostentatiously displaying human power over nature and showing the extension of one's culture (Baridon 1998: 137). Through contact with and colonisation by the Roman Empire, the Roman garden culture was brought to Western Europe and England. Traces seemed to remain or re-emerge long after the fall of the Roman Empire, especially in the cloister gardens that appeared during the early eighth century AD. Initially without floral decoration, these comprised four rectangular paths arranged around a central juniper bush. A well-known example is the gardens of the abbey of Saint-Gall which included a cloister, vegetable gardens and cemetery with fruit trees (Baridon 1998: 543). Later variations of this 'medieval garden' included elevated beds that were used for the cultivation of plants, especially herbs. Through continued contact between Northern and Western Europe and the Eastern Mediterranean during the following centuries, different garden models, especially that of the Islamic garden, saw a wide distribution throughout Europe.

Since the fourteenth and fifteenth centuries, the early medieval gardens in Western Europe have transformed into profane gardens of delight, displaying the newly accumulated wealth of their owners and serving to cultivate and refine the pleasures of the human condition. Plots planted with flowers were arranged around a central fountain; grassy areas under the shade of fruit trees invited people to dance, listen to music, socialise or read poetry. The early Italian and French Renaissance gardens that appeared from the sixteenth century reintroduced once again certain aesthetic elements of the classic period. These would sometimes work as a means to subtly proclaim the social and political emancipation of some newly powerful North Italian clergymen, traders and bankers. This period saw in particular the re-appropriation of the concept of the Roman countryside residence, which in form of the villa would become a new social institution, incorporating the royal and noble pleasures of hunting and the cultivation of leisure in its original classical sense, creating distance from the city and political life, nurturing human refinement and enabling reflection upon life. The villa was built within gardens based upon the three formal principles that would inspire the later Renaissance garden: the geometrisation of planted forms and structures, the omnipresence of water freely projected into the air or filtering down the walls of grottos, and material references to the classical age (Baridon 1998: 593). Furthermore, it introduced the idea of landscape; according to the late sixteenth-century Italian architect, Leon Battista Alberti, it opened up the view to a 'pleasant' countryside, with fields of flowers, hidden pastures, woods that offered shade, clear sources, rivers of pure water, and lakes to swim in (Alberti 1568). The baroque garden developed in France during the seventeenth and eighteenth centuries – the most famous example is probably the garden of Versailles – pushed the principles of the Italian and French Renaissance garden further. It was not only open to the countryside, but used different visual and architectural tricks, such as the calculated use of straight lines, water mirrors and shadow games to create a point of escape on the horizon, to generate an effect of infinitude. Seen as the embodiment of the human ability to control nature and force it into certain forms, a symbol of absolute power that reflected the dominant political order of the absolutist regimes in Europe, this garden model was widely copied in Italy, England, Germany, Austria and Russia.

The eighteenth century witnessed a clear break with the aesthetic of the baroque garden. England had expanded its militaristic and colonial enterprise to become a global empire. It was fashionable to see it as a new Rome. Once again, the invocation of classical references would supply a powerful allegory for a newly enriched social class made up of traders and the landed nobility and would allow them to articulate their economic and political emancipation. This was seen in the renewed interest in antique temples and gothic ruins, the organisation of grand tours to the sites of the classical age in the Eastern Mediterranean and North Africa, and, particularly relevant to this study, a revolution of the aesthetic principles of baroque gardening culture (Assunto 1988). The English garden broke away from the straight lines and geometry of the French garden – by then reconsidered as signs of political despotism and absolutism – and elevated asymmetry to a new aesthetic ideal. Breaking with the geometry believed to be inherent to nature, the newly invented sinuous lines and arbitrary forms staged in the garden became celebrated as signs of liberty. At the same time, the act of forcing nature into such non-geometrical forms emancipated history as a category enabling reflection on time and marking the triumph of the human being over an archaic natural or wild condition (Baridon 1998: 813). From this point of view, nature was seen as no more than a 'thing' to be tamed, studied and understood in terms of positive laws.

In turns, the empirical and scientific philosophy underlying the English garden became contested by new garden models, among others those created in the politically up-and-coming Germany. Stressing the 'irresistible growth of life' based on a quasi-divine 'force of nature', these translated into a new body of philosophical thinking that emerged during the industrial revolution at the end of the eighteenth century. They laid the grounds for a romanticist vision of nature that would mark the nineteenth and early twentieth centuries (Mosser and Teyssot 1991). In the German context, a new garden format built according to the idea of perfection in nature allowed people to engage with nature's perceived sublime, quasi-divine quality. During the same period, other forms of gardens developed in parallel; for example, public gardens as allegorical flower, plant and animal displays for the emerging nationalisms of the nineteenth century, or the private and working-class gardens vulgarising concepts of the utilitarian and of the contemplative garden at different levels of society.

Gardening as Cultural Technology

Through these historical readings, I understood that forms of gardening, especially of contemplative gardening, had long existed as a cultural practice and multipurpose technology. It appeared that contemplative gardens have always been multi-functional places, secluded environments in which to indulge in ideas about nature, time and the cosmos and the ostentatious display of wealth and power. As a result of contact and cross-appropriations during the past 5000 years, forms of contemplative gardening have been diffused across a wide geographical area encompassing large parts of South and South-East Asia, the Middle East and Mediterranean basin, and Europe.

While the perception of gardens and garden displays may have depended on the individual and cultural dispositions of garden visitors, the historic repetition of a specific gardening aesthetic within this historical 'ethnoscape' (Appadurai 2003a) – e.g. the principle of symmetry used in Arabian, Persian and later European gardens – is likely to have led to significant 'garden consciousnesses' and shared sensibilities among certain populations, e.g. those social elites who actually cultivated and enjoyed contemplative gardens. The historical 'success' of contemplative gardening within this Eurasian ethnoscape may lie in its ability to formulate, mediate and naturalise forms of political and moral order. Contemplative gardens appear here to be persistently conceived of as miniatures of a wider world, a form of visual art which compresses a specific interpretation of the mysteries of nature, time and being within a comprehensible and experienceable realm. They seem to represent what Alfred Gell (1988: 7) called a 'technology of enchantment' capable of luring humans into submitting to the rules of often highly unequal social and economic systems. In this sense, garden design can be understood as a technical tool and strategy that, through metaphor, mimetic practice and the use of metonymic matter, tries to convince visitors of what Susan

Steward (1993) defined as an 'authentic link' between the tangible space of the garden and a more or less imagined distanced cosmos – the past, the future, the classical age, foreign countries, the worlds of gods and ancestors, the nation. Accordingly, most contemplative gardens incorporated or worked with metonymic matter – flora and fauna, 'original' relics, public and personal souvenirs, etc. – taken, or believed to have been taken, from such distanced worlds. They also saw the cultivation of highly metaphorical embodied practices – poetry reading, music, nurturing the spirits, etc. – that seemed capable of bringing alive, in the imagination of the practitioners, the spirit and values of an imagined authentic world, such as the classical garden during the Renaissance.

In many historical contexts, the garden became self-referential where the in situ arrangements made reference to an imagined garden of delight located in some distanced realm. For example, the imaginary places created by the liturgies of the 'book religions' are largely based on the allure and promise of a garden of heavenly delight. The latter represented a powerful tool with which to legitimate and govern social asymmetries and ontological boundaries between ethnicities, classes and existential conditions. The image of such a heavenly garden, cultivated by means of often sophisticated political and moral economies, made the hardship imposed upon agrarian and later working classes look normal and natural. It provided an imagined future world to be accessed by the dead that not only made the incertitude of death bearable, but also rewarded the submission to the rules and will of the powerful while alive. In many cases, the contemplative and ostentatious gardens built by the politically powerful within the immediate here and now were presented as glimpses of the gardens to come. Contemplative gardens thus appear as places in society where political power is exercised in society. Their technology appears to be based on two complementary political acts. The first consists of the formulation and fashioning of distanced worlds that, through their allegorical dimension, can help to legitimate specific sets of social and moral order and authority, and make uneven social relations appear normal and natural. The second consists of the political governance of flows and contact with these distanced worlds made visible and brought alive in the garden.

Historically, the common tendency was for the ostentatious character of these gardens to seem heightened in contexts marked by strong political and economic asymmetries – political regimes dominated by oligarchies, dictators, monarchs, central governments, hyper-capitalist elites – while their opulence seemed to diminish and their aesthetic to 'flatten' in more egalitarian contexts. This could be understood in terms of a process of social mobility. For example, throughout European medieval and modern history, the newly powerful nobilities, clergies and later commercial middle classes used gardens as an art form to formulate and make visible their revolutionary claims against established forms of political power. They often used references to 'classical' themes and garden cultures, as a means of asserting 'democratic' rights and thus of legitimating their own political emancipation. A distinction should, however, be made between these rather opulent neo-classical gardens – where classical themes were used merely as part of the ostentation by the newly powerful elites – and 'flattened' gardens where many opulent and ostentatious elements disappeared, for example in the original Greek agora or the late nineteenth century public gardens in England and Germany (Baridon 1998).

From a more intersubjective perspective, it can be asserted that humans have always created forms of enchantment that allowed them to poeticise the incertitude and mystery of distance, time and being. These forms of enchantment were not always, or not necessarily, instituted by the state, but often emerged within the intersubjective space between social actors (Jackson 1998). From the gardener's perspective, gardening can therefore be seen as a specific tool with which to engage the world and consider its incertitude; as a way to humanise the margins of the immediate here and now, to 'work the ground' (Appadurai 2003b). It can be seen as a technique to create a personalised poetics of everyday life, capable of rationalising the more or less arbitrary events and traumas of being into a coherent story, into a chain of causalities, into a 'mistaken causal belief' (Gell 1988: 7). Gardeners are normally social actors and therefore usually employ only those technologies that are at their disposal, e.g. those they have learnt to execute in society. In this context, gardening can be seen as a culturally embedded 'technology' (Gell 1988) that imposes certain rules and moral orders upon the gardener. From this point of view, both gardeners as social actors and gardening as a cultural technology have agency upon each other (Latour 2007). At the same time, the gardeners can mobilise the technology of gardening in their own terms and resignify it through subtly personalised forms of gardening. However, submitting to the general rules of gardening – or at least to their visual signs: making beds, walking around being dirty, cultivating life, etc. – appears to be a necessary condition for gardening to work as a form of social participation; a thing people do and through which they can personalise public symbols and generate social connections and sociability. Similarly, participating in modernity, e.g. by adopting a form of modernist thinking, may merely be a means of enabling social participation within the social realms generated by what is then called modernity, a global soap opera of moralists, academics, and post-tribal populations who play out modernity as a specific sign-world, who cultivate it as a specific sign-culture.

Towards a Global Gardening State

The idea of 'gardening' human society had explicitly entered the language and thinking of public policymaking around the late nineteenth century, if not earlier. Zygmunt Bauman (1998) powerfully demonstrates how, in the early twentieth century, it had been applied to the idea of 'cultivating' the human as a gardener would cultivate flowers, by 'purifying' human 'races' through the control of genetic reproduction, by creating human species according to the racist aesthetics of an ideal nature. During the second half of the twentieth century, a consideration of the horrors of the holocaust, of repeated 'ethnic cleansings' and racial segregation and apartheid led to strong opposition to the concept of a 'gardening state' and its objective of cultivating humans according to a phenotypical ideal. The continued struggles against racial discrimination resulted in the progressive abolition of segregation and apartheid regimes.

The fundamental principles of the gardening state appear, however, to have remained, shifting into new contexts and embracing different social scales. The sometimes politically conscious promotion of people of non-white phenotype in the media, politics, education, global fashion and beauty competitions witnessed a subtle change in racial ideals, a subtle change of the 'colour line' (Bonniol 1988; Bonniol and Benoist 1994). Perhaps not unrelated to this same trend, in the academic world, especially in anthropological research, the focus seems to have shifted away from the study of 'pure cultures' and the way in which they work within a totalising closed realm, embracing instead approaches based on historical change and creolisation processes (Hannerz 1987, 1992; Picard 2010c).During the 1980s, some landscape architects and ecologists claimed that the planet earth constituted the ultimate garden that humanity had an obligation to cultivate (Berque 1995, 1996; Mosser 1999).

The body of texts on the cultural history of gardening made me understand that the concept of gardening had entered realms not explicitly referred to as gardens. In this sense, as with contemplative gardens, many planned urban environments, churches, museums, city centres and exhibition sites were made to mediate dominant ideas about political order and human relations to nature, time and being (Panofsky 1971; Bouquet and Porto 2005). At the end of the nineteenth century, the concept of gardening was used in the field of spatial planning. Public gardens were developed as spaces for physical and moral recreation, and also for public education. Moreover, utopian models suggested by the garden city movement[4] – combining workplace, communal institutions, utilitarian and contemplative gardens, and residences – heavily influenced the urban planning models from the early twentieth century. Moreover, the emergence since the eighteenth century – or 'invention' – of specific rural (Marie and Viard 1988), mountain (Joutard 1986), seaside (Corbin 1988) and underwater (Picard 2008b) landscapes has been considered as a form of *in visu* gardening, of imposing forms and frames of ideal landscapes – captured in paintings that circulated among the urban aristocracies and emerging bourgeoisies – upon the land and thus transforming it into picturesque, alpine or bucolic landscapes (Roger 1997).

The emergence of environmentalist movements fuelled by the early environmental crisis in the European colonies (Grove 1997: 117) and the creation of nature conservation areas that had become prominent during the nineteenth century seem to have translated the concept of contemplative gardening onto an even larger scale. Throughout the nineteenth and twentieth centuries, vast extensions of land dominated by the Western colonial empires were transformed into nature and game reserves. The ecology of these places was often remodelled according to an idealised vision of endemic wilderness – purified and protected from 'exotic' plants, animals and 'anthropogenic impacts'. Roderick Neumann (2002) demonstrates how humans, especially indigenous peoples, became ontologically and aesthetically assimilated with such imagined gardens of wilderness and were made to contribute to their tourism related exploitation. Certain groups living inside the newly developed natural parks in the postcolonial period in Tanzania were required to remain in a condition which was considered by the makers of these parks as 'natural' (for example, the building of concrete houses, and the use of cars and modern weaponry was prohibited). More recently, the discourses of sustainable and ecotourism development – emphasising the use of low-tech infrastructures and local supplies in building materials, techniques and produce – seem to have had a similar effect of 'cultivating' certain populations, usually those who are politically marginalised, as parts of culturally codified ideal landscapes (Picard 2008a).

In many cases, it seemed to me that part of the legitimisation protocol of newly formed 'modern' states was to identify and study, or otherwise invent and ostentatiously subdue, specific 'local' populations considered as 'primitive'. Through the creation of museums, reserves, interpretation sites, and children's plays, the alleged 'authentic wilderness' of these populations and the territories they inhabited became a part of newly created ritual processes, that implied the ceremonial invocation of, and often also symbolic violence toward, these 'Others'. Many contemporary states who consider themselves as 'modern' have started to engage in such ritual processes, often elevating those populations whose discrimination or massacre marked a founding moment in their own history.[5] They became part of what was considered as the 'national heritage', a concept legally formalised in France, England and the United States two centuries earlier, which provided a way to display, historically ground and materially embody (for example in public gardens and landscapes) the public stories of kingdoms and emerging nation-states (Anderson 1991; Héritier 2003).

In the postwar period, international organisations such as UNESCO[6] projected this concept at a global scale. During the postwar period, UNESCO engaged in several projects aiming at the preservation of 'cultural heritage of outstanding value'. Its first major project consisted of the relocation of the Abu Simbel temple in Egypt, threatened by the construction of the Aswan dam. With the financial support of all major Western nations, including those of Eastern Europe, the Abu Simbel temple was cut into pieces and relocated to a higher location. Abu Simbel became a symbol for the will of this international community of experts to 'preserve' the remnants of 'past civilisations', with or without the agreement of national governments. In the following years, architectural remnants of various other 'civilisations' or 'high cultures' were preserved. The organisation's involvement was legally formalised through the creation of a set of normative actions, in particular the 1972 Convention Concerning the Protection of the World Cultural and Natural Heritage. The principles of this convention, especially the understanding of the concept of heritage, were heavily influenced by French and Anglo-Saxon policy models which had been used as part of nationalist policies during the early nineteenth century. It seemed to imply a projection of the concept of heritage, hitherto used to define the nation, at the level of a world society, to identify, preserve and instrumentalise a set of 'world heritages' as the social connectors of a human nation. Through its 2001 Universal Declaration on Cultural Diversity, the legally binding 2003 Convention for the Safeguarding of the Intangible Cultural Heritage and the 2005 Convention on the Protection and Promotion of the Diversity of Cultural Expressions, UNESCO developed new normative actions aimed at creating conditions that allowed nations, communities and individuals to officially 'recognise', 'protect', help to 'value' and 'preserve' different forms of local, artistic and indigenous culture.

Through these more recent actions, the organisation was reacting to an epistemic dilemma underlying its initial approach to cultural heritage, based upon a conception of culture as a thing and the assumption of the possibility of a positive science of culture, an anthropology or art history that could reveal positive laws underpinning the cultural dimensions of the human condition. UNESCO's early cultural policy was founded on the idea that a community of experts was able to identify a positive morphology of human culture and to judge it according to an objective system of moral and aesthetic ideals. The dilemma mentioned above was perpetuated in the operational structures of UNESCO's activities during the post-Second World War period. The community of experts that developed UNESCO's activities mainly consisted of university-educated white middle- and upper-class males from European urban backgrounds. This community of experts, whose idiosyncratic values were taken as the moral and aesthetic ideal, heavily influenced UNESCO's early actions in the field of culture, as well as the selection of sites placed on the World Heritage List which initially included mainly archaeological sites. Most of these were found in the Mediterranean peripheries, and included many classical sites that had previously served the dominant Western states as places where people could consider their philosophical groundings and establish 'authentic' links with the creation myths of European humanistic culture – the Greek *agora*, the Roman *cite* – and their 'correspondents' in other continents – the Maya Temples of South America, the Pyramids in Egypt, the Hanging Gardens of Babylon, the Great Wall of China. Through their selection, these sites seemed able to evoke and make visible a particular vision of world history and cultural order on the global scale. The stories told about these newly preserved sites were usually disconnected from their immediate social environments. They were defined within the wider stories of a global cultural history based on the rationale of human evolution, progress and cultural refinement.

While there is no single logic behind the working of international organisations, one idea of how to use 'heritage' seemed to have generated a new social realm on the global scale, founded on a network of heritage clusters, a global 'heritage-scape' (di Giovine 2008). In the game of multiple, but significantly collinear, forces appropriating and diffusing this idea, UNESCO's World Heritage Centre seems to have taken control here of the 'content' of sites. Through its policies, it has popularised a global model of how to think about heritage and how to contextualise it within the wider fabric of the global heritage-scape. On the other hand, the World Tourism Organisation (WTO), through its 1999 Global Code of Ethics for Tourism, appears to have taken on the role of managing the technical, administrative and economic aspects of tourism infrastructures, site access and economic exploitation. Finally, the World Bank, through its advocacy of tourism as a form of economic development (de Kadt 1979) – the organisation financed the tourism master plans of developing countries such as Tunisia, Bali, Senegal, Mauritius, and the Dominican Republic – seems to have taken on the role of donor and economic development promoter. In this context, tourism development appears to have become governed by post-nationalist 'global polity format', a 'set of cultural rules or scripts specifying how institutions around the world should deal with common problems' (Lechner and Boli 2000: 51). It seems to have instituted a post-national state which redefines entire territories, sometimes entire countries, as contemplative gardens evoking ideas of nature, progress and the passing of time; a new form of global governance culture where the preservation of specific places, practices and environments was subjected to entirely new forms of transnational political authority (Duffy 2002). The conservation or preservation of heritage started to constitute in itself a new form of governance at the local level of destinations (West 2006). In many countries, it became an economic and symbolic resource mobilised in the – often controversial – processes of nation-building and modernisation which marked the postcolonial or postwar contexts in places as varied as Bali (Picard 1992), Kenya (Bruner 2001), Sri Lanka (Crick 1994), Spain (Greenwood 1989), Turkey (Tucker 2002), Indonesia (Adams 2006), Japan (Hiwasaki 2000), the Philippines (Ness 2003), or Mexico (Van der Berghe 1994).

These developments were mostly marked by a major ambivalence linked to the co-presence of two seemingly antagonistic economic systems. While on one hand international policy makers, academics and some global tour operators have started to stress the need for the 'sustainable development' of tourism resources, the inclusion of 'local communities' and the social economic integration of tourism sites, the global tourism industry, on the other hand, has put into place a capitalistic, aggressive and profit oriented economic system. This ambivalence immediately generated controversies among the development community, the cultural elites of developing countries and the tourist audiences themselves. Marie-Francoise Lanfant and Nelson Graburn (1992) explain this ambivalence as the tension between two concurrent but respectively – seemingly – exclusive dynamics, one of advocating progress through economic development and one of protecting the idealised landscapes and 'authentic cultures' of tropical islands through conservation polity. In other words, tourism development was caught up in one of the most striking contradictions of modernist thinking – on one hand it was considered a pragmatic economic alternative, on the other hand a spiritually loaded 'economy of the alternative' (Lanfant and Graburn 1992; Wheeller 1993). This ambivalence was partly solved by the development of policies which reconsidered 'culture' and 'nature' as 'resources' of a transnational and transgenerational symbolic economy; as resources which could unite humanity through a common world-historical narrative of humanistic development, cultural refinement and diversity, and the embodiment of this narrative in the material culture of initially mainly historical sites, to be 'preserved for future generations'.

Through careful stage management and the use of tricks of rhetoric by the tourism industry and policy makers, this realm is positioned outside the capitalist logic of the tourists' 'own' society, while it remains of course part of the tourist product and the capitalist logic of the global tourism economy. In this sense, economic production modes identified as 'integrated local development' and the use of various fair trade labels can be seen as part of the touristic commoditisation process. The popular doctrine of 'sustainable development' provides here a powerful ideology invoking the idea of a 'responsible' tourism that preserves natural environments and the cultural authenticity of natives, that does not impact upon or transform the local worlds, that somehow preserves a condition of timeless happiness. Just as many nation states cultivated and continue to cultivate 'their' national savages as part of their modernity, the global nation seems to mobilise similar figures to legitimate its modernity. Tropical islands, governed as tourist destinations, appear to constitute a powerful realm in which to make visible this global modernity and physically engage its moral foundation.

Garden Economics

Many authors interested in the global integration of tropical islands have focused their attention on the political economy of material commodities produced within the realms of global capitalism (Ortiz 1995; Mintz 1986). In a way they were more interested in the cash crop, than in the contemplative aspects of these colonial island gardens. The historical enchantment of tropical islands as paradises was often approached in terms of a 'symbolic superstructure', a moral aesthetic legitimating their exploitation and making hierarchies between centres and peripheries appear normal and natural (Said 2003; Hall 1997). Yet, it is not clear whether there is any connection at all between the political economy of material commodities in tropical islands that developed since the sixteenth century and the far older, pre-Christian imaginaries of tropical island paradises. Both phenomena seem parallel in register rather than conspiratorially intertwined, with only occasional (as opposed to systemic) connections. In this sense, the formation of tropical islands as large contemplative gardens of delight seems to point to a yet so far little discussed facet of global modernity, a form of gardening on a global scale that, I believe, requires the formulation of new ways of thinking. It implies a different form of world order and world society in which tropical islands and other tourism-related spaces are cultivated and accessed in terms of a specific, highly symbolic realm; in terms of gardens.

The model underlying these 'gardens' appears to be largely independent from the social realities that mark social life a the local scale. Indeed, most islands developed for tourism seem to conform, or are made to conform, to a widely generic pattern emphasising aspects of 'pristine nature', 'eternal sunshine', 'pure water', 'clear blue skies', and 'beautiful islands indigenes'. It seems that this model finds its source in the age-old idea of an eternal garden bringing to life images of a primordial time and nature. This idea is not new but, as the environmental historian Robert Grove (1997) has shown, it has been formative for modernity and modernist thinking themselves. In various historical contexts, tropical islands have provided a visual and symbolic theme representing and nurturing ideas of those mythical places that have helped humanity to think about time beyond death, myriad variations of imagined gardens of delight, heavens, islands of the dead, and other places of origin and eternal return that have been studied by anthropologists around the world. The modernist ambiguity with regard to 'nature' both as a nostalgic past and as a condition to be overcome by rational science and moral can be seen here as a variation playing out this same theme. The contradictory, yet complementary, narratives of a utopian return to nature and of the unavoidable forces of history that mark modernist thinking to such an extent seem to derive their symbolic underpinning from pre-modern representations. The innovation brought about by modernist thinking seems to lie in the idea and quasi-religious doctrine that the rational study of nature would ultimately lead to Enlightenment and God (Habermas 1985; McGuigan 1999).

The specific tourism related semiotics of island territories lend themselves to an allegorical reading. Islands appear as microscopic images embodying the various, ambivalent and contradictory modernist narratives of being in the world. Through their arrangements, they evoke specific philosophies of time and being. The modernist nostalgia of a homogeneous, pure and innocent *ur*-condition frequently appears to be projected here onto the 'interior' of the island space. Through this specific structure, tropical islands thus make visible a morally charged idea of a time, defined by a linear connection between a 'pure' and 'authentic' condition located in the past (and embodied in the islands' interior), leading (following the metaphorical flow of the rivers) to the heterogeneous, contradictory, historical condition of the present (found in the clashes of life in the coastal sites), ultimately losing itself in a somehow celestial, undetermined anticipation of the future (following the gaze toward the sunset over the horizon, the indefinite sea, the sky).

From this point of view, tropical islands appear indeed as 'large gardens', as Marie-Françoise Lanfant suggested, allowing modern subjects to recognise and remediate different facets of their 'modernist' selves. In particular, they seem to be connecting a specific cultural logic of time which moves from a primordial condition of innocence toward a historic condition of social melange. This particular conception of time finds an *ur*-model in the genesis of the Garden of Eden and its subsequent loss. Adam and Eve, the characters of an allegorical golden age, initiate time by committing the first crime. Harmony is broken, languages and diversity emerge, and all beings live with the burdens of earthly existence. Adam and Eve's story seems to remain one of the fundamental myths organising the modernist thinking of time and being, while the newly prominent story of Creoleness suggests an optimistic model for thinking of the future.

Formations and Ambivalence of Local Modernity

As I have shown throughout the chapters of this book, the new social role of being a 'garden', or being part of the matter exhibited and made visible in the garden, triggered a new form of economy and a new form of collective self-understanding in the island. To understand how this new economy was both formalised and normalised, I would like to suggest the use of the Lacanian concept of 'mirror stage'. The intersubjective contact between various social actors involved in tourism and the development of tourism related infrastructures seems to have generated a 'cultural' mirror stage, in its structure similar to Jacques Lacan's (1966) observation of young children becoming conscious of their selves by seeing themselves in a mirror while their mother is watching. From a local perspective, faraway, mythical France became here a mirror, embodied in the eyes of 'outsider' representatives: administrative agents, tourists, European migrants, the media, and people performing Frenchness in the public and private realms of island social life. These agents and mediators reflected back a partial vision of a local self. Recognising and valuing specific aesthetic forms in the ocean of sheer indefinite possibilities, they rendered such a self in a specific format. In many cases people in La Réunion recognised that these 'outsiders' attached a certain aesthetic value to forms of their selves, yet they were initially unable to identify the forms that this value related to. In a way, they searched the gaze of the outsiders, trying to see what specifically was 'beautiful' or 'magical' in them, trying to recognise what the outsider saw and valued when looking at them. 'Giving a good image', the quasi-omnipresent logic of action observed among the populations in the island, could here be understood in terms of the motherly mediation which affirmed the narcissistic processes of becoming conscious of self as a 'beautiful' and 'magical' entity. In this sense, the third social actor involved in this process is the imagined or real gaze of the social quarter within the island, observing individual and collective action, and disciplining deviation through the powerful practice of public mockery. Engaging with a self formulated in terms of the attributes thrown back by the outsiders' gaze, a 'magical' and 'beautiful' self, represents here initially a form of social deviation. Different social actors studied in this work were clearly marginalised, sometimes very violently, when engaging with outsiders or adopting new forms of practice or ideas about self. They were publicly mocked by neighbours or their immediate residential quarter. Many were very careful not to step outside the bounds of what appeared to be acceptable, especially where they engaged wider social entities, e.g. where a project was seen as involving an entire village and thus had to make sure to 'give a good image' of this village within the wider social gaze of the island.

Over time, certain fashions of doing and thinking flowed into what seemed to be socially acceptable practices and then were quickly adopted by large parts of the island's population. One new idea which was soon popularised in local thought was that of thinking about the island's being in the world through a dialectics of inside and outside. Initially mediated through the artistic work of nineteenth-century poets and later mobilised by both the island's autonomy movement and public policy development programmes, this idea was at the heart of a new aesthetic of everyday life quickly adopted within the island. Describing a social phenomenon that has been observed in various other contexts of human societies (Bachelard 1994a; Waldren 1996), this aesthetic allowed the formulation of an island 'locale' (Appadurai 2003b) in La Réunion whose identity emerged from the symbolic delimitation from various ontological others, e.g. the contemporary French mainland, the 'past' as a space of ancestry, the geographical neighbourhood in the Indian Ocean. Yet, these ontological others were not consigned to an absolutely different space of belonging, but were made to entertain relationships with the actual here and now of the island's present. They became a network of relations that made this here and now plausible and whose maintenance was fundamental to the maintenance of a collective island self. The paradox underlying this process is that the very aesthetic and moral order of the dialectic between inside and outside only became a socially accepted category for thinking about the (local) world because it was mediated and gained validity through outside social actors and institutions.

At a different level, the local implementation of the political doctrine of unity-in-diversity, advocated by Western political institutions and the intergovernmental agencies dominated by these during the 1970s and 1980s, led to a decentralisation of power and ownership within the French state and allowed a wider degree of cultural self-determination in La Réunion. This could be seen in the strengthening of regional governance bodies, new local development initiatives, the liberalisation of the local media, the full introduction of the French welfare state, and the development of a mass consumption society. It led to the development and emancipation of cultural policy divisions in the island's locally elected governance bodies, the Regional Council and the Departmental Council. It also generated a new paradox. While on one hand, these new institutions defended a narrative of cultural self-determination, they adopted on the other hand precisely the techniques of heritage management, interpretation and site selection they had learnt in France. The form and substance of the narratives used to make visible the new local selves remained largely identical to that of 'outside' curators or site developers from France. As shown in the third chapter, contestations only seemed to occur where 'non-locals' started initiatives to present 'local heritage'. In some cases, they were violently rejected. This paradox may be explained in that the adoption and performance of the very narratives of locality, diversity and cultural self-determination were, once again, embedded within a form of magical thinking related to a powerful outside. Symbolising and evoking the power of the former coloniser, France, they allowed the appropriation of a 'magical' quality associated with France. In this sense, these ways of thinking about the local indentity gained legitimacy as a result of their association, metaphorical or metonymic, with the mythical colonial mother who ultimately remained an important symbolic and political reference and cultural model.

For the ethnographer, the localised 'fetishisation' and colonial mimesis of such 'outside' concepts and the social integration of the subsequently formed localities into a wider global society imply yet another striking paradox, this time on a global scale. From a local perspective, conceiving social and spatial entities through concepts such as 'diversity' or 'locality' may initially manifest the mimesis of concepts adopted from the former colonisers, a kind of cargo cult[7] invoking the presumed 'magic' of this former to legitimate specific power positions in the island's society. However, as an effect of time and repeated nurturing within tourism and other contact realms, this initial fetishisation may lead to the emergence of more stable social practices and forms of organisation. It may lead to the normalisation of new modes of social participation in a transnational world, a specific performance acted out within a global social theatre. It may generate new systemic forms of transnational reciprocity and social roles. In tropical islands, populations may be thought of as a global priest class fed by modern tourists in search for spiritual and physical recreation. From here, a new world order appears to emerge, with vast territories transformed into gardens for the delight and symbolic maintenance of ideas and institutions governing modern society.

On the other hand, the phenomena described in this book address only one layer of global society. The conditions of life in tropical islands are generally marked by other, often competing phenomena and interests, usually related to economic development, the exploitation of resources, geopolitical strategies of global powers, urbanisation issues, etc. which often follow different logics and aspirations. They generate what Anna Tsing (2005) calls 'frictions', conflicts but also sometimes unexpected collaborations between interest groups and epistemic communities who see their objectives realised in common actions or lobby work. As I have shown in chapters four to six, within the wider realm of tourism development and conservation policy in La Réunion, a widely heterogeneous group of environmental lobby groups, commercial tourism developers, postcolonial autonomy militants, tourists, international cultural policy makers, global and local media and local development agencies often share interests in 'conserving' (which usually means to invent altogether) an 'endemic natural environment'. Domestic hospitality, tourism site developments and nature conservation activities constitute here new forms of social participation, usually translating established local forms of governance – especially the culture of the *kartié* – within the emerging tourism-scape. In La Réunion, many forces work towards the reimaging and redeveloping of the island as a 'human garden' within a global tourism-scape. As a result of these heterogeneous yet co-linear forces, 'magic' seems to become a polysemic symbol, enabling a wide variety of social actors to think about a local self and to participate in social life. It also generates new dilemmas and antagonistic forces. While the majority of people in La Réunion today have started to subscribe to a logic of conservation in terms of a Western model of island idyll, many are unemployed and live in miserable housing conditions. Many have left the island to look for jobs on the French mainland. In this context, from a pragmatic position of development politics, it would make sense to promote the development of large-scale hotels in order to generate jobs. The new narratives of an island locale, imbued with magical qualities that need to be preserved, can also become an intellectual prison that hinders the establishment of new projects, that has generated an ambiguous culture of local self-admiration, and that leaves the newly created locals in an indefinite position as the victims of history.

Endnotes

Prelims

1. Rosenbloom's article summarises recent research on expenditures of money, prompted by the harsh recession in the USA. The bulk of the findings by psychologists, home economists and market researchers show that the change from buying things to buying experiences increases reported 'happiness' and that frequent expenditures, e.g. long weekends off, are more satisfying than large lump sum expenditures, such as an expensive "holiday of a lifetime." The advantages of the consumption of experience over things lie mainly in the anticipation and the reminiscence, as has long been pointed out by tourism theorists, strengthening the parallel with the paradigmatic ritual sequences of preparation/separation and re-incorporation along with memories, photographs and souvenirs.

Introduction

1. If language is an 'intuitive' technique to articulate meaning and to verbalise emotions, thoughts and perceptions by putting them into meaningful words and phrases, it relies on the existence of what Roland Barthes called a 'significant consciousness' (1957). Roland Barthes' concept seems akin to Jerome Bruner's concept of 'folk psychology' (Bruner 1992) or Pierre Bourdieu's *habitus* (1977), defining acquired patterns of thought, behaviour and feeling that are shared among social groups and thus constitute a collective consciousness that transcends the individual subjectivities and perceptive modes of social actors, not in a metaphysical sense but as a historical result of socialisation. It hence constitutes what Emile Durkheim (2001 [1894]) defined as a social fact, 'manners of acting, thinking and feeling external to the individual, which are invested with a coercive power by virtue of which they exercise control over him'.
2. Stanley Tambiah explains that, from the beginning of its use, the word magic was employed to stigmatise 'Others'. The word first seems to have occurred in an early Greek text on epilepsy. It was used to denounce 'occult' theories, instead explaining this disease by naturalistic explanations anchored in a conception of nature governed by laws that can be studied in their regularity (Tambiah 1990: 9). In this early historical context, the term magic referred to the arts of divination used by

the Magi, a Zoroastrian priest class feared in Greece for their power to intervene in domestic politics. Magic subsequently became a more generic term to designate the use of occult forces assigned to a presumed super-nature and this firmly established itself as a common concept in modernist thinking. The Enlightenment movement of the eighteenth century, reiterating the Greek idea of logic and reason as a means of knowing the rules of nature, made the struggle against forms of magical and 'irrational' thinking one of its endeavours.

3. Interpretations of tourist experience spanned from the total denial of meaningful experiences by tourists (Boorstin 1962) to categorisation systems in terms of motivations (Cohen 2004a). John Urry (1900) suggests that tourism was governed by the hermeneutics of the 'tourist gaze', the idea that tourists were looking out for signs ('symptoms') of a certain attraction, yet that the signs had become the attractions in themselves, and that tourism was fundamentally void of deeper meaning.
4. The concept of ethnoscape was originally coined by Arjun Appadurai (2003a) and has been taken up in the field of tourism. Among others, Michael di Giovine (2008) applies it to a study of the global heritage-scape that emerges within the realm of UNESCO policies.
5. I am thankful to Joao de Pina-Cabral (2002) who suggested that I consider here the concept of 'reciprocal compatibilities' that he developed in order to study the colonial and postcolonial contact zones of Macau. His idea here is that contact does not necessarily lead to cultural diffusion, acculturations or creolisations, but in many cases to the maintenance of difference.
6. Dean MacCannell (1976) deconstructs romantic and existentialist notions of 'authenticity' as the ideological underpinning of modernity. He asserts that tourism is motivated by a quest for authenticity where a modern self attempts to achieve a condition perceived as being more 'real', yet now 'lost' as a result of the disenchantments brought about by modernist thinking. Ning Wang (1999) nuances this proposal by suggesting that not all forms of tourism are motivated as such by a quest for what he calls 'existential authenticity'.
7. According to the classical works by anthropologists such as Emile Durkheim (2001 [1894]), Marcel Mauss and Henry Hubert (2006 [1902]), James Frazer (1993 [1911]), Edward E. Evans-Pritchard (1976 [1937]), Branislaw Malinowski (1992a [1948]), and Claude Levi-Strauss (1966), magic is defined as that which is believed capable of altering what is conceived of as 'natural laws' and the 'rules of causality', a supernatural quality or power embedded in talismans and fetishes, or invoked through the creative virtue of words, spells, forms of mimesis or the intervention of supernatural beings such as gods, spirits or ancestors. For believers, the use of magic increases chance and protects against bad luck or malicious forces. The use of magical spells is often believed to be effective in controlling people and subduing them to the magician's will, possessing them, making them ill or killing them. Magic is also believed to be effective in invoking different types of spirits and spirit powers assumed to live in parallel worlds and, in many cases, to make them work for one's purpose. For James Frazer, magic is commonly believed to relate to sympathetic connections between objects, people and places that had previously been in contact and that are believed to continue to exert power upon each other after being separated

(Frazer 1993 [1911]). He explains that objects that have been part of, or in contact with, specific material or spiritual realms are often believed to retain a metonymic quality that allows the invocation of the original – the relative who has passed away, the sacral shrine that has been touched, the original artworks of which a fragment has been taken home as a souvenir (Benjamin 1999 [1970]; Hennig 1999). In what he defines as the 'law of analogy', James Frazer observes that the magic of an original – a place, a person, a spirit, an object, a story – is frequently invoked not only through metonymic matter, but also through forms of mimesis and metaphor which, through specific aesthetic features associated with an original, invoke the power of this original in order to generate a certain effect.

8. The phenomenological works by Eugen Fink (1976), inspired by Edmund Husserl, stress the relationship between proximity and distance as a central element in the configuration of selfhood and being in the world. Susan Steward (1993) discusses the political economy of generating an 'authentic' link between a here and now and a realm situated in a distanced geography, sociability or mythical time. For Mike Taussig (1993), this does not necessarily relate to a spatial or temporal distance, but in many cases stems from a process of concealment where a 'magical' realm is generated through a political economy of limiting access to specific spaces, spirits or other symbolic resources.
9. Zymund Bauman (2000) stresses the fluid nature of the human condition and those institutions formed to maintain its ontological stability. For him, constituting and maintaining selfhood is an ongoing process and struggle of engaging the uncertainties of social life and embedding them in symbolic forms and narratives of continuity. Arjun Appadurai (2003b), in a similar vein, talks about the ongoing work of socialising the social, spatial and temporal boundaries of social life, not primarily with an aim of economic production, but as a means of affirming being human. Bruno Latour (2007) uses the metaphor of assemblage to describe the human efforts made to maintain identity through multiple relationships with different social actors, which can be human, but also material objects or invisible entities such as gods and spirits. Diana Espírito Santo (2010) considers self as a fluid realm; to maintain itself, it requires ongoing ontological work to entertain relations with spirits which are not only inhabiting, but are also constitutive of a person.
10. Ideas assimilating magical thinking and primitivism are present in many of the pioneering ethnographic texts, including those by Edward Tylor (1913 [1871]), James Frazer (1993 [1911]), or Marcel Mauss and Henri Hubert (2006 [1902]). In these works, magic is usually explained as a purposely-performed 'trick'. Jeanne Favret-Saada (1977, 2009), in her reconsideration of witchcraft in rural France, suggests an approach to magic in terms of a social practice whose internal logic (and pertinence) will remain widely incomprehensive for the ethnographer's eye. Yet, she suggests, it can be observed through its effects, namely as an important social and therapeutic function linking individuals within their social environments.
11. For Jean Delumeau (1978), this aesthetic emerges from a Western history of enchantment of the world, which he sees as being rooted in the fears of 'Western ancestors', conscious about the temporal, spatial and social limits of their existence. Neo-Marxist authors such as Immanual Wallerstein (2004) root this aesthetic in the

history of mercantilism and logic of capitalist production systems in the Western world. For this author, the idea of subduing nature provides a moral legitimisation for the modern project of global economic expansion. For James Clifford (1989), the paradigm of cultivating nature as a means to reach a higher moral state is projected onto the scale of world society. It becomes a metaphor articulating power relations between core and peripheries, where the latter are respectively ascribed with qualities related to the degree by which they have managed to cultivate nature and elevate themselves above the 'natural condition'.

12. In German, the term *ur* describes an overarching order or model, also an 'initial', 'earliest' or 'first' condition which serves as a reference to measure – and morally judge – change, but also the authenticity of an original. The term was adopted into English during the nineteenth century.
13. For the Catholic church, the ability to achieve 'moral perfection' (assisted by divine guidance) remains a key concept to define human 'culture'. The 1992 edition of the Catholic Catechism stresses accordingly that 'Creation has its own goodness and proper perfection, but it did not spring forth complete from the hands of the Creator. The universe was created "in a state of journeying" (*in statu viae*) toward an ultimate perfection yet to be attained, to which God has destined it. We call "divine providence" the dispositions by which God guides his creation toward this perfection' (1994, p. 302).
14. The critiques of European historical philosophy proposed by authors such as Friedrich Nietzsche, Georg Simmel, Theodor Lessing, Walter Benjamin, and Michel Foucault suggest that two complementary types of historic narrative, with different moral and ideological underpinnings, emerged in this context (Bischof 1983). Theodor Lessing (1983 [1919]) distinguishes between 'optimist' and 'pessimist' views of history. History, he claimed, has either been considered in terms of a painful, yet necessary progress, according to the optimistic view, or as a means of establishing and reproducing systems of exploitation, according to the pessimistic view. Lessing also stresses that both optimistic and pessimistic views of history evolve within a common ideological framework, referring to the past as a condition out of which the material realities of the present have emerged, a condition variably signified in terms of the ideological projects that dominate the present. According to this argument, for the optimists, the past is frequently formulated as an archaic condition that is slowly, often painfully, being overcome through social and technological progress. For the pessimists, it often represents an idealised condition of innocence and authenticity from which capitalist systems of exploitation emerged, alienating humans from a primordial condition of happiness. In Lessing's terms, both types of historical narrative situate a form of 'initial condition' at the beginning of time and symbolically legitimate the political orders of the present and the projects for the future through the invocation of, and the 'magic' that stems from, these imaginary primordial conditions.
15. I am thankful to Camila del Marmol for the delicacy of her thought and for pointing me towards the texts of this author. In his collection of essays, *The Aleph and other stories*, Borges (1970) sublimely joins content and form by leading readers through a process of learning tropes, weaving them into more complex stories and eventually culminating in the confrontation with the aleph.

16. Sigmund Freud (1981) analyses the pain of rupture that people tend to encounter when a beloved one dies and explains this, in line with a Hegelian interpretation of love as a dialectical process, as the effect of having become part of the other and the other being constitutive of the self. Boris Cyrulnik (1997) talks about the 'bewitchment of the world' to describe how social relations between people and things emerge from the 'bewitchment' and cross-appropriations of each other and each other's spirits.
17. Peter Pels stresses that forms of magical thinking penetrate almost every level of modern social life; that magic is not only in modernity, as some kind of 'pagan remnant', but essentially belongs to modernity (Pels 2003). He suggests reconnecting to the classical anthropological theorisations of magic as a phenomenological quality of social life by authors such as Marcel Mauss (1902). Since the 1990s, different commentators have embraced the concept as an analytical category to study a wide range of phenomena or practices that do not explicitly refer to forms of magical or religious practice or thinking: science (Tambiah 1990), commodities (Taussig 1993), cinema (Meyer 2003), museums (Bouquet and Porto 2005), governance (Taussig 1997; Graeber 2007), art, technology and gardening (Gell 1988, 2005).
18. Ning Wang (1999) later nuanced MacCannell's proposal and summarised the debates that ensued by stressing that not all forms of tourism are motivated by a 'quest for authenticity'. Wang distinguishes between different forms of authenticity – 'objectivist' (relating to the true nature of objects, persons, etc, 'constructivist' (relating to socially constructed values attached to the concept) and 'existential' (relating to the embodied 'real' experience and feelings).
19. The idea of 'reverse magic' follows Stuard Kirsch's (2006) approach to reverse anthropology where 'magic' (as an emic category) becomes magical (from an etic perspective) by means of indigenising an initially exogenous concept to define the self.
20. The idea of islands and island-like territories being imbued with specific transforming or otherwise 'magical' qualities is not uncommon in the history of human societies. Examples of islands believed to be inhabited by powerful gods or spirits have been reported from the very beginnings of empirical ethnography: Alfred Radcliffe-Brown (1933 [1922]) described the spirit god *Pulga* in the North Andaman Island, Bronislaw Malinowski (1992 [1948]) the *Baloma* spirits of the dead in the Trobriand Islands, Raymond Firth (1963 [1936]) the *atua* spirits in the Polynesian Tikopia, and Clifford Geertz (1969 [1960]) the *kipua* spirits in Java. These earlier works emphasise the religious dimension of such beliefs and their role in the organisation of political order within a group or society. Soliciting the power of specific islands or island-like territories, and the spirits which inhabited them, can prove highly efficient when the appropriate procedures and socially recognised mediators are being used. The accidental, malicious or unsolicited access to, or use of, specific islands and island spirits, on the other hand, is often seen as highly perilous; the accidentally shipwrecked, the curious or the thugs risk being transfigured or transformed, literally petrified or otherwise being held prisoner, only released with the help of magical practice or tricks. Some commentators have interpreted the constitution and mobilisation of these socially assumed magical qualities in terms of political economy, as a tool to legitimate and exert political power, especially in view of governing access to rare resources, secure harbours or geo-strategically important passages. The archae-

ologists Brian Bauer and Charles Stanish (2001) relate the worship of shrines in the islands of the sun in the Titicaca Lake in Peru to ancient forms of regional statecraft; the control of these islands, believed to be the place of origin of the Sun, and of the rituals related to this belief, helped the Tiwanaku and later Inca rulers to legitimate their position within social hierarchies (245). In a more contemporary context, Phillipe Chaudat (1993) demonstrated the political economy of fishing resources underlying the *vorombe* cult in the Malagasy island of Nosy Ve, near Anakao; the political monopoly held by one lineage group to establish contact – by means of possession – with these powerful spirits attributed to this group the power to govern access to the rich fishing grounds believed to be inhabited by these spirits. Similar 'power mechanisms' have been reported from other places in Madagascar (Fauroux 1997) and the Western Indian Ocean (Lambek 1993) as well as from a variety of other places in the world. For other commentators, the belief in magical qualities as part of the logic of island imaginaries is less related to a form of political economy of material resources or geopolitical positions than to a form of enchantment related to the geographically peculiar form of islands as land surrounded by sea. For Roger Caillois (1973), the enchantment of curious or mysterious forms is related to the tendency by humans to translate material discontinuities into forms of symbolic continuity. Islands represent a specific form of 'spatial discontinuity' (Gay 1995) whose mystery may be related to their 'roundness', evoking the experience of being in the world from a subjective perception (Bachelard 1994b [1958]). From this perspective, islands may appear as miniatures that translate a common conception of being in a circumscribed material space, a kind of garden that evokes and hence gives access to the wider ideological and ontological underpinning of existence. As a consequence of such enchantments (whether or not they are based on a political economy of resources), islands commonly appear embedded in powerful imaginaries that objectify them in forms of symbolic continuity and frequently ascribe specific – 'magical' – qualities and powers to them. In many societies, these imaginaries of islands and the evocation of their related magical qualities are brought alive through forms of ritual and festivity. In many cases, pilgrimages to specific islands and island-like spaces such as mountains or valleys (that sometimes host monasteries and permanent priest populations) are part of the social festival calendar. While their access frequently remains prohibited or highly regulated during the time-space of secular life, the festive periods allow and often purposely imply a transgression of such spatial proscriptions (Caillois 2001). Through various festive and ceremonial practices – sacrifices, performances, consumptions, prayers – festival participants seem able to bring alive the specific space related imaginaries and connect to what is often perceived as a primordial space, power or event legitimating the order and separations of social life. Both the individually perceived connection to the – magical – qualities of such a primordial space and the largely ritualised and socially differentiated forms of participation that mark such festivals seem able to recreate the being in the world on different individual and collective scales. Individuals are able to recreate the social and symbolic relations that define their personal life-worlds, while social hierarchies poetically embedded in specific island myths are reproduced, reaffirming the authority by the powerful who usually control access to the islands and the spirits that guard them.

21. Jacques Lacan (1966) observed young children candidly becoming conscious of themselves through recognising themselves in a mirror, while their mothers watched.

Chapter 1

1. During the Romanian revolution of 1989, the communist regime of Nicolae Ceausescu was overthrown after violent street fighting. Following a swift trial, Ceausescu and his wife Elenea were executed.
2. The 2007 *Compendium of Tourism Statistics* edited by the World Tourism Organisation includes general data on tourist flows by country or dependent territory. Fifty-eight of these countries or dependant territories are geographically located in the 'intertropical zone', between the tropics of Cancer and Capricorn (two imaginary lines that lie at 23.5 degrees latitude north and south of the equator where the sun is directly overhead respectively at noon on the June and December solstices). These countries or dependent territories (the latter emphasised in italic) are, in alphabetical order: *American Samoa (US)*, *Anguilla (UK)*, Antigua and Barbuda, *Aruba (Netherlands)*, Australia, the Bahamas, Barbados, *Bermuda (UK)*, Bonaire, *British Virgin Islands (UK)*, Cape Verde, *Cayman Islands (UK)*, Comoros, *Cook Islands (New Zealand)*, Costa Rica, Cuba, Dominica, Dominican Republic, Fiji, *French Polynesia (France)*, *Guadeloupe (France)*, Grenada, *Guam (US)*, Haiti, Indonesia, Jamaica, Madagascar, Malaysia, Maldives, Marshall Islands, *Martinique (France)*, Mauritius, Federated States of Micronesia, *New Caledonia (France)*, New Zealand, *Niue (New Zealand)*, *Northern Mariana Islands (US)*, Palau, Papua New Guinea, Philippines, *Puerto Rico (US)*, *Réunion (France)*, Saba, Saint Eustatius, Saint Kitts and Nevis, Saint Lucia, Saint Maarten, Saint Vincent and the Grenadines, Samoa, Sao Tome and Principe, Seychelles, Solomon Islands, Sri Lanka, Taiwan (Republic of China), Tonga, Trinidad and Tobago, *Turks and Caicos Islands (UK)*, Tuvalu, *US Virgin Islands (US)*, Vanuatu. Strictly speaking some countries (e.g. the Bahamas, Taiwan, etc.) are not, or not entirely, situated in the tropical zone, but have still been included. For other places, especially those that are part of national territories and that actually qualify as tropical islands from a geographical point of view, no data has been available. Based on the country or dependant-territory specific data (reprocessed by means of an Excel spreadsheet), it was possible to generate a general overview of the 2005 global tourist flows to tropical islands in terms of parameters such as tourist arrivals, expenditures, lengths of stay, origin of tourists, scope of travel, etc.
3. MINTEL's *Long-haul Holidays – UK reports* (2007) indicates that, in the United Kingdom, more than 66% of people questioned aspired to spend holidays in long-haul destinations with, as the main motives, good weather, beaches and the opportunity to 'switch off and relax'.
4. Different authors have pointed out different methodological issues related to research on the flows and connections that constitute various global ethnoscapes (Tedlock 1991; Marcus 1995; Clifford 1997, Amit 2000; Appadurai 2003a; Burawoy, M., J. Blum, S. George et al. 2000). In the field of ethnographic tourist studies, some

of these issues have been taken up by Graham Dann, Dennison Nash and Phillip Pearce (1988). For a recent discussion of these issues, see Naomi Leite's and Nelson Graburn's 'Anthropological Interventions in Tourism Studies' (2009).

5. Nelson Graburn (2002) discusses the outputs of different approaches based on the ethnographer taking on the role of tour guide. Such approaches had previously been tested by anthropologists including Rachid Amirou (1995), Eric Cohen (1985, 2004b) and Edward Bruner (2005).
6. Among the tourists guided in these round trips, the motivations underlying their holiday on a tropical island seemed to emerge from various social contexts and personal circumstances. Many were, as they told me, 'busy professionals', 'usually working long hours' with not enough time to 'cultivate' their life as a couple, or relations with close relatives and friends. The tourist journey was expected to 'make them leave this busy environment' and 'forget about it all for some time'. It was to 'offer' them 'quality time' spent in an 'amazing environment' with their partners and friends. Other people appeared so existentially bored with their everyday lives back home that the time of the holiday seemed to constitute one of their principal aspirations in life. Some months after one of the trips, I visited a man in his mid-fifties at his home near Frankfurt. He had attracted my attention during the trip for being such a 'perfect tourist': he was dressed in safari wear and always had appropriate shoes, all the right medicines that he shared with his fellow tourists; he was very knowledgeable about how to negotiate on markets, how to avoid sunburn; he was exceptionally knowledgeable about hotels and tour operators in 'more than 60 countries'. I was amazed by his house which was stuffed with tourism souvenirs wherever I looked. It was hard to get through the living room. He talked me through some of the objects that were places on shelves or on the wall. There were model boats from Mauritius, spears and black wood sculptures from East Africa, masks from Indonesia, Inuit handicraft from Alaska, a marble chessboard from Madagascar, prints from China, and more. In a similar fashion, an elderly woman I revisited in Berlin had several themed collections of souvenirs, different types of small objects: animal sculptures, stones and miniature handicraft objects that she had arranged in wooden boxes. Each of her trips was 'filed' in an album in which she retraced the time-frame of the journey and had added written personal reflections next to photographs, maps, entry tickets or other paper souvenirs of the journey. She told me that these albums were for her own pleasure only. It was rare that she would show them to anyone, 'only to very nice people – like me', she added. Both the middle-aged man in Frankfurt and the elderly woman in Berlin told me that they were, in one way or another, socially alienated. The man from Frankfurt told me he never managed to build up friendship networks in his home environment; he did not know anyone 'here'. The elderly woman in Berlin had never been married (her fiancée died in the Second World War) and her friends and family had passed away. Both repeatedly told me, during the journey and in the post-tourism context, that they were longing for human contact in their everyday lives and that the framework of the organised tour enabled this contact. For other tourists, the trip seemed to imply a deeper existential dimension. Some said they had realised their 'childhood dream' of travelling to a tropical island. They explained to me how the idea of such a trip had been often nurtured from a very young age, repeatedly pushed back for various social, economic or

political reasons, and was finally made to come true through this very journey. Ernest repeatedly explained how much he had desired to see a tropical island. Only once the Berlin Wall had fallen did it become possible to realise this dream. A woman, nearly eighty years old, told me about a picture of her father in front of the Victoria Falls. It was one of her only personal souvenirs after he died during the War. After almost giving up her life-long dream to travel there, she had booked a trip the year before which, as she said, had allowed her to 'close a circle'. Others, especially people who had previously gone through 'difficult times' (in their words), hoped the trip would mark what they called a 'cut' and 'generate a more positive outlook for life'. One woman in her mid-forties told me she had booked the holiday together with her best friend, to 'get over her divorce' and the depression that followed. An elderly couple told me that their parents had recently died. They had been looking after them for fifteen years and now wanted to 'bring colour back into their lives'. While the tourist journey appeared motivated by quite different contexts and aspirations, the common underlying principle seems to be that it allows subjects to mark breaks between different cycles of social life and to recreate symbolic order. This idea possibly first appears in Nelson Graburn's theorisation of tourism as a 'sacred journey' (1977, 1989). Graburn suggests here that tourism represents a 'sacred' time-space alternating with the 'profane' time-spaces of everyday life especially the obligations of work; an emotionally heightened time-space that allows tourists to engage with forms belonging to the 'sacred' realms of different modern myths: nature, culture, art. Similar ideas, discussed by authors such as Dean MacCanell (1999), Victor and Edith Turner (1978), Jean Viard (1986), Eric Cohen (1992), Christoph Hennig (1999), Ning Wang (1999), and Badone and Roseman (2004), have attempted to theorise tourism as a form of 'modern' pilgrimage to sites that represent powerful symbolic references for modern social life. These breaks define, on the one hand, wider structural time-frames that give rhythm to social life in modern society. They typically articulate the transitions between different agricultural, industrial and business administration cycles. On the other hand, these breaks mark changes in personal life circumstances which result from expected social transitions (e.g. coming of age, career advancement, death), unexpected ruptures (career changes, separations and divorce) or the life-changing realisation of dream journeys (pilgrimages, once-in-a-lifetime journeys, honeymoons, etc.). As I have shown elsewhere, wider structural changes and economic revolutions challenging the symbolic and political order of societal life are, in many cases, accompanied by the emergence of new festivals, often an increased tourism phenomenon – which thus can be said to mark such a form of historical break (Picard and Robinson 2006).

7. Stephanie M. Hom (Hom Cary 2004) has defined these touristic epiphanies as 'tourist moments', which appear to carry the touristic subject temporarily beyond the frameworks of conventionalised forms of tourist performance or travel culture. It seems to me that what made these moments 'peak' is a sudden, deep connection perceived by the tourists, a shock of beauty that left them temporarily speechless, that induced a set of symptoms that have elsewhere been conceptualised in terms of a 'Stendhal' syndrome (also 'Paris syndrome', 'Jerusalem syndrome'). The psychiatrist Graziella Magherini from the Santa Maria Nuova Hospital in Florence, Italy observed, over a period of almost twenty years, hundreds of cases of tourists who, after being ex-

posed to artworks considered as particularly beautiful, started suffering from rapid heartbeat, dizziness, confusion and hallucinations. In her 1989 publication based on these observations, she coined the term 'Stendhal syndrome' to describe these 'psychosomatic' conditions. The term is named after Stendhal, the pseudonym of the nineteenth-century French author Henri-Marie Beyle who, in his book *Rome, Naples and Florence* (1817), had described similar symptoms that occurred during his visit to Venice in 1817. A similar 'Paris syndrome' has been reported, mainly for Japanese individuals moved by the 'romanticism' of Paris (Viala, Ota, Vacheron et al. 2004) and a 'Jerusalem syndrome' for visitors to various religious sites in Jerusalem (Bar-el, Durst, Katz et.al. 2000; critiqued by Kalian and Witztum 2000). The term has also been used to describe similar effects of sublimation experienced by some individuals when confronted with specific forms of 'beauty' in the natural or human world.

8. Once or twice it happened that tourists had brought the travel catalogue from which they had booked the trip and asked me to find the exact spots from where some of the photographs in this catalogue had been taken. They would then take photographs from these same spots. When I later revisited these tourists in Germany, I was shown their photograph albums which included several pages with images from the catalogue juxtaposed with those they had taken themselves.
9. Elvi Whittaker suggests the use of Abraham Maslow's concept of 'peak experiences' to approach such 'strong moments' (Whittaker, forthcoming). After the first couple of guided tours, it became relatively easy for me to anticipate the type of places, people or stories that would generate such 'strong moments', that would induce more or less powerful emotional reactions among the tourists. I realised that the time-space frame of the journey, built in collaboration between the German tour operator and the agency I was working for in La Réunion, was actually structured around such 'strong moments'. Each half-day of the tour included at least one, usually the visit to a spectacular landscape viewpoint or 'cultural site'. The production of the particular tourist space of this five-day round trip hence seemed to be based on a sophisticated empirical or intuitive knowledge, by the tourist agents, of the collective aesthetic dispositions of the tourists that would book this trip.
10. In the weeks following each trip, I asked the tourists to send me what they considered as the '10 most significant photos' of their journey and to comment on each of them briefly. Seven tourists responded to this call and sent me between eight and twelve photographs respectively. The visual content of these photographs can broadly be grouped into four content-related thematic categories: panoramic shots of landscapes; hotel and service spaces; local populations; and cultural sites. The analysis of the photographs in terms of these categories revealed a standard variation (a measure of how spread out data values are around the mean, defined as the square root of the variance) lower than 15%. This means that, among this very small sample, the different tourists sent me sets of photographs that were more or less similar in content; the different samples varied only by one photograph in average. This significant homogeneity allowed me to analyse this sample based on the average distribution of visual contents. The largest percentage of photographs by far showed panoramic shots of landscapes (83%), followed by equally distributed percentages for the three other categories (hotel and service spaces, local populations, and cultural sites), which represented about 5% each of the visual content of the photographs.

11. Today, writing up these observations, I remain baffled by this 'miracle of consensus' (MacCannell 1976: 42) among people (including myself) from widely different social backgrounds, apparently with no other link than 'being German'. I remain bewildered about how the very personal emotions of the journey emerge within what seems a wider collective frame of the tourism. Tourists would often become aware of such a collective frame when talking to other tourists and realising that they were moved by the same sites. This realisation generated another effect of tourism which was far away from the actual sites of the journey; a feeling of belonging to a community of common sense. Some tourists talked about such a realisation ironically, stating that 'we are never free'. Others seemed to use it to confirm that their shared experience related to a deeper truth (e.g. 'nature is unconditional'). In any case, it allowed tourists to relate the conditions of their personal being to a wider public imagery and conceptualisation of what constitutes a tropical island.
12. Following Arnold van Gennep (1961), liminality defines a time-space of social fluidity, sometimes of structural 'carnivalesque' inversion (Turner 1969; Bakhtin 1993), where ontological and social boundaries are symbolically weakened, inversed or disappear. Liminality is part of various forms of social festivity, which, according to van Gennep, typically follow a three-part structure of exclusion, liminality and re-integration. Roger Caillois, in his *Théorie de la fête* (1950), explains that the liminal time-space of festive events allows people to evoke playfully a mythical time of cosmogonic unity when heavens and earth, gender and age groups, dead and alive, humans and gods 'still formed one'.

Chapter 2

1. *Brevet d'Aptitude Professionnelle d'Assistant Animateur Technicien de la Jeunesse et des Sports.*
2. The vast majority of the tourists Orom interacted with can be categorised as 'French urban middle class'. The almost systematic repetition of conversational themes in a given moment of the guided tour hence could be related to a more generic 'French middle class culture of communication', a cultural epistemology historically formed within a specific frame of the French nation-state and its strongly centralised social institutions (e.g. education, media, army, public service, governance corps).

Chapter 3

1. Pseudonym. Alexandre Delarge, Raphael Folio and Jean-Ives Loufo are all highly charismatic local actors.
2. *Colonage*: the land owner would lend land to *colons* who exploited it at their own cost and paid a rent in kind, usually 30% of the crops produced.
3. This initiative was finally rejected by a special commission put in place by the National Forestry Office (ONF).

4. The choice of using these particular media to communicate the predefined themes of 'earth', 'first part of the 19th century' and 'first colonisation of the valley' emerged from a second brainstorming session involving Crouzet Richard and the professional display designer. A written note found in the archive of this exhibition, dated 02/99, indicates a list of associations that resulted from this brainstorming session and that summarises the initial approach to the museography of this room: Anchaing/Heva – Marooning – Legend/Myth – Piton d'Anchaing – Hunter/Game (Animals-Fugitives)/Bronchard – First settlers/concessions – hell/paradise – forest – waterfalls/canyons/ridges – mountains – islands/isolation – dirt road/paths – hunting/gathering – river culture – abolition/slaves/freed slaves – owners/concessionaries – wood/smoke/deforestation – cabana – colours: greens and black (green of the vegetation/black of the rock, penetration in a virgin space, black of the skin of the maroons and of obscure spaces).
5. Crouzet Richard and I had frequent discussions about the value of the romantic references used to illustrate the theme of slavery in the first room. In response to my criticism about the use of these sources and the possibility that they induced a mystification of history based on the romantic and exoticising tropes popular during the heyday of nineteenth-century French romanticism, he insisted that they constituted historical documents that needed a form of mediation.
6. Mary Louise Pratt (1992) adapted the concept of transculturation from Fernando Ortiz (1995 [1947]).
7. Article 5 of the *Memorandum of Understanding* signed between Salazie Ecomuseum and MNATP specifies that, where possible, all objects were to be collected in duplicate, one destined for the collection of Salazie Ecomuseum, the other for the MNATP.
8. Françoise Vergès, the scientific co-director (with Carpanin Marimoutou) of this new 'museum without collection', wrote in 2008 that 'diversity is the condition of [the Reunions] unity' (Vergès 2008: 220). She stressed that the new museographic space was less interested in being a contemplative place in which to display the social worlds of the island, than in generating a space of exchanges and frictions, which enable alternative approaches, *bricolages* and emerging arts to be reflected. While stressing the dynamic and lively nature of Creole society, she seems to perpetuate the idea that the asset of the island lies in its 'rich' and 'singular' 'immaterial culture' (Vergès 2008), a Creole culture of *bricolage* that serves as a model for both internal and external worlds.

Chapter 4

1. This text is the result of several years of direct observations and repeated informal and formal conversations with the principal characters of the study, Adamsky, Eve-Marie and Claudette (pseudonyms). The latter initially hesitated to make the intimacy of their social and family life public. However, they supported the underlying idea of generating debate about the tragedy, heroism, tenderness and violence that marked the contexts of change La Réunion has been going through, and that usually remain

hidden to the public eye – precisely to avoid public mockery. To preserve the anonymity of the persons whose lives have been described in this text, all names, precise dates and references to places have been omitted or substituted with pseudonyms.

2. The anonymous reviewer of an earlier draft of this text asked me to insert here a review of the academic literature on 'hospitality'. The focus of this chapter is ethnographic, yet it appears indeed useful to point the reader toward ideas which engage with the concept of hospitality on a more general level. Many contemporary theoretical and philosophical engagements with this concept refer to Emmanuel Kant who explained, in 1795, that a world of universal peace would only be achieved by means of a 'law of world citizenship' based upon conditions of 'universal hospitality'. He claimed that the 'right of a stranger not to be treated as an enemy when he arrives in the land of another' would allow 'the human race [to] gradually be brought closer and closer to a constitution establishing world citizenship' – a claim more recently re-uttered by French philosopher, Jacques Derrida (Derrida and Dufourmantelle 2000). Kant thus set the scene for later sociologists writing on notions of hospitality, both in terms of its underlying moral claims and the ontological distinctions between the social actors – hosts and guests – involved. In the early twentieth century, Georg Simmel produced one of the first sociological analyses of hospitality. He discussed how the ambivalent unity of nearness and remoteness involved in every human relation is organised in the specific phenomenon of the stranger. The latter, Simmel explains, is able to challenge notions of strangeness and possibilities of commonness among hosts and guests, and thus to accentuate conceptions of Self and Other. Hocart, in his study on the divinity of the guest, stresses the a priori uncertain nature of guests, who, he asserts, were seen in various contexts – in ancient Greece, India and Fiji – as potentially divine messengers or returning ancestors. Similarly, for Julian Pitt-Rivers strangers belong to the 'extra-ordinary' world, which makes them, in the belief of hosts, a 'suitable vehicle for the apparition of the Gods' (1977: 101). He defines the social logic of hospitality in terms of a double strategy aimed both at socialising and containing strangers, by transforming them into guests, and at anticipating a form of future reciprocity based on the idea that God will repay what was given for free. In a more abstract sense, hospitality also includes forms of symbolic consumption where ontological others are symbolically or literally ingested, by means of naming them, eating them, exhibiting or destroying them or the specific matter or food believed to contain their magical power. Claude Levi-Strauss (1966 [1962]) extensively describes the symbolic logic of consuming 'others', sometimes quite literally, as a means of appropriating their magic and power. With some exceptions (Lashley and Morrison 2007; Rosello and Leff 2003; Roberts, Selwyn, Andrews 2007; Lenz 2010), the recent literature on hospitality focused almost exclusively on commercial host-guest relationships, usually without relating to the earlier literature on the social logic of hospitality. The anthropological literature on hospitality also touches upon the idea of carnival as hospitality for the deaths, gods, and other visitors from the invisible world. In carnivals, participants become host and guest at the same time. The weakening of social boundaries transforms them into travellers into the world of social others. At the same time, others penetrate into their own social realms which are ostentatiously disguised in order to cater for, but also to protect against, different

'guests', including visitors from 'beyond' – spirits, gods and the deceased. For further reading see Roger Caillois (2001) and Mikhail Bakhtin (1993 [1941]).

3. In the mid-1990s, she gained access to the *Revenu Minimum d'Insertion* (RMI), a modest income that helped her to survive. At the end of the 1990s, more than 100,000 households in La Réunion lived on the RMI and family allowances for their children.
4. Jacques Simonin and Eliane Wolff (1993), in particular, analyse the projection of the culture of the *kartié* into the newly emerging public sphere of the school.
5. Other important immigrations emanated from the Indian Ocean, especially Madagascar, Mauritius, the Comoros and Mayotte.

Chapter 5

1. All names are pseudonyms.
2. In the sense of what Marc Augé (1992) calls 'Non-Places'; however, the 'non' here only applies to the formal aspect, not to the emic meanings of the place which, as this study has shown, persists underneath the largely interchangeable objects and types of plants of the site.

Chapter 6

1. On the 'other' side, the seaside, the limit of the public domain was defined in 1982 by the *United Nations Convention on the Law of the Sea*, UNCLOS, fixing the limits of the territory at 12 nautical miles from the shore and exclusive economic zone 200 miles along the shore. Along with these ownership rights, the convention defined certain obligations, especially the one to 'prevent, reduce and control pollution of the marine environment' (Gray Davidson 2002: 528).
2. All data related to catalogues were collected from the Thomas Cook archive in Peterborough, England, which holds a collection of most of the annual catalogues produced by this tour operator since the beginning of the twentieth century.
3. Based on PADI figures (Mintel 2003).
4. An accessible text about their biology and ecology can be found in the popular science book *World Atlas of Coral Reefs* by leading marine ecologists Mark D. Spalding, Corinna Ravilious and Edmund P. Green (2001).
5. The *2002 World Summit on Sustainable Development Plan of Implementation* stressed the promotion of sustainable tourism through a) enhanced international cooperation, direct foreign investment and partnerships with both private and public sectors, at all levels; and b) the development of programmes that encourage participation in eco-tourism, enable indigenous and local communities to develop and benefit from it, and enhance stakeholder cooperation. Other regional programmes with a strong focus on ecotourism development include the Indian Ocean Commission's Regional Coastal Management Programme (RECOMAP), Kenya's Tourism Trust Fund and the Western Indian Ocean Marine Science Association (WIOMSA).

6. 'The reef, veritable city of corals, is populated by a multitude of animals living amidst the corals. The corals which look like curious sculptured stones are made of thousands of miniscule animals. These strange animals which construct the coral are called polyps. The polyp is an animal with a soft body in the shape of a millimetre long bag. Its mouth is surrounded by numerous tentacles and it eats minuscule animals. You have never seen a polyp? That's normal, they only go out by night. [...] When the polyp touches a rock, it starts constructing a base. Then, it constructs a calcium wall around itself, a little lodge which is called the chalice. This lodge forms its skeleton and its house. It protects it and prevents it from getting taken away by the current. The polyp never stops building. Once it has finished its lodge, it will close it with a floor and start building the next level. The polyp never lives alone. Once it has settled on a rock, it creates a twin polyp. This phenomenon is called budding. As each new poly will start budding, a big family is very quickly formed. All joined together, these polyps construct a veritable building of several levels of which they only occupy the last one. This building is called a coral colony or simply the coral. [...] In the past centuries, the water level of the oceans has increased and the coral colonies have continued to build on each other in order to stay in the sunlight just under the water surface (the polyps can't live in the darkness). In the meantime, the sand that the waves have taken behind the reef has formed beaches and the ground of the lagoon. This is how the big coral reefs of St-Gilles and La Saline have been formed.' (Gabrié 1999)

Chapter 7

1. All names are pseudonyms.
2. Chou-Chou Festival in Hell-Bourg, Curcuma Festival in Plaine-des-Grègues, Lentil Festival and Wine Festival in Cilaos, Mango Festival in Saint-Paul, Pineapple Festival in Saint-Denis, Milk and Goyavier Festival in Plaine-des-Palmistes, Agaves Festival in Entre-Deux, Coffee Festival in Saint-Louis, Palm Festival in Saint-Philippe, Orchid Festival in Tampon, Garlic Festival in Petite-Ile, Green Honey Festival in Plaine-des-Cafres, Bichiques Festival in Bras-Panon.
3. The concept of 'life crisis' is borrowed from Arnold van Gennep (1961), with the idea that particular forms of festivity are organised in situations of societal rupture, transition or alienation. While such forms of festivity seem to mark all forms of social life in more or less organised or cyclically recurring ways (Turner 1969), the approach underlying this chapter will focus on longer lasting 'cycles of festivity' accompanying or following shortly after periods of wider economic and social change. I have shown elsewhere (Picard and Robinson 2006) that such long festivity cycles can be consistently observed in various historical and social contexts characterised by forms of economic, political or scientific rupture and revolution in which established forms of common sense fail to provide meaningful metaphors for the individual and collective being in the world.

Chapter 8

1. Marie-Françoise Lanfant is an emeritus research director at the French National Centre for Scientific Research (CNRS). Through the studies carried out at her research unit, the Unité de Recherche en Sociologie du Tourisme International (URESTI), she has pioneered, from the late 1970s onwards, an approach to tourism as an international and transnational social fact. Major outputs by the URESTI team and associate researchers include papers by Marie-Françoise Lanfant focusing on internationalisation processes (1980), identity (1992, 1995), heritage (1992), the principle of the 'alternative' (1992, with Nelson Graburn), and the gaze (2009); Jacques de Weerdt's work (1987) on the construction of 'deep rurality' in France; Danielle Rozenberg's research (1990) on the touristic myth of the Balearics; Jean-Didier Urbain's work (1991, 1994) on the semiotics of tourism and tourist spaces; Rachid Amirou's studies (1995) on tourist imaginaries and the sociability of the journey; and Michel Picard's works (1992) on nationalism, identity and the historic emergence of 'tourism cultures' in Bali. Marie-Françoise Lanfant supervised the earlier stages of my doctoral research between 1999 and 2001; she visited La Réunion in May 2000, to participate in a workshop at the University of La Réunion and to see the actual sites where I carried out my fieldwork.
2. The terminology of the 'gardening state' is borrowed from Zygmunt Bauman (1998) who describes forms of race politics that, in the early twentieth century, attempted to literally 'garden' human forms, especially their genetics, through the positive selection of certain, and the prohibition of other, forms of human biological reproduction, namely through planned fertilisation, on one hand, and euthanasia, on the other. He shows how the idea of the gardening state legitimated discrimination based fundamentally on social-historical and cultural criteria and led to the horrors of the holocaust.
3. The word garden originally derives from the Persian *apiri-daeza* ('verger enclosed by a wall') and was adopted by ancient Hebrew as *pardès*, which became *paradeisos* in the early biblical texts (Delumeau 1992: 13) to designate a garden of delightful felicity inside a happy countryside, Eden.
4. The ideas that generated the garden city movement are usually attributed to Ebenezer Howard (1898). As an urban planning concept, it heavily influenced later architects and spatial planners, among them Le Corbusier (cf. Beevers 1988).
5. For a recent article comparing the relationship between genocide and nation building in different Western countries – Turkey, the USA and Germany – read Elizabeth Kolbert's 'Dead Reckoning: The Armenian genocide and the politics of silence', published in the *New Yorker Magazine* of 6 November 2006.
6. UNESCO is an UN agency created in 1945 to develop global policies and normative actions in the fields of culture, education and science.
7. Cases of 'cargo cult' were reported from New Guinea and Micronesian countries where islanders, after contact with strangers – especially colonial administrators, missionaries and soldiers – from Europe, Japan, Australia and the USA, started to engage in rituals that imitated certain behaviours of these strangers. According to

the ethnographies by Peter Worsley (1957), Judy Inglis (1957), Kenneth E. Read (1958), Bill Stanner (1958) and others, the background to these rituals was the belief among the islanders that the cargo – equipment and manufactured tools thought to be imbued with magical qualities – that planes had dropped and ships discharged to supply the foreigners, was actually destined for them. In an attempt to attract planes and ships, and the cargo these carried, these islanders started to imitate the strangers, e.g. by setting up mock airstrips, fabricating 'radios' made of coconuts and straw, and painting Western symbols on their cloth or bodies.

Bibliography

Adams, K.M. (2006). *Art as Politics: Recrafting Identities, Tourism, and Power in Tana Toraja, Indonesia*. Honolulu: U Hawai'i Press.

Aerni, M.J. (1972). 'Social Effects of Tourism', *Current Anthropology* 13(2): 162.

Albers, P. and W.R. James (1988). 'Travel Photography: A Methodological Approach', *Annals of Tourism Research* 15: 134–158.

Alberti, L.B. (1568). *L'Architecture et art de bien bastir*. Transl. by J. Martin. Paris: [unknown publisher].

Allaire, J.-C. (1964). *Projet directeur de Salazie-Hell-Bourg: enquête monographique*. Saint-Denis: Préfecture de La Réunion.

Amirou, R. (1995). *Imaginaire touristique et sociabilité du voyage*. Paris: PUF.

Amit, V. (ed.) (2000). *Constructing the Field: Ethnographic Fieldwork in the Contemporary World*. London: Routledge.

Anderson, B. (1991 [1983]). *Imagined Communities: Reflections on the Origin and Spread of Nationalism*. London and New York: Verso.

Appadurai, A. (1981). 'The Past as a Scarce Resource', *Man* 16: 201–219.

———. (1996). 'The Production of Locality', in A. Appadurai, *Modernity at Large*. Minneapolis: University of Minnesota Press, pp. 178–200.

———. (2003a). 'Global Ethnoscapes: Notes and Queries for a transnational Anthropology', in A. Appadurai, *Modernity at Large: Cultural Dimensions of Globalization*. Minneapolis: University of Minnesota Press, pp. 48–65.

———. (2003b). 'The Production of Locality', in A. Appadurai, *Modernity at Large*. Minneapolis: University of Minnesota Press, pp. 178–200.

Arendt, H. (1977 [1954]). 'Tradition and the Modern Age', in H. Arendt, *Between Past and Future*. London: Penguin Classics, pp. 17–40.

Assunto R. (1988). *Ontologia e teleologia del giardino*. Milan: Guerini.

Augé, M. (1992). *Non Lieux*. Paris: Seuil.

Bachelard, G. (1994a [1958]). 'The Dialectics of Outside and Inside', in G. Bachelard, *The Poetics of Space*. Transl. by Maria Jolas. Boston: Beacon Press, pp. 211–231.

———. (1994b [1959]). 'The Phenomenology of Roundness', in G. Bachelard, *The Poetics of Space*. Transl. by Maria Jolas. Boston: Beacon Press, pp. 232–241.

Badone, E. and S.R. Roseman (eds) (2004). *Intersecting Journeys: The Anthropology of Pilgrimage and Tourism*. Urbana and Chicago: University of Illinois Press.

Bakhtin, M. M. (1993 [1941]). *Rabelais and His World*. Trans. by Hélène Iswolsky. Bloomington: Indiana University Press.

Barat, C. (1978). *Les Paillotes de l'île de la Réunion*. Saint-Denis: CUR.

———. (1989). *Nargoulan. Culture et rites malbar à la Réunion*. Saint Denis: Editions du Tramail.

Bar-el, Y., R. Durst, G. Katz, J. Zislin, Z. Strauss, H.Y. Knobler (2000). 'Jerusalem syndrome', *British Journal of Psychiatry* 176: 86–90.

Baridon, M. (1998). *Les jardins. Paysagistes, jardiniers, poètes*. Paris: Laffont.

Barthes, R. (1957). *Mythologies*. Paris: Seuil.

Bataille, G. and R. Hurley (1988). *The Accursed Share: An Essay on General Economy*. New York: Zone Books.

Baudrillard, J. (1972). *Pour une critique de l'économie politique du signe*. Paris: Gallimard.

Bauer, S.B. and S. Charles (2001). *Ritual and Pilgrimage in the Ancient Andes: The Islands of the Sun and the Moon*. Austin: University of Texas Press.

Bauman, Z. (1998). 'The Scandal of Ambivalence', in Z. Bauman, *Modernity and Ambivalence*. Cambridge: Polity, pp. 18–52.

———. (2000). *Liquid Modernity*. Cambridge, UK: Polity Press.

Beevers, R. (1988). *The Garden City Utopia: A Critical Biography of Ebenezer Howard*. Abingdon: Olivia Press.

Benjamin, W. (1999 [1970]). 'The Work of Art in the Age of Mechanical Reproduction', in W. Benjamin, *Illuminations*. London: Pimlico, pp. 211–244.

Benoist, J. (1983). *Un développement ambigu. Structure et changement de la société réunionnaise*. Saint-Denis de La Réunion: FRDOI.

———. (1998). *Hindouismes créoles*. Paris: Editions du Comité des Travaux historiques et scientifiques.

——— and J.-L. Bonniol (1994). *Un ordre étagé mis à bas*. Aix-en-Provence: Laboratoire d'écologie humaine et d'anthropologie.

Benoit, G. (1988). *Séminaire de réflexion sur le développement de Salazie*. Saint-Denis: Commissariat à l'Aménagement des Hauts (CAH).

Berger, J. (1979). *Ways of Seeing*. Harmondsworth: Penguin.

Berque, A. (1986). *Le sauvage et l'artifice: les Japonais devant la nature*. Paris: Gallimard.

———. (1995). *Les Raisons du paysage. De la Chine antique aux environnements de synthèse*. Paris: Hazan.

———. (1996). *Etre humains sur la Terre. Principes d'éthique de l'écoumène*. Paris: Gallimard.

Beyle, H.-M. (aka Stendhal) (1964 [1817]). *Rome, Naples and Florence*. New York: French & European Publications.

Bischof, R. (1983). 'Entzauberte Geschichte (Postface)', in Theodor Lessing, *Geschichte als Sinngebung des Sinnlosen*. Matthes and Seitz, Munchen, pp. 265–291.

Bloch, M. (1986). *From Blessing to Violence: History and Ideology in the Circumcision Ritual of the Merina of Madagascar*. Cambridge [Cambridgeshire]: Cambridge University Press.

———. (1992). *Prey into Hunter: The Politics of Religious Experience*. The Lewis Henry Morgan lectures, 1984. Cambridge: Cambridge University Press.

Bonniol, J.-L. (1988). *Couleur et identité. Le miroir des appartenances dans la genèse de populations créoles*. Aix-en-Provence: Université de Provence.

——— and Benoist, J. (1994). 'Hérédités plurielles. Représentations populaires et conceptions savantes du métissage', *Ethnologie française* 24(1): 58–69.

Boorstin, D.J. (1962). *The Image; Or, What Happened to the American Dream*. New York: Atheneum.

Borges, J.L. (1970). *The Aleph and Other Stories, 1933–1969*. New York: E.P. Dutton.

———. (2004 [1949]). 'Tlön Uqbar Orbis Tertius', in J.L. Borges, *Fictions*. Transl. by R. Caillois. Paris: Gallimard, pp. 11–31.

Bouquet, M. and Porto, N. (2005). 'Introduction', in M. Bouquet and N. Porto (eds), *Science, Magic and Religion: The Ritual Process of Museum Magic*. New York and Oxford: Berghahn Books, pp. 1–28.

Bourdieu, P. (1977). *Outline of a Theory of Practice*. Cambridge: Cambridge University Press.

Bruner, E.M. (1995). 'The Ethnographer/tourist in Indonesia', in M.-F. Lanfant, J. Allcock, E. Bruner (eds), *International Tourism: Identity and Change*. London: Sage, pp. 224–241.

———. (2001). 'The Maasai and the Lion King: Authenticity, Nationalism, and Globalization in African Tourism', *American Ethnologist* 28(4): 881–908.

———. (2005). 'The Balinese Borderzone', in E.M. Bruner, *Culture on Tour: Ethnographies of Travel*. Chicago: University of Chicago Press, pp. 191–210.

Bruner, J. (1992). *Acts of Meaning*. New Heaven: Harvard University Press.

Burawoy, M., J. Blum, S. George, Z. Gill, T. Gowan, L. Haney, M. Klawiter, S. Lopez, S. O'Riain, M. Thayer (eds) (2000). *Global Ethnography: Forces, Connections, and Imaginations in a Postmodern World*. Berkeley: University of California Press.

CADOQ (1998). *Déclaration d'association – Modification des Statuts*. Saint-Paul: Sous-Préfecture de Saint-Paul.

CAH (1995). *Pays d'Accueils à La Réunion. Note de synthèse*. Saint-Denis: Commissariat à l'Aménagement des Hauts.

Caillois, R. (1950). *L'homme et le sacré*. Paris: Gallimard.

———. (1973). *La pieuvre: essai sur la logique de l'imaginaire*. Paris: Editions de la Table Ronde.

———. (2001). 'The Sacred as Transgression: Theory of the Festival', in R. Caillois, *Man and the Sacred*. Chicago: University of Illinois Press, pp. 97–127.

Cambefort, J.-P. (1988). 'Dynamiques des situations et des relations sociales en milieu institutionnel', in C. Ghasarian and J.P. Cambefort (eds), *Rôles et Enjeux. Approches d'Anthropologie Généralisée*. Saint-Denis: Université de La Réunion, pp. 201–307.

Carr, L. and R. Mendelsohn (2003). 'Valuing Coral Reefs: A Travel Cost Analysis of the Great Barrier Reef', *AMBIO* 32(5): 353–357.

Carret, J. (2002). *De l'autre côté du mur: socialisation et institutionnalisation des tagueurs et graffeurs à Saint Denis de la Réunion*. Saint-Denis: Université de La Réunion.

Catechism of the Catholic Church (2010). *Catechism of the Catholic Church*. http://overkott.dyndns.org/ (accessed 24 June 2010).

Cesar, H. (2001). 'The Biodiversity Benefits of Coral Reef Ecosystems: Values and Markets', in *International Workshop on Market Creation for Biodiversity Products and Services*. Paris: OECD.

Chane-Kune, S. (1996). *La Réunion n'est plus une île*. Paris: L'Harmattan.

Chaudat, P. (1993). 'La possession Vorombe dans la région de Tuléar', *Galaxie Anthropologique* 2–3: 130–136.

Cherubini B. (1996a). 'Les mises en scène du monde agricole : foire, fêtes, identités locales', in B. Cherubini (ed.), *Le monde rural à La Réunion*. Paris: L'Harmattan, pp. 61–84.

———. (1996b). 'La construction symbolique des identités dans le monde créole: exemples réunionnais', in B. Cherubini (ed.), *De la tradition à la post-modernité. Ecrits en hommage à Jean Poirier*. Paris: PUF, pp. 267–277.

———. (1996c). 'Du local mythifié à la sociabilité villageoise: Les nouveaux cultes de l'identité', in *Droit et Anthropologie de la complexité. Mélanges dédiés à Jean Mas*. Paris: Economica, pp. 95–108.

CI (2008). *Economic Values of Coral Reefs, Mangroves, and Seagrasses: A Global Compilation 2008*. Arlington, USA: Conservation International.

Clément, G. (1997). *Traité succinct de l'art involontaire*. Paris: Sens et Tonka.

Clifford, J. (1989). 'The Others: Beyond the 'salvage' Paradigm', *Third Text: Third World Perspectives on Contemporary Art and Culture* 6: 73–77.

———. (1997). *Routes: Travel and Translation in the 20th Century*. Cambridge (USA): Harvard University Press.

Cohen, E. (1985). 'Tourist Guides: Pathfinders, Mediators and Animators', *Annals of Tourism Research* 12(1): 1–149.

———. (1992). 'Pilgrimage and Tourism: Convergence and Divergence', in A. Morinis (ed.), *Sacred Journeys: Anthropology of Pilgrimage*. Westport: Greenwood Press, pp. 47–61.

———. (2004a). 'A Phenomenology of Tourist Experiences', in E. Cohen, *Contemporary Tourism: Diversity and Change*. London: Elsevier, pp. 65–86.

———. (2004b). 'The Tourist Guide: The Origins, Structure and Dynamics of a Role', in E. Cohen, *Contemporary Tourism: Diversity and Change*. London: Elsevier, pp. 159–177.

———. (2004c). 'Youth Tourists in Acre: A Disturbance becomes and Lifelong Preoccupation', in D. Nash (ed.), *The Study of Tourism: Anthropological and Sociological Beginnings*. London and New York: Elsevier, pp. 50–59.

Colwell, S. (1999). 'Dive-Tourism and Private Stewardship of Small-Scale Coral Reef Marine Protected Areas', in I. Dight, R. Kenchington, J. Baldwin (eds), *Proceedings of the International Tropical Marine Ecosystems Management Symposium, 1998*. Townsville, Australia, pp. 217–221.

Conand, C. (2002). 'Marine Ecology of La Réunion: An Overview of Recent Research', *AMBIO: A Journal of the Human Environment* 31(7): 602–605.

Corbin A. (1988). *Le Territoire du vide. L'Occident et le désir du rivage. 1750–1840*. Paris: Aubier.

Crick, M. (1994). *Resplendent Sites, Discordant Voices: Sri Lankans and International Tourism*. Camberwell, Victoria, Australia: Harwood.

Crouch, D., R. Jackson and F. Thomson (eds) (2005). *The Media and The Tourist Imagination. Converging Cultures*, London and New York: Routledge.

Csordas, T.J. (1997). *The Sacred Self. A Cultural Phenomenology of Charismatic Healing*. Berkeley: University of California Press.

CTR/GB2 (1998). *Etude sur les comportements des touristes non-résidents*. Saint-Denis: CTR.

Cyrulnik, B. (1997). *L'ensorcellement du monde*. Paris: O. Jacob.

Dann, G., D. Nash, P. Pearce (1988). 'Methodology in tourism research', *Annals of Tourism Research* 15: 1–28.

DATAR (1996). *Note sur la filière Guides de Pays*. Saint-Denis: CAH, pp 1–4.

De Bollivier, P. (2005). 'Spécificité de l'art contemporain à La Réunion: une question de regards', in L. Medea, L. Labache, F. Verges (eds), *Identité et société réunionnaise: nouvelles perspectives et nouvelles approches*. Paris: Karthala, pp. 43–66.

De Kadt, E. (1979). *Tourism: Passport to Development*. New York: Oxford University Press (for UNESCO/World Bank).

De Weerdt, J. (1987). 'Espace rural et tourisme en France: Orientations de la recherche', *Problems of Tourism* 2 (36): 83–93.

Defos du Rau, J. (1960). *L'île de la Réunion. Etude de géographie humaine*. Bordeaux: Université de Bordeaux.

Delumeau, J. (1978). *La peur en Occident: 14e–18e siècles*. Paris: Fayard.

———. (1992). *Une histoire du Paradis*. Paris: Fayard.

Derrida, J. and A. Dufourmantelle (2000). *Hospitality: Anne Dufourmantelle Invites Jacques Derrida to Respond*. Transl. by Rachel Bowlby. Palo Alto: Stanford University Press.

Di Giovine, M. (2008). *The Heritage-scape: UNESCO, World Heritage and Tourism*. Lanham: Lexington Books.

Dirks, N. (1990). 'History as a Sign of the Modern', *Public Culture* 2(2): 25–32.

Doumenge, J.-P. (1984). 'Enjeu géopolitique et intérêt scientifique des espaces insulaires', in *Nature et Hommes dans les îles tropicales*. Talence: CEGET-CRET, pp. 1–6.

Dove, S.G. and O. Hoegh-Guldberg. (2006). 'The cell physiology of coral bleaching', in J.T. Phinney, W. Skirving, J. Kleypas and O. Hoegh-Guldberg (eds), *Coral Reefs & Climate Change: Science and Management*. American Geophysical Union, pp. 1–18.

DPCS (1998). *Compte-rendu de la réunion des chefs d'équipements culturels du vendredi 14 juillet 1998 à la DPCS*. [no place]: DPCS.

Duffy, R. (2002). *A Trip Too Far: Ecotourism, Politics, and Exploitation*. London: Earthscan.

Durkheim, E. (2001 [1894]). *Elementary Forms of Religious Life*. Transl. by Carol Cosman. Oxford: Oxford University Press.

Ecomusée Salazie (1996). *Rapport de programmation*. Hell-Bourg: Ecomusée Salazie.

——— and Université of La Réunion (1998). *Avenant N° 1 à la convention cadre*. Saint-Denis: Ecomusée Salazie and Université de La Réunion.

——— and Université of La Réunion (1998). *Convention cadre*. Saint-Denis: Ecomusée Salazie and Université of La Réunion.

Edensor, T. (1998). *Tourists at the Taj: Performance and Meaning at a Symbolic Site*. London and New York: Routledge.

Espírito Santo, D. (2010). 'Spiritist Boundary-work and the Morality of Materiality in Afro-Cuban Religión', *Journal of Material Culture* 15(1): 64–82.

Evans-Pritchard, E.E. (1976 [1937]). *Witchcraft, Oracles and Magic among the Azande*. Oxford: Oxford University Press.

Eve, P. (2003). *20 Decembre 1848 et sa Celebration a la Reunion: Du Deni a la Rehabilitation: 1848–1980*. Paris: L'Harmattan.

Fabian, J. (1983). *Time and the Other: How Anthropology Makes Its Object*. New York: Columbia University Press.

Fauroux, E. (1997). 'Les représentations du monde végétal chez les Sakalava du Menabe', in J.M. Lebigre (ed.), *Milieux et sociétés dans le Sud-Ouest de Madagascar*. Talence: CRET, pp. 7–26.

Favret-Saada, J. (1977). *Les mots, la mort, les sorts: la sorcellerie dans le Bocage*. Paris: Gallimard.

———. (2009). *Désorceler*. Paris: Ed. de l'Olivier.

Featherstone, M. (ed.) (1990). *Global Culture*. London: Sage.

Fink, E. (1976). *Proximité et distance: essais et conférences phénoménologiques*. Transl. by Jean Kessler. Munich: Karl Alber.

Firth, R. (1963 [1936]). *We, the Tikopia. Kinship in Primitive Polynesia*. Boston: Beacon Press.

Floch, F. (1999). 'Saline-les-Bains: Barrage et râlé-poussé au nom de la tradition', *JIR* 28 January 1999.

Follea, B. and C. Gauthier (1994). *Etude Grands Paysages de l'île de La Réunion*. Saint-Denis de La Réunion: DDE.

Frazer, J.G. (1894). *The Golden Bough: A Study in Magic and Religion*. New York: MacMillan.

———. (1993 [1911]). *The Golden Bough. A Study in Magic and Religion*. London: Wordsworth.

Frey, N.L. (1998). *Pilgrim Stories: On and Off the Road to Santiago: Journeys along a Way in Modern Spain*. Berkeley: U. California Press.

———. (2004). 'Stories of the Return', in E. Badone and S. Roseman (eds), *Intersecting Journeys: the Anthropology of Pilgrimage and Tourism*. Urbana: U. of Illinois Press, pp. 89–109.

Freud, S. (1981 [1915]). 'Considérations actuelles sur la guerre et sur la mort', in S. Freud, *Essais de psychoanalyse*. Paris: Payot.

———. (2003). *The Uncanny*. London: Penguin Books.

Fukuyama, F. (1992). *The End of History and the Last Man*. New York: Free Press.

Gabrié, C. (1999). *Le monde merveilleux du récif à la Réunion*. Saint-Denis de La Réunion: Région Réunion.

Gattuso, J.P., M. Frankignoulle, I. Bourge, S. Romaine and R.W. Buddemeier (1998). 'Effect of calcium carbonate saturation of seawater on coral calcification', *Global Planet Change* 18: 37–46.

Gauvin, G. (1996). *Michel Debré et l'île de la Réunion*. Paris: L'Harmattan.

Gay, J.-C. (1995). *Les discontinuités spatiales*. Paris: Economica.

Geertz, C. (1969 [1960]). 'Spirit Beliefs', in C. Geertz, *The Religion of Java*. New York: Free Press, pp. 16–29.

Gell, A. (1988). 'Technology and Magic', *Anthropology Today* 4(2): 6–9.

———. (2005). 'The Technology of Enchantment and the Enchantment of Technology', in J. Coote and A. Shelton (eds), *Anthropology, Art and Aesthetics*. Oxford: Oxford University Press, pp. 40–63.

Ghasarian, C. (1988). 'Salazie: Espace social quotidien d'un village des hauts de La Réunion', in C. Ghasarian and J.-P. Cambefort (eds), *Rôles & enjeux. Approches d'Anthropologie Généralisée*. Saint-Denis: Université de La Réunion, pp 1–37.

———. (1991). *Honneur, chance et destin*. Paris: L'Harmattan.

———. (2002). 'La Réunion: acculturation, créolisation et réinventions culturelles', *Ethnologie française* 32(4).

Gilbert, P. (1993). *Murs de la Réunion et culture rap: représentations identitaires et territoriales des groupes de tagueurs et de graffeurs de Saint-Denis de la Réunion*. Saint-Denis: Université de La Réunion.

Graburn, N.H. (1977). 'Tourism: The Sacred Journey', in V. Smith (ed.), *Hosts and Guests: The Anthropology of Tourism*. Philadelphia: University of Pennsyvania Press, pp. 17–31.

———. (1983a). *To Pray, Pay and Play: The Cultural Structure of Japanese Domestic Tourism*. Aix-en-Provence: Centre des Hautes Etudes Touristiques.

———. (1983b). 'Introduction: The Anthropology of Tourism', in N.H. Graburn (ed.), Special Issue of *Annals of Tourism Research* 10(1): 9–33.

———. (1989). 'Tourism: The Sacred Journey', in V. Smith (ed.), *Hosts and Guests*. 2nd ed. Philadelphia: University of Pennsylvania Press, pp. 22–36.

Graburn, N.H. (1995). 'Tourism, Modernity and Nostalgia', in A. Ahmed and C. Shore (eds.) *The Future of Anthropology: Its Relevance to the Contemporary World*. London: Athlone, pp. 158–178.

———. (2002). 'The Ethnographic Tourist', in G.M.S. Dann (ed.), *The Tourist as a Metaphor of the Social World*. Wallingford: CAB International, pp. 19–40.

Graeber, D. (2007). *Lost People. Magic and the Legacy of Slavery in Madagascar*. Bloomington: Indiana University Press.

Grasseni, C. (2007). 'Introduction', in C. Grasseni, *Skilled Vision: Between Apprenticeship and Standards*. New York and Oxford: Berghahn Books, pp. 1–19.

Gray Davidson, M. (2002). 'Protecting Coral Reefs: The Principal National and International Legal Instruments', *Harvard Environmental Law Review* 26(2): 499–546.

Greenwood, D.J. (1989). 'Culture by the Pound. An Anthropological Perspective on Tourism as Cultural Commoditization', in V.L. Smith (ed.), *Hosts and Guests*. 2nd ed., Philadelphia: University of Pennsylvania Press, pp. 171–186.

Grove, R. (1995). *Green Imperialism: Colonial Expansion, Tropical Island Edens, and the Origins of Environmentalism, 1600–1860*. Studies in environment and history. Cambridge: Cambridge University Press.

Habermas, J. (1985). 'Modernity: An Incomplete Project', in H. Foster (ed.), *Postmodern Culture*. London: Pluto, pp. 3–15.

Hall, S. (1997). *Representation: Cultural Representations and Signifying Practices*. London: Sage and Open University.

Hannerz, U. (1987). 'The World in Creolization', *Africa* 57: 546–559.

———. (1992). *Cultural Complexity: Studies in the Social Organization of Meaning*. New York: University of Columbia Press.

———. (1996). *Transnational Connections*. New York and London: Routledge.

Hansmann, L. And L. Kriss-Rettenbeck (1966). *Amulet und Talisman: Erscheinungsform und Geschichte*. München: G. D.W. Callwey.

Harrison, J. (2003). *Being a Tourist: Finding Meaning in Pleasure Travel*. Vancouver: UBC Press.

Hastings, J. (1988). 'Time out of Time: a Schooner Voyage across the Pacific', *Anthropological Research on Contemporary Tourism: Student Papers from Berkeley* Special issue of *Kroeber Anthropological Society Journal* 67–68: 37–54.

Hatziolos, M.E., A.J. Hooten and M. Fodor (1998). 'Coral Reefs: Challenges and Opportunities for Sustainable Management', in *Proceedings of the 5th Annual World Bank Conference on Environmentally and Socially Sustainable Development*. Washington: World Bank.

Hennig, C. (1999 [1997]). *Reiselust: Touristen, Tourismus und Urlaubskultur*. Frankfurt and Leipzig: Suhrkamp Taschenbuch.

Héritier, A. (2003). *Genèse de la notion de patrimoine culturel: 1750–1816*. Paris: L' Harmattan.

Hiwasaki, L. (2000). 'Ethnic Tourism in Hokkaido and the Shaping of Ainu Identity', *Pacific Affairs* 73(3): 393–412.

Hobsbawm, E. and T. Ranger (eds) (1983). *The Invention of Tradition*. Cambridge: Cambridge University Press.

Hocart, A.M. (1952). 'The Divinity of the Guest', in A.M. Hocart, *The Life-Giving Myth*. London: Methuen & Co, pp. 78–86.

Hoegh-Guldberg, O. (1999). 'Climate Change, Coral Bleaching and the Future of the World's Coral Reefs', *Marine and Freshwater Research* 50(8): 839–866.

Hom Cary, S. (2004). 'The Tourist Moment', *Annals of Tourism Research* 31(1): 61–77.

Houat, T. (1844). *Les marrons*. Saint-Denis: Archives Départementales de la Réunion.

Howard, E. (2008 [1898]). *Garden Cities of To-morrow*. www.forgottenbooks.org (accessed 25 December 2008).

Huchet, C.-D. (1990). *Pour un centre de patrimoine dans le cirque de Salazie. Sources pour des temps présents*. Saint-Denis: Pays d'Accueil de Salazie.

Husserl, E. (1964). *The Idea of Phenomenology*. The Hague: Martinus Nijhoff.

Idelson, B. (1999). *La presse quotidienne régionale (P.Q.R.) acteur social local. Analyse d'un discours de presse: le cas du 'Quotidien de La Réunion' (1976–1997)*. Saint-Denis de La Réunion, France: Université de La Réunion.

———. (2002). 'L'espace mediatique reunionnais, hier et aujourd'hui', *Hermes* 32–33: 101–110.

Inglis, J. (1957). 'Cargo Cults: The Problem of Explanation', *Oceania* 27(4): 249–263.

IPCC (2007). *Climate Change 2007: Synthesis Report. Contribution of Working Groups I, II and III to the Fourth Assessment Report of the Intergovernmental Panel on Climate Change*. Geneva: IPCC.

Jackson, M. (1998). *Minima Ethnographica: Intersubjectivity and the Anthropological Project*. Chicago and London: University of Chicago Press.

Joutard, P. (1986). *L'Invention du Mont Blanc*. Paris: Gallimard/Julliard.

Kalian, M., E. Witztum (2000). 'Comments on Jerusalem Syndrome', *British Journal of Psychiatry* 176: 492.

Kant, I. (1795). *Perpetual Peace: A Philosophical Sketch*. http://www.mtholyoke.edu/acad/intrel/kant/kant1.htm (accessed 19 January 2009).

Karsenti, B., and M. Mauss (1994). *Marcel Mauss: Le fait social total*. Philosophies, 49. Paris: Presses Universitaires de France.

Kirsch, S. (2006). *Reverse Anthropology: Indigenous Analysis of Social and Environmental Relations in New Guinea*. Stanford, Calif: Stanford University Press.

Kirshenblatt-Gimblett, B. (1998). *Destination Culture: Tourism, Museums, and Heritage*. Berkeley: University of California Press.

Kolbert, E. (2006). 'Dead Reckoning: The Armenian genocide and the politics of silence', *New Yorker Magazine*, 6 November.

Kristeva, J. (1991). *Etrangers à nous-mêmes*. Collection Folio/essais, 156. Paris: Gallimard.

Labache, L. (1996). *La question de l'ethnicité à la Réunion. Vers un melting-pot?* Unpublished PhD dissertation. Paris: Ecole des Hautes Etudes en Sciences Sociales.

Lacan, J. (1966). 'Le stade du miroir comme formateur de la fonction du Je telle qu'elle nous est révélée dans l'expérience psychanalytique', in J. Lacan, *Ecrits*, Paris: Seuil, pp. 93–100.

Lambek, M. (1993). *Knowledge and Practice in Mayotte: Local Discourses of Islam, Sorcery, and Spirit Possession.* Toronto: University of Toronto Press.

Lanfant, M.-F. (1980). 'Tourism in the Process of Internationalisation', *International Social Sciences Journal* 17(1): 14–43.

———. (1992). 'Le tourisme international entre tradition et modernité. Pourquoi ce thème?', in *Actes du colloque 'Le tourisme international entre tradition et modernité'.* Nice: University of Nice.

———. (1995). 'International Tourism, Internationalization and the Challenge to Identity', in M.-F. Lanfant, J.B. Allcock, E.M. Bruner (eds), *International Tourism: Identity and Change.* London: Sage, pp. 24–43.

———. (2009). 'The Purloined Eye: Revisiting the Tourist Gaze from a Phenomenological Perspective'. Transl. by D. Picard, in M. Robinson and D. Picard (eds), *The Framed World: Tourism, Tourists and Photography.* London: Ashgate, pp. 239–256.

——— and N. Graburn (1992). 'International Tourism Reconsidered: The Principle of the Alternative', in V.L. Smith and W.R. Eadington (eds), *Tourism Alternatives. Potentials and Problems in the Development of Tourism.* Chichester: John Wiley & Sons, pp. 88–112.

Lashley, C. and A. Morrison (eds) (2007). *In Search of Hospitality. Theoretical Perspectives and Debates.* Oxford: Butterworth-Heinemann.

Latour, B. (2007). *Reassembling the Social: An Introduction to Actor-Network-Theory.* Oxford: Oxford University Press.

Lechner, F.J. and J. Boli (2000). 'Introduction', in F.J. Lechner and J. Boli (eds), *The Globalisation Reader.* Oxford: Blackwell, pp. 49–51.

Leite, N. and N. Graburn (2009). 'Anthropological Interventions in Tourism Studies', in T. Jamal and M. Robinson (eds), *The Sage Handbook of Tourism Studies.* London: Sage, pp. 35–64.

Lenz, R. (2010). 'Hotel Royal and other Spaces of Hospitality: Tourists and Migrants in the Mediterranean', in J. Scott and T. Selwyn (eds), *Thinking Through Tourism.* Oxford: Berg Publishers, pp. 202–229.

Lessing, T. (1983 [1919]). *Geschichte als Sinngebung des Sinnlosen.* München: Matthes and Seitz.

Levi-Strauss, C. (1966 [1962]). *The Savage Mind.* Chicago: University of Chicago Press.

Lilette, V. (1999). *Le mythe du marronnage. Symbole de 'résistance' à l'île de La Réunion.* Unpublished MA dissertation. Saint-Denis de La Réunion, France: Université de La Réunion.

Live, Y.-S. (1999). 'Sociologie de La Réunion: Mutations, paradoxes, representations, migrations', in B. Cherubini (ed.), *La recherche anthropologique à La Réunion.* Paris: L'Harmattan, pp. 185–204.

Lodge, D. (1991). *Paradise News.* New York: Viking Press.

Loupy, S. (2001). *Les pêcheurs du lagon à La Réunion*. Unpublished MA dissertation. Paris: University Paris X-Nanterre.

MacCannell, D. (1976). *The Tourist: A New Theory of the Leisure Class*. New York: Schocken.

———. (1999 [1976]). *The Tourist: A New Theory of the Leisure Class*. Berkeley: University of California Press.

Maestri, E. (1998). *Groupe Bourbon – 1948–1998*. Saint-Denis: Gaphica.

Magherini, G. (1989). *La Sindrome di Stendhal*. Firenze: Ponte Alle Grazie.

Maillot, A. (2002). *Le surf: logique du micro-social*. Saint-Denis: Université de La Réunion.

Malinowski, B. (1935). *Coral Gardens and their Magic. A Study of the Methods of Tiling the Soil and of Agricultural Rites in the Trobriand Islands*, 2 Vol. London: George Allen and Unwin.

———. (1992a [1948]). 'Baloma: The Spirits of the Dead in the Trobriand Islands', in B. Malinowski, *Magic, Science and Religion, and Other Essays*. Long Grove: Wavelandpress, pp. 149–274.

———. (1992b [1948]). *Magic, Science and Religion, and Other Essays*. Long Grove: Wavelandpress.

Marcus, G. (1995). 'Ethnography in/of the World System: The Emergence of Multi-sited Ethnography', *Annual Review of Anthropology* 24: 95–117.

Marie, M. and J. Viard (1988). *La campagne inventée*. Arles: Actes Sud.

Martin, A. (1998). *Mission MNATP à la Réunion – Juillet-août 1998*. Hell-Bourg: Ecomusée Salazie.

Mauss, M. and Henri H. Hubert (2006 [1902]). *A General Theory of Magic*. Transl. by R. Brain. New York and London: Routledge.

McGuigan, J. (1999). *Modernity and Postmodern Culture*. Buckingham, Philadelphia: Open University Press.

MCUR (2008). *Maison des Civilisations et de l'Unité Réunionnaise*. http://www.regionreunion.com (accessed on 4 November 2008).

Medea, L. (2002). 'Creolisation and Globalisation in a Neo-Colonial Context: The Case of La Réunion', *Social Identities* 8(1).

———. (2003). 'La construction identitaire dans la société réunionnaise', *Journal des anthropologues* 92–93.

———. (2005). 'Hégémonie et Hétéronomie: les conséquences du processus d'occidentalisation à travers la Départementalisation. Repenser l'Identité dans une Situation Pluriculturelle', in L. Médéa, L. Labache, F. Vergès (eds), *Identité et Société Réunionnaise. Nouvelles Perspectives, Nouvelles Approches*. Paris: Karthala.

Medea, L., L. Labache, F. Vergès (eds) (2005). *Identité et société réunionnaise: nouvelles perspectives et nouvelles approches*. Paris: Karthala, pp. 171–206.

Merme, C. and L.A. Roussin (1852). *Promenade à Salazie*. Saint-Denis: Archives.

Mespoulhe R., R. Troadec, M. Martin (1994). *Suivi expérimental sur le nettoyage et la sauvegarde des plages balnéaires de la Réunion*. Saint-Denis: Université de La Réunion.

Meyer, B. (2003). 'Ghanaian Popular Cinema and the Magic in and of Film', in B. Meyer and P. Pels (eds), *Magic and Modernity*. Palo Alto: Stanford University Press, pp. 200–222.

Milani, R. (2005). *Esthétiques du paysage*. Trad. by G.A. Tiberghien. Arles: Actes Sud.

MINTEL (2003). *International Diving Market – December 2003*. London: Mintel International Group Ltd.

——— (2007). *Long-haul Holidays – UK*. London: Mintel International Group Ltd.

Mintz, S.W. (1986). *Sweetness and Power: The Place of Sugar in Modern History*. New York: Penguin.

Mirault, E. (2004). 'Approche socio-économique du territoire littoral récifal de l'île de La Réunion', in B. Cherubini (ed.), *Le territoire littoral: Tourisme, pêche et environnement dans l'océan Indien*. Paris: L'Harmattan, pp. 57–98.

MNATP (1999). *Tropiques métis*. Paris: Ministère de la Culture.

MNATP and Ecomusée Salazie (1998). *Convention cadre*. Paris: MNATP / Ecomusée Salazie.

Mosser, M. (1999). 'Le XXIe siècle sera jardinier', in H. Brunon (ed.), *Le jardin, notre double. Sagesse et déraison*. Paris: Autrement, pp. 231–240.

——— and G. Teyssot (eds) (1991). *Histoire des jardins de la Renaissance à nos jours*. Paris: Flammarion.

Ness, S.A. (2003). *Where Asia Smiles: An Ethnography of Philippine Tourism*. Philadelphia: University of Pennsylvania Press.

Neumann, R.P. (2002). *Imposing Wilderness: Struggles over Livelihood and Nature Preservation in Africa*. Berkeley: University of California Press.

Niollet, L. (1999). *L'habitation en bois-sous-tôle*. Hell-Bourg: Ecomusée Salazie.

Norlander, B. (2003). 'Coral Crisis! Humans are Killing Off These Bustling Underwater Cities. Can Coral Reefs Be Saved?', *Science World*, December 2008.

Ohnuki-Tierney, E. (1993). *Rice as Self: Japanese Identities through Time*. Princeton NJ: Princeton University Press.

Ortiz, F. (1995 [1947]). *Cuban Counterpoint: Tobacco and Sugar*. Durham and London: Duke University Press.

Ottino, P. (1999). 'Quelques réflexions sur les milieux créoles réunionnais', in B. Cherubini (ed.), *La recherche anthropologique à La Réunion*. Paris: L'Harmattan, pp. 65–95.

Pandolphi, P. and E. Quezin (1998). *De hier à aujourd'hui. La case en paille, un patrimoine à préserver*. 17 min. Saint-Denis: Université de La Réunion.

Panofsky, E. (1971). *Renaissance and Renascences in Western Art*. New York: Westview Press.

Parc Marin (1999a). *Note de presentation*. Saint Gilles: Parc Marin.

——— (1999b). *Document d'orientations et de gestion*. Saint Gilles: Parc Marin.

Pels, P. (2003). 'Introduction', in B. Meyer and P. Pels (eds), *Magic and Modernity*. Palo Alto: Stanford University Press, pp. 1–38.

Pendleton, L.H. (1995). 'Valuing Coral Reef Protection', *Ocean and Coastal Management* 26(2): 119–131.

Picard, D. (1999). *Terre de vie: systèmes contestés de transmission foncière à La Réunion*. 18 min. Official selection at the 2000 CNRS Scientific Film Festival in Nancy, France.

———. (2004). 'International Tourism and Cultural Transformation: Variations of the Creole Garden in La Réunion, Indian Ocean', in P. Tsartas and J.K. Steen Jacobsen (eds), *Understanding Tourism – Theoretical Advances*. Mytilini, Greece: University of the Aegean, pp. 503–522.

———. (2005). 'La fable des coraux ou la mythification de l'économique: tourisme international et protection des récifs coralliens à La Réunion', in B. Cherubini (ed.), *Le territoire littoral – Tourisme, pêche et environnement dans l'océan Indien*. Paris: L'Harmattan, pp. 147–166.

———. (2006). 'Gardening the Past and Being in the World: A Popular Celebration of the Abolition of Slavery in La Réunion', in D. Picard and M. Robinson (eds), *Remaking Worlds: Festivals, Tourism and Change*. Clevedon: Channel View Publications, pp. 46–70.

———. (2008a). 'La relation à l'étranger à La Réunion', in C. Ghasarian (ed.), *Anthropologies de La Réunion*. Paris: Editions des Archives Contemporains, pp. 77–93.

———. (2008b). 'Coral Garden Economics: International Tourism and the Magic of Tropical Nature', *Etudes Caribéennes* 3(9/10): 99–121.

———. (2009a). 'Through Magical Flowers: Tourism and Creole Self-Fashioning in La Reunion', in S. Moorthy and A. Jamal (eds), *Indian Ocean Studies: Indian Ocean Studies: Cultural, Social, and Political Perspectives*. London and New York: Routledge, pp. 374–396.

———. (2009b). 'Giardinaggio creolo: turismo e resistenza culturale nell'isola della riunione', transl. by V. Simoni, in C. Cipollari (ed.), *Scenari turistici. Sguardi antropologici sulle località turistiche*, Roma: CISU, pp. 45–58.

———. (2010a). 'Cultivating Human Gardens: Tropical Island Tourism in the South Western Indian Ocean', in P. Gupta, I. Hofmeyr and M. Pearson (eds), *Eyes Across the Water. Navigating the Indian Ocean*. Pretoria, South Africa: University of South Africa Press, pp. 326–343.

———. (2010b). 'Tropical Island Gardens and Formations of Modernity', in J. Scott and T. Selwyn (eds), *Thinking Through Tourism*. Oxford: Berg, pp. 139–160.

———. (2010c). '"Being a Model for the World": Performing Creoleness in La Reunion', *Social Anthropology* 18(3).

——— and M. Robinson (eds) (2006). *Festivals, Tourism and Social Change*. Clevedon: Channel View Publications.

——— and M. Robinson (eds) (forthcoming 2012). *Emotion in Motion: Tourism, awe and Inner Journeys*. London: Ashgate.

Picard, M. (1992). *Bali. Tourisme culturel et culture touristique*. Paris: L'Harmattan.

Pina-Cabral, J.D. (2002). *Between China and Europe: Person, Culture, and Emotion in Macao*. London School of Economics monographs on social anthropology, v. 74. London: Continuum.

Pitt-Rivers, J. (1977). 'The Law of Hospitality', in J. Pitt-Rivers, *The Fate of Shechem, or the Politics of Sex*. Cambridge: Cambridge University Press, pp. 94–112.

Pocock, C. (2009). 'Photography and Tourism on the Great Barrier Reef', in M. Robinson and D. Picard (eds), *The Framed World: Tourism, Tourists and Photography*. London: Ashgate, pp. 229–238.

Poirier, J. (1999). 'Culture créole, hétéroculture réunionnaise', in B. Cherubini (ed.), *La recherche anthropologique à La Réunion*. Paris: L'Harmattan, pp. 125–144.

Pratt, M.-L. (1992). *Imperial Eyes: Travel Writing and Transculturation*. London and New York: Routledge.

Radcliffe-Brown, A.R. (1933 [1922]). *The Andaman Islanders.* London: Cambridge University Press.

Read, K.E. (1958). 'A Cargo Situation in the Markham Valley, New Guinea', *Southwestern Journal of Anthropology* 14(3).

Région Réunion (1995). *Schéma d'Aménagement Régional.* Saint-Denis: Conseil Régional.

——— (1998). *Compte rendu de réunion. Séance de travail du 24 juillet 98.* Saint-Denis: Conseil Régional, Direction des Affaires Culturelles.

Roberts, L., T. Selwyn and H. Andrews (2007). 'Hospitality and Eroticism', *International Journal of Culture, Tourism and Hospitality Research* 1(3): 247–262.

Robinson, M. and D. Picard (2006). *Tourism, Culture, and Sustainable Development.* Paris: UNESCO.

——— (2009). 'Moments, Magic and Memories: Photographing Tourists, Tourist Photographs and Making Worlds' , in M. Robinson and D. Picard (eds), *The Framed World: Tourism, Tourists and Photography.* London: Ashgate, pp. 1–38.

——— (2009). 'Tourism and Photography: Magic, Memory and World Making', in M. Robinson and D., Picard (eds), *The Framed World: Tourism, Tourists and Photography.* London: Ashgate.

Roger, A. (1997). *Court traité du paysage.* Paris: Gallimard.

Roos, D., G. Bertrand and E. Tessier (1998). *La chasse sous-marine à La Réunion.* Le Port: IFREMER La Réunion.

Rosello, M., and A.A. Leff (2003). 'Postcolonial Hospitality: The Immigrant as Guest', *The French Review* 76(6), 1294.

Rosenbloom, S. (2010). 'But Will It Make You Happy?' *New York Times* [NY edition] 8 August: BU1.

Rozenberg, D. (1990). *Tourisme et Utopie aux Baléares. Ibiza, une île pour une autre vie.* Paris: L'Harmattan.

Ryland, J.S. (1982). 'Reefs of Southwest Viti Levu and their Tourism Potential', in E.D. Gomez, C.E. Birkeland, R.W. Buddemeier, R.E. Johannes, J.A. Marsh, R.T. Tsuda (eds), *Proceedings of the 4th International Coral Reef Symposium.* Manila: University of the Philippines, pp. 293–298.

Sahlins, M. (1968). 'Notes on the Original Affluent Society', in R. Lee and I. DeVore (eds), *Man the Hunter.* Chicago: Aldine, pp. 85–89.

———. (1994) 'Goodbye to Tristes Tropes: Etnography in the Context of Modern World History', in Robert Borovsky (ed.), Assessing Cultural Anthropology, New York: McGraw Hill, pp. 37–395.

Said, E.W. (1979) *Orientalism.* New York: Vintage Books.

———. (2003). *Orientalism.* London: Penguin.

Saville-Kent, W. (1893). *The Great Barrier Reef of Australia: Its Products and Potentialities.* London: W.H. Allen & Co.

Selwyn, T. (2007). 'The Political Economy of Enchantment: Formations in the Anthropology of Tourism', *Suomen Antropologi* 32(2): 48–70.

Serageldin, I. (1997). 'Coral Reef Conservation: Science, Economics, and Law', in M.E. Hatziolos, A.J. Hooten, M. Fodor (eds), *Coral Reefs. Challenges and Opportunities for Sustainable Management.* Washington D.C.: World Bank, pp. 3–7.

Serviable, M. (1983). *Le tourisme aux Mascareignes-Seychelles*. Saint-Denis: Université de la Réunion, collection des Travaux du Centre Universitaire.
Simmel, G. (1950). 'The Stranger', in *The Sociology of Georg Simmel*. Transl. by Kurt Wolff. New York: Free Press, pp. 402–408.
Simonin, J. and E. Wolff (1996). 'Ecole et famille à La Réunion: le télescopage des modèles', *RIAC Lien social et politique* 35: 37–46.
———., M. Watin and E. Wolff (1993). *Medias, école, 'kartié' à La Réunion: des espaces en contact*. Saint-Denis: CNRS UR1041-Université de La Réunion.
Spalding, M.D., C. Ravilious and E.P. Green (2001). *World Atlas of Coral Reefs*. Berkeley: University of California Press.
Stanner, W.E.H. (1958). 'On the Interpretation of Cargo Cults', *Oceania* 24(1): 1–25.
Steward, S. (1993). *On Longing: Narratives of the Miniature, the Gigantic, the Souvenir, the Collection*. Durham and London: Duke University Press.
Tambiah, S.J. (1990). *Magic, Science and Religion and the Scope of Rationality*. Cambridge: Cambridge University Press.
Taussig, M. (1993). *Mimesis and Alterity*. New York and London: Routledge.
———. (1997). *The Magic of the State*. New York and London: Routledge.
Tedlock, B. (1991). 'From Participant Observation to the Observation of Participation: the Emergence of Narrative Ethnography', *Journal of Anthropological Research* 47(1): 69–94.
Thomas Cook (1968). *Holidays Overseas 1968/9*. Peterborough: Thomas Cook Archive.
——— (1975a). *The Cunard Caribbean 1975–1976*. Peterborough: Thomas Cook Archive.
——— (1975b). *Far and Away. The Best in Egypt, Africa, Far East, Indonesia, Australia, Caribbean and the Americas 1975–76*. Peterborough: Thomas Cook Archive.
——— (1979). *Far Away Worldwide Holidays & Tours 1979/80*. Peterborough: Thomas Cook Archive.
——— (1980). *Getaway America 1980*. Peterborough: Thomas Cook Archive.
——— (1985). *Faraway 1985–1986*. Peterborough: Thomas Cook Archive.
——— (1986). *Activity Holidays 86 / Marlboro Adventure Travel*. Peterborough: Thomas Cook Archive.
——— (1990). *The Faraway Collection: Caribbean, Bermuda, Indian Ocean, Kenya, Hawaiian islands, Thailand, Far East 1990–1991*. Peterborough: Thomas Cook Archive.
——— (1995). *Worldwide Faraway Collection 1995–96*. Peterborough: Thomas Cook Archive.
——— (2001). *Worldwide Signature 2001*. Peterborough: Thomas Cook Archive.
——— (2003). *Neilson 2003–2004*. Peterborough: Thomas Cook Archive.
——— (2006). *Worldwide Signature 2006*. Peterborough: Thomas Cook Archive.
Thompson, K.A. (2006). *An Eye for the Tropics: Tourism, Photography, and Framing the Caribbean Picturesque*. Objects/histories. Durham: Duke University Press.
Tsing, A. (2005). *Friction: An Ethnography of Global Connection*. Princeton and Oxford: Princeton University Press
Tucker, H. (2002). 'Welcome to Flintstones-Land: Contesting Place and Identity in Goreme, Central Turkey', in S. Coleman and M. Crang (eds), *Tourism: Between Place and Performance*. New York and Oxford: Berghahn Books, pp. 143–159.

Turner, V. (1969). *The Ritual Process.* Chicago: Aldine.
———. (1973). 'The Centre out There: Pilgrim's Goal', *History of Religions* 12(3): 191–230.
——— and E. Turner (1978). *Image and Pilgrimage in Christian Culture.* New York: Columbia University Press.
Tylor, E.B. (1865). *Researches into the Early History of Mankind and the Development of Civilization.* London: J Murray.
———. (1913 [1871]). *Primitive Culture,* 2 Vol. London: John Murray.
UNCED (1992). *Rio Declaration on Environment and Development.* Geneva: UN Publications.
UNEP (2003). *Agenda 21,* http://www.unep.org/Documents.Multilingual/Default.asp?documentID=52 (accessed on 4 December 2008).
——— and WWF (2003). *Conventions and Coral reefs: Fourteen Multilateral Environmental Agreements, Programmes, Partnerships and Networks Relevant to the Protection and Conservation of Coral Reefs, and the World Summit on Sustainable Development Plan of Implementation.* UNEP: Nairobi.
UNESCO (1972). *Convention Concerning The Protection Of The World Cultural And Natural Heritage.* Paris: UNESCO Publishing.
UNWTO (1999). *The Global Code of Ethics for Tourism.* Madrid: UNWTO.
Urbain, J.-D. (1991). *L'idiot du voyage. Histoires de touristes.* Paris: Plon.
———. (1994). *Sur la plage: mœurs et coutumes balnéaires.* Paris: Payot.
Urry, J. (1990). *The Tourist Gaze.* London: Sage.
Van den Berghe, P. (1994). *The Quest for the Other: Ethnic Tourism in San Cristobal, Mexico.* Seattle and London: University of Washington Press.
Van Gennep, V. (1961). *The Rites of Passage.* Transl. by G.L. Caffee. Chicago: University of Chicago Press. (French ed. 1906).
Vergès, F. (1999). *Monsters and Revolutionaries. Colonial Family Romance and Métissage.* Durham and London: Duke University Press.
———. (2001). *Abolir l'esclavage: une utopie coloniale. Les ambiguïtés d'une politique humanitaire.* Paris: Albin Michel.
———. (2008). 'Mémoires et culture(s) à La Réunion', in C. Ghasarian (ed.), *Anthropologies de La Réunion.* Paris: Archives contemporaines, pp. 209–234.
Vergès, P. (1993). *D'une île au monde. Entretiens avec Brigitte Croisier.* Paris: L'Harmattan.
Viala, A., H. Ota, M.N. Vacheron, P. Martin, F. Caroli (2004). 'Les Japonais en voyage pathologique à Paris: un modèle original de prise en charge transculturelle', *Nervure Journal de Psychiatrie* 17(5): 31–34.
Viard, J. (1986). 'Les vacances: une modernité sous le signe de l'archaïsme', *Loisir et Société* 9(1): 183–192.
Waldren, J. (1996). *Insiders and Outsiders.* New York and Oxford: Berghahn Books.
Wallerstein, I. (2004a). 'The Rise and Future Demise of the World Capitalist System', in F.J. Lechner and J. Boli (eds), *The Globalization Reader.* Oxford: Blackwell, pp. 63–69.
———. (2004b). *The Modern World-system in the longue durée.* Boulder: Paradigm.
Wang, N. (1999). *Tourism and Modernity.* New York: Pergamon.

Watin, M. (1991). *Habiter: approche anthropologique de l'espace domestique à La Réunion.* Unpublished PhD dissertation. Saint-Denis: Université de La Réunion.
——— and E. Wolff (1995). 'L'emergence de l'espace public à La Réunion', *Etudes de communication* 17: 19–39.
West, P. (2006). *Conservation is Our Government Now: The Politics of Ecology in Papua New Guinea.* Durham: Duke University Press.
Wheeller, B. (1993). 'Sustaining the Ego', *Journal of Sustainable Tourism* 1(2):1–29.
Whittaker, E. (forthcoming). 'Peak Experiences in Tourism', in D. Picard and M. Robinson (eds), *Emotion in Motion: The Passions ofTourism and Travel.* London: Ashgate.
Wilkinson, C.R. (1998). 'The 1997–1998 mass bleaching event around the world', in C.R. Wilkinson (ed.), *Status of Coral Reefs of the World (1998).* Australian Institute of Marine Science, pp. 15–38.
Wolff, E. (1991). *Quartiers de vie: approche ethnologique des populations défavorisées de l'île de la Réunion.* Paris: Meridiens-Klincksieck.
Worsley, P. (1957). *The Trumpet Shall Sound: A Study of 'Cargo' Cults in Melanesia.* London: MacGibbon & Kee.
Zitte, W. and A. du Vignaux (1993). *Nouveaux mondes.* Saint-Denis: Artothèque.

Index

Lightning Source UK Ltd.
Milton Keynes UK
UKOW03f0709130913

217130UK00003B/15/P